OATH UNDO ME

OATH UNDO ME

Megan Formanek was born and raised in Australia on the bright, and sometimes very stormy, Illawarra region. At University she studied History and after graduation worked in Law before moving abroad, first to South Korea, and later to Italy and then England. During this time, she began writing to escape the brutal Korean winters and has continued ever since. She, her partner, and her son, now live in the wet tropics of Far North Queensland.

www.meganformanek.com

/meganformanekauthor

OATH UNDO ME

VIKING TRADING LANDS BOOK ONE

MEGAN FORMANEK

LIFE ITINERANT PUBLISHING

First printing edition, 2022
Copyright © 2022 by Megan Formanek

Map of Northern Europe adapted from European Lake
Location Map by Alexkr under the Creative Commons
Attribution-Share Alike 3.0 Unported license.

Aldeigjuborg map © 2022 by Dean Haynes, Megan Formanek

Published by Life Itinerant Publishing
Cairns, Queensland, Australia

www.meganformanek.com

A catalogue record for this
book is available from the
National Library of Australia

Paperback ISBN: 978-0-6488808-0-0
eBook ISBN: 978-0-6488088-1-7

Cover design, map design and photography by Dean Haynes

For my boys Dean, Archer and the one who
will forever be missed, Bjorn.

PLACE NAMES

Below is a list of place names, generally contemporaneous with the time period of this novel. As is common in modern times, each place may have been known by several names by different language speakers. As the predominant language of the characters in this book centres on Old Norse, those names as used by that language are, mostly, chosen except when used by people speaking different tongues.

In the ninth century, spelling was inconsistent and largely phonetic, changeable with dialect and accent, resulting in some contention surrounding place names themselves. Obviously, in part, I have preferred spellings that are more accessible to those accustomed to the English language, omitting special letters that are especially difficult to pronounce. It is also noted that as more archaeological evidence emerges and our understanding of all things Viking improves, so does it change our perception of borders and the lands these names may refer to. No one approach is without its issues. The place names adopted have been done so for the readers benefit for ease of reading whilst keeping the lilt of the original language.

Aldeigjuborg — Staraya Ladoga, Russia.

Birka — Town on the island of Björkö, Sweden.

Austmarr — Baltic Sea.

Gardarike — Garðaríki in Old Norse, the lands of the Rus' (Kyivan Rus') which now includes Belarus, Russia and Ukraine.

Karlstad — Located in Sweden.

Miklagard — Constantinople/modern day Istanbul, Turkey.

Holmgardr — Town that pre-dated present day Novgorod, Russia, and contained the stronghold Rurikovo Gorodische.

Serkland — Abbasid Caliphate, including modern-day Middle East, West Asia and North-East Africa.

Svealand — Sweden.

Uppsala — Region within Sweden.

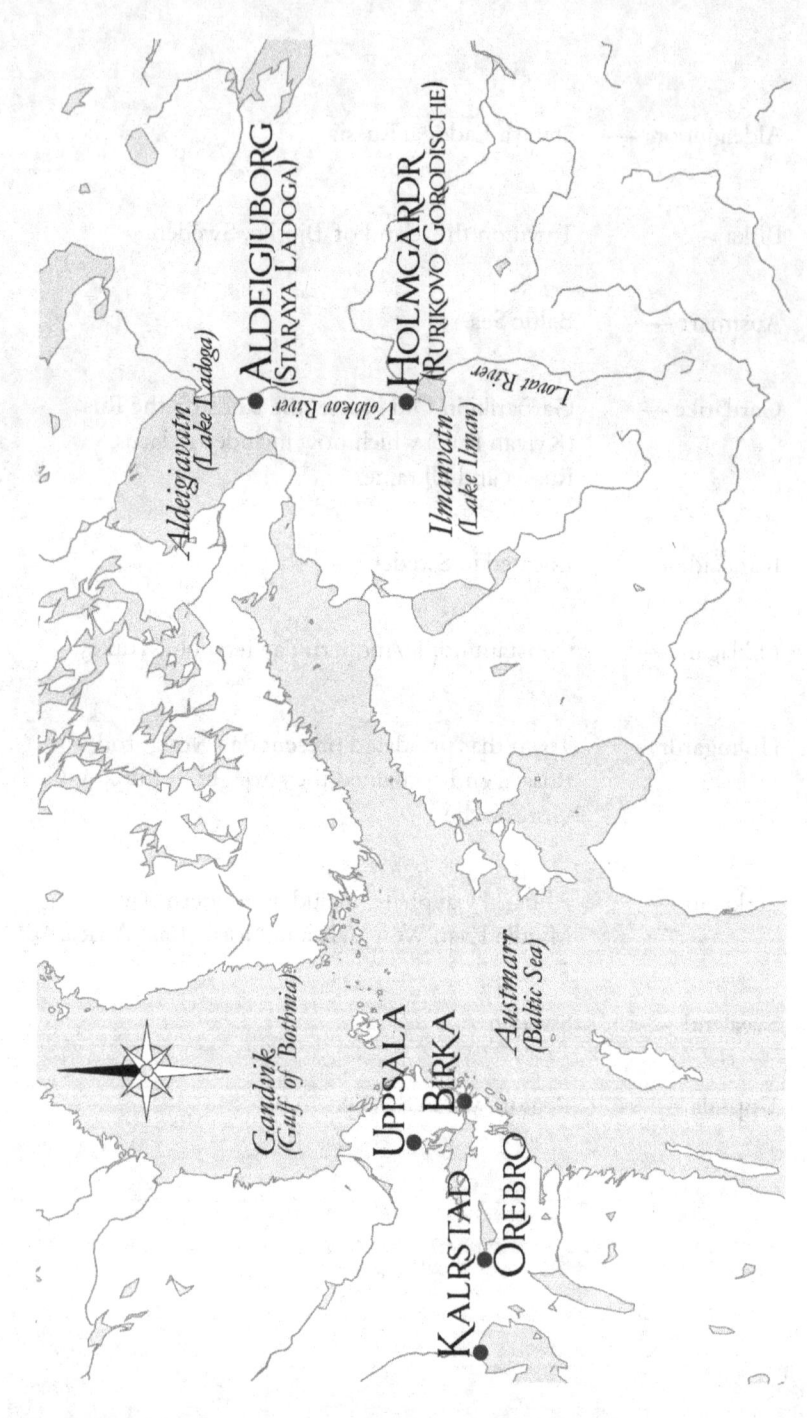

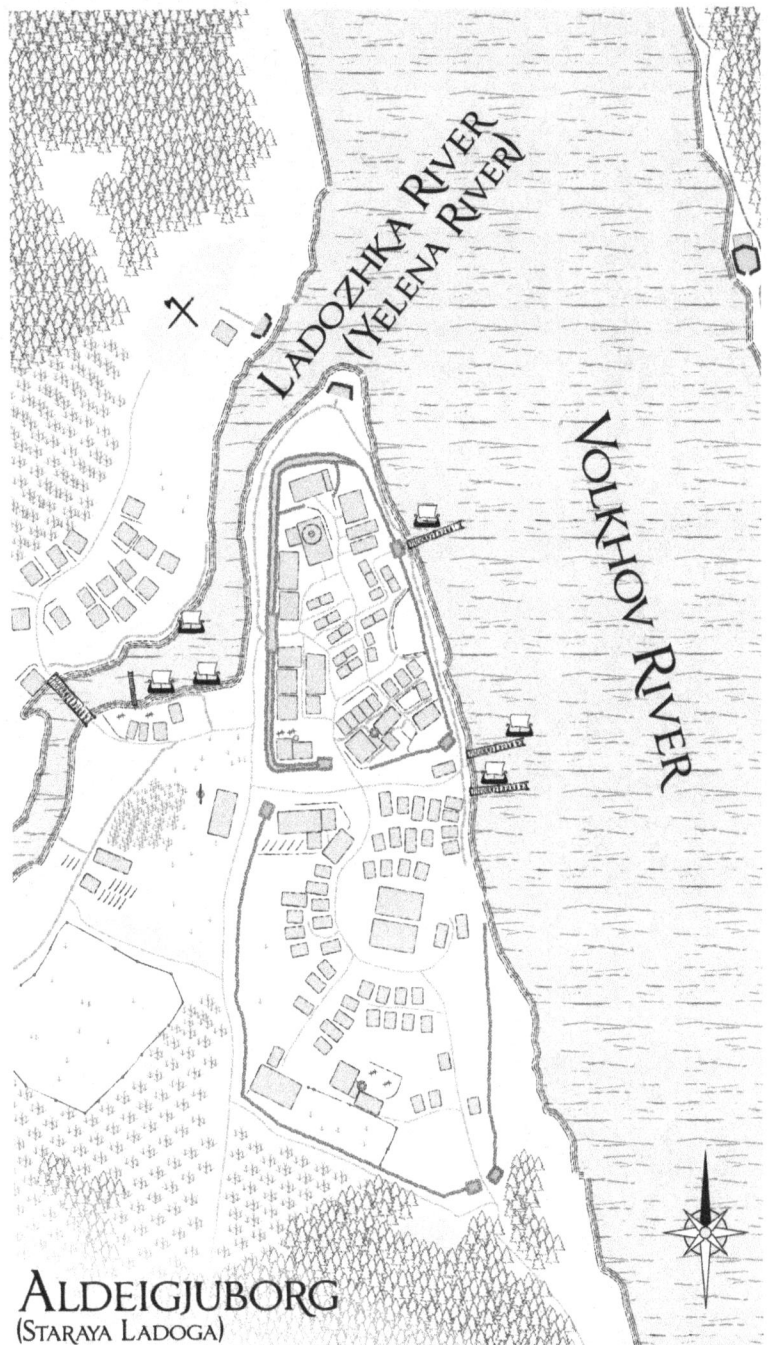

LADOZHKA RIVER
(YELENA RIVER)

VOLKHOV RIVER

ALDEIGJUBORG
(STARAYA LADOGA)

PROLOGUE

SPRING 879CE, SVEALAND

I had not wished for my husband's death.

Yet, he lay before me, cold in our bed, covered in thick animal furs. His death would bring me what I desperately desired for two long years: escape. But for him, there would be no Valhalla, the desire of all men. There was no honour in dying in your sleep.

Huddled on a low stool in the corner of the room, I sat watching my husband Auden's dark outline, knowing he would never again spring from our bed with the same vigour he exhibited each morning before. I stared through the gloom and listened to the gentle whistle of the icy wind outside.

My thin *serkr* did little to keep me warm and still, I sat on that stool, with my feet tucked beneath me, thinking. Alone in the night, I could imagine the walls did not contain me. The wood of the structure and the earthen floor were still there, but my mind was free to remember my father, whose wisdom I required more at this moment than ever before. I traced the familiar spiralling pattern of my armring under the sleeve of my nightdress, closing my eyes and letting my mind wander to the last time I saw him.

My father and I had sat side-by-side on the soft green grass, with a great expanse of water before us, enjoying the gentle breeze. It was spring, and that was always an exciting time, bringing with it much opportunity.

'Don't tell your mother, ever!' He made me promise with a whisper and a wry smile. His thick golden beard covered the corners of his mouth and the beads tied into it jiggled when he talked.

I was eager to keep my word, without knowing what I agreed to. 'I won't,' I promised with a nod.

My father and I kept many secrets from my mother, who made no effort to understand either of us. We shared many a giggle or covert smile behind her back, much to her annoyance.

His fingers tugged at his armring worn tightly around his wrist, attempting to remove it. Made from silver interlocking pieces and a strand of silver wrapping around the band, it was distinctive, different from all the others I had seen. Where Freki or Geri, the wolves who so often shadowed Odin, were traditionally represented by a wolf's head on either side of the opening, my father's armring bore the head of another animal, his namesake, Tarben, the bear of Thor. The jarl had gifted the armring to my father upon his oath.

'Father, no! You can't,' I protested as he twisted and pulled at the armring.

He had received it as a young man and at that time, it would have fit snugly around his forearm then. Over time, as he had grown, it had become embedded into the flesh of his wrist, making it near impossible to remove. 'I can,' he said forcefully, though his voice was strained as he twisted his arm this way and that, extracting the skin that had become one with the metal.

'You will need it for the summer raids,' I tried to argue, though no one ever successfully argued with my father.

'Astrid, something tells me I will not. I know you will need something to keep you on your path when I am gone,' he said with a wink.

In his blue eyes, surrounded by weathered skin and deep wrinkles, I thought I saw the glint of a tear. It was not possible. My father never cried. 'Have you had your runes cast?' I asked him.

'No.'

'Then how do you know?'

'I feel it in my bones,' he responded and continued the struggle to remove his armring.

The force he was exerting caused me to think he would push the bones out from within his skin. Eventually, the ring popped off with such force that it flew into the air and curved down to land on the grass between his feet. He shifted closer to me and, scooping up the ring and taking it between his thumb and forefinger, lowered it into the lake before us, waving it back and forth as he washed it. The metal glittered beneath the thin sheet of water, distorting its proportions.

'Now it has a new purpose - to protect you,' he said, handing it to me with a smile.

I could see the effects of its constant wear on my father's skin, his wrist indented with the twisting pattern of the metal. A white band of flesh, the tell-tale sign of years of wear, where the sun darkened the skin around it but could not reach under the metal. There were two deep indents where the nodes of the ring pressed into his flesh.

'I thought you got an armring when you took an oath to protect someone else - like the jarl?' I asked. I had never been to the *thing*, the great meeting, though I heard many people talk about them.

'That is true.'

'Then I do not deserve it. I've taken no oath to protect anyone,' I huffed.

'You must make an oath to protect yourself, Astrid. In this life, you will need to use your instincts. There is a natural order. Such as when the jarl asks something of you for which, in return, you too will receive. This is life. But beware of those who are generous without demand. The time will come when they call on the debt you have unwittingly accepted.' He paused. 'Daughter,' he added seriously. 'You have to make an oath to me that you will protect yourself. Do not fall for tricks and do not allow yourself to be led easily.'

'I promise.' I nodded, accepting the armring and slotting my hand into the opening where it rattled around, loose on my wrist.

'Not like that.' He took my arm in his hand. 'You should wear it here,' he said, pushing the armring onto my forearm and disguising it beneath the rough brown wool of my shirt sleeve. 'Should you ever need me, when I am not here, know that you have my strength - that is my gift to you.'

I glanced at my father, this enormous warrior who was staring out over the water. I removed my armring, breathing it in. Though metal itself did not have a smell, the wear upon it kept a fragrance that encompassed my father's life: farm animals, perspiration, mead, and home. To me, it smelled like adventure. It was everything my father was to me: a farmer, raider, explorer, and above all, him. I knew the scent would fade with time and each time I touched it, it would bring the memory of my father back to me, comforting me in his absence.

'Even if what you say is true, I would like to think you will do your best to come home.'

Without acknowledging my comment, he continued to stare across the water, where the hills mirrored our embankment. As he stared, I watched him. He had allowed me to tidy his hair, which I had fastened back against his neck with a leather lace, but I had missed a strand and it protruded obviously like a rat's tail. When I had pointed it out earlier, he laughed, patting the back of his head, feeling for the hair. 'It adds more character to my appearance. Now every man and woman will know me from the back.' I doubted anyone could mistake my father's massive form, for he was a giant of a man. I desperately hoped he would fix it once he left. I couldn't bear him facing the battle, looking anything but his best.

As I had many times before, I begged my father to take me with him.

'Astrid, you are barely fifteen - too young,' he had said to me, shaking his head.

'Father, you have trained me. I know how to use an axe and I am ready.'

'To use an axe?' He laughed.

'I can.'

'I know you can, but there is a great world of difference between knowing how to use it and actually using it to take a man's life.'

'Or a woman's,' I interjected.

'Huh?' He stopped.

'A man.' I paused before continuing. 'Or a woman's life. I've seen both go into battle,' I explained.

A wry smile that told me my indignant comment had entertained him crept across his lips, 'Yes, there is a substantial difference between using your axe on a wooden figure and using it to kill a man, or a woman.'

'I could do it,' I protested.

'I know you could.'

'Then you will speak to the jarl on my behalf?' I was hopeful.

He paused as if to consider it. 'You are a fine fighter, but it would not be right to allow a girl so young to go and besides, your mother would never agree to it.' It was true; my mother would not appreciate my father carting me off for adventure and untold dangers. 'You will go one day,' my father promised.

It irritated me that his promise had not been more immediate, for I had always thought that it would be better to die on the battlefield than in a childbed.

'Astrid,' he said, turning to look at me. 'There are things I see in your future that will require much strength. It is my hope that, even though I may sup with the gods, I will be there when you need me.' I instinctively touched the armring as if it brokered some secret connection between us. Bjarndýr, I had named it, bear, like my father who would always be there to protect me.

My awareness came back to the room, the hard stool I was sitting upon, and the reality of the situation I found myself in. My fingers still traced Bjarndýr's intricacies, and I felt I now had the strength to approach Auden's body. Lying on his side as he usually did, his arm untucked and laying atop the furs whilst his body was nestled among the layers. His slightly open mouth and gently closed eyes did not betray any difficulty in his passing; it appeared he merely slept his way into death. *A peaceful way to pass*, I thought to myself.

My mother had chosen Auden as my match because of his age and wealth. A man to curb my rebellion. Auden, I was told, had chosen me for lack of other suitable young ladies and had been told I would cause little disruption to his already well-established life. Mother had not known him, for if she had, she would have known he had no stomach for discipline. That much was evident from his grown children. What had curbed my rebellion was boredom, isolation, and disinterest, the most certain of ways to kill the fire within a person.

Auden was grey when I first saw him, an old man who I had begrudged at first. He had been kind to me from the start, which was more than I expected, and more than many women received as their wedding gift. Though we had spent years tied together in union, we had never developed more than a mutual understanding to let the other be, which suited me well enough and for that, he had earned my respect.

In the darkness, I stood over him, examining his white hair, wrinkled face and gnarled hand that held fast to a gathering of fur. I had not screamed when I discovered his senseless body beside me, though it had startled me when I shook him to stir. I had not raised our house. He was long gone, and I knew I needed to make my decision before anyone could remove that possibility from me.

As a widow, I had two options: remain with the family of my deceased husband and be married once more at their pleasure or return to whatever family I had.

My mother had died shortly after my marriage. I cared not for my sister, and that left my aunt Torfid. She had remained in Karlstad her entire life. I could not know what I would do when I arrived in Karlstad, but I would be free of Auden's sons, who had not treated me as kindly as he had.

Where Auden managed his estate with an even hand, his two sons desired power and, although I knew there was no possibility of my being with child, they did not and any child I might have been carrying would have stood in their way. Once the morning came and Auden's death became known, it would topple me from my position of importance as his wife and I would be tossed out or re-shelved to marry again when the time presented itself. I spun my armring around my forearm, tracing the bear heads with each turn.

Finally, I felt the sun rising from where it slept, sunlight creeping into the room through the gaps in the wood, soaking beams and doorways with light. The chatter of the female thralls on their way to clean the room and help me dress was the first noise to reach my ears. I rushed to meet them, pulling a shawl around my shoulders before one of them entered the room.

'Has he risen for the day?' asked Isla, a slight girl with hair of fire and a fair face.

'No,' I answered.

She must have been scarcely older than me, I wasn't sure, and had been owned by Auden before I arrived but gifted to me upon our wedding. I refused to acknowledge owning a person and, though they deprived her of her home and family across the sea, I attempted to show her as much kindness as I was able.

'He is still asleep?' she asked, shocked. She knew, as I had come to, that he never slept past sunrise.

'Auden is dead.'

She stared at me, her green eyes round with disbelief, silence on her lips.

'Did you hear me?' I asked.

She nodded. 'What should I do?'

'Tell his sons.'

She glanced at Auden's shrouded body. 'Would it be better if you told them?'

'Absolutely not!'

'They will beat me,' she cried.

I took her hand. 'Isla, I have no reason to expect that this would cause them to have any violent outburst. On the contrary, I expect them to welcome the news of their new position and inheritance.'

She sniffled back tears.

'They will not hurt you,' I assured her.

'How could you know that?'

'Did you kill him?' I asked her, knowing the answer.

'Of course not. I would never,' she blundered.

'Then you have no reason to fear retribution.'

Her eyes wandered over Auden's body, narrowing with thought.

'How did he die?' she asked.

'I do not know. I woke in the night and found him like this.'

'Do you want me to dress you?'

I waved her away. 'Go, I will dress quickly before you return with his sons.'

She looked again at Auden, took a deep breath, and scuttled out of the room to deliver the news. I knew it would be a matter of moments before the room would fill with people coming to see the truth of Auden's death.

Gathering my garments, I changed my night dress for a simple woollen underdress in cream and an outer dress of thicker spun woollen fabric in dark blue, which did a decent job of keeping out the chill. I pushed Bjarndýr high on my forearm to my elbow, out of view, and pulled my sleeve down to my wrist. The stiff fabric of my outer dress swept the floor, the light grey trimming a stark contrast

9

to show that I was wealthy enough to wear light-coloured fabrics that would stain with any laborious work. Dark, sturdy fabrics were made for people who would inevitably spill the earth upon the weave.

As I tied a strand of leather with a bronze pendant around my neck, I could hear the approach of voices engaged in anxious conversation. Hurriedly I fastened my thin leather belt, with pouch attached, around my waist, tying it and tucking the excess on the other side. They drew nearer, the voices louder. I stood in the centre of the room as I threw my cloak around my shoulders where it lay heavy and to the ground, the grey fabric matching the hem of my dress. I didn't have time to place the grey fox fur around my shoulders before the men entered the bedroom. I snatched it from the bed and held it in my hands, using the soft fur to comfort me in what I knew would be a trying exchange of words. Isla appeared in the chamber door. Behind her, heavy footsteps approached.

'Where is he?' Harald, the eldest son, asked me, pushing Isla out of the doorway. He was barely taller than me, though he had the self-assurance of a man twice his size. He appeared to have dressed as hurriedly as I had, his tunic crooked and his feet without shoes. Half of his brown hair was fastened at the top of his head with a leather lace, the rest left to fall to his shoulders in an untidy mess.

I motioned to Auden lying in our bed and went to stand aside him as the members of our house craned their heads into the chamber to look.

'Why didn't you call for us sooner?' Harald asked, annoyed.

'I sent for you as soon as I woke,' I lied.

I glanced around for Isla. Our eyes met as she took the sign to slink out of sight.

'How did he die?' Gorm, the younger of the two sons, asked.

I shrugged. 'I don't know.'

Gorm was younger but towered above his brother. Childhood illness marked his face, unlike his brother, who proved far too proud of his own good looks. As was the case for younger sons, who had less to prove, Gorm had an easier, more relaxed nature.

'It appears Father expired because of his advanced age,' said Harald, having pulled Auden's eyelid back and inspected his eyes. 'There are no marks, nothing to hint to any cause,' he continued, opening his father's mouth to check for any malady upon his teeth and tongue.

'What a shame he had no appetite for war, or he could have been feasting with the gods instead of festering in his bed.'

'Hush, that's a horrible thing to say, Harald,' I rebuked him, smoothing the fur atop the bed he had rumpled in his assessment of his father's corpse.

'Brother, Astrid is right,' Gorm said, looking around the room.

'He was a good man, and he left you a good inheritance,' I added. Gorm sent a sideways glance at Harald. He, too, would be unsure of his position now.

'When it is my time, when the gods deem it, I will not allow myself to die old in my bed. No! I am fated to die in battle and go to Valhalla! Everyone, get out!' Harald dismissed the room. 'Astrid, not you,' he ordered me to remain.

I turned towards him, his gnarled nose broken many times, distorting his face like a wavy line down the middle, though it served to only make his eyes and mouth even more remarkable. 'I did not know any sooner than I sent for you,' I lied again, worried he was about to punish me, as was his right to do. Gorm lingered in the doorway.

'What will you do?' Harald asked me. 'Will you stay here?'

Why did he care? I wondered. He wouldn't want to marry me himself. Harald liked pretty things, and I was nowhere near what I considered pleasing to his eye. It concerned me he might want to shackle me to his brother Gorm as some strange form of punishment, a way of keeping us both out of the way. My dearest hope was that he would have no argument about my leaving. Glad I had taken the time to think before sending for Harald, I knew what my answer would be without hesitation.

'I will return to my family.'

'What family do you have? Your mother and father are dead, are they not?'

We both had that sad fact in common, but I ignored his careless remark. 'I have an aunt, my mother's sister, in Karlstad. I will go to her, as my father would have wanted.'

'You have no other kin? A sister remains, I recall.'

'That is true, though we were never close. I prefer to go to my aunt in Karlstad. It is not far, so I will not trouble you for a horse or escort. I can walk alone.'

'If that is what you wish, though I could choose to take you as my wife,' he spoke slowly, lingering on each word as if to relish my visible unease at the suggestion. He clicked his tongue, 'No, you're not pretty enough for me and far, far too wilful. What kind of man would it take to break you, I wonder? I could try, I guess, but the reward,' his gaze wandered from my face down the front of my dress, 'would be hardly worth the effort.'

I jutted my chin out and stood to my full height, refusing to be intimidated. He had thought to insult me with the comment, but I found my wilfulness something of a virtue. 'I am sure you will find a suitable mate soon Harald and she will surely see you for the prize that you are.'

He narrowed his eyes, though I was sure he did not grasp my thinly veiled affront. 'You will stay for the funeral and the obligatory mourning period. Once we are done with you, then you may leave.' He drew close enough for me to feel his breath as he spoke.

'I will stay for the funeral,' I agreed, taking a step back. 'I won't stay any longer than that.'

'It is customary that you remain here for the mourning period. You should know that!'

Refusing to be terrorised by Harald's arrogance, I would not be the one to break eye contact first.

'If you should discover yourself with child, then that child would be my father's heir,' Harald baited with malevolence in his eyes.

'You are his eldest Harald. You are Auden's heir. This is the way it should be,' I corrected, my tone softening. Was he really worried that I was with child?

'Another child, a girl, could mean a profitable marriage alliance; a boy in the family could become my warrior. Either way, their place would be here in this house.'

'There will not be a child.'

'How could you possibly know that right now?' He raised his eyebrow. 'There could be a child. Do you have any signs or lack of a sign?'

'Harald!' I admonished, shocked that he would dare to ask such a thing in front of anyone.

His brother was obviously undeterred by the question and pressed his own. 'How could you be so sure?' Gorm asked from the doorway.

Was their plan to humiliate me into admitting that my marriage was one that would leave me either proven as barren or undesirable? 'There's not a child and you both know it. I will stay for the funeral and then I will leave.'

Having succeeded in his embarrassment of me, he relinquished, 'Fine, leave when you are done. I will not stop you.'

'You are so generous,' I whispered, bowing my head in dutiful deference and just as much to hide the grimace at having to do so.

'Why you would want to return to the life of a farm girl, I cannot understand, but that is your mistake to make.' He nodded and left the room with Gorm to make preparations for his father's funeral.

The event would be consistent with his station in life. We would make a *blót*, an offering to the gods on Auden's behalf, ensuring his safe passage to the afterlife. There would be feasting to be enjoyed by all who knew him.

The morning after the funeral, I packed my things. Not wanting to be burdened by belongings, I took with me only a rucksack containing bedding, food and supplies, and the clothing that I wore, along with the axe and shield I received from my father. When I was first married, I hid my weapons from Auden. One day, when I slipped out to practise in the woods, he had seen me. Thinking I would receive a reprimand, I knelt before him. To my surprise, he raised me up, looked me in the eye, and gave me the greatest compliment I had ever received. 'You are not who your mother described, but that does not displease me,' he said with a gentle smile. From that day on we were more gentle neighbours than our previous feeble attempts at husband and wife.

The journey to Karlstad was not difficult. It would be two days walking through mostly flat or undulating green lands. I stopped at the bottom of the longhouse to look back. I hoped I would never see it again.

'You have all you need?' Gorm asked me. He was the only one to see me off.

'I think so. I have enough provisions to see me to Karlstad.' Inside my bag were smoked fish, some bread, and a few berries to last me on my travels.

'Once you leave, you cannot return,' he warned. I knew the conditions. 'You are sure?' he asked.

'I have never been surer,' I replied calmly.

'Was my father such a terrible husband?' Gorm had known there was no love between Auden and me, though we had confined that unhappiness to ourselves.

A smile tilted the corners of my mouth at some of the fonder memories. 'He was a kind man.'

'He was a good father.'

'And a fair landowner,' I agreed.

'A trait Harald does not possess,' Gorm lamented.

'I would wish you good fortune, but I fear it would not help you. You will have to make your way in the world soon enough.' I knew it would be a short time before the brothers found conflict with one another.

'I know it.' Gorm nodded. 'Will you miss any of this?'

I had to stop myself from laughing. Missing part of a life I never wanted seemed preposterous. 'Not a single bit.'

'Well then, I wish you good fortune and farewell, Astrid,' he bid me goodbye.

It had been many years since I had seen my aunt Torfid and I was looking forward to having a familial connection. There was also some freedom in being a widow and I fantasised about finally joining in on the summer raids. My father had kept me from them as a young woman and my mother had persisted with the prohibition until marriage chained me to Auden and the pretence had stopped there. My mother believed the only dangerous activity a woman should engage in was childbirth, something I did all in my power to avoid.

I stopped on the crest of a small hill to admire the distance I was putting between myself and Auden's, now Harald's, land. To the west was my past and with every step I took towards the east, to the settlement of Karlstad, I felt as if I was dropping the stones that had weighed me down since my marriage. The land around was mostly family farms with fringes of forest-green everywhere. I would be safe enough on my own, I reasoned. The only people I expected to encounter were farmers. Having made the reverse journey two summers prior, I knew what to expect: long days of walking with little change in the scenery.

Crouching down at a small inlet to splash water on my face, I remembered my arrival as an unwilling bride. Not knowing what to expect, save for a marriage to an old man, I had not imagined the isolation I would experience. I had made few friends, forged no connections, found no comfort. Now every breath I took felt like the sweetest air I had ever breathed, releasing the pressure put upon me. The coolness of the water trickling down my cheeks brought blood to the surface of my skin, prickling like a thousand insects marching across my face. The sky above me was a rippling fabric, almost close enough to touch. Grass grew in thick green tufts, fertile lands that would feed a herd of sheep year-after-year; such lands had kept Auden and me in obscene wealth. I wondered if Harald would have the ability to maintain it. That was no longer my concern, and I shook my care for them off as I removed my cloak, draping it over the crook of my left arm.

Dinner was preserved herrings and dry bread. I savoured their strong flavour; salty, smoky, and sweet. As night came, I unrolled some furs I would use as a camp bed, laying down and covering myself with my cloak. By this time tomorrow, I would be in Karlstad and as I closed my eyes, I imagined what my new life would be like. With a smile, I drifted into the darkness of my first night, unencumbered.

'*Kona.*'

I could hear, but my eyes remained closed, fused, willing it to be part of my dreaming.

'*Kona.* Lady. You should wake up.' His voice sounded childlike.

I opened my eyes to see the boy who had been calling out standing above me in the morning light. I had slept all night.

'You should move on, *kona*. My sheep graze here.' He motioned towards his flock of black sheep behind him. 'They particularly like to *skita* on that spot there.' He pointed to a clump of dung right next to me. I bolted out of my bedding.

The boy stood barely as tall as my shoulder and was likely half my age. 'There, this is where they *skita*,' he repeated with a giggle.

I shook my bedding to dislodge the droppings, and the boy helped me by attempting to flick the straggling pieces off with his stick. 'You

15

must have been tired when you set up your bed.' He laughed as he dislodged the last of the stubborn excrement.

'I was,' I agreed, as I rolled and wrapped my bedding into a tight bundle and attached it to my rucksack. 'Do you know how far Karlstad is from here?' Many people in the villages, most never leaving their small farms, would not have made the journey themselves, but would have some idea of the distance and direction.

'No more than half a day, if you don't stop too many times,' he riddled.

I wondered how many times would be too many, and what half a day was to him. Planning on walking steadily, I hoped it meant I would arrive long before nightfall. He watched me secure my cloak around my shoulders. The morning air had a chill, but I would have to remove it once the sun was at its full heat and the walk warmed me from the inside.

'That is a fine cloak,' he observed.

'A gift from my dead husband.'

'Was he a jarl?' he asked, tapping his stick on the ground.

'No, just a rich landowner.' The well-practised answer tumbled from my mouth. Auden never had the stomach for warfare, though many would have considered him a chief among his otherwise equals, though he had never hungered after it. His sons, I knew, would find their way to that title by whatever means necessary.

'What will you do now?' he asked innocently.

'I am going to Karlstad to be with my aunt.'

He nodded, as if satisfied by the answer. 'My parents will be wanting me,' the boy remembered. 'The sheep graze here until the afternoon, but my brother will be up soon to watch over them. It's his job to make sure they don't get into trouble.' He grinned, running away, tapping the sheep's backsides with the stick as he raced by. Honest interactions with children were my favourite; they had no need for niceties and felt no compulsion to keep the conversation going once it had served its purpose.

I threaded my arms through the straps of my rucksack and made sure it sat comfortably on my back. The load was not heavy. I moved quickly, skipping over some rocks that lay in the shallower inlets, allowing me to pass by them with ease. Everything around me melded into green. It was everywhere, so strong it hurt my eyes. These lands fed their farmers well; not so in the lands surrounding Orebro, where I had grown up. The town was upon the Narke plains, surrounded by tall trees and harder to grow good, strong crops. As I walked through dividing lines, I smiled and greeted farmers. They were lucky to live on such fertile lands and, so long as their families did not grow large, they could feed them all. With large families came splitting property until there was scarcely enough to support any of them. It was a problem facing many of my people. Fertile land had already been allotted, and others took less viable land, hoping to succeed. Squabbling broke out everywhere, leading to many seeking their fortunes through raiding, devoid of other options. My family had not owned their own land. My father was a warrior, a Viking, and worked the land for others when he was not away searching for riches. It was the way of the men who lived near the settlements and larger villages. There simply was not enough land for everyone to have their own slice of it.

Opening the pouch, I had secured to the belt around my waist, I retrieved what remained of last night's bread for my breakfast. If it had been dry last night, it was now so hard and unyielding that I thought it was almost inedible. Ideally, it would have been warm and freshly baked, but after two days of travel, it was hard as a rock and quite unappealing. I smeared what small pieces of herring remained, attempting to add some moisture to the meal. Crunching through the dough was impossible, but if I left it in my mouth for a moment, it softened enough to break apart. It was a slow and frustrating way to eat when my stomach was already grumbling hungrily.

Overhead, a flock of birds flew towards the open ocean. My favourite bird was the swan, with its graceful long neck and large white feathers, elegant without frivolity. The large wings meant it could cover great distances with ease. Life would have been easier had I had my own wings. I could have flown to the ends of the earth, made my own life and moved on when I wanted to. The distance between me and the birds was too great, and I could not make out if they were my favourite swans, but I continued watching them anyway until they were out of sight.

As I wandered along, away with my thoughts, I hadn't noticed the tall *mullein* flowers brushing against my clothing. Sneezes erupted from me as a cloud of yellow covered me, their hairy little flowers irritating my nose. It covered me in pollen, and it clung to my dress as if life depended on it. Beating the persistent powder from my clothing only irritated me further, sending me into another sneezing fit, my nose running and my eyes watering from the ordeal. Water was the only way to rid myself of the irritant. I splashed my face until I felt relief, the prickly sensation replaced by the cool tingle of refreshing water. The sun beat down on me and from its height I knew it was near noon, which meant I would soon arrive in Karlstad. I found the path that was worn into the ground and followed it towards the town, people nodding in greeting as I passed.

There was little time to think as my heart beat loudly in my chest, anticipating my reunion with my aunt. Torfid was a lot like my mother in appearance, but nothing alike in nature. Where my mother was authoritarian and austere, Torfid was a relaxed and generous woman. My mother had married young, like many women, and given my father two children. Torfid had no children of her own, preferring to remain unmarried, or at least that was the story she told. My aunt had long stayed in the town, providing weaving services for the townspeople. She made a decent living from it and thankfully it had been this skill, learned from my aunt, that had been the only womanly pursuit my mother had been proud of me for. Torfid was popular. She had many friends and seemed to enjoy her life. How she would react to my situation, I did not know. She had no forewarning of my arrival, as I had sent no word - still, I was sure she would be happy to see me. I was always her favourite, as she had been mine. That was likely part of the reason there had been a rift between my mother and me. Her own daughter reminded her too much of her sister, the carefree and unconstrained Torfid.

Over the rise, wooden longhouses came into view with silhouettes of people and animals going about their daily life. I entered through the rear of the settlement, where the livestock sheltered, and they built homes. Most new arrivals came via the water, where trade and travel occurred. It had been a long time since I had smelled the mingling of dung and marketplace that hung heavily in the air of a town with tightly packed buildings and small muddy walkways. It was glorious.

Walking past a pig pen, I saw a young girl with dirty blonde hair sitting on the fence with a blade of grass sticking out from between her teeth.

'Where can I find Torfid?' I asked. In a place like this, everyone knew everyone.

'In there,' she said, pointing to a large longhouse across the muddy path. I thanked her and made my way towards the building.

It took a moment for my eyes to adjust to the darkness inside the longhouse. Light spots flashed before my eyes as the sunlight outside gave way to the windowless interior. I steadied myself in the doorway. The inside of longhouses was always dark, built for protection against the elements, their only light source the central fire which also provided much-needed warmth. I had previously seen some buildings that had windows, but windows meant that wind, rain, and snow could enter along with the light, and if one was shut out, they all were.

'Have you seen Torfid?' I asked a woman inside nursing her infant. She threw her head to her left, and I looked around her. My aunt, tall, with beautiful grey eyes, stood behind her.

'Astrid? Is that you?' she asked, coming close to embrace me.

'Oh Aunt, how I have missed you!' I squeezed tighter.

'I am so happy to see you, but why have you come? Is everything alright?' It was not unusual for women to visit their families, but they seldom arrived without their spouse, and never alone.

My mouth curved into a smile. 'I no longer find myself married.'

Torfid shook her head slightly, trying to understand my meaning. 'He divorced you?'

'Odin's beard! Never! He died and I couldn't bear another moment in that place.'

'I see.' Her eyes narrowed and in a hushed voice she said, 'I never forgave your mother for packing you off to that old man.'

'That is why I had to come to you.' I still clung to her.

'Come, sit down. We have much to talk about.' She guided me towards a bench and plopped me down, standing in front of me, facing the doorway. She stopped smiling and squinted at the figure that had appeared.

'Ah, Sven,' Torfid addressed the man who had entered.

'Torfid.' He smiled, kissing her cheeks. 'Have you finished the detailing for my mother?' he asked, sitting down beside me, even though he had taken no notice of my existence.

'Yes,' my aunt answered, handing the fabric to him. 'Sven, this is my sister's daughter, Astrid.' She sent a nod in my direction.

'*Hej*, I know Astrid.' A broad grin flashed upon his handsome face.

'I only just returned this very day.' Heat rose in me, and I thanked the gods for the dim light that hid my flushed face.

His smile did not fade. 'I did not think I would ever see you again after I moved away. If you recall, I was very reluctant.'

'As was I.' Our eyes held for longer than was comfortable. 'And are you back living in Karlstad now?'

He nodded. 'Things did not work out in Orebro for my mother and me.'

I turned to my aunt to explain our acquaintance, 'We used to play as children, but I have not seen him since I left to marry Auden!' The knowing look on Torfid's face told me I needn't have bothered, for she well remembered my acquaintance with Sven, and no doubt the trouble we used to cause together.

'And have you returned on your own?' Sven did not miss the look Torfid flashed in his direction, barely veiled by a flutter of eyelashes.

I nodded.

'And recently widowed,' Torfid offered, to which I responded with a cautionary glare.

'Your husband will be feasting with the gods in Valhalla by now.' Sven spoke the line we all reiterated when a warrior died, and we offered comfort to the family of the deceased.

'No, I know for sure he is supping with none other than the worms and I'm certainly not sorry to be widowed.' My aunt looked shocked, but Sven laughed.

'Oh, how I remember you, Astrid,' he said, slapping me on the back.

Torfid looked down at the embroidery piece in her hands, her eyebrows raised and a smile curling at the corners of her lips.

'Be assured, we will see a lot of each other, *minn Svanr*. So much to catch up on.' His arm wound around me, squeezing our bodies together before releasing me.

'Curse my readable face,' I grumbled to myself as I felt my face glowing red again. 'Still intent on calling me by that ridiculous nickname?'

'Always, *minn Svanr*. Graceful without frivolity, just like your favourite bird, if I remember correctly. You were forever looking up to the birds, eh?' He kissed my aunt again on the cheek and left the longhouse with his commission in hand.

'I hope no one else remembers anything so embarrassing about me,' I groaned to my aunt as she slipped her bony arm around my shoulders.

She eyed me sideways and looped a lock of my hair around her finger, twirling it. 'He certainly remembers you, my girl, but I think the question at the frontmost part of my mind is, why does he think you are his?'

PART ONE

Tell me a tale,
We have hope, we have dreams.
To have a little more
Than the scraps we need to feed.
Tell me why we should not wander
To far off, distant lands.
And take what we may
By the strength of our hands.
When those who reside there
Do not protect their riches
They do not deserve them.
For they know not our names
Only of our deeds.
They care not to know more.
We are brutish
To those outsiders.
We are fearsome

In the eyes of ignorance.
They know not our lives,
We have families and loved ones
We are farmers and merchants.
But above all
Optimistic and opportunistic.

ONE

Spring 880 CE, Karlstad, Svealand

My skin itched under the woollen fabric of my clothing. The midday sun was intolerably warm and only made the itching worse. Sven was in the field before me, pulling weeds out at the root, and his shirt soaked with the exertion of hard work. I raised my hand to my brow, shielding my eyes from the sun, and leaned against the rail of the wooden fence. The gesture caught Sven's attention.

'Just making sure everything is in order before our departure,' he yelled. He waved as he walked towards me.

'Will your mother be happy?' I replied as he came nearer.

'The season has been kind. She has no cause for concern.' The fence bowed under his weight. Sven leaned against the rail as he grabbed a handful of his tunic to wipe away the sweat dripping from his face.

'Enough to get the family through until you return?'

I was lucky. Aside from my aunt, who was more than capable of looking after herself, I had no one to worry about.

'She will need to do maintenance, but I think she will have plenty to eat,' he answered. Hunger was always a genuine threat. Mouths to feed were ever-increasing and, it seemed, the fertility of the land was on the decline.

'Who knows when we will be back? It could be a few months or more. She will be fine. She's a smart woman.' Sven threw one leg over the railing, hopping over the fence with ease. 'Are you ready?' he asked with a grin, throwing his left arm around my shoulders as we walked back to town.

I tossed my head back with a laugh. 'Of course. I have been waiting for this moment since I was a little girl. I'm not sure I could be any more ready than I am now.'

'You're all packed?' Sven already knew the answer. My bag had been packed and waiting for weeks. I shrugged off Sven's heavy arm and continued to stride purposefully toward our destination.

'Finally sold that dress,' I reported.

'You should have kept it.'

'What would I need such a fine dress for? The coin I got in exchange for it is far more valuable to me,' I responded. Fortunately for me, the man I sold it to had a pretty wife he wished to adorn. 'And I certainly don't need it for any memory of Auden,' I added. My foot struck a rock, and I stumbled back, Sven catching me by the elbow.

'You're far too clumsy to wear such fine things anyway.' He chuckled, releasing my arm.

'I prefer to be distinguished by my skills and not my choice of clothing.' A quick brush down wiped away my damaged pride and the dirt on my dress. Now that I had sold my impractical garments, I wore the typical long *serkr* underneath a woollen hangerock, a combination far easier to move in. A closer cut gown threatened to rip at the seams at the slightest unwomanly movement. The simple brooches that fastened the dress at the straps meant all I had to do was put my head through the opening rather than fuss with any laces or fastenings. No, I would never regret shedding my fine attire. They were stifling.

We climbed the incline of a small hill on the approach home, our breath labouring with each step. The grass underfoot was springy and green, made full by drenching rains and plenty of sunshine.

'I rather liked the dress, *minn Svanr*.'

'URGH! Why do you continue with that stupid name?' I asked for the umpteenth time, quickening my step to walk ahead of him.

'I'll stop when you do something with that mop on your head,' he teased as he ran behind me, messing my hair with his giant hands.

'What's wrong with my hair?' I wore it loose down my back like an unmarried woman and I thought it looked neat enough. I scooped it up and let it hang in a mass over my right shoulder.

'A warrior should always look her best,' he quipped.

'You sound like my father.'

'And he would have told you to comb it,' Sven remarked.

As we neared the town, the earthen pathway crunched beneath our leather shoes.

'It might have been left to grow wild for too long now,' I agreed.

'Luckily, I didn't mistake it for a weed, or I might have just… pop!' He accompanied the sound with a plucking motion, as if he had pulled the weed straight from the ground.

'And then you might have received a beating from my aunt,' I joked. 'I could ask her to help me.' Aunt Torfid could braid in her sleep, and the style would keep my hair from my face. It would also give me the chance to spend some time with my aunt before my departure.

'Will she miss you?' Sven asked. He paused for a moment to let an old lady pass as we navigated the narrow alleyway between the animal stalls, the air strong with dung and rotting fruit.

'Oh, I guess so. She may miss my help with the spinning and weaving, but she was alone for so long before I returned, she will manage without me.' As an accomplished craftswoman, my aunt had instructed me in the art of weaving fine fabrics on the loom, a task that had kept me busy during the cold months.

'You've been alone for a while now, too. Do you think you will want to marry again?' A mischievous glint was in his eye. We had talked about my previous marriage but seldom spoke about marrying again with any seriousness.

'Not unless I meet someone tall, handsome, and funny.' The pathway was too narrow to walk side-by-side, so I shouted back to him over my shoulder.

'He would have to be funny?'

'Oh yes, he would have to make me laugh,' I answered seriously, stopping to look at him.

'What about a strong warrior type?' Sven asked, wrapping his arms around me and squeezing the air from within me.

'I wouldn't rank gratuitous muscles highly,' I jibed, finding myself pushed against the side of a merchant's log house.

'Not even if he was very, very handsome.' Sven smiled, releasing me from his arms without stepping aside.

'Most of all, he would have to let me go raiding and wouldn't leave me at home.' I poked his stomach with my fingertip. He recoiled, and I took my chance to escape.

'So, you would consider marrying again?'

'Why? Do you have a friend who can't ask me himself?'

'I just want to know if my raiding partner is searching for gold or for love.' Sven was breathless, as he fought to keep up with my pace.

'Not love, that much is certain.'

Sven joined me as we walked along the buildings. 'What about marriage?'

'No marriage,' I agreed. 'So, you can tell your friend I'm not interested.'

'You only have eyes for the gold?' He waved his hands about as if he could conjure the metal into being.

'When I find my wealth, I'll never have need of a man again.'

Sven cackled.

'Not as a husband anyway,' I retorted, stilling his laughter. 'What about you, Sven? When is your mother going to tire of you being home and goad you to take a wife?'

'When the time is right,' he answered enigmatically.

I rolled my eyes. 'When the time is right, ha! Is there such a time? Your mother wishes you were married yesterday or even longer before.'

'She does,' he conceded, 'but it is not so straightforward.'

'Are you going to tell me who she is?' I asked as we walked towards the longhouse.

'I would ask you to be patient, but I know that's not possible for you,' he jibed. 'Do you remember when we were little *barns* and your mother made bread?'

'She was forever making bread.'

'One time she had made so many discs of bread for both of our families and she put it on a rod to cool. Of course, she warned us not to eat any of it, but you did not listen. Even though it was scorching hot, you snuck off with two of them and burned your mouth eating it. Your mother was furious,' he recalled.

'I don't remember that!' I lied.

'She was so mad! And your tongue was so raw you had no taste for a week!' He laughed until his eyes leaked with tears.

'That sounds more like you.' I pretended I didn't remember, but I did. My tongue had been so badly burned that not only was food tasteless, Sven had relentlessly teased me because I could not speak properly until it healed.

'It seems I remember more of your childhood than you do.' He wiped a tear of laughter from his cheek.

'Pfft. I remember the fireside stories of adventure and the first time I held Skara, my axe, but none of the tales you keep making up,' I provoked him, and enjoyed the look of irritation it brokered.

'As you keep telling me. But I remember you back then,' he spoke in a low tone and winked as he left me at the door of the longhouse. As he sauntered down the path, I wondered which of the women who so often swooned over my friend would wed him. Would it be Gislaug with her pretty brown hair or would Freydis' mother, Unna, shove her daughter into Sven's bed? He might be young and attractive, but he did not own land. If he returned from the raids having made his fortune, then marriage would be beyond doubt. No, I was certain he would wait until his adventure was done. He was not ready yet.

It was always dark inside the longhouse. There was a central hearth with only a small opening in the roof for its escape, so it clouded the inside of the building, filling my nose with its acrid smoke. My eyes adjusted to the dim light inside and I searched for my aunt. The benches built onto the walls of the structure housed napping women with their children and various articles of clothing and blankets, were also used for sleeping. Children were playing, running between benches disregarding any delineated territories. Their mothers attempted to control their wayward manners and when they could not, a simple dip of the head indicated their apologies. I looked down as a boy no taller than my knees ran into me and squeezed between my legs, under my dress, and shot out from behind, running away, squealing with delight. I could not help the small laugh that escaped my mouth.

Everyone had their place in the longhouse, and mine at the very back corner was, in my opinion, the best position. In the summer, fingers of cool air reached through gaps in the wood, refreshing my skin as I slept. When winter came, the icy wind would chill me and I would creep down further under my fur linings to keep warm until the holes would freeze over in the most brutal depths of winter, stopping the cold air from reaching me. During those times, I would push my cloak against the wall and create a cosy little nook. When I closed my eyes,

I imagined the wall was my father's back. As a little girl when the loud winds howled, I would crawl in behind him, and his broad back with its unyielding muscles brought me comfort enough to sleep.

Privacy was scarce in a house shared with others. The longhouse was home to, at the last count, ten families, besides a few single women and a handful of the elderly. The single men lived in another building, not so coincidentally situated close to the tavern. In my corner, I could close my eyes and be alone if I could drum out the incessant noise that accompanied the vast number of people within. Today it was deafening. So many men and women were already preparing to leave and were spending their last moments with loved ones in animated conversation. Next to me, a young couple were parting. The woman stroked her newborn's soft hair as she nursed the child. A timid smile and a quiet farewell were all she managed as her husband left, then she turned her face from him to hide her tears. As soon as he was out of sight, the baby erupted with high-pitched wailing and the mother's sadness soon forgotten.

'Astrid,' I heard my aunt's voice before I saw her. We embraced, and as we did so, I felt her tug on my hair.

'You cannot leave looking like this,' she said disapprovingly. 'Sit.'

I plonked myself on the bench obediently as her nimble fingers combed through my hair, forming tight braids. 'Your father would have been very proud. Once a warrior's daughter, almost one herself.'

The words were compliment enough, but the mention of my father made me beam. 'It is all I've ever wanted.' For as long as I could remember, I had dreamed of sailing for far off places, crashing into forbidding coastlines, setting ashore, clashing sword to sword with ugly strangers and discovering their riches. I wanted to live those fireside stories my father had told.

'You are well prepared. This is your time, and you must take your chance, whatever the cost,' she whispered into my ear.

My father had sired no sons, and, in their absence, he had to make do with two daughters. He had insisted I learned how to fight, not just defend myself. My sister had been disinterested in anything other than those pursuits considered befitting for a young woman and was patently my mother's favourite. Not only had I taken to becoming a warrior at my father's behest, but I thoroughly enjoyed it. I lived and breathed the warrior lifestyle. I dreamed about it. Occasionally, I would sneak away from the overprotectiveness of my mother, finding my father fireside. In his hand, a horn of ale, listening with rapt attention to the tales of the raid from returned warriors. Someone would always send me home before the proper celebrations would begin, at my father's insistence and to my most vehement protestations. At first my mother had been reluctant to allow my father to train me, but in the end, she gave in to his will. Not long after my father died, my mother became intolerant of me. I could not wholly blame her. I was steadfast in my insistence to train, neglecting all my other duties. Without my father to command her, she no longer allowed me to go to the practice yard, nor would she hear my complaints. Clipped into feminine demureness, she whipped me with domestic lessons until I fit the mould she deemed acceptable for her daughters. When I had become befittingly docile, she found me a suitable marriage, and I was then someone else's erstwhile rebel to deal with. I certainly did not agree with her on the suitability of the man she had chosen, nor my new vocation as a wife and mother of two adult children who were older than me. Superficially, I possessed the virtues for the wife that my husband-to-be required: young, presumably fertile and a face unmarked by illness. It became apparent that they did not permit me to have my own criteria, but I ultimately accepted that the union would benefit my family, so I acquiesced. Despite pleading with my mother for more time before my marriage, she would not allow it.

It turned out to be unfortunate timing - within the year my mother would be dead, dying in childbirth struggling to provide her new husband with issue, and I would remain married to a man I never wanted to marry to benefit a family that no longer existed. My husband, Auden, was much older than I, and I was his third wife, but he was kind enough with me. I, at best, tolerated my necessary duties and he, sensing I had neither the love for him nor the task, imposed it upon me less frequently until he left me alone entirely. And now, the only family I had left was my dear aunt Torfid.

'That is the last one. Does it feel secure?' Torfid asked.

'It feels as if it stretched my skin around my head,' I groaned, running a hand over the intricate braiding.

'Good. It will hold for weeks if it is hurting so much now,' she advised reassuringly.

My scalp was on fire.

Torfid and her younger sister Aeilar, my mother, had always looked so much alike. Both had long, ash-blonde hair and grey eyes. They were often being mistaken for twins with their perfectly shaped noses and high angled cheekbones. Their strangely pointed ears made them seem otherworldly entirely, 'children of the gods' they had been called, and it fit them quite rightly. I had not inherited this particular feature. It was this ethereal combination that had attracted the attention of my father and he often joked that my mother was the goddess Freyja's own daughter. Growing up so close in age, the two girls spent much time in each other's company. They were both disobedient, stealing away from their mother to play tricks on the other children. They were harmless usually. However, one incident led to another child almost drowning in the lake. I never learned the details, but it chastised my mother sufficiently, who from then on was a model obedient child. I could not say the same of my aunt, who continued her defiant manner straight into adulthood, and there she had remained. My father would often say I took after my aunt rather than my mother. To me, it was a compliment, but to my mother, it only set us further apart.

'The style suits you.' My aunt smiled, standing back to admire her work. 'You will turn many heads - make sure they are the right ones.' She winked knowingly.

Like so many others who hoped I would soon make another match, she meant well. They hoped I would produce playmates for the other children of the settlement and sit in the dark halls to spin and weave cloth with their mothers during the winter months. It was all that their expectations demanded of me. So, I leaned in to plant a kiss on Torfid's cheek and she embraced me tightly.

As I scooped up my rucksack, I almost forgot the two things I would certainly need. The first was my axe, given to me by my father and named Skara, the carver, and I kept her sharp enough to live up to her name. The second was my shield, made from linden wood with an iron boss and rimmed with an iron band for reinforcement. Neither was decorated, as others had adorned their weapons. They were merely practical, well maintained, and deadly, just as I needed them to be. And both were leaning against the foot of my bench, and I cursed myself for being so absent minded in misplacing them.

Mossy banks hedged my path to the river. When I arrived at its banks, the stunningly blue water greeted me, reflecting the full sun on its surface. My hand dipped into its blue depths. It was crisp. It would be some weeks until one could comfortably submerge themselves, though there were always those who enjoyed the shock of an icy bath. For now, a brief scrub would suffice.

The water stilled enough for me to view my blurry reflection on its surface. My hair was the colour of golden rushes, like most of the women in my family, though, unlike my mother's eyes, mine were a deep shade of blue. My hand ran through my image on the water, and cleaned my hands, face, and neck.

Behind me, I heard a shuffling noise. My body lurched forward, and my hands tried to stop my fall, but found water instead of solid ground and I fell, face first, into the shallows.

'Sven!' I gasped, cold water stealing my breath. 'You are as sneaky as a cat.'

'And, I wasn't even trying to stalk, *minn Svanr*. You startle much too easily.' He snorted. 'Are you finished taking a bath?'

I knelt, but my clothing, now sodden, weighed me down.

'Usually, you would take off your clothes to bathe,' he teased. 'Here, take my hand.'

I got up, ignoring his proffered grip, and wrung the water out of my clothing. 'You're so funny, Sven.'

'Don't forget, I am also strong, and very handsome,' he continued as he approached. He reached a hand towards my shoulder and fastened the corner of my overdress with my embossed brooch, which had come loose.

'Was there ever a man who was more conceited?' I asked as he thumped me on the back, causing me to cough up a lungful of water.

'Of course!' he answered. 'Have you met Eric?'

'Please say he is not coming with us to Birka,' I groaned. Eric was so full of himself it was likely he would just float away into the sky one day.

'He's not on our boat. If we don't run for it, we might not have any other option.' Sven grasped me by the elbow and together we ran to the boats where everyone was preparing to leave, my dress still sodden and the water in my leather slippers sloshing as I ran. 'This is us,' Sven called, waving me over to a small boat at the edge of the water.

I threw my belongings in with the other jumbled rucksacks. 'Move over then.' I pushed past Sven's hulking frame.

'Still have to push her out, you two!' Leif, an older, well-seasoned raider, shouted.

Sven chuckled. 'I knew that. Come on out,' he said, sliding me along the seat with his backside.

With our entire party ready, we pushed each vessel out and when the boat was afloat and away from the shore; we jumped in one by one, careful not to capsize. Shoes off, clothes rung, and basking in the sunshine, our oars lapped the water, and we were slowly on our way.

'Row. Row!' Sven demanded, throwing instructions over his shoulder.

I rolled my eyes. 'What do you think I'm doing here with this oar?' I huffed between breaths as I pulled it with both hands. Sven made it look easy.

'Relax your shoulders or you won't be able to move them tomorrow,' he yelled.

'Worry about yourself,' I shouted back.

'Why are you so stubborn?'

He might have been right, but I didn't like people telling me what to do, so I ignored him.

The small boats which left Karlstad each contained sixteen people and could easily navigate the small rivers and inlets on our way to Uppsala, our first stop being the island of Björkö. Every man and woman would take their turn at the oars, and when the wind and current were right, we would rely on the sail to power us to our destination. This would be the furthest I had ever travelled from my home.

The land surrounding us was overwhelmingly green. Behind the flattened banks of the river, the soft curve of hills and mountains stretched as far as my eyes could see.

After the first day, I found Sven had been right. My shoulders hurt. I reluctantly followed his instruction and improved my technique, and thereafter, the discomfort, while still present, lessened. The day was calm, a light wind, and the current steering us, allowing our party a moment of respite.

'This will be my first raid too,' Sven whispered as we watched the hills go by, taking a seat next to me.

'Why have you waited so long?' I asked.

'My father never wanted me to go. He never went himself. It was more important to him to farm the land.'

'And that's not important to you?'

'We are the same, Astrid, you and me. We want adventure, and I want to bring riches to my family,' he dreamed. It was every man's desire. That was why we went raiding. Now that Sven's father was gone, he had no one to hold him back. Many people of our age had lost a parent. To grow old was to become a burden.

The sky darkened and instead of sleeping inside our vessel; we made a camp on land that night. As we heaved the ship onto the embankment, the sunset stretched fingers of orange and yellow into the dark blue sky.

'I want to find a quiet place for a while, away from all the others,' I told Sven as I slipped away from those unpacking their belongings onto the grass. The evening sky was clear, pleasant enough to enjoy with minimal bedding. I sat away from the others lying down in the tufty grass to watch the stars above. It was impossible to count them all, no matter how many times I tried. I closed my eyes. A moment later, I heard someone approaching. Sven crouched down next to me.

'You shouldn't be alone here. Don't worry,' he said as I shot him an annoyed grimace, 'I'll be quiet.'

'If you must.'

'There are too many men here with no one to check them. It would be safer if I stayed with you, even if that means putting up with your snoring.' He rolled out two sets of bedding.

I sat up. 'Snoring?' I had taken the bait before stopping myself.

We both laughed.

'Are you cold?' he asked.

'The air has a chill on it tonight,' I agreed.

His arm snaked around my shoulders.

'What are you doing?'

'Huh? You said you were cold!'

'So, throw me a fur! Do I have to worry about your advances too, Sven?' I chided him. 'Take a man away from his settlement and suddenly he loses all his senses.'

His cheeks reddened. 'No, it's not like that. Perhaps I am unsure what is to come.'

'We all are. That's part of the adventure.'

He nodded. 'I don't feel like myself,' he confessed.

'And you were looking for comfort?'

'In the wrong place,' he agreed.

'We should join the others,' I suggested, 'a drink and some raucous company might be what we need.'

Our belonging left where they were, we walked back to the fire to listen to the tawny-bearded storyteller regaling the crowd with stories of previous raids. When I was a small girl, my father would send me home before these fireside tales could get going. Sometimes I would sneak back and crouch behind the people gathered. There, I would hear the reality of raiding, the brutality, fatality, and auxiliary damage that was deemed acceptable. The gore and glory were exciting, but for me, learning about the different people and their beliefs captured my interest. Before my father left, I would ask him to observe his opponents and, when he returned, I would expect a report. I recalled believing that every man and woman who went into battle must have felt honoured. Every one of them sought the glory of Valhalla, and those who did not return would go there to be celebrated.

Once the tawny-bearded man concluded his tale, a tall man with dark hair took his place. Everyone leaned forward, for he was a well-known raconteur. I squeezed between enrapt bodies to inch closer to the fire. The tale was one of my favourite stories; it told of a group led by two famous jarls that raided an island across the Austmarr. The inhabitants of the island were no match for the raiders, who easily cleaved heads from shoulders and left with their rival's riches. They returned heroes, and their rank exalted.

'It was a daring feat, for they did not know what land they might have encountered when they travelled there. Would they make it? Would there be anything worth the journey once they arrived?' the dark-haired man asked the crowd. What he didn't tell us was that years later, the same men made that exact journey once more, but this time met with slaughter. The enemy had fortified the island, and what had once been easy prey turned into a viper's nest. Those previously undefeated bands of warriors lost, buried in the ground in foreign lands. Their story brought back with the few survivors that remained. But no one was interested in hearing that story.

I had dreams of exploring settlements in the east, and of visiting exotic cities such as Miklagard, the great city. There was nothing more thrilling than the treasures within its walls. I did not want to remain in my small town, marry and produce children to perpetuate the never-ending cycle of what I perceived to be nothing better than being a slave to one's own husband and family. The Norns had destined me for something more, and I was determined to have it.

My eyes drifted from the storyteller. No matter how many times a story was told, it could still capture its audience with the correct dramatic aplomb. There was one uninterested member of the audience, Sven, stood behind a group of men. He turned away and wandered off into the darkness; I followed. Once out of the crowd, I shadowed Sven until we reached our camp away from the others. In the dim evening light, he sat on the grass and appeared to be deep in thought. I approached slowly and quietly, shuffling my light leather shoes on the dirt underfoot. He was talking, but there was no one around. My feet scuffed the dirt as I crept forward, giving myself away.

'You would be terrible at a stealth attack Astrid,' he said clearly and looked over his shoulder to where I stood, barely two feet from him. I hunched my shoulders in defeat and perched myself on the grass next to him. 'Ah,' he sighed, 'we will be there before we know it.'

He was referring to Uppsala, our first major stop. Birka was still a while longer.

'Are you nervous?' he asked.

'Of course,' I answered. 'Did the drinking help?'

He made a gesture with his hands but stayed silent.

I shoved him with my shoulder. 'What is it? You don't keep anything from me. Has something happened?'

'Something is always happening,' he answered cryptically.

'You are so frustrating.'

He remained silent for some time; his head still turned away from me whilst I stared expectantly at his dark profile. Exasperated at his evasiveness, I drove the point of my elbow into his ribs.

'Ow!' he exclaimed in a combination of pain and surprise.

'Tell me,' I demanded.

He swallowed hard, turning to face me and grabbed my hands, holding them in his own. 'Astrid, we have been together ever since your return to Karlstad,' he began.

'You never leave my side,' I agreed.

He exhaled. 'And it is time for me to take a wife.'

That explained his strange behaviour. He was saying goodbye to our carefree ways. Perhaps his mother had chosen for him or pressured him to decide. Mothers had a way of doing that.

'Oh, Sven.'

He laughed. 'I guess it won't be so bad.' He managed a weak smile. 'I promise to teach your children how to wield an axe, even if their mother will not approve. And even if they're girls!'

He smiled, taking my hands. 'I know you will.' He wrapped his arms around me. Though we had embraced before, this was different. His body was tense.

'Did you just sniff my hair?' I asked, recoiling. 'Or are you crying?'

We broke apart. His hand lingered awkwardly on my back. 'If you don't want to marry, just tell your mother you won't!'

He groaned and buried his face in his hands.

'I should go back,' I said, looking back towards the fire.

Neither of us moved. Sven looked towards me, lowering his face to be heard. 'Please don't.'

'Tell me what's wrong,' I urged.

'I can't,' he whispered. In the same breath, his lips brushed mine, and I was too shocked to respond. I froze as he kissed me. For a moment, I thawed. My mouth responded, and then I pushed him away.

'This can't happen! Even if we are both scared of what is coming.'

He didn't reply but furrowed his brow. 'Astrid,' he started. Even in the dark, I could tell he was blushing deeply.

'What is wrong with you?' I raged. 'Whatever is happening in your head, you better stop it now!'

His mouth opened and closed without sound.

'Don't even think about following me,' I growled as I pushed past him, grabbing my bedding and lugging it back to camp amongst the safety of others. The storytelling had concluded, and all were bedding down for the night, and I found a place to sleep there. I squeezed my eyes shut, still unable to process what had happened. The chorus of surrounding snoring distracted me until I heard the crunching of the ground under my shoe. I knew it was him even before I heard the timid whisper of my name. 'Astrid?'

My back was towards him, but I still squeezed my eyes shut, willing him to go away.

'Astrid?' he tried again.

'Go away!' I seethed as I buried myself deep into my covers.

He gave up and must have put himself to bed. Within moments, his breathing grew heavier. I resolved myself to stay awake, but the energy I exhausted being angry with him drained me and I drifted off to sleep.

The morning light grazed my face, and I opened my eyes in time to see the first rays of the sun casting shades of gold against the dark sky. I turned over sleepily and stretched my limbs out over the uneven ground, feeling my bones creak and realign. A small groan of embarrassment escaped me as I remembered the night before and I thanked Freyja it had gone no further. Sven was around somewhere. I rolled over and saw him kneeling a short distance away from me, unaware I was now awake. He was two strides from me and bare from the waist up. His broad shoulders were lit by the morning light and his hair ruffled in the gentle breeze. He rolled his bedding together and tied it with a rope. I pulled my blanket above my head, hoping to hide away from any interaction.

'Too late. I've already seen you,' he bellowed, whipping my blankets off me with a huge smile on his face. I assumed this meant he was going to act like the kiss had never happened.

'How did you sleep?'

'Well enough.'

'Would you put your clothes back on?' I asked, shielding my eyes, but something happened when he roguishly smiled. It is discomfort, I told myself.

He puffed his chest out as if he were a bird displaying his beautiful plumage before grabbing his tunic and putting it on over his head. He was obviously built for fighting, built to be powerful. I rolled my eyes.

Despite my earlier embarrassment, I realised he was now tormenting me to break the tension.

'Enough of that! I get it, you're built like Thor,' I joked as I threw my shoe at his head. He ducked, but it was too late, and the shoe hit him between the eyes.

'Careful! You could have blinded me.' He laughed, lopping the shoe back in my direction gently. The shoe fell into my lap.

'Perhaps then you would stop staring at me that way.'

'Do you really think I could be a god?' he asked, missing the point entirely.

'I said you look like a god, not that you are one,' I corrected.

'Well then, do you really think I look like a god?'

'Careful or I'll throw my shoe at you again,' I threatened, laughing.

He struck a pose, arms flexed above his head. 'Call me Harbard from now on, *minn Svanr*. A god disguised as a man. No mere mortal looks as I do.'

I waved my shoe in mock threat. 'That will never happen.'

'Or Thor, either is acceptable.' He winked, catching my shoe as I sent it sailing towards his head for the second time.

Two

Uppsala, Svealand

Sven sat next to me on the mossy rise. He was intent on apologising to me for the fifth time, but I put my hand up to stop him. 'Don't.'

'I don't know why I did it. I'm sorry.'

'Just promise me it won't happen again.' My voice was soft but laced with disappointment that I hoped he would not miss.

'I'll try.'

He was oblivious to my chagrin. 'You can do better than try.' Something had been different in Sven since our arrival in Uppsala. His thoughts consumed him, and he seemed on edge.

'The gods keep so much from us,' he riddled as he tore a blade of grass lengthways. 'They play with us as it pleases them.'

'And it's in your power to either smile or to scowl at them.'

The beat of the drum interrupted our musings, and we made our way into the woodlands. We walked side-by-side in silence as I waited for him to divulge what gnawed at his insides. The woods were quiet, except for the sound of that far off rhythm. There was no one within their dark cover except for the small creatures that occupied the place and tried to keep out of sight. Lengths of the sun's rays penetrated the treetops, where it was possible to catch glimpses of the cornflower blue sky. Though summer had come and so had the warm days, the tree cover provided shade enough to cool the air, the ground covered by soft leaves breaking down into the earth. My dress skimmed my ankles but did not pick up any dirt as we walked. It swirled in the wind so much I had to hold the sides of it against my legs so it would not blow above my knees.

'What if the gods had tied you to another?' Sven asked, breaking the silence. His face was serious as he stopped to look at me.

'Me?'

'You, me, any of us? What if the gods tie our fate to that of another?'

'Then you just have to wait for them to die before you are free,' I dismissed, as my hair whipped around my face.

'Not like Auden. Not just being sent off to marry someone. I mean, what if the Norns had tied your heart to another?'

'You truly believe that?' I asked, tucking my hair into the neckline of my underdress to stop it from catching in the wind again.

Sven's face was lined with concern, his brow creased, and his mouth down turned. 'Of course, I believe it. The Norns have woven our destiny, as you know, but my fate is not possible without the woman they have tethered me to.'

'The gods entertain themselves.'

'I've seen it, Astrid. Sometimes they speak to me; they tell me it is so.'

'If the gods have told you so, then it will come to pass,' I replied, as we continued to walk through the tree cover. It had always been the way. Whatever was pre-determined would come to be. Those who occupied Midgard could face their fate with good humour or ill, but destiny would not change. Why Sven would have cause to doubt that I wondered as I sped up to catch him.

He was breathless as we mounted the rise, 'I have to chase my destiny and take what the gods put before me.'

It seemed he was still intent on riddles. 'What are you really talking about?' I stopped walking and stood, a little breathless myself, waiting for his response.

Slowly, Sven took my hand, and with a voice that was none too sure, he answered. 'Astrid, the gods tell me to marry you.'

My mouth opened, but no sound came out. The wind blew through the trees and tendrils of my hair whipped my face as I willed my ears to have been mistaken, but still he spoke, his mouth moving and at first, I heard nothing, just an ebb in my ears.

'We are bound, you and I.'

'It's not the first time I've heard such a declaration,' I replied callously, 'and I doubt it will be the last.' The look he gave me was tender and unsure and, suddenly, I feared hurting my friend, but not enough to entertain his advances. 'Sven, I have shut that part of me away.'

'Why?' he asked.

'Because love only brings misery. It might have been different if they had not forced me to marry Auden, but now...' I hesitated.

He latched onto the pause. 'Now, you are free to decide for yourself. Have we not always been good to each other?'

'It's been too long, Sven,' I began. 'You are a brother to me now.'

The words wounded him like a seax to the guts. 'They forced me to leave too,' he started, 'when my family left for Orebro, and they sent you away. There was something you should have...'

'It's too late.' I stopped him.

'We are meant to be, Astrid. The gods tell me it is my fate.'

'It is your fate the gods whisper, not mine!' I responded, blood thundering in my ears.

'There is no one else. I need you.' He stood before me, staring, waiting for my response. 'Do you hear me, Astrid? Are you listening?'

My hand shot up, hoping to ease the rambling and give me a moment to think. 'I hear you,' I stumbled over the words. 'I just can't believe it.'

His belligerence knew no bounds. 'You will see it in time. I know you will.'

The trees constricted the space around me; the grove shrouded in darkness; the air hard to breathe. 'I don't want to marry,' I gasped.

'It would be different with me.'

Sick rose in my throat. 'Sven, please listen. It does not matter if it was you or anyone else. I don't want to marry again. Not now, not ever!'

'I would give you everything you wanted if we married,' he pleaded.

'How could you give me what I want when the very thing I do not desire is marriage?' I yelled, his arrogance infuriating me.

'One day Astrid, you will have to marry again. You cannot avoid it. As a widow, you may choose a match for yourself but wait a while longer and you may feel the pressure to take who they put before you. If I love you, then why not take me? Why wait until you have no say in the matter?'

'Understand this Sven.' I drove the point of my finger into his shoulder. 'Hear what I am saying, I do not want to marry you!' I didn't care if I was being abrasive, just as he didn't seem to take any notice of my rising anger. 'You say I have a choice but, if my only option is to choose you, what choice is that?' Locked eye-to-eye, I stared him down and refused to submit.

His face softened as he approached me, pushing me back against the trunk of a tree. 'Astrid, listen. If we marry, I will insist you come with me to raid. We will have adventures together. I will give you what you want.' He took my hands in his, urging me to accept his offer.

'You don't understand, do you?' I asked, pushing him back. 'Anything you give me would also be in your power to take away. I want to earn it.' Then no one could take it from me.

'That is not how it works, Astrid.'

'I will not be traded to a man like a barrel of salt!' I spat the words at him and turned to walk away.

Behind me, he called for his pet, '*minn Svanr,*' a name I had come to hate.

'Never call me that again,' I screamed, sending my voice down the cavern of trees that carried it in the wind to his ears. He bowed his head, and I left, cloaking myself in seething anger. Now I would wear it for protection.

As I walked, the grove opened into a clearing. The flat ground made the perfect place for a market, and all the merchants who had travelled to Uppsala had set up their stalls. A crowded place, full of pretty distractions, was exactly what I needed. I stopped at a cloth-covered table laden with trinkets. The beads and jewels reflected the light from the sun, but it was a green bead mottled with a grey that caught my attention, distracting me from my anger.

'Pretty green, no?' asked the merchant, noting my interest and picking it up, holding it in front of me. He was a tall man, wiry, with thin legs. The brown tunic he wore came to his knees, hiding his billowy pants, and had the effect of making him look as if he were standing on wooden stilts. His long beard jingled with bronze and silver beads wound around and clamped onto his beard hair.

'It is,' I agreed, narrowing my eyes. The colour was special, and somehow familiar.

'The shade suits you well,' he suggested, holding it up to my collarbone. His long fingers emphasised the delicacy of the workmanship.

'Do you think so?'

He had captured my interest until I realised the bead was the same colour as Sven's eyes. The swirling of green and grey together, but without the black at the centre, it was strangely unnerving. 'I have no need for such fine things, as beautiful as they may be,' I replied politely.

The hat on his head clung tightly as he bowed low to return the bead to his table. 'Perhaps something else?' He waved his weathered hand over the pretty things on his table.

'Not today.' It was the customary polite refusal of an uncommitted browser who was more interested in watching people than making a purchase.

He smiled and redirected his efforts to a dark-haired woman admiring a silver and antler hairpin. The merchant's well intended, albeit sales driven comments stoked my frustration. I didn't need a distraction; I needed distance. The snaking river sparkled in the afternoon sun, and I followed it upstream from the stationary vessels to find a quiet spot on my own. The noise of the celebrations could still be heard above the gentle lapping water on the shore, but it was good enough. On the water's surface were small birds, taking turns to dive below in search of edible morsels. On a rock, I perched myself and was surrounded by thick bushes.

Had Sven really been harbouring feelings for me all this time? He knew I didn't want to marry; he's been told enough times. So why did he think I would want to marry him? Or didn't he care what I wanted? I was angry at myself for being so oblivious, angry at him for keeping it from me. A little time to think would do us both good. Sven would realise he was wrong, and I could calm down. And, once we were on our ship, heading for the raids, we would think about success, not romance.

The shadows of the evening approached slowly, covering the land around the water. I sat and watched the birds until the only light came from the stars and moon above. The stars twinkled, and I thought, *this cannot be my fate.* It was not what the gods wanted for me. They destined me for more than marriage. I had denied Sven, but he would understand, and we would put this all behind us.

I lay against the rock and relaxed, convinced that this too would be forgotten in time. The darkness cloaked me as I lay still, indiscernible from the element of earth. My ears were alert with the sound of water lapping against wood and oars breaking its tensioned surface. The sound grew louder until it drowned out the celebrations. If the newcomers meant me harm, my calls would not be heard above the distant revelries. It was more likely they were travellers arriving for the celebrations, but I could not know for sure, so I lay as still and close to the rock as possible and watched for the approach of the boat. In the dim light, I could make out the outline of two men. They jumped into the shallow waters and dragged their small craft onto the land. It was too small to be a seagoing vessel, which meant they had not come far. They had probably left their knar on the nearby island of Björkö. The longer I watched, the better I could see them, as my eyes adjusted to the dark. They had hiked their pants up to the knee, and they had removed their shoes to avoid damaging them in the water. I could hear them talking, but at this distance, could not make out the words until they drew nearer.

'Glad to be home, Björn?' asked the taller of the two men, who wore a triangle cap. They sat on the grass to put their shoes back on.

'Yes, and no. It's a quieter life here, but the gods bless those who live on the other side of the Austmarr,' Björn answered.

His tall companion seemed to be in a lamentable mood, 'We do all the hard work of transporting their goods while they sit around and count their gold.'

'If I did not have a wife and another child on the way, I would not come back here. Could stay over there and make my fortune and make my mistress my wife.' Björn laughed.

'But you already have one of those!'

'How would they know, eh?' he replied, chuckling.

The men stood up and walked towards Uppsala, carrying a small bag each. Aside from their height and head coverings, it was difficult to make out any detail without moving.

'The settlements of Gardarike are just the beginning. If we dared to go further, we could make more money than we ever dreamed. I've even met a few merchants from as far as Serkland. I never knew there were men like that out there with their dark features and such hair all over their faces. If I had not seen it for myself, I could not have imagined it,' the tall man exclaimed as they drew nearer.

They spoke of different lands, but I had not heard these names before, and I needed to know more.

'Next time we should travel further to see what these other settlements offer. Maybe we could get a better deal for these furs up the river,' Björn suggested.

'It might not be as easy as that. We'll need an introduction,' the tall merchant grumbled as they passed me, taking no notice.

'We should try. I will ask Neflaug if she has a connection.'

'What is she like, your pretty lady?' the tall point capped merchant asked Björn. There was some obvious heckling going on as the first man goaded the second into divulging specific details.

'She is a widow,' the second man gave in, stopping and adding hand gestures to his description. 'And now she has no husband, so she is free and she's a merchant herself and has a fair bit of power and wealth,' he bragged.

'Liar. If she is as rich as you say, why would she want you?' the other man scoffed in fits of laughter.

'Ah, come now! She is, I swear. She has a fortune.'

'Alright, alright, but what of her looks? Surely, she is ugly. Why else would she choose you?'

'Oh no! She is as delightful as summer itself: hair the colour of sand, green eyes, not too tall and a good handful at the top and the bottom. She has a particular talent for warming my bed in the most wicked way.' Björn chuckled. I wished I did not have to listen to this part of their conversation and hoped it didn't devolve any further.

'Then why are you back here?'

'Sometimes I ask myself the same thing. Ah, I think she would not have me as a husband and so I return here.'

'You are already married! And besides, Neflaug is using you for all the trinkets you bring to lie before her bed,' the tall man teased.

'I know, I know, but they would never know. Anyway, my wife is heavy with child. I must do my duty and provide for them, and I don't mind being used for trinkets if Neflaug welcomes me to her bed,' his voice faded as they disappeared from earshot.

I waited a while before moving, slipping off the rock onto my feet. The celebrations were dwindling, and the drumming had stopped. My mind was abuzz with the conversation I had overheard, and my imagination was conjuring images of a far off land with limitless opportunities, but my body was exhausted and longing for sleep. As I walked up the path towards Uppsala, a man's enthusiastic grunt and a woman's playful giggle emanated from the nearby bushes. The darkness obscured them, but I could hear their frantic encounter as I hurried past.

With little effort I located my camp, rolling into the bed I made up earlier next to Sven. Lying on my back, I observed the stars. When I was a small girl, my mother told me, 'The Norns have written each person's fate, and the gods show us in the stars,' as she put me to bed each night. My mother had once been a dreamer, before the reality of hard work and daily life had set in.

My mind wandered to the foreign lands called Gardarike and Serkland. I repeated the words over and over in my head until my body melted into the ground, and I surrendered to Nott. Sleep was fitful that night. In my dreams, I wandered alone in the pitch black of night. There was a man. I wanted to run away but found myself rooted to the spot. Somehow, he had the power to draw me to him, even though my body and mind resisted. He laughed. No, not laughed, cackled a menacing, evil sound that filled the forest.

'Sven?' I called.

But the man did not answer.

'Sven?' I cried, beseeching him to explain the terror he caused me.

He bared his teeth and suddenly I found I was bound with rope, unable to move.

'Sven, why are you doing this?' My voice echoed in the tree hallows as I thrashed, trying to free myself from the bindings, but it only made it tighter. 'Get me out of this,' I pleaded, struggling until I woke myself.

It was a nightmare. I told myself lying still, coiled in my bedding and separating real from imagined. Deep breaths calmed my racing heart, and with the rising sun, the darkness disappeared. The camp was sleeping and feeling the need to drive out the night's horror, I grabbed my axe and walked to the clearing where the day before Sven had confessed his feelings to me. The eeriness of the grove sent a shudder through my skin. It wasn't the place; it was the memory. A little exercise would soon make me forget, and I manifested an enemy to take my frustration out on.

Before me stood my imaginary foe, a stocky dark-bearded man wearing a leather jerkin and armed with a sword. The curved hilt nestled against his hand as he raised it to strike me. I countered, defending his assault with the clang of metal upon metal as Skara met his sword. Over and under, I whirled my axe over my head and brought it down upon him. His sword, much heavier than my agile axe, blocked me. Our eyes locked, both full of concentration.

It was this war practice that had kept me sane after my return to Karlstad. In it, I could lose myself, thinking of nothing but the next move. When I was younger, I practised with my father and when that was no longer possible I did so alone, in secret. After I got married, I stole away in the evenings into the forest. It was my outlet - my own, in a world where everything was decided for me. Hand to hand combat was a dance of death, one moving, unknowingly, to their end and the other to their preservation. Both thinking they would be victorious. In that most dangerous exchange, each had the unbiddable desire to kill the other.

The quickening beat of bloodlust flowed through me as I gave in to the trance of early morning practice. My axe came down in a sweeping motion, finding the space between my opponent's neck and shoulder, causing a great emission of blood that fell on the ground at my feet. In a last attempt, my foe grasped his sword with his left hand and lunged towards my right. Seeing the consequence of this motion before he made it, I moved to the side. I blocked with my shield, making contact with a mighty thud, and he collapsed to the ground. Knowing he was spent, he fixed his eyes on the sky as I carved my axe down, splitting him through the middle and sending him to Valhalla. He had been a worthy opponent, if only in my mind. I never lost when there was no one to fight against.

The soft tufts of grass met my body as I flopped onto my back and stared into the blue of the morning sky. I could not stay for long. My crew would wonder where I was. We had to leave for Birka, the town on the island of Björkö, to attend the *thing* by the afternoon. I still had time. My armring shone in the smattering of light. My father had been here in Uppsala many years before and had consulted with a *völva* to know his fate. At that moment, I knew he was guiding me to do the same. Uppsala was rife with those seeing women who could portend one's fate, some more attuned to the voices than others.

It was early as I made my way back to the camp, but merchants and merrymakers were already gathering. Many had gathered in Uppsala for the great meeting of the important men of the land that the *blót*, a celebration of our gods where we made offerings, would follow. I found a woman sitting halfway up a sloping mound covered in green grass and surrounded by willowy trees. I knew her to be a *völva* at once for she wore a dark hooded robe, her skin painted, and her eyes seemed to be distant and seeing all at the same time. She watched me with those dark eyes. Anxiety constricted my throat, stealing my voice.

'You wish me to cast your runes?' she asked in a soft voice, smoothing the linen cloth covering a stump before her.

I nodded.

She held out her hand, waiting for me to give her something for her wisdom. I removed a bone hairpin from the pouch around my waist, placing it within the smooth skin of her palm. She turned the adornment over, inspecting it and satisfied of its worth, placed it out of sight beneath her and gestured to the grass before the tree stump.

'Sit,' she ordered. 'We will see what the gods have to say about you.' She narrowed her eyes, assessing me. 'What questions do you have for me to put before them?'

I closed my eyes and thought of the events that had caused me to seek her out. 'What destiny have they decided for me?' I asked.

'Oh,' she breathed, 'the gods have a plan for each of us that will be revealed only when the time is right, unless that time is now, they will not show you. They will only show us small parts of where your path will lead.'

'Have they tied my destiny to any man?' I leaned forward, feeling the desperation to be told otherwise.

'Hold these questions in your mind as you choose your stones. Maybe the gods will reveal something to us on this day.'

I sat back and nodded.

'Are you ready? Close your eyes.'

I did as instructed. 'Yes.'

She sipped from her cup, setting it down on the ground beside her. With her chin on her chest, she lolled her head side-to-side, chanting in a low voice. When she was done, she rattled a cloth bag in front of me, gently placing my hand at the opening. 'Take nine runes out of this bag. Don't look at them, just hold them in your hands.'

I collected one piece at a time with my right hand, putting them into my left until I had nine. There was no way I could know what any of the runes said with my eyes closed, for they were all roughly the same size and shape, carefully carved from small even stones.

Her hand shot out across the stump. 'Give them to me.'

I pressed the runes into her open palm. Her wiry fingers snapped closed around them. The *völva's* lips grazed her own knuckles as she muttered softly into her clenched fist, eyes closed and body swaying as she shook the rune stones. My eyes darted around the fabric, expecting to interpret their meaning at once as the runes scattered and landed in their places. Some fell upside down.

'A rune on its head will have a different meaning than if it were facing up.' She glanced at me. 'You really don't enjoy doing things as you should, do you?' she asked with a mischievous smile.

I shook my head.

'Loki might like to whisper mischief in your ear and, I see you might even have wont to listen but, you think too much,' her voice was light and melodic.

She was not wrong.

The *völva* inspected the runes closely before looking up. 'See these three here,' she said, pointing to a cluster of runes marked with yew, wood, and wheel, closest to me and all face up.

I nodded.

'A journey comes for you. When you arrive, your life will change. You will be born anew.'

My heart leapt in my chest. *A warrior*, I thought. After all this time, I would become the shield maiden I had always dreamed of.

'But this one here,' she mused, tapping the rune I knew to be wood, 'see how it is reversed? Your world will change that much is true, but not without sacrifice. You will lose everything you have ever known. These here,' she continued as if she had not foretold my ruin, explaining as she turned over a group of three runes, being careful to not adjust their position. 'These are dice, elk, and birch. They show us a destiny further in the future.'

'I see.'

'You hide a secret within you. It is not yet something even you recognise, but it will cause you great anguish. You will find yourself used by others, betrayed, and your secrets spilled for their gain.'

A feeling of sickness rose in my throat. 'What of love?' I asked hesitantly.

'I do not know what games the gods intend to play with your heart.' Her eyes glossed over, clouding the mortal world from view. 'There is a babe in your arms while your husband seeks his riches.'

My eyes widened. Did she say baby and husband? That was not what I had in mind for myself.

Had the runes proved Sven's dreams true? Was my fate to bear his children while he adventured? The Norns did not weave that destiny; the gods did not guide me towards that, surely not. 'Is that all you see?' I asked the *völva*, my voice cracking.

'There are two more,' she spoke softly, 'those furthest from you are horse and ox. It is interesting that they should appear together.' She considered the objects more closely. 'Trust and health, usually, but as you can see ox is on its head.' She closed her eyes as I watched, waiting for the gods to speak their wisdom into her ears. 'The gods reveal little. All they show me now is a long life and...' she trailed off.

I leaned forward.

'You must learn to see what is in front of you.'

I laughed. The seer cocked her head, narrowed eyes and silent lips. 'Well, thank you,' I said, rising to leave. Scarcely more enlightened than I had been before I parted with my bone hair pin.

'Wait.' She stopped me. 'One, two, three, four, five, six, seven, eight. Eight?' She looked around. 'We've missed one,' her voice strained as she searched for the ninth rune. Then she bent to the ground where it lay down turned.

'What wisdom does it speak, *völva*?'

'This one speaks the loudest of them all. It should guide you in all things- the sun. You, the Norns, have decided, shall find glorious victory in the path they have laid before you. Learn to see, learn to trust and you shall find yourself rewarded.'

Rooted to the spot, silent, I watched the seer gathered up the runes and placed them gently back into the bag. 'Thank you,' I mumbled.

On my way back to camp, I stopped to lean against the trunk of a tree. I was not ready to face Sven again, not yet, and certainly not if the *völva* foretold our union. But I still had hope. She told me I would take a journey, that could be a raid, it could have been anything. The vagueness of it irritated me. I wanted certainty. There was never any certainty with the gods. They were capricious and able to make mistakes, just like the rest of us. The *völva* was meant to bring me peace, to help me towards my future. All I felt was frustration.

The betrayal and motherhood, as much as that concerned me, wasn't in my immediate future. I would worry about that later. Now, I needed to make an offering to the gods and ensure they were looking at me with a smile and not a grimace.

Statues of the gods were placed in the sacrificial grounds- the grove and were north of three large burial mounds that dominated Uppsala. As I walked past the intimidating structures, the curved land seemed to meet the sky as if the *jotunn* had pushed the earth up from below. But these were made by men, a feat that was impressive to behold.

Drums beat in a constant low rhythm, accompanied by the hum of mumbled chants as I made my way into the solemn grove. It was not the time for the *blót*, the traditional time to make a sacrifice, it was the moment for individual worship. Men and women had encircled the wooden carvings of the gods. Smooth, beautiful faces, etched into the effigies depicting our gods Odin, Frigg, and Freyja. Visitors lay their offerings at the feet or in the god's mouth. Others were standing a short distance away, chanting and dancing. A man with a long white beard sang from his throat, the deep echoing sounds filling the space like a cavern.

As was customary in Karlstad, I lay down my offerings of foraged berries at the feet of the idols of Freyja and Frigg. First, I took some mead and poured it at the feet of Frigg, wife of Odin and queen of Æsir, goddess of marriage and motherhood. 'Frigg, goddess of so many things,' I whispered to her. 'Guide me. What do you see of my future, oh, goddess?' I turned from Frigg, 'And Freyja, look on me in favour so you can make the thread of my life golden. What do the Norns weave for me? Give me a sign so I know the way forward. Your wisdom is my hope.' As I had with Frigg, I offered berries at Freyja's feet and poured a little mead into her mouth. At their feet, many others had made similar offerings of bread, eggs, glass beads, coins, silver, and fabrics. People offered their most valuable items. There was no limit, and in a few short weeks, gifts of life would replace offerings of gold. Every nine years there was an ultimate offering made, the *Dísablót*. At this sacred gathering, nine males of each kind of animal, including people, would be gathered, sacrificed, and hung in the grove at Uppsala. This time coincided with the meeting of all our people at Uppsala at the *Disting*, which was held alongside the *thing*, similar to the one we would attend in Birka.

With eyes closed, I offered my voice to the gods. Every note increased the vibration through my body, as calm covered me like a blanket against the cold. The music slowed, and when it stopped; I eased into the world again. Blinking slowly, my eyes brought my surroundings back into view and I knew it was time to face what was coming. Only one small body of water stood between me and my dreams of raiding. We would make the brief trip to the island of Björkö for the *thing*, and it was there that my fate would be decided.

THREE

'Where have you been?' Sven grabbed my arm, concern etched on his handsome face.

I shook off his grasp, still annoyed by him but willing and wanting to forget the whole mess. 'I needed some time to think.' If he wanted a further reply, he wouldn't get one. The best I could manage was a petulant shrug.

'You had me worried. Left all your belongings here, and you vanished.' He ran his fingers through his hair, once, twice, and again.

'Stop doing that,' I chided. 'And I didn't leave everything behind. I took Skara,' I explained, tapping the weapon secured to my belt.

'So?'

'Sven, I just went into the forest this morning to practise and, after that, to the clearing with everyone else to give offerings to the gods.' I wasn't sure why I felt compelled to explain myself to him, especially given he was the one who had behaved so obnoxiously.

'You were gone for a long time.'

'Since when did I need your permission?'

His mouth stretched into a tight line; his jaw set square. 'You don't. I was worried. That's all.'

'I am still my own person, Sven. You do not need to worry about me!' I huffed, trying to push past him. It was useless. Unless I wanted to hack at him with my axe, I was not getting through his broad frame. He gently clamped his hands around my shoulders. 'Would you stop grabbing at me?'

'Astrid, with everything that has happened, I thought you had run off,' he whispered. 'I didn't intend to make you feel like my possession,' he added, releasing me.

'Pffff,' I replied childishly, and glared at him.

'And I wouldn't blame you. I caused all of this.'

My arms felt as awkward as the rest of me. Not knowing how to stand, I landed on a stance with arms akimbo, not allowing Sven to think he could deflect my annoyance with his change in attitude. 'Can we put this all aside?'

Sven watched me curiously and nodded slowly.

'But I am warning you, Sven. This is your last chance. Any more surprises and I will….'

'Alright, I understand,' he interjected. He toyed with something small between his fingers. The glint of it caught my attention.

'What is that?'

He hid the thing deep into his clenched palm, and raised his arms above his head, far out of my reach. 'It's nothing,' he replied with a mischievous grin.

I stood on my tiptoes, trying to reach up to snatch at it. 'Show me!'

'You made me promise there'd be no more surprises,' he teased, hiding his hand playfully behind his back. But the smile on his face told me it was something I would want to get a look at.

'Is it for me?'

'I bought it yesterday, but after telling you I loved you; I wasn't sure if….' With caution, he held his fist and slowly parted his fingers.

'Show me,' I demanded as I pried at the treasure beneath.

'So, you want surprises now?'

'Come on,' I laughed, trying harder to prise it from his enclosed fist.

He opened his hand, offering it towards me. In it was a small silver pendant of a woman, wrapped in a cloak or perhaps wings, 'A Valkyrie?' I grinned. 'She looks like she's ready to calmly lead me to Valhalla or Folkvangr.'

'Something to protect you,' he explained.

'You are optimistic that I will join the raids.' I couldn't help but be pleased with a gift that echoed my own dreams.

'Do you like it?' he asked me nervously.

I nodded, trying to tie it around my neck.

'I'll help you.' Sven hurried to tie the waxed linen cord.

The pendant slipped from view against my skin under my *serkr*. 'Now I have two amulets of protection,' I said with a wink, my left hand finding my father's arm ring, Bjarndýr, hidden beneath the sleeve of my underdress.

'And soon you may not have to hide that,' Sven said, motioning to my armring. 'Once you have sworn to raid with the jarl, you can wear it, just as I will wear mine when I swear my oath to him.'

In the distance, a horn sounded for the gathering of our band to leave for the island of Björkö.

'Neither of us will have any entitlement to wear one if we don't run for the boat! We should hurry.' We had been away too long, talking instead of preparing. I grabbed Sven's hand, running back to our campsite. 'They would not leave without us,' Sven cried in between panting. 'Come on,' he teased. 'I am only going this slow because you can't keep up,' he continued in between strained breaths.

'Is that so?' I laughed as I sped up to overtake him. We met again on the shore where the small vessel was banked in the sand.

'I was at an obvious disadvantage,' Sven complained breathlessly as we clambered into the boat.

'It cannot be obvious if I cannot see it. Unless you are going to complain that your looks have had some play in the matter.'

'My bag is much heavier than yours,' he managed between heaving breaths, stowing the bag in question between his legs as he sat on the bench seat.

'Perhaps next time you could leave some of your beautification tools at home,' I teased. Sven was notorious for his hygiene and appearance.

'I absolutely need a comb for my hair and a different comb for my beard,' he explained, 'unlike you, who doesn't even bother to comb her hair for weeks at a time.'

'And what about your bronze ear scoop?' I asked. His bag was full of items I deemed useless for a raid.

'Astrid, that is even more essential than the two combs.' He looked around at the others in the boat with us. 'Who wants mucky ear holes?' he asked, addressing our companions. A chorus of laughter, but a general agreement with Sven surrounded me. I rolled my eyes.

'After I, Sven is the next most beautiful,' a deep voice chimed in.

'Thank you, Eric,' Sven chuckled. 'That means a lot coming from you,' he added, sending a wink in my direction.

'Fine. You were under a disadvantage owing to your beauty tools,' I conceded. Our eyes met as we heaved the oars, and I couldn't help but feel entertained by his enthusiasm. It was impossible to be mad at my great buffoon of a friend.

The waters surrounding the island were still and, approaching from the south, we came into the port. There was no other easy way to enter the enormous trading town, for rock face enshrouded its remaining three sides. Atop the cliff, a fortress sat surveying the lake beneath, a mighty deterrent for invaders. We rowed to the moorings within the harbour, exiting onto a floating platform making its way to land. As every man and woman approached the main gate, it reduced them to the size of an ant, the city walls looming high overhead. The ramparts were taller and thicker than any man or army could ever breach.

'Can you believe more than one thousand people live within these walls?' Vali, a farmer from Karlstad, asked me as we walked through the city gates. The land beyond was covered by tall birch trees which gave the island its name.

'One thousand?' I repeated in disbelief. It was a number that was difficult to fathom. I had seen a thousand blades of grass, perhaps a thousand drops of water, but a thousand people in one town I had never seen.

'They have a Christian church,' Gedda, Sven's neighbour who both farmed and dabbled in fishing, blurted, pointing at a great wooden structure in the middle of the town topped with a cross. I stared, perplexed by the building in the distance. Gedda looked as if he was going to laugh at me but stopped himself. 'It's a religion. We have our gods, and they have a God,' he informed me.

'Just one? How can he listen to all his people? That's, that's just…' I trailed off.

'So different?' Sven questioned with a laugh.

'Quite right,' Vali replied. Gedda nodded his head in agreement.

I turned to probe Gedda further. 'What do you know about this religion?'

'Nothing really. Only the one God thing.'

'I heard they crust everything they can in gold,' Vali interjected.

Gedda elbowed Vali in the ribs. 'Where are they getting all that gold from, eh?'

'Raiding, I suppose.'

Gedda shook his head vehemently. 'Churchmen aren't raiding nothing, Vali. They just wear their pretty dresses and wave their crossed sticks around.'

Vali shrugged. 'It's what I've been told, that's all. Hey! And you said you knew nothing else about them Christians, Gedda. What else have you got rattling around inside that head of yours?' The teasing continued with the flattening of Vali's hat, which he smoothed out with a face that had tolerated his old friend's antics for a long time.

'Are you curious?' Gedda asked me.

'I want to see it.' A giggle bubbled inside me, overcome by childish curiosity.

'Be careful they don't hook you in with some free food and wine.'

Sven's head shot up. 'Free wine?'

'It's how they get you,' Gedda replied seriously.

'I'm only interested in the free food.' I laughed, dragging Sven by the hand away from Gedda and Vali.

'Do you really want to eat? There is so much food in the marketplace, but we must be back with our men by the afternoon,' Sven asked.

'No, I'm not hungry. More curious. Aren't you?'

'Probably not as much as you are.'

No, Sven was almost certainly always hungrier than he would ever be curious. 'Do you really think they've crusted everything in gold?'

'Not possible,' Sven said with a shake of his head.

I eyed him disbelievingly. 'Just because you haven't seen it doesn't mean it isn't true.'

'Where is this church, anyway?' Sven asked as we walked the streets crowded with traders and people gathering for the raids.

'I'd say that was it.' I pointed to the decorated log structure with a tall roof.

'So, you are really dragging me in there?' As if my pulling on the sleeve of his shirt was not enough to dictate the direction of our adventure.

'I want to see this Christian church. Let's go look at it, and all of its gold,' I whispered as we made our way to the steepled building.

FOUR

BIRKA ON THE ISLAND OF BJÖRKÖ, SVEALAND

Far too anxious to sleep, I had been wide awake since the night birds began their midnight hunt. Before anyone else had even stirred from their bedding, I was clothed and packed, with my axe leaning upon my shield, ready to go. When the sun finally rose, it sent rays into the sleeping city, waking the inhabitants of the longhouse we lodged in, crowded with bodies and belongings that would be soon gone to raid wherever the jarl sent us. The horn for the gathering sounded and I watched the people around me as they hurriedly dressed and threw scrumpled belongings into bags, their heads spinning from the previous night's revelries. A short, fair-haired man struggled to pull on his trousers, hopping until he lost his balance and fell to the ground. Jumping up quickly, his foot became tangled in his cape, yanking at the fastenings around his neck, and almost choking him. As funny as the scene was, I found myself unable to laugh.

As I left the longhouse, I was carried away in a tide of people, moving towards the great hall that would host the *thing*. Even if I had wanted to change direction, it would not have been possible. Everyone moved to a singular destination as our bodies pressed tightly together. The dusty ground, kicked up by passing feet, and the ash from extinguished fires mingled in the air and irritated my throat. I coughed as we entered the hall, where the crowd dispersed to find friends. I stood on my toes, craning my head in search of Sven, his golden hair, and broad shoulders visible at the front of the hall. He had found a seat on a bench and was in animated conversation with a man on his left. On his right was a vacant position I knew he had saved for me. I manoeuvred myself through, squeezing myself between shoulders and tightly packed bodies, until I found my place on the bench next to Sven.

'Good morning.' The words found Sven's ears as I stumbled to catch my breath.

'That church,' he began, 'I've seen nothing like it, almost enough to make you want to become a Christian,' he gushed over the building as if it were a woman.

'Never,' I replied, 'and anyway, I cannot think about a church right now. This moment will decide my entire life. I feel like my insides are being eaten by insects,' I groaned, holding my stomach.

His chest pressed firmly against my shoulder as more and more people packed onto the bench until I thought I might just pop out of my seat. I wanted to see his face, so I twisted as best I could in my seat to turn and look at him. Being so close made it difficult for me to take in his profile. His jaw was set square, as he did when he thought much too hard, and his blue eyes were staring straight into the void of the raised platform before us. I continued to stare at him and after a few moments; he turned his head and shot me a mischievous smile and my mouth cracked into a wide grin. He bowed his head and pushed his shoulder into mine. The bugs in my stomach calmed.

'See that man over there?' He indicated with a nod towards the man on the raised platform, dressed in a fur cloak fastened by a bronze chain. 'He is Soren, Jarl of Birka. He dispatched the previous jarl last year and married his wife.'

The story was well known, but I had never seen the man for myself. The previous jarl I had seen was a much older man who had been challenged and defeated by someone younger and more capable.

'And his woman,' Sven began, 'was the widow of the previous jarl.' She was young, perhaps the same age as I, and was round as a cauldron, heavily laden with the belly of childbearing and it looked as if she was close to her birthing time. Following my thoughts, Sven nodded towards the woman. 'When her husband was killed, she was pregnant but lost the child because of the stress of it all. It seems she is fecund. I've never seen her in any other condition. She had provided the previous jarl two children in as many years and married less than a year now to this jarl and, as you can see, is ready to burst at the seams.'

I could think of nothing worse than being handed from one man to another with no other purpose than bearing children. The woman looked positively exhausted. I had seen many young pregnant girls before, but so many pregnancies at such an age took a toll on the body and often the women of her position died well before their children were old enough to remember them. No doubt if his current wife died in childbed, she would be replaced quickly with a younger and just as fertile trade-off. I uttered a silent mumble of thanks to Frigg that my fate would not be the same as the jarl's wife.

'He already has children by his handfast wife but his marriage to that one,' Sven nodded toward the Soren's young pregnant wife, 'means more, and besides, can a man ever have too many children?'

'Too many sons, of course,' I whispered. 'Fine while they are young, but as they grow, so will the trouble, unless he plans on gaining more lands to divide between them.'

Sven nodded. 'More daughters, though, pretty brides to make alliances.'

'But you never know what you will get before they deliver the child,' I replied, watching the jarl's wife as she waddled to take a seat behind her husband on the dais.

Soren was a man in his prime, strong and, I wondered, if his wife found him more likeable than the old man. He whispered with his wife; his long tawny coloured hair fastened at the nape of his neck with a metal ornament that caught the light as he moved his head in surveying the room with his intelligent icy blue eyes. It took brawn to fight the pack leader and win, but it took brains to keep it.

A short, dark-haired man approached Soren, who, inclining his head, allowed the man to speak in his ear. The jarl contemplated something for a moment before nodding. The smaller man scuttled off to the back of the hall. Readying himself for the presentation to come, Soren drew himself up to his full height and spread his arms out, signalling the commencement of the thing. A hush fell over the room, and all eyes were upon him. He cleared his throat with a cough and began.

'There has been much speculation regarding the target of this season's raids,' he began. 'I do not seek to draw it out any further and so, will announce it presently.' He drew a deep breath. 'We will be raiding Frankia with Konugr Erik of Uppsala and his son Bjorn, to whom we are sworn,' he bellowed, loud and clear.

The hall erupted with noise, a loud rumbling of excitement, chanting, and men slapping other men on the back. Some shocked faces appeared in the crowd, but overall, the feeling was one of excitement.

'QUIET!' he raised his voice again above the din and the room obeyed his command. 'We have vastly improved our knowledge from our previous raids, but there is always more to learn, and we must not be complacent. I am sure of our victory with Thor's help,' he roared, and battered his clenched fists against his chest.

At once, the loud rumbling of drumming feet on the floor began, and cheering filled the room. Soren turned to face his wife, tenderly touching her shoulder, and she mustered a weak smile. I found myself carried away in the excitement of it all, hooting and bellowing with those around me. Boisterously I slapped Sven on the leg, instantly regretting it as my hand smarted from the impact. I shook it to regain sensation, watching Soren as he motioned for the crowd to go still again.

'This is a raid like no other, so we will need many warriors. The usual exceptions apply; those with child or debilitated should remain to care for the families, crops, and livestock. My men will assign those who are able, to groups and ships. Please stay until you have all been attended to. Later we will discuss issues from your homelands, and I will hear petitions.' He concluded his address and strode from the raised platform and towards the back of the hall, shaking hands and greeting leaders from other areas.

The excitement dispersed with the crowd as they were assigned to groups, and the celebration resumed outside, many excited by the prospect of looting a land renowned for its wealth. Sensing my anxiety, Sven put a protective arm around me and drew me into his side. 'You need not be worried, Astrid.'

'No?'

A grin curved the sides of his mouth with a bristling smugness. 'I have arranged everything to make this happen for you.'

'Sven, what have you done?'

'Just wait. Promise me you will do nothing hasty.'

'You are worrying me now Sven,' I murmured, though I could barely hear my voice above the thundering of my heart.

'We already know what is going to happen, Astrid.'

'We do?'

'See it as an arrangement if you want to. At least it might start like that, but the gods tell me they are sure about this.'

'I thought we had laid that to rest?' I was bewildered at Sven's comment, unsure if he had made it in jest.

My mind was confused, caught up in the day, and unable to think clearly. So, when Soren's short assistant read aloud each name and where that person would be assigned, I was convinced my name had already been spoken. The Karlstad list concluded, and I approached the short clerk who had been earlier speaking with Jarl Soren.

'I am Astrid of Karlstad, come to raid with the jarl. I have my own weapons, an axe, and a shield, with the skills to use them. So, where have you assigned me?' My voice was calm despite the lack of confidence I felt inside as I addressed the clerk.

The short man looked up at me from his seat, his eyes straining with focus. He clicked his tongue and narrowed his gaze, continuing to assess me. 'Mmmm yes, Astrid of Karlstad, did you say?'

'That is me.'

He bared his teeth in an attempt at a smile. 'You will raid with the rest of your village.' He assessed me with his narrowed eyes. 'On the condition your marriage takes place before departure. Betrothal, heathen or otherwise, I care not, just that it is done.'

'My what?' I stammered in disbelief.

'Your husband-to-be kindly negotiated your participation in the raids on your behalf. It is because of him you may go about such an unwomanly endeavour,' he said matter-of-factly.

'He is not my husband-to-be!' I raised my voice.

'Do you have any male relative to speak for you?' he asked, raising one eyebrow.

'No, but I am a widow, so I could surely speak on my behalf?'

He ignored my protest. 'If you have no one to speak for you, then I suggest you leave it to your husband to resolve the matter. If you were my wife, I would have beaten you at the first suggestion,' he said, waving me away with his hand.

I opened my mouth to argue but couldn't find the words. I could not believe Sven was capable of this kind of betrayal. I didn't want to believe it. In disbelief, I exited the hall into the morning sunshine, where I met Sven's smiling face.

'Now you don't have to worry about anything,' he beamed.

'What have you done, Sven?' Unsure if he comprehended his own stupidity.

'This was the only way. They wouldn't let you go without being spoken for. They said, "father or husband" and, well, you didn't have either.'

Fury fumed inside me. 'Are you actually an idiot or are you so wilfully blind to what I want?'

'Honestly, Astrid, I thought maybe you loved me. There is something between us I cannot ignore. You walk my dreams, waking and asleep! Is it too much to imagine that you felt the same?'

'So, you are an idiot!' I screamed, pushing past him.

'An idiot for loving you?' he pleaded, grabbing at my hand to stop me.

I turned on him, anger searing the blood coursing through me. 'If you loved me, you would not do this to me. You know I don't want to marry so you concocted a plan to force me to be with you? Are you even aware of how evil that makes you seem?'

'*Minn Svanr,*' he mustered a tender voice.

'How dare you!' I cried. 'I will never be yours.'

'I cannot help that I love you,' he said, as he came to stand in front of me, holding my face so we were eye-to-eye. 'I will not be ashamed of my feelings. You want to raid, and I could not bear to think of you with another man.'

'It is not as simple as that. There is a big difference between thinking of me with another man and you being my husband.' My body shook with rage. 'You still don't understand, do you?' I asked, drawing nearer to him. Looking at the ground gave me a moment of reprieve. I took a deep breath and raised my eyes, and the fury would have been clear. 'I am not something to be owned,' I whispered with tears in my eyes, more from frustration, but still could not be contained.

'Own you? Never! That's not what I want. All I want is for you to be yourself with me.' His lips brushed mine and my body froze as it had when I spent so many nights doing my duty as Auden's wife. My mind and body were separated from each other. 'If it was not now with me, it would be someone else soon enough,' he replied.

'That's your excuse? That it might be someone else?'

'I couldn't bear it.'

'Yet you could bear it when your own inaction caused my very unwanted marriage to an old man. Hmm? You had the opportunity then, Sven. You did nothing, you only committed to the point that you wanted and left me in the dark, all alone. What consequences were there then for you? I would wager none so onerous as there were for me.'

'We were young.'

'Youth gave me no reprieve.'

'I know you and you know me,' he breathed, his lips forcing a kiss upon my own. The sensation sent a jolt of repulsion coursing through me, bringing my mind back.

'It's too late, Sven. You had your chance, but that time has long passed.'

His hand grasped for mine in desperation. 'You know me and my heart.'

'I thought I knew you,' I seethed, pushing him away. 'You took no responsibility for what happened. You never tried to help me. It was your fault then, just as it is now, and if this truly is you, then I want nothing more to do with you.' Whether by arrogance or ignorance, he had unforgivably betrayed me.

Walking away was difficult. He was my best friend. *Friends don't betray each other*, I reminded myself as I felt the pull to seek him out and resolve it again. Not in my worst nightmares had I ever imagined that Sven would continue with this ludicrous proposition after he understood my feelings. And with his refusal to back down, I found myself nestled between impossible decisions, crushed by their impending weight. Feeling exhausted, I looked for a calm spot to think. I walked to the high rock face overlooking the city, away from the noise and crowds. There, in the heather, I lay down and looked up at the sky, dreaming of that far off land that I had heard those merchants discussing nights before. A land where it was possible that a woman could make her own wealth and live her own life. That was the sort of freedom I wanted for myself.

My mind drifted to a strange land with green mossy hillsides protecting me and at the centre, a city bustling with activity. As I wandered inside the walled city, turning left, I found myself in an open marketplace. I had seen many markets before, but none like this. The ground beneath me was compacted and hard underfoot. The buildings towered above my head, much taller than the one level buildings of my hometown. My nose was filled with the smell of fresh-baked bread, mixed with the familiar stench of livestock, and the warm musty scent of fodder that accompanied them. People pushed past me, busy with their own business. A man with a long face and sharp features was locked in conversation with another man with a round smiling face, small eyes, and a mane of blazing red hair. Between them they passed a fabric of whimsy, catching the sunlight, it appeared to change colour from blue to green. It ran through their hands like liquid as they examined its beauty.

Suddenly, my dreams took me back to Karlstad, with all its familiar sights and smells. The rising mountains were behind me and, in the distance, the longhouse I called home. In my dream, I strolled to a lonely spot on the hill and sat down atop the rough grass, spreading my hands behind me for support. I leaned onto my hands and let my head gently flop back until I was looking directly into the blue sky above. I closed my eyes and when I opened them again, my father was standing before me smiling the smile that always made me feel at the centre of his world.

'Astrid, what are you doing here?' he asked me, his voice warm and full of concern.

'I don't know, Father.' The helplessness forced my hand to Bjarndýr, my armring, aglow on my arm as I touched it.

'You still have it,' he said, smiling.

'Of course.' I smiled. 'Oh, Father! I don't know what to do.' All I wanted was comfort, to be held in his arms as he did when I was a child.

'Yes, you do!' He would not allow me to wallow in anguish. 'You know exactly what you need to do. It is right before you,' he said, waving his hand towards the water.

'How will I see it?'

'Trust yourself, Astrid,' he said kindly as I blinked back my tears.

The early morning air was chilly as I woke from my dream. I slept there all night nestled in the heather above the city. Though my father was not with me as I wished, I would have to make do with his words of encouragement as I replayed memories over and over. My feet seemed to follow a path separated from my mind as I trusted my instincts, just as my father had told me to. Heading back to camp, I quietly packed my belongings and found Sven sleeping heavily as he did when he drank. His back was turned to me and the rest of our people, his body facing away from the camp, down the hills and towards the water as if keeping watch against some silent foe.

I sat beside him on the small patch of bedding behind his back and huddled close to him. He did not rouse but made a small noise and shuffled over to make more room for me. I waited a moment until I was sure he was still asleep. I wanted to talk to him, explain to him, without interruption, but I knew it would only make things more difficult to leave. Thinking I would never see him again was painful, though staying, after all that had passed between us, seemed like torture. I stifled a cry and pushed my heart from my throat, nestling it safely back in its rightful position in my chest and willing it to turn to iron. A deep breath steadied my nerves, and I parted my lips, licking them to allow the words to escape unfettered.

'It is not your fault for loving me,' I started as tears welled in my eyes. 'Perhaps I could forgive you for putting me in this position. Maybe one day I will thank you. This could be the best for me, even though we don't know what is coming yet.' The pain choked me, and I hesitated, unsure if I could continue. The words felt like they would tumble from my mouth in a painful ramble. I paused, taking a deep breath.

'Choosing you would mean giving up on me, my dreams, and my life. You have your own life to live, and I am sure it will be full of love and adventure. It will not be the adventure that I need, that I am looking for.' He could not hear me, his deep breathing unbroken, still it helped to unburden myself.

'I'm sorry it has to end like this, but I cannot forgive this betrayal, not yet, and perhaps never,' I whispered, taking up my sack, shield, and axe and walked away from everything I knew. Tears streamed soundlessly from my eyes, stinging the dry skin on my cheeks. I didn't hate Sven, I couldn't hate him, and after all, he was just doing the same thing as I was; going after what he wanted.

With one foot in front of the other, I made my way down to the docks we had arrived at the day prior. As I walked, the handle of Skara, my axe, thudded rhythmically against my shield like a battle drum urging me forward. I had thought no further than getting to the docks and somehow getting aboard a vessel, wherever it was bound for. I could not go back to Karlstad, to the life I had known.

My mind was busy manufacturing a way to win my passage when my feet reached the banks, the area already alive with action. Around me, men were loading goods into merchant ships able to cope with the journey across the sea. Unlike the vessels which had brought us to the city, the byrding ships used by merchants were sturdier and were equipped with a tented cloth for coverage during the night's rain or stormy seas. I drew closer, inspecting the workmanship of the surrounding ships. My eyes dissected the construction of the wood that was split and layered in a way that made the boat strong, buoyant and hopefully watertight. Even in the darkness of early morning, I could see the smoothness of the wood, planks of timber carefully laid over one another to ensure an aqua dynamic surface. It was beautiful. I ran my hand over the surface of the wood; someone had polished it until unblemished to the touch, and I stooped low before it, admiring the forward curling detail on the prow of the ship.

So absorbed in my admiration of craftsmanship was I that I did not hear the footsteps that signalled someone's approach. I remained oblivious until I felt someone standing behind me, watching me. Startled, I stepped back to find an escape and stepped directly onto the foot of the man, who emitted a curious squeak upon impact.

'Calm yourself, girl, I didn't mean to startle you,' he said kindly. I smiled weakly in response. 'Are you my precious cargo girl, Signe?'

'Err.' I opened my mouth and hesitated, unsure how to proceed.

'No need to be afraid, my girl. Neflaug has provided me with your description and told me to meet you here this morning.' He nodded his head.

My mind told me this could be a trick. I had heard of women being captured and sold as slaves in far off lands. 'Neflaug of the Rus' trading city?' I asked, trying to sound as if I were merely confirming details already known to me.

'Just the same. She is waiting for you and wants you as quickly as we can journey there. She ain't known as a patient woman and I won't be wanting to endanger myself to her wrath.'

I knew well enough that my name was not Signe, that I was likely taking someone else's hard-earned position. It was wrong of me to assume another's name, but it was as if the gods were speaking directly to me. There was something about the man's smile that calmed me, even though he lacked a few teeth. His voice sounded like the man I had heard in Uppsala that night by the docks. It struck me, just as the *völva* had predicted, and it couldn't have been any plainer. This was my opportunity; my time to act.

'Of course. We will sail now?' I asked, glancing behind me. The town would be still asleep. No one would know where I had gone for some time. But the real Signe might be along at any moment.

The man looked over and shouted to his men and a small group of people huddled together. 'Yes, everything is loaded. Put your belongings inside and we can take to the water.' I did as he instructed, placing my sack of clothing onto the ship, but my axe and shield landed with a clatter. 'What do you need that for?' he asked, pointing to my weapon.

I shrugged, trying to seem indifferent. 'It was my father's.'

'A warrior?'

I nodded. 'And you can never be too prepared.' A smile my reply, hoping that would be the end.

He asked no further questions and at his word; we pushed the ship off the sand and one by one we jumped into the ship until we were powering through the water and out of the harbour. I wanted to look back, to tell Sven not to look for me. He would still be asleep, but when he woke and noticed me gone, he would not understand where or if it was of my own will. Only would I allow myself to look forward to where I was going, not what I left behind, refusing to think about anything but the future.

'My name is Björn,' the gap-toothed man introduced himself. 'You must be excited to start this new life, huh?'

I turned, looking towards the horizon and the brilliant rising sun streaking the grey sky with orange and gold. 'More than you will ever know.' The words were spoken softly as the bow of the ship parted the water and away from Björkö and everything I knew.

Björn leaned towards me and patted me on the back in a fatherly manner. ''Tis a few days' journey, my dear. I hope you have strong sea legs. You'll be thankful that we are only passing, not going into Gandvik, for that would be even wors'a journey.'

FIVE

ON THE AUSTMARR

Air inside my body escaped my mouth with a loud expletive as I lurched
with the tossing waves. The sky and water were almost indistinguishable
in the darkness, an expansive stretch of angry swell. My eyes were too
tired to see the difference, even if there were any.

Sea spray soaked my clothing and mingled with my sweat, causing
damp discomfort. My stomach turned. I tried my best to keep the
meagre amount of food I had consumed from spilling onto the deck
of the vessel, as my hands searched the darkness for something to
steady myself against. Close by, I found the softness of a body who had
not roused with the lolling byrding. How anyone could sleep through
this was beyond my comprehension. At last, I located a large chest,
likely containing trading goods, and then another. I nestled myself
between them, finding a place that felt as comfortable as lying over a
bed of thistles. My back wedged against one chest, I closed my eyes
and imagined myself back in Karlstad, pressed up against my wall side
bed, safe. I conjured images of those I had left behind. Sven's stupid
smiling face flashed in the darkness, and my eyes shot open.

My stomach lurched again as I tried to move myself to a seated
position. Slowly, I eased myself onto my elbows. They gave way beneath
me as a jolt violently returned me to a horizontal position. My head
rocked from side-to-side on the floor as I summoned the energy for
another attempt. To conserve my strength and the remaining contents
of my stomach, I lay as still as I could. Mikel lay to the right of me.
He was small for his age, all gangly limbs, and smooth cheeks for

pinching and not growing a beard. His chest was rising and falling with each deep breath, blissfully unaware of the ruckus occurring around him. Pitching violently once more, the ship's movement launched me straight towards the sleeping boy. Startled by the impact, Mikel cursed, catapulted from his sleep.

A garbled sound escaped my lips. 'Mikel, are you alright?' I asked, intending to pat his back softly in apology, but it came off more like a rough shove.

He shifted his body away from me, closed his eyes, and went back to sleep. Some people just had the ability to sleep through anything, unlike me, who, I discovered, was not at all comfortable on the water. Despite my initial hopes I would make a fine sailor, it turned out that the illness never left during our days on the sea. I could scarcely keep any food down. Thankfully Björn had told me our destination was not far now and I willed my body to find the energy to survive the rest of the journey.

My eyes strained to see around me. As I lay on my back, I could just make out the canvas roof stretched over the vessel to protect the travellers from the elements. The fabric rippled and snapped in the wind like a whip cracking the parched earth. It did a poor job of keeping out the rain, I thought, as sea spray soaked my face. During the day, we removed the tent, and all the passengers were expected to help man the ship. Everyone needed to row for the byrding to navigate the narrow waterways or when there was insufficient wind to fill the sails. I would assist under instruction but, mostly, did not know what I was doing, and discovered early on that I was not cut out for seafaring.

When the water had calmed and the worst of the night became a memory, I took my place at the oars, seated next to my new friend. Mikel was a boy of only fifteen, though he could not tell me for sure. Small in stature and unlike the boys of my hometown, most of whom could pass for a grown man by his age, his size was likely because of underfeeding in his early years. His mother had abandoned him as a child, his family had given him nothing, not even a name, nor ever laid eyes on him. Mikel had grown up alone on stoops and in alleys, thieving a meal where he could. At ten, he had the good fortune of finding a benefactor who offered him a chance to apprentice in the carpentry trade to a well-known master. This man became more than his master, himself never having married or fathering any children. He had treated Mikel as a son. For years, Mikel worked hard for his adopted father to show his appreciation, working night and day to develop his skills and progress in his trade, though it would be many years until he could become a master himself.

His 'father' had died a week before the beginning of our journey, and Mikel had found himself without a benefactor, home, or employment. He had been lucky enough to find a position in the new lands, with their constant requirement for a skilled workforce, and found himself next to me on a ship headed for an unknown land. For Mikel, he felt this was his only choice, so he took what little belongings and money his 'father' had left for him and took his chances.

During our journey, as much as we were able, we sailed close to the coast, save for the crossing of the Austmarr, particularly where the body of water was at its widest. I was told, after the rough crossing between my homeland and the land of the Rus', the water would become calm again and the only issue would be the maze of rivers and inlets of Gardarike. Björn had made this journey many times and told me that there were some rivers so shallow, narrow, or so riddled with rapids that the byrding had to be portaged by the crew. He explained that was the reason they constructed the ship to be light, a much different ship from those used for raiding or war.

As foretold, the water became calmer after the crossing and I could sit on the deck and enjoy the sight of being surrounded by water, my eyes resting on the horizon where the clear blue sky met the water, merging into one.

'Signe,' a voice called from behind me.

My new name rang prettily from Björn's mouth as he came to sit by me, far nicer than Astrid had ever sounded; hard and angry but responding to Signe would take time.

'Are you excited about all this?' He seemed to have taken a genuine interest in my new life. There was no doubt it was likely because of his involvement with Neflaug, my new mistress.

'I suppose I am looking forward to the opportunity to start again in a new place.' It was as close to honesty as I would tread.

He watched me for a moment before whetting his lips to speak. 'Was your husband's death sudden?'

Shocked by his forwardness and not having been prepared for the question, I drew on reality as my only inspiration. 'It was sudden in that it was not expected, but he was old, and it is not possible to live forever,' I replied, hoping it would be a sufficient answer.

'Will you marry again?' he continued. The kindness in his eyes spoke to honest interest rather than malicious intent.

'I hope not!'

He laughed at my candour. 'And why should you have to? A woman should be able to choose just as a man can. You are fortunate the woman I am taking you to, Neflaug, is industrious and unmarried. No one even bats an eye. And if they do, it's not 'cause she is unmarried, if you catch the flow of the water, eh?'

My eyes narrowed, though his mischievous face gave nothing further away. 'I must be fortunate then, Björn. Even though you say that no one thinks Neflaug's position as odd, you know, there would not be many men who think as you do.'

'How's that?'

'Well, many men think that a woman is there for the taking. Few believe that a woman may have her own choices or know her own mind.'

'What did your husband think about all that?'

I raised my eyebrows and shrugged. 'Not sure. I never asked him, and he certainly never asked me.'

'Did you not love your husband?' he asked plainly.

'Can't say I had a choice in the matter. When we married, I was only a girl.' What was love other than an inconvenience, anyway?

'Ah, I see.' He nodded. 'Not all men treat their woman with kindness. Is that why you don't want another?'

The water sparkled as I stared, contemplating the question. 'Even a burnt child learns to stay away from the fire,' I whispered.

He murmured in assent, and we were both silent for a moment.

Was that really why I didn't want to marry again? Was I set on living a life alone in search of adventure, or did I truly believe that a fulfilling life and marriage were inconsistent with one another?

'This is a new world you are about to be living in,' Björn began, bringing me back from my thoughts. 'You will see the differences when you have been there for some time. There are some men in Aldeigjuborg that think and do things differently. They have to!' He squeezed my shoulder as he stood. 'Though the old breed still gets their fingers into everyone's business, you will find some there that believe a woman should be free to choose her own destiny and her own man, should she want one,' he said, staring out over the water. 'Remember, possession is not love, Signe.'

'It is quite refreshing to hear that.' My response was meant to be light, tinged with a laugh, but the sound caught in my throat.

Björn looked back at me, narrowing his gaze. 'Are you worried about what she expects of you?'

That was the problem. I had no idea what I was approaching. 'A little,' I managed. All I knew was that Signe was employed as one of Neflaug's women who spun and wove textiles. Nothing more.

'I'm sure you do not need to be.'

Bright fingers of light appeared on the horizon. Grey mist drifted over the dark sky that lightened to a spectrum of dusty pinks, yellows, and oranges as the sun rose from behind the river. It was the most amazing sunrise I had ever seen, and it transfixed me. A perfect representation of my new life - through adversity we will come until we see the dawn of the new sun on our horizon, and we will start again.

Sitting on the platform at the bow of the ship, I basked in the early morning sun with my young friend Mikel, sharing the little food we had remaining between us and reminisced over our former lives. I let out the tight braids my aunt had woven and shook out my long hair. A gentle breeze blew through my loose locks.

'How are you feeling?' Mikel asked.

'A little of everything, I think. It's not just new positions we are travelling to. We are leaving our old selves behind. Now we can be anyone we want to be when we arrive, even if that is someone different. There won't be anyone telling us what we should be.'

Mikel tapped his smooth chin before replying. 'I had not thought of it like that, but it might be nice to be someone new.' He smiled. 'And if I don't want to be the boy abandoned by his family, I don't have to be.'

'Your father loved you enough to provide you with a skill. That should be all that matters.'

Tears beaded in his eyes. Mikel turned his face away and swallowed, swatting away the drops that threatened to fall. 'He was as close to a father as I have ever and likely will ever know. Taught me my trade, treated me well. That's all people need to know.'

'Argh, watch yourself, boy, don't let anyone catch you simpering over a woman like that!' Björn laughed from behind as he approached and sat down beside us in the sun. He lounged back, his skin leathered by the wind and harsh sun unprotected by the trees that a non-seafarer would have the benefit of.

Mikel feigned being sick. 'Never! Awful things girls are.' He wretched.

'One day you will want after one, I promise you that, boy,' Björn said, grinning, revealing a missing right canine tooth. 'Oooh, just wait until you see the marketplace. The goods on offer are like never you would have seen before. And the people, oh the people, in all different colours. Short ones, tall ones, fat, and skinny, some pretty and some looking more like animals,' he added knowledgeably. 'And the food. Mikel. You'll be fattened up in no time.' He licked his lips. 'Soon you will forget about all you have left behind.'

I proffered a nervous smile to Mikel.

'Feel sorry for us, eh?' Björn faked forlorn. 'We have families tying us to the old lands. We may enjoy ourselves while we are here, but we must return some time, though I'll be taking my time getting back,' he lamented.

As we approached our destination, the other men on board were in high spirits. Apparently, Aldeigjuborg as a major trading port, contained delights they dreamed of long after they left it.

'There she is, boy!' Björn said, clapping Mikel on the back and gesturing to the town, which appeared as we sailed around the bend in the river. 'That's Aldeigjuborg, your new home.'

With a deep breath, I reminded myself that everything would be alright. Under the sleeve of my shirt, I felt my father's armring, Bjarndýr, safely hidden. All I had to do now was to put one foot in front of the other and trust the Norns had woven a path that would lead me towards adventure and, hopefully, not to my end.

SIX

ALDEIGJUBORG,
GARDARIKE THE LAND OF THE RUS'

My hand tightened around the handle of Skara, my thumb pressing her eye to distract me from the rising bile in my throat. The axe was almost a protective talisman, close by to prevent trouble, but her very presence symbolised a danger I would need to hide. Over my shoulder, I slung my bag, allowing it to slip forward to hide the weapon under its sagging fabric.

Björn chortled. 'You'll not need to battle your way into the city, Signe. Fear not.'

An awkward smile was all I could manage as I slumped back into the seat in a restless battle of standing and sitting as we traversed the narrowing river. The water parted gently as we rowed towards the city and as we neared the bend of the Volkhov as it flowed into the Ladozhka River, which was incredibly shallow in parts, preventing the heavy, deep hulled boats from entering. Passing the fork, we continued to the harbour outside the city gates. Men hurried to shout greetings to others on the jetty as we slowed, approaching the moorings protruding from the reeds. With a hefty bang, the ship hit the wooden pole and made my teeth clatter in my head.

'Steady on! I almost spat out my teeth,' Mikel called, his fingers tracing his teeth to make sure they were still there.

Björn grinned broadly, making a show of his gap smile. 'What, are you afraid of having a beautiful smile like mine, boy?'

The crew laughed as they passed planks between them to join the jetty path. Boats joined hull-to-hull. Around us were twenty-or-so similarly sized vessels, each moored to a pole around the central walkway of planks leading to a gently sloping grassed hill. Beyond that, I could not see much more than the wooden *tyn* walls, a palisade taller than two men standing end to end, but I assumed it led the way to town.

'Odin's beard!' I cursed under my breath, bringing Mikel's attention to the sharpened stake at the end of each spear in the wall. He seemed more interested in everything else that was happening around us.

'Not going to get any easier if we just stay here.'

I tore my eyes away from the walls, I passed a sack of something heavy to Björn, who was clamouring across the other moored boats to access the jetty. The ship next to us was also unloading. Men were shouting and birds were flying overhead, hoping to scavenge a morsel thrown their way. With the boat unloaded of goods, there were only us to remove.

On Mikel's shoulder, I placed a steadying hand, more for my comfort than for his. 'Come on, let's see what is inside.' I threw one leg over the gunwale and into the ship alongside; we made our way along the vessels. On the last one, just before reaching the jetty, I misjudged the distance and stumbled. Mikel caught me by the elbow as I stumbled onto the deck.

His boyish face did not hide his amusement. 'Why do you even carry those?' He pointed to Skara and my shield. 'Were you a warrior woman or something?'

Embarrassment coloured my face. 'My father gave them to me, and I would never be without them,' I snapped, regretting my tone instantly. 'They are all I have.'

He nodded in understanding; he too had precious little of his previous life.

When we finally made it to solid ground, I felt as if I had been drinking. My legs were disobediently sensing uneven ground and my mind told me the world swayed like the flow of water. The distance between me and Björn, who watched with interest, seemed much further than it ought to have.

'Follow me, you two!' Björn called from the top of the jetty, beckoning us forward. 'It's a little way, but you'll get the lay of the farming lands on our walk in, at least.'

The land surrounding the walls appeared to be a mix of marshland and arable farmland that was divided up into small allotments. Easily able to feed themselves, the farmers would surely grow fat and supply surplus to the inhabitants of the fortification. The walled town, I was assured, was not overly large itself and certainly nowhere near the size of Birka, though some said it was the capital of the Rus' cities. Someone else said it once was, but no longer. Björn explained that the wealthy dwelled within the city and overflowed during trade time and market days. Those who worked in the city came and went as needs be.

We crossed the bridge with our belongings in tow. The walls were just as impressive as they had been at a distance. They seemed expansive, high and thick. Some parts of the wall were *tyn* construction and others were a type of cell construction that would make them difficult to breach the multi-layered structure. How would one even breach such a wall?

'So Björn, is it dangerous here?' I asked, motioning to the impending wall.

'Hmm,' he pondered and shrugged, 'no more dangerous than anywhere else I would imagine. You know, warring tribes, raiders, and bandits. Aldeigjuborg is an important town, one of the first on the river- the gateway to the trading route, from here onto Holmgadr. That's kind of the capital of the Rus, and where the present Grand Prince Oleg is living.'

'You keep saying this word "Rus'," but what does it mean?'

Björn looked at me, disbelievingly. 'Do not tell me you have never heard of the Rus'. That's what they call our people who settled here. We've changed a bit over the years. Letting go a bit too much of the old ways I say, but they like to build and trade, so I'll keep my complaints to myself.'

My decision to come to Aldeigjuborg had been swift, and not considered, and now I wondered what kind of danger I was walking into. 'And the raiders, do they cause much damage?' I asked nervously.

'To the people or the city?'

'Er, both?'

'We are less than a day's sail from the sea, so it is not hard to reach. The problem for them would be the fine protection that the city guards offer. If you can get past that unnoticed,' he said, pointing to the watchtower on the left embankment of the river partially covered by trees, 'and then sneak into the gates, or get over those walls somehow they'd have to have all the Æsir behind them.'

'I am not sure that puts me at ease,' I grumbled, trudging along after Björn.

'Then why worry about it? The gods have already made their plan for you. We are all going to die. Nothing you can do about that. And anyway, you'll be alright as you've got your little axe right there, eh?' He chuckled.

His teasing eased my nerves, and laughter followed. It was strange that I would live in a town with so much to offer others who might want to take it by force when only a few days prior I had been hoping to raid a town just like this one. 'Björn, why do you come to trade here?' I asked breathlessly after running to catch him, lost in my thoughts since I had lagged.

'Hmm,' he mumbled, thinking. 'I can get the best price for anything, and I can get almost anything Svealand landowners want or need from here too, or through here as it flows from both ends.'

'Many people pass through here?'

He nodded emphatically. 'Traders from lands far away come in the warm months. This is the last stop before our homeland, and few will venture that way. Why would they when I will make the trip for them?'

'What about glass beads?' I asked, thinking about the time Auden had gifted me a necklace made from fine glass beads from a passing merchant.

'Of course.'

'And would they have come from some far-off land?'

'It is possible, though more likely they came from the glass makers of Birka.'

'Oh.' My shoulders slumped. I had hoped that at one time, I had owned some kind of exotic foreign finery.

'Here in Aldeigjuborg,' Björn continued, 'I get paid, mostly, in Arabic dirhams. None of this trading for broken bits of metal that I cannot be sure of its value. Though everyone still accepts hack because being paid is always preferable than not.'

'Coins?'

'Getting coins instead of hack silver means I know what I am getting and the more money I make, the happier my wife is. The happier my wife is, the more I get away with.' He laughed with a roguish smile.

His humour was infectious, and I found a broad smile taking over my face. Distracted by the conversation, we now found ourselves at the main gate to the town. Glancing at Mikel, I watched his mouth fall open in awe as his eyes followed the height of the walls.

'They are so high,' he whispered.

'Plenty more to make your eyes bulge within the walls, I promise you,' Björn joked as he pushed Mikel towards the forming crowd that bustled to the entrance.

I wondered, looking up at the height of the wall, if the walls of the great cities looked similar. Could it be possible that they were larger? Was it even possible to build walls any bigger?

The many people passing by me interrupted my thoughts. I scanned each face, their skin coloured in distinct tones and their features so dissimilar to my own. Some had dark eyes with broad noses making their face seem wide and flat whilst one had flesh the colour of oiled oak, large round eyes framed with thick bushy brows that moved like insects when he spoke. I had been staring at a young man with dusky coloured skin engaged in lively conversation with a beautiful woman with round, green eyes. Their exchange bordered on intimate. Perhaps I should have looked away, but I couldn't. The man leaned close to the woman's ear and whispered something. She giggled, and he bit her on the neck. My mouth fell open in shock at the brazen act. The man turned towards me and, with a mischievous grin, winked before returning his mouth to the woman's lips. My face flushed with embarrassment.

Björn was engaged in a discussion with the guard at the gate. Their talk had turned to directions. I could tell by the way they gesticulated, throwing their arms about, pointing and nodding. Our shipmaster, Björn, turned to beckon us to follow. We passed through the gates, and Björn turned to me. 'It's quite a sight, isn't it?' I did not need to reply, sure my face was sufficiently awe struck.

Once through the gates, the arrangement of the houses seemed to be in the shape of a rough circle enclosing rows of buildings. Unlike Karlstad, where I was accustomed to family living, many did not live as communally. Longhouses were in the few, save for the outline of farming lands. No, here, familial dwellings comprising a few rooms seemed to be the norm. Each building stood tall. The roofs were angular rather than curved, some with small landings out the front to keep the mess of the muddy roads out of the dwellings.

Directly inside the walls, I saw a building that housed the town's guard. Behind it, a series of steps, I assumed, led to the wall's ramparts. On my right was the tavern and to my left the guildhall, with large double doors which were closed to the masses that passed it. A row of merchant homes with small stalls set up out front were on the next street. The surrounding sounds were unfamiliar too. The ground crunched underfoot from some sort of hard-packed dirt which formed the primary thoroughfare. There was much commotion occurring as we walked. The noise was deafening, and I could discern none of the words spoken over the din. My ears felt assaulted. I raised my hands defensively over them to stifle the sounds. Mikel, instead, seemed to be entertained by the hubbub, grinning.

Björn patted me roughly on the back and I could see his mouth forming the words, 'You will get used to it.'

How it would be possible for anyone to adjust themselves to cope with such volume? I thought, was beyond me. Surely one would go deaf. A waft of deliciousness floating on steam found my nose and my mouth watered. Björn ushered us to a small table surrounded by stools, and I plonked myself down. An old woman hunched over a vat, stirring it with a large wooden paddle. No words were uttered, just three fingers waved in the woman's direction that resulted in three small bowls of whatever she stirred in her vat. She placed each one before us on the table. Perspiration covered my body, making my clothing stick to my skin. I pulled at it uncomfortably and rolled my sleeves above my elbows to ease my discomfort.

'Is it always so hot?' I moaned.

Mikel cast a sideways glance, 'It's not that hot.'

'Maybe it's just all the people. But Odin's beard I am sweating.'

'It's likely weariness from the journey,' Björn offered helpfully. 'Here, eat,' he added, pushing the bowl under my face, 'it will help.'

My stomach grumbled. I had not eaten a hot meal in nearly two weeks. 'What is it?'

'Who cares?' Mikel managed with a mouthful. 'It's delicious.'

I shovelled a spoonful into my mouth. 'I'm so hungry I think even if they boiled wood, I would eat it.' Lucky for me, the stew woman had not been boiling wood, but a very savoury, thick stew-like concoction of vegetables and some kind of tender meat seasoned with strong herbs.

'Good to see you both have a healthy appetite. Some people are too nervous to eat when they first arrive,' Björn announced proudly as he prodded into his own bowl.

I laughed. If there was one thing I should be proud of on this day; it was my 'healthy appetite.' I would never turn down a good meal.

'Are you nervous, Signe?' Mikel asked as he finished his bowl.

Setting my bowl down to answer him, the withered old lady whipped the bowl from under my nose. 'But I'm not finished,' I called out to her. She shrugged. 'A little,' I replied to Mikel.

Björn pulled us both to our feet as people were already clamouring to take our seats. 'You will have to learn to be quick.' He chuckled, leading us away. 'But I am sure you'll both come to enjoy it here and your hometowns will be but a distant memory, eh?'

The words 'hometown' and 'distant memory' hit the pit of my stomach and made me feel uneasy. I had been ignoring the significance of the decision I made since I left and now that I was here, I would have to live a new life. I wondered if Sven had been terribly mad when he found I had fled, or if he would have thought that some tragedy had befallen me. Perhaps it would have been easier if he thought I had found some horrible end. He could move past that. But Signe knew no man named Sven. She knew none of the trials and disappointments that Astrid had encountered in her life and Signe, my new identity, was all I had.

'Your new lives here can offer you more than anything you would have hoped to find in the lands of your families,' Björn reflected ruefully.

We left the tent together in the direction of the merchant homes, which all backed onto the town walls. After a short distance, we stopped outside a work yard that was obviously used for carpentry work. It had a small residence attached to it as well as a covered work yard which housed carpentry tools. A man, a little older than I, was sitting just inside the doorway sipping from a cup.

'Luca!' Björn called out.

'Yes?' the man answered in a slow voice, standing up and walking out to greet us.

The men embraced. 'Luca, how are you?'

'In good health and good business, and you?'

'Being back in Aldeigjuborg has improved my happiness, friend.'

'And your wife?' Luca enquired.

'She is well. Big with yet another child. I am truly blessed by the gods.' Björn stepped back and put his arm around Mikel, ushering him forward into the yard. 'This is your new apprentice, Mikel.' he introduced the two. Mikel still seemed nervous. That was natural, but Luca, by all appearances, was a nice, friendly man. 'I hope you will find him skilful, and I hope in time you will work well together and make a good business.'

'I am confident of it,' Luca replied with a toothy smile and welcomed Mikel into his home, into which they disappeared. We waved a farewell as we turned away from the carpentry yard.

Björn exhaled slowly. 'I think they will be a good match. Luca is a kindly man, and he needs good help. They will learn a lot from each other.'

'Will I see him again?' I asked, having grown fond of Mikel during our journey.

'I expect so.'

As it turned out, I would not be far from him at all and, should I want to, could check on him easily. We stopped outside of a house with a small, planked area sheltered by a wooden awning. An entrance door led to the residential area, but I could see that the building extended some way back into what appeared to be a warehouse. The home solidly constructed on a single level with a flourish of stylised archives and windows.

Björn was fidgeting with something inside his satchel, pulling a small box from within before knocking on the door. 'This is you,' he whispered over his shoulder towards me.

The door opened slowly. Even from my obstructed view, I could see the tall, beautiful woman who appeared on the threshold. She stood, at least, as tall as me, with long tawny hair, tumbling in loose curls over her shoulders and down the front of her dress. Soft lines formed at the corners of her eyes but did nothing to diminish her beauty. Her green eyes highlighted by the shade of her dress, which was cut to cling provocatively at the curves of her body. She was all soft edges, nothing sharp save for her mind, if the intellect I detected in her eyes would be anything to judge by.

Suddenly conscious of my appearance, I felt like a farm girl in my rough spun woollen dress, a simple undershirt and tangled locks soaked in sweat and likely odorous. My fingers combed through my hair, and I pulled my sleeves down to cover my arms and Bjarndýr. Neither Björn nor the woman paid any attention to me. Their eyes were locked on each other, regardless of their apparent mismatch. Björn handed her the small box. From inside, the woman withdrew a necklace on a long strand of some material I could not quite see. She seemed to like it and turned so he could fasten it around her neck. He kissed her on the cheek and turned, red-faced, to me.

'This is Signe,' he said, motioning for me to step forward.

I stood up straight and walked forward into her line of sight. '*Hej*,' I greeted the green-eyed woman.

A slight smile graced her lips, and she sent a wink in Björn's direction. '*Hej*, Signe. I am Neflaug.'

Björn nudged me forward.

'I am Signe.'

'I know.' Her eyes flashed with amusement.

She probably thought I was dim. I cursed myself.

'Why does she have an axe and a shield?' Neflaug directed the question to Björn.

'A gift from her father.'

'Strange,' Neflaug replied, but dismissed it as a quirk.

'Well, I have delivered all I need to. I'll leave you two to get on with it. My crew will be here for a few more days should there be any trouble.' He chuckled. 'Neflaug, if you have any business that you need me to attend to.' He stopped before saying any more.

'I know where to find you,' she finished for him, gently touching his forearm.

'Hmm, alright then. Good luck, Signe.'

I proffered a grateful smile to Björn as he left. Neflaug turned to walk inside the house. I followed. The first room was a living space that contained a large hearth on the left and on the right, a long trestle table with one bench on either side. It was mostly dark inside except for the sun, which crept in from the doorway. It was small for the size of the house, informing me that there must have been additional rooms to make up the size I had perceived from the outside.

'How is your native tongue?' Neflaug asked.

It tempted me to stick it out and show her, but I resisted the urge. Still, I was not sure what she referred to.

'Do you speak well?'

Oh no! She thought I was stupid. I hurried to correct myself. 'Good. I think. I speak well and can make marks,' I answered, showing that I could count and keep account when required.

'There is no need for modesty, Signe. I need to know what skills you have. What kind of woman have I brought into my house?'

'I know my runes, but I have little practice with writing them.'

'Can you count?' she asked.

'Yes.'

'We use a special method for ordering and writing here. It's a simple shorthand of strokes to count. You will learn,' she detailed. 'Any other languages?'

'I'm sorry?'

'Do you speak any other languages?' she asked.

'Like what?'

'*Mal*, Signe, like *Fransk, Latin, Engelsk*?' She searched my face for a response, some twinge of recognition.

My face blanked; it mortified me how ignorant I seemed. Nothing more than a simple farm girl who did not know people spoke any other language than her own. Of course, I knew people spoke other tongues. It's just that I had never given it any thought. Thank the gods, Neflaug and I could understand each other, though she might not have thought so by the lack of reply.

'No need to fret. At least I know what I am working with,' she said and turned away from me. 'When I first arrived, I could barely read and now I can communicate in three languages. If you work hard, you will learn a lot. At the moment, I just need you to read and write the orders. The rest will come as we go.' She smiled kindly for the first time, sat a hot cup of nettle tea on the table, and motioned for me to sit down. 'How are the men where you are from?' The question caught me off guard.

'Big,' I answered matter-of-factly.

She laughed. The sound made me giddy. 'Of course, they are, but are they modest?'

'Is any man modest?'

'No, I suppose not,' she agreed. 'And the women? How about them?'

'I guess I would consider them modest,' I replied, reflecting on it.

'That always seems to be the way. We live in a world designed for men, in which only they should succeed. If we learn to take the opportunity where it arises, then we will achieve more than most.'

My cup seemed bottomless. The water tinged green from the nettles that floated, suspended in the liquid. I did not dare look up to meet her eye, afraid she might already know me as a pretender. And, in my exhausted state, I continued to stare into my cup as if it held all the answers in the world, petrified that it would be too easy to give myself up.

Neflaug drew a deep breath and continued in a serious voice, 'But first you must wash the muck of your journey away, burn that awful dress, and rest. I need you at your best and never at any less.'

PART TWO

On oceans, they sailed
Without fear in their hearts,
Their sails billowed with excitement.

In search of fortune, to prosper.
No longer poor farmers,
With Thor at our side.

We shall run toward victory
Screaming, 'Valhalla, Valhalla,'
We will feast with the gods in paradise.

SEVEN

SPRING 880CE, ALDEIGJUBORG, GARDARIKE

Through the shuttered window, the sun peeked, kissing my face with its warm rays. I stretched lazily, too comfortable to get up, and slowly blinked my eyes open. The room was still and bare; apart from the bed, only a small table occupied the space. I could walk from wall-to-wall in four paces even so, having my own room seemed strange. Privacy was a luxury, and I had always shared my sleeping place with either my husband or an entire longhouse full of people. A purpose-built bed, not a bench, was for the rich. Yet, there was one in my room. It made me wonder what exactly it was that Neflaug expected from me. More than that, I was concerned if I would live up to them.

I pulled the furs covering the bed over my head, stealing a moment away from my anxieties, but the clanging of pots from the hearth room told me they would expect me to rise soon. My arms reached high in an appreciative stretch and my feet found their way into my leather slippers. Skara and my shield lay on the floor where I had hastily discarded them the night before in my desire for sleep. For now, they would need to live under my bed. Any marker of my previous life might give me away. *I have to be careful*, I thought, slipping the Valkyrie pendant that Sven had given me from around my neck.

You need to forget about it all. Especially him, I chided myself. I wrapped the necklace in my travel worn clothes, tucking it under my shield and out of sight. 'You can do this,' I whispered as I slipped on a clean *serkr* that Neflaug had left in the room and pulled the door open and walked out into the hearth room. It was already warm, the fire stoked, and a young woman was fussing over a bubbling pot.

'*Dóbro útro*,' she greeted me with a smile.

I stared at her, ignorant of her meaning.

She moved behind me, collecting a couple of bowls from the shelf, 'Good morning.' She smiled politely over my shoulder.

'What did you say before?' I asked, watching her gracefully move around the hearth, busy with her chores.

'Good morning.'

'No, before that.'

'Good morning,' she repeated.

'No, I mean before you said, "good morning"?'

She giggled shyly. 'They both mean good morning, miss,' she explained, returning to the thick porridge over the fire. The local tongue lightly accented her voice.

'Oh,' I breathed. The feeling of inadequacy had returned now, having not been long forgotten. Neflaug would no doubt hear about my inability to understand a simple greeting, though I hoped she would put it down to nerves.

'Don't worry yourself, miss. Sit,' she said kindly, guiding me to the bench seat and plonking a bowl of gloopy oats before me.

'You do not need to call me miss. My name is Signe.' Besides, it made me uncomfortable to be in a position of rank again, especially one that brought with it any deference. It reminded me of being married, and that was not something that put my mind at ease.

'I must call you that, miss. If Neflaug heard otherwise, I would be out the door, but you can call me Helga.' She winked as she collected a small earthen pot from the table. Inside was a small utensil which resembled a stick with a ball on the end. A golden liquid dripped from the dipper onto my porridge.

'What is it?' I asked, watching her spill long threads of the viscous syrup onto my breakfast.

Helga dipped her finger into the bowl and smacked it against her lips. 'Honey.'

'Honey?' I dabbed my finger in the goo and tentatively licked it. It was sweet.

'The nectar made by bees.'

Of course, I knew what honey was. Traditionally, we used it for mead. It was drunk on special occasions such as weddings and honeymoons where newlyweds drank whilst becoming acquainted with each other, but seldom used to top porridge.

'How do you usually have it, miss?' she asked.

'I have never eaten porridge this way. Usually, it would be berries or nuts.'

'I can forage for some if you like.'

'No need, Helga, this is delicious,' I mumbled appreciatively as I shovelled breakfast into my mouth.

She sat down beside me and watched me as I ate, but I was too hungry to care. As I crammed my last mouthful in, I heard the warehouse door open and Neflaug entered the room. She wore a modest gown of fine wool; the shade of blood red. Weary around the eyes; she must have been awake for some time. With a heavy sigh, she fell onto the bench next to me and without a word began spooning her porridge from a bowl that appeared before her into her mouth. When she stopped for a breath, she addressed me without looking up from her meal. 'How did you sleep?'

'Well, thank you.'

'Good. Your room. How do you like it?' She continued to stare into her bowl.

Her refusal to look at me was unsettling, whether it was on purpose or because of her own fixation on something. 'The room is lovely, thank you. Who will I share it with?' Feeling a question was easier to pose than assuming it would be my own.

'Share? Who else will live there with you?' She finally looked up from her bowl. Immediately I wished she had not, for her eyes were ablaze with something between annoyance and amusement. 'I would not have thought you would presume to take a husband so soon.' There was a sharp intake of breath as she waited for my response.

My face reddened, and I stumbled over my response. 'Oh no, no, nothing like that. I have no desire for a husband, it's just… it's a large room and all of my own. I, I…'

'Desire is another matter entirely, though bringing any man into this house would not meet my approval.' She clicked her tongue in reproach, then shrugged. 'My room is much larger and grander, but the other women in my employ live outside the walls. They only sleep here, when need be, so if you ever need to share with anyone it's likely only ever going to be Helga.' Neflaug glanced at the young girl busying herself with the pot over the fire, who, no doubt, was trying to remain well out of the way.

Neflaug set her spoon into her empty bowl and without so much a breath between, Helga scooped them up, removing them from the table. 'Finish your bowl, Signe, and I shall show you the warehouse and then the actual work will begin.'

Though only a small amount remained for me to eat, my stomach turned with nervousness, and I found I could not finish. Helga swept the utensil and bowl away without a word and followed Neflaug through a door. The warehouse was a cavernous space lit only by a central fire and the small amount of light that penetrated the planks of wood which formed its structure. It was as much as a longhouse, though much smaller, as I had seen since my arrival in Aldeigjuborg.

Neflaug walked towards the double doors and called to me over her shoulder, 'Help me open these.' She unlatched the bolt and together we pushed them open, letting a bright stream of light inside. The warmth was delightful on my skin. Even the sun shone brighter in Aldeigjuborg, I thought.

Against the walls, I recognised the tools of the spinning and weaving trade: drop spindles, spinning wheels, and, in the corner near the large doors, a very large table which I assumed was for sorting and packing the wool. Against the wall furthest from us was a standing loom. I had used one before, but I had little skill in it. The small weights held the vertically hanging threads taut at their ends, swaying gently as if measuring time. Behind us, the sounds of approaching women gave me hope that one of them would be the master of the standing loom. If Neflaug had expected that skill of me, I would prove a bitter disappointment.

Four neatly dressed women entered through the doors. One walked with grand purpose, ahead of the others. Plump and short, she had the appearance of a friendly woodland creature with mouse-brown hair falling to her shoulders under her hood. She smiled kindly, and with a nod of acknowledgement to Neflaug, sat upon a stool and began untangling wool. Another taller woman gently placed a package of blue cloth on a long bench next to the loom.

Neflaug fingered the fabric. 'It is beautiful, no?' she asked, turning to ask my opinion.

'The dye is beautifully fixed; the colour is so even.' I didn't dare touch it, but even without doing so, I could tell the work was finely done.

'We were so used to those drab, muted tones of brown, grey, and creams of our homeland. What we see here is luxury and wealth. The likes of which we could have never imagined in our most outlandish dreams,' Neflaug continued, running her hands over the fabric. 'This is the sort of colour one dreams about wearing. If you step out of the house with a robe made of this, all eyes will draw to your body,' she said proudly, holding the fabric against her own shapely figure.

'What kind of lady here would buy such a luxury?' I asked curiously.

'Not you or I, that is for sure. Someone will make it into a dress for a rich man's wife,' she scorned.

'I thought even a woman can amass good wealth on her own in Aldeigjuborg.'

'What we are discussing is more than good wealth. Some things may be different here, others will always remain the same, and having a rich husband will make you a kept woman anywhere,' she glowered, setting the fabric gently down on the table. 'If business continues to go well, I could use some to make a dress for myself and use it as a demonstration of our business.' There had been lightness to her voice as she spoke, almost a suppressed girlishness mirrored in her eyes that saw more than the reality around her.

'If I may?' I interjected. 'It may not be such a far-fetched idea. You would not need to make the entire dress out of such costly fabric. Instead, use it as a trim to outline the parts of the body you wish to draw attention to.'

'That could work.' She stroked her right cheek thoughtfully. 'We often have a scrap here or there when evening out the bolts, so I may not even need to take away from the saleable goods. You are a bright girl. I see I have chosen well,' Neflaug congratulated herself. She took my arm gently and smiled. 'Come, let's get you started.' As she led me to the other side of the warehouse where two women were speedily spinning clumps of wool into fine strands. 'Do you prefer the drop spindle or wheel?'

'Drop spindle,' I replied, having only ever seen a wheel once but never used it.

She ran her hand over the spinning wheel. 'This is so much more efficient, but so many are reluctant to use it.' She shook her head.

A plump woman behind a spinning wheel called out.

'What did she say?' I asked, leaning close to Neflaug.

'Oh Hilde! She said that one day you will all come around to the idea of a spinning wheel. It's her accent. You cannot understand her meaning then?'

'Perhaps if I listen closer, it sounds like her mouth is full of something.' It was possible to be more descriptive, but I did not want to sound rude.

'You will grow accustomed to it. She was born in these lands, as were her family many generations before, though she speaks our tongue well. She can be a little difficult to listen to. Thankfully, her daughter Helga's speaking is a bit more refined.' Neflaug turned away from the others. 'I expect you are still tired from your journey, so do your best, but I'll not expect much from you right now.' Neflaug grinned, but something told me she would do the exact opposite.

I took the spindle in my right hand and felt the smoothness of the wood. Its length was ideal. I always preferred my spindles about the length of my forearm and no thicker than my finger. On its notched length, a whorl made from clay and of middling weight sat perfectly even. At the top was another notch, deeper, and only on one side, which made a hook for the wool to feed in to. With my left hand, I picked up a small ball of grey wool.

'I believe this comes from the sheep near your homeland,' she spoke, watching me intently.

'It comes all the way from Svealand?' I asked, puzzled why someone would ship in wool when there were so many sheep just outside the town walls.

'Of course not, that would be expensive. No, they brought the Gotland sheep here.'

My eyes did not hide my surprise. The wool was fine indeed. The finished garment would be light and beautiful, providing good warmth.

It was expensive, but for good reason. In its natural colours of silver and charcoal, it was beautiful. The key was that it took particularly well to being dyed, so it could produce a variety of colours.

'Go on,' Neflaug urged.

From the bundle, I teased out some of the soft fibres. Weaving them through the loop at the end of the spindle, I wound the thread around the shaft twice to secure it so it would not dislodge once I started spinning. With a steeling breath and standing upright, I held the spindle by the whorl whilst my middle finger and thumb pinched the length of the wood and spun it. A couple of attempts were all it took to get it spinning smoothly, then I only needed to repeat the process to keep the momentum of the whorl. As it spun, I let it hang whilst using both hands to continue feeding out the unspun wool, and as it became yarn, the spindle drooped lower and lower to the ground. Before it stopped, I took it up, winding the now beautifully smooth spun wool around the shaft above the whorl and beginning the process again. I kept going until I had enough to make a skein, counting eighty turns, more-or-less.

Neflaug had stood without moving, watching me for the entire time. When I looked up to seek her approval, there was a slight smile on her full lips. 'Very good. Very good.' She nodded.

'I'm a little out of practice, but I can assure you I will increase my speed,' I promised.

'You already match the speed of my experienced ladies. If you get any faster, I think you will be the fastest I have ever seen. We not only produce wool for yarn here, but as you can see from the loom there, we also make cloth,' she explained, removing my spindle from my hand and placing it on the table.

Wool that became cloth was finer and needed to be combed so that it aligned the fibres before they spun it into small and neat yarn. Once it was in yarn, it would be woven into fabric using the loom, but it needed to be pressed tight so that the fabric would be strong and keep its shape.

'I want you to concentrate on spinning. I have other plans for you and do not intend to waste you before the loom.' She walked away and through the big door and out of sight without saying another word.

Such relief I felt at knowing Neflaug had brought me to the town to do something I was competent at. Though her abrupt departure had been surprising, I assumed she meant me to stay with the other ladies and spin for the rest of the day. So, picking up the spindle, I walked around the warehouse, enjoying the meditative process. I could lose myself in the repetitive nature of the work and my mind would wander on to different things. The beauty of a drop spindle was that once you were in the rhythm, you could do just about anything whilst spinning: cooking, walking, nursing a baby, and kissing your husband - as long as you could dedicate one hand to keeping that spindle spinning.

Two women, also pacing the length of the warehouse, sang. I didn't know the words, unsure if they were even in my language, or if they just had a strange accent, but after a couple of rounds, I could mimic the words well enough to join in. They giggled at my first few attempts, but they were warm in repeating some of the more difficult phrases slowly so I could try to break them down. It was nice to be a part of something as we took it in turns leading the song, and then singing it in rounds. I swayed from side-to-side, singing and spinning. We must have been working for hours without Neflaug's oversight. There did not seem to be any hierarchy between the women. Everyone knew their jobs and got on with it.

Lost in my work, later that afternoon, it surprised me to hear Neflaug's voice when she whispered beside me, 'There are a few things we need to attend to.'

Did I do something wrong? I wondered but didn't dare ask. Neflaug had, with a simple command, made me feel like a child about to be chided by their mother. Without dallying, I followed her to the hearth room where she faced me, no hint of any meaning on her beautiful face.

'We need to arrange your day.'

More confusion, 'I don't understand.'

'My intention for you was to study the trade every afternoon and work in the morning. I need you to learn other languages, as well as our recording techniques, and I need you able to do both as soon as possible.' Her hands rested on her hips. 'You will work in the warehouse from breakfast to midday, then you will go to my friend, who will instruct you in language and trade. You must adhere to this routine. Do not take these responsibilities or these opportunities lightly,' she warned.

The weight of my commitment bore on me, 'I will not disappoint you.'

There was a flash of something in her eyes; something that I understood might be a temper. 'You should know better than to disappoint me, Signe. I did not bring you here to be a simple spinning maid. There are plans for you. Here we run a large endeavour, with clients that speak in different tongues, and I have tried to do it alone, but I cannot do so any longer. You are here to help me run things, to be my right hand.'

Her words stunned me. My mouth opened and closed without words like a fish desperate for breath out of water.

'You must have wondered why I brought you here directly. Why you had lodgings in the main house?'

Of course, I had wondered, but my mind had not gone so far to imagine that she had planned to hold me in such a position. She did not wait for me to answer.

'From you, I expect loyalty, unflinching, unrivalled, unquestionable loyalty. If I so much as think you have cast your eye elsewhere, I will put you out onto the street. It is not a friendly place outside of my circle. However, if you are inside it, you will experience a golden paradise.' She bared her teeth in what could have been a smile.

'I know no one else,' I tiptoed gently back into the conversation.

'You know what loyalty is, don't you?'

My head bobbed up and down in agreement.

'It is not a great demand when, in return, you will receive much. Signe, to me you are an investment and in me you shall find many opportunities.' She proffered her right hand to me. 'You agree to our fair arrangement, then?'

My hand buzzed with apprehension. Was loyalty all she was demanding? Before I could question any more, my hand jolted out to meet hers and the two shook, binding our deal. Neflaug clicked her tongue in approval and opened the door onto the street.

'No time to waste. Let's go.' She held the door open, waiting for me to exit.

I didn't ask where we were going. My mind was still trying to piece together the commitment I had made. Stepping onto the street, I had not realised how bright the day was. It was much warmer than the summers at home and I could feel a little perspiration accumulating on the small of my back. The fabric of my dress was thick and did not let air through to cool me. I fanned myself with my hand as we walked up the street. We reached a grand house, Neflaug rapped her clenched fist on its large ornate wooden door. She stood expectantly before me, waiting for the door to open, and when it did, there was a loud creak.

'Eryk!' Neflaug greeted her friend.

'How wonderful to see you! Neflaug, it is always a delight to see you outside of our normal town meetings,' he welcomed her in a loud voice.

Neflaug shot a glance at me over her shoulder.

'And who is this?' he asked, directing his attention to me.

Neflaug stepped sideways, allowing me to approach the doorway. 'This is Signe and Signe, this is Eryk, Aldeigjuborg's Jarl, of sorts.'

'Not so much a jarl,' he tutted, 'but I am Prince Oleg's man. That is true. So, this is your new girl? You have finally arrived, huh?' Eryk asked, shooting a quick glance up and down Neflaug's body and I was thankful it was her he was appraising, and not I. He obviously liked what he saw. To me, he looked like a massive lump, the same size around as he was in height. A mound of land, or a large rock, the rolls of his flesh natural indents in the landscape. He stepped forward off the landing onto the street, his enormous belly jiggling before him. 'How are you, Signe? Pleased to meet you.' He pressed my hand into his.

'I am well, thank you,' I hesitated, unsure how to address someone so grand. 'Eryk?' I added.

'You call me Eryk. I don't want to hear any "master" or such. If you give me too much deference, I will feel all important and my head won't fit through that door.' He chuckled, motioning to the door behind him. 'How was your journey? Are you now a sea hand? I am not much for the water myself.'

'My journey was mostly uneventful, except that we took on some water, but we avoided any serious danger. As for comfort at sea, well, I think that is something I shall never get used to.' I laughed to myself. If I ever saw a boat again, it would be too soon.

'Quite true. If I could avoid travel by water, I would do so altogether. It's a horrible way to get anywhere. Such a dangerous method of transport and so bad for digestion,' he said, patting his bulging belly fat.

'Yes, well,' Neflaug interrupted. 'Signe needs you for your expertise in accounts. I need her to help me with the business and once she has mastered that, I want her to take on a second language. She shouldn't have much trouble with it. She appears to be quite bright.'

Eryk peered down at me. Even though I was quite tall, he still towered above me by at least a head. 'How often should she come?' he asked.

'Each afternoon, if you can spare the time?' Neflaug suggested.

'Yes, of course. I like to see a fledgling bloom,' he mumbled, smiling to himself as he devoured Neflaug with his eyes.

Was there something between them? It certainly seemed as if Eryk would welcome whatever advances Neflaug might broach, but I could see no sign that my mistress returned the desire. Neflaug propelled me forward with a hard shove, and I tripped over the threshold. 'Come straight back to the house when your lessons are done,' she instructed.

I had been busy trying to make sense of the pledge Neflaug had extracted from me and hadn't been taking notice of directions. I shot an uneasy glance at Eryk.

He nodded reassuringly. 'If she does not know the way, I can walk her there.'

Inside Eryk's home were all smooth wood surfaces. Not a rough edge in sight. Each panel was richly decorated, polished, or covered with some ornament.

'This is....' I started. I had meant to say something admiring, but it came out as a stutter that stifled any further words.

He chuckled. 'It's a little over the top, but that's the way my wife likes things to be done.'

They had covered the tall ceilings and walls in ornately embroidered tapestries or furs. Eryk was obviously a man in power, and I made a note in my mind to study the tapestries when I had the chance, if I got the chance.

'Take a seat,' he offered.

It was a beautifully carved chair. Unsure, I looked around for a simpler stool in case this was Eryk's pride of place, but all of them were similarly opulent, save for one that was obviously built for Eryk's ample frame.

From the end of the table, Eryk eyed me curiously. 'Shall we begin?'

'Baaaa- tteeer,' Eryk corrected me, over enunciating the word.

'Ba-tier,' I tried to repeat.

'Closer that time, but make sure you really roll your Rs.' He stopped. There was a knock at the door.

I sat back. Despite struggling with some words in the Frankish language after a month of dedicated learning, I was pleased with my development.

It was Neflaug at the door. I could hear her honeyed tones as Eryk greeted her and they chattered away. I gathered my belongings.

'But are you happy with her progress?' Neflaug pressed Eryk as we walked home together. She pressured him for honesty.

'A model pupil, really, Neflaug. Would I lie to you? I may even start her on the language of the Arabs soon.'

'Excellent news.' Neflaug grinned as we neared the house. We said goodbye to Eryk and walked into the hearth room.

'I have something for you,' she said, pressing a folded garment into my hands. It was soft against my hands, and as I unfurled it, I saw it was a cream-coloured dress made from fine wool. An ankle length garment, with long sleeves, and finished in a flattering V neckline. At the hem was a flash of colour.

'What is this?'

'It is obviously a dress, no?' Neflaug tossed her curls back and pressed the robe against me. 'I thought the blue would look more appealing on you. Look, it matches your eyes.' She held the trim up for me to inspect the brilliant blue I had seen on my first morning in Aldeigjuborg. 'I cannot have you wearing that horrible brown sack you arrived in any longer. You represent me and my business and now you need to look the part.'

I threw my arms around her. 'Thank you.'

She patted me on the arm without returning the embrace. 'It's just good business,' she finished, pulling away.

That seemed to be Neflaug's way, to be generous with her gifts but not with her attention, leaving me forever careful in her company. One moment she was sunshine and smiles, the next a dark storm cloud bringing rain upon those close to her.

Neflaug ventured a grin, 'Go on. Put it on.'

I needed no encouragement, running from the room to dress in my bedroom. The door had barely closed before I discarded my old dress for the new, feeling the softness of the fine weave against my skin. If only I could have seen my appearance. I was sure the dress fit perfectly, firm and well fitted across my chest and waist, but hanging loosely from that point, stopping at my ankles to keep the trim from skirting the floor.

'You can ask Helga for help with dressing,' Neflaug suggested from the doorway, where I had not noticed her watching. 'Do you like it?'

'Stunning. It's wonderful.' The garment felt like perfection on my skin as I spun around.

Neflaug leaned against the door, assessing my appearance. 'Soon we will have cause to make you something finer.'

'Finer than this?' I laughed girlishly. 'Is there such a thing?' If there was, then I could not imagine it. This was finer than anything that I wore as Auden's wife.

Leaving her position, Neflaug stilled my whirling, toying with my hair as she piled it upon my crown. 'I think the time has come for us to make you a more visible part of what we do here.'

EIGHT

'What are you doing, miss?' Helga asked me as I stirred a pot of *orredsuppe*, the heady aroma of onion and chervil delighting my nostrils. Helga gently steered me away from the pot. 'That's my job,' she reprimanded in her sing-song voice.

I stood aside but refused to be dismissed. 'But, oh, Helga, the fish needs to go in right now,' I protested, lifting the board from the table. I tried to slide the chunks of fresh fish into the bubbling pot, but Helga's expert efficiency brushed me out of the way as she took the board from my grasp.

'That is not your job, miss, and if she sees you, we will both be in trouble.'

'It's best that neither of us gets in trouble with Neflaug. Though I miss cooking and all I wanted was to do something nice for them,' I grumbled, finally accepting that this was a battle I would not win against Helga.

'For who?'

'The other women. I thought an enjoyable meal would make them warm to me.'

'They don't dislike you. They are just wary of your closeness to Neflaug. After all, she is the one they rely on to pay them.' She tried to comfort me.

'I know,' I groaned, as I sat down on the bench. It had been months since my arrival and, whilst polite, the women had kept their distance.

Hilde entered the hearth room, looking at both of us warily. 'Vat are you two doing in here?' Her accent was heavy, though I was becoming accustomed to understanding it with careful listening. Her matronly appearance made me think of a wise old woman, though she could have been scarcely over fifteen years my senior.

'I'm making you all a meal.' I smiled, using the distraction to edge closer to the pot.

Hilde glanced at her daughter with a disapproving tut. 'That's Helga's job.'

'Yes, Mama. Signe wanted to do something nice for you all,' she replied, sending an "I told you so," look in my direction.

'They like you vell enough.' Hilde smiled, answering my thoughts.

'That is what I told her, Mama.'

I slumped over the table. 'Then why won't they talk to me?'

'It's your accent. They cannot understand vat you say,' Hilde replied, twisting her mouth to enunciate the words.

My eyebrows arched with shock. 'My accent?!'

Helga appeared as surprised by this revelation as I was.

Hilde shrugged and nodded, '*Da!*'

'They have trouble understanding my accent?' I laughed.

'At first, they didn't even think you vere speaking the same tongue. I put them right.'

'What a relief!' I breathed, not having considered that their reluctance to embrace me as their own had been but a matter of understanding. My mind had simply gone to their pure dislike of me without further evaluation.

Hilde wandered over to the boiling pot, peering inside. 'Vat are ve eating then?'

'Quick, Helga, take it off the fire. We don't want the fish to overcook.' I jumped up, helping Helga to take the pot off its hanging and onto the stand for serving.

'Vat is it?' Hilde asked again.

'*Orredsuppe,*' I replied, collecting the bowls from the shelf.

'Vat a treat. I love trout.' She rubbed her hands together excitedly and sat with her bowl at the table.

'Lunch!' I yelled at the ladies through the warehouse door.

'That's my job, miss,' Helga said in mock admonishment.

I stepped to the side to allow her to pass. 'Go on then.'

'LUNCH!' she yelled with the power that defied her small stature.

Hilde, not waiting for the others, tore at a hunk of bread, dipping it into her soup. 'Her lungs she got from her father.'

The women filed into the room, holding out their bowls to be filled. Each greedily consumed their contents as fast as their carved spoon would shovel before returning to work. I smiled at each of them. If they could not understand my words, at least a smile would mean they would understand I did not think I was above them. They thanked me in turn for the delicious meal and trudged back to their work with what I could only assume were satisfied stomachs.

Soon I would have to leave my work for errands, and I desperately wanted to finish the staple of wool I had been spinning that morning. Next to me, Hilde whistled along while her foot pumped at the spinning wheel. 'I used to do all this vork from my home before Neflaug came along.'

'It was the same in my hometown,' I replied, finishing my spinning and winding off the thread.

'It's unusual, yes, but I quite like having a reason to leave the house each morning.'

Unlike the others, I worked where I lived so, aside from my lessons, I had little reason to leave. 'Do you live far away, Hilde?'

She stopped peddling, 'Oh no, not at all. I live just outside the town valls. My husband is a farmer, as are my boys, and they are around all day, so the little ones do not get into too much trouble.'

'Even if we wanted to, I do not think that Neflaug would allow us to work from home,' the quiet Elin piped up from behind the loom. 'No, she wants to watch everything we do.' She giggled, surprised by her own comment. Her hand covered her laughing mouth.

Hilde went back to spinning. 'I don't mind so much, but it is difficult ven the babes are tiny.'

'Mmmm,' I murmured in agreement.

Helga crept into the warehouse, standing before me. 'Excuse me, miss, but aren't you expected to be at the market?'

Odin's beard! I had almost forgotten! 'Yes, I am.'

'You best leave now before Neflaug returns.'

I hastily shoved the completed spinning into my basket. 'I will go now.' My dress was rumpled from work, but my hands made quick work of smoothing the fine cream fabric and the blue trim was as perfect as it had been the day Neflaug had presented it to me. I pushed a comb into each side of my hair, holding my loose locks back from my face. 'Please don't tell her I left so late, will you?' I pleaded with the ladies.

They sympathetically smiled at me in unison. 'You have no cause to worry,' Helga replied gently, hurrying me through the hearth room and onto the street. 'No one will say a word, miss.'

The day was warm, and I was glad I had not decided on a hood or a shawl. There was no need when the weather was so fine. The sound of clanging pots on the iron stove from the food stalls, shouts of stall-holders, and the loud chatter of passers-by assaulted my ears. Whilst my ears may have been accosted, the colours and people it devoured during my weekly outing delighted my eyes. Market day was my favourite day. Usually, I would attend accompanied by one of the other women from the warehouse, however this time I had garnered Neflaug's agreement to leave alone upon the promise that Mikel would meet me there and return me home. He had not. Instead, we had agreed to meet at the marketplace and, as I scanned the square, he had not appeared.

Something had caught my eye though, a trestle table full of captivating trinkets. Spread on the simple brown cloth was an eclectic mix from the merchant's travels. A brooch captured my interest, most likely in well-polished silver. A thick ring of metal formed the basis of the piece, upon which a long pin, attached only on one side, would fasten the fabric around its wearer. At the bottom of the ring, instead of making a complete circle, were pieces of silver atop a flattened plate arranged in a winding pattern. On either side of the cleft that separated the design was a spherical node which caught the sunlight as it sat in my hand.

'It's a pretty thing, isn't it?' the salesman prompted.

'It is,' I agreed.

'Celtic,' the man informed me.

I raised an interested eyebrow.

'Those who live in the west,' he explained further, 'though *valskr* might be more recognisable a word for you, if,' he hesitated, 'I am not mistaken.'

'You are not mistaken. I have heard of these people.'

How exotic, I thought, but without money of my own I couldn't purchase it no matter how coveted it was. Neflaug had promised me payment before the end of summer, once I had proven myself. Until then, I had to make do with the small stipend she provided.

My finger traced the intricacies of the brooch lightly, but stopped when I felt a shiver creep up my spine, as if I were being watched. Chancing a glance over my shoulder, I found him; a handsome stranger sitting on a stoop across from the trinket stand. Embarrassed at his attention, I turned away, pretending to examine the other offerings spread before me. A second glance over my shoulder told me enough to figure the man was a merchant, judging by the amount of silver adornments hanging off him. Just then, Neflaug's voice ran in my ears, a warning to stay away from any man whilst I remained in her employ. Don't make eyes with strangers, I chastised myself, turning away from the table so my eyes could rake the crowd in search of Mikel. Still no sign of him, but that stranger. Is he still watching me?

This time I didn't look away, challenging him to be the first to break our connection. Instead, he laughed, his green eyes so intense, his smile so inviting that against my will, my mouth curved at the sides into a smile. A brief laugh escaped my throat before I could stop it. Odin's beard! What am I doing? Neflaug told me not to speak to anyone. What exactly did I think was going to happen? She wouldn't find out. It was harmless; I decided. But when I glanced over my shoulder, he was gone.

'*Hej*,' a deep voice uttered from beside me. Startled, I threw my hands out. He grasped my hand in his. It was rough against my soft hand, treated daily with the lanolin of sheep's wool.

Faking confidence, I met his certain tone with my own. 'Is it so obvious that I am from Svealand?'

'Without a doubt,' he replied without releasing my hand. 'Please, let me introduce myself. I am Kjarr.' He paused, allowing his grasp to slide to the end of my fingertips. 'And what name would such a woman from Svealand have?'

'Karr?' His name did not sound quite right on my tongue.

He seemed amused. 'Well now, that seems rather like my name though you say it more like this… Yah! As if you were spurring your horse on.' As he spoke, he acknowledged nothing around us, and

I found myself pulled in by his commanding voice. His presence was intoxicating.

'Kjarr.'

'Yes, that's right.'

Suddenly aware that my hand was still in his, I wiggled my fingers. 'Well, Kjarr,' this time perfecting the pronunciation, 'can I have my hand back now?'

Chuckling good naturedly, he released his grip. 'You are still to give me your name.'

It was my turn to smile, bemused. 'Signe.'

With a slight inclination of his head and a down turned gaze, he mumbled to himself before his eyes flicked up to mine with the strangest sense that he looked into me. 'I feel favoured by the gods to have met you and, if I can ask, what brings you to Aldeigjuborg?'

'It is where I live now, but today I've come to the market.'

'That much is obvious. You would not need to be a *völva* to know that,' he teased at my awkwardness. 'How often do you come here? I ask, only to understand if there should be any hope that I will see you here again.'

'Every week,' I answered. I couldn't help myself.

For a moment, he seemed distracted. 'To fetch food for your pantry?' He was playing with me.

'Oh no, it's far more secretive than that.' I rose to the game.

'Hmm, a secret, is it?' he mused, taking my hand in his again. 'Do not divulge your secrets to me if it will land you in peril.' He stooped his head over my hand. 'I would never forgive myself if your demise came at my persistence.' Without hesitation, he lowered the remaining increments to land a light kiss on the back of my hand, and my breath caught. 'Now you know my name, you may call on me whenever you like. If you like,' he added quickly before he turned to walk away.

In his departure, confidence found me. 'How will I find you?'

A brilliant smile swept his face, as I knew I had fallen right where he wanted me. 'I am the silver merchant. Everyone knows me,' he answered before disappearing into the crowd. If I wanted to see him again, it would be me who would be searching.

'Who was that?' Mikel asked, finding me before I could compose myself.

'He said his name was Kjarr,' I whispered. 'And where were you? I have been waiting for ages.'

'What were you talking about?' Mikel asked, ignoring my protest.

'You're nosy today, aren't you?' I said, shoving him playfully with my shoulder.

'What did he want with you, or from you?' he added protectively.

'That, I do not know.'

Mikel shrugged. 'Let's eat something. I am so hungry I could eat one of those terrible bug things that always find themselves in my bed,' he grumbled.

'Does Luca feed you enough?' I knew he did, but Mikel was a growing boy. Even in the two months we had been in Aldeigjuborg, it seemed he had grown substantially. A little upward, but mostly his size had increased in his body. The hard and regular work had put muscles on his lanky frame and, he found, the more meat he had to him, the more he needed to eat. Work kept him far busier than when he worked for his father, but the days went by fast and every day that passed brought him closer to being a master himself.

'Here, let's try this.' Mikel stopped before a stall selling vegetables and meat encased in pastry.

'They look tasty,' I answered, handing over the money Neflaug gave me for food, as he ordered one for me and two for himself. 'With this appetite, you will need to pay for yourself.' I laughed, watching him scoff the parcel down with greed. I nibbled a little more daintily on mine. It was hot. I waved it around to cool it. Mikel seemed impervious to the heat as I watched him wolf down another pastry. 'Ah, I'm late. I really have to go. I'm sorry Mikel, but Eryk is expecting me for my lesson.' Mikel waved me goodbye as ordered yet another pastry and stuffed it into his mouth.

Eryk left his door unlocked for me and, letting myself in, I found him working at his table in the large room. 'A little late today, Signe,' he said without looking up.

'I'm sorry. I hope you weren't waiting for long,' I apologised.

'Not at all. I could catch up on some work I have been putting off for some time, so really, I should thank you,' he said with a smile, pushing a small box to one side.

I sat down opposite him and exhaled deeply.

'Something troubling you?' Eryk asked, peering across the table.

'No, not really,' I dismissed.

'You are clearly thinking about something.'

Unsure if I should proceed, I started neutrally. 'There are some interesting people here in town.'

Eryk's eyes sparkled with curiosity. 'Oh, yes?' he nodded, prodding me to continue.

Fidgeting with some papers strewn about the table, I ventured a little further. 'And I suppose you know most of them.'

'Naturally,' he cracked his knuckles and shifted his backside backwards in his seat. 'Is this about anyone in particular?'

'Perhaps, are you familiar with the silver merchant?' Why was I asking him this and what was I hoping to achieve? Surely, I knew that anything I asked of Eryk would somehow make its way back to Neflaug's ears. Still, I could not stop myself.

'Kjarr? I know him well.'

'And what do you think of him?'

Seriousness overshadowed Eryk's face. 'He is a good man, excellent business mind with a commanding presence.' His fingers drummed loudly on the table as his eyes drifted to the left, thinking for a moment.

'What is it?'

'Best not tell anyone that you find this man interesting, huh?' he suggested, but I was unsure if his concern was now fatherly or a warning. 'Neflaug did not bring here you to get married and spout offspring.'

'No, it's not.' I felt my cheeks reddening at the inference.

Eryk wet his lips. Darkness filled his eyes that made me shift in my seat. 'Just keep this between us, little bird. It will be our secret.'

NINE

'Why does he call you little bird?' Neflaug demanded. She cornered me as I tried to reconnect a piece of fine, unspun wool that had come apart.

'I told you, I don't know,' I replied through gritted teeth. Eryk had persisted with the pet name for weeks, but never in front of Neflaug. The name made me uneasy, but I did not dare speak against the most important man in the town.

She stood over me. 'There must be a reason!' she growled.

'Perhaps he thinks of me as a daughter?' I offered, setting down my spindle.

'Is that it? Have you done anything to make him think anything else?' She looked at me, waiting for me to say something only she was anticipating.

'Like what?'

Neflaug edged closer. 'You know what I am talking about. More than a daughter.'

I caught her meaning and felt my face flush red. 'Of course not.'

'Don't you dare make him think you are something you are not! Don't think you can trap a great man like that in whatever you may be planning.'

'I swear to you I have done nothing other than what you had bid me to.' I took her by the arm and led her into the hearth room, where we were alone. 'It's just a pet name. You said yourself that he takes an interest in growing the skills of those less than him.' I hoped that would placate her.

'Fine,' she said, relaxing her shoulders.

I breathed a sigh of relief.

Her mood changed. 'Go to the market and buy me some honey,' she commanded as I caught the basket she threw at me.

'Is Helga busy?' Usually, she would run those types of errands.

'She is sick, and I am asking you to do it, so get yourself ready and go. Now!' she ordered aggressively, hands on her hips.

I removed my apron and took the coins she held in her hands, slotting them into the pouch around my waist. I counted them. 'This is too much.'

'Keep the rest.' She shooed me out the door.

Surprised by her sudden outburst, I stood on the street in a stupor. Was it something more than Eryk's pet name? Did she doubt who I was? I worried as my feet moved in isolation of my mind, leading me to the marketplace. Neflaug seemed suspicious of me, yet put me in a trusted position, and now gifted me coin. She was either magnanimous or dangerously brutal. I never knew which side of her I would see. Touching Bjarndýr, I wished for my father's guidance. He would probably say that it was wise to question everyone's motive. Perhaps that was all Neflaug was doing.

I stopped at a small stall and purchased the honey. Not wanting to return to chance another encounter with Neflaug's rage, I started towards Luca's workshop, hoping to see Mikel. Exiting the central marketplace, I ran headlong into Kjarr, my pot of honey falling from my grasp.

'Got it.' He smiled, catching the pot before it reached the ground.

'Thank you. I cannot afford to make any more mistakes today,' I groaned, as he handed it to me.

'Trouble with the master?'

'Nothing I cannot handle,' I replied, trying to laugh off my earlier miseries. 'How is business?'

He flicked his dishevelled brown hair from his eyes; he smiled. 'I feel the seas calling me again. Soon it will be time to set off on another adventure.'

'No matter how loud the seas called me, I would never go to them,' I joked, recalling the lurching feeling in my stomach during my journey to Aldeigjuborg.

'Not a good sailor?'

'You could say that. Remind me to tell you about it sometime.'

'Sounds like quite a tale.'

'Will you be gone long?'

'Who knows?' he answered, 'but I didn't seek you out to bore you with my business plans. I wanted to give you something.' In his hand was a package tied with a string.

'Why?' I asked before I could stop myself.

'Why not?'

'I don't mean to seem ungrateful, just wondering why you would buy me a gift.'

'I find you interesting, Signe. And this,' he said, thrusting his hand forward again, 'is a token of that intention, a gift of friendship.' He took my empty hand and placed the package in it.

'You don't know me,' I blurted.

'I don't need to know you to find you interesting.'

Slowly opening my hand, I saw the brooch I had admired the week before. 'How did you know?'

'Last week, I found myself in this marketplace. I saw a woman admiring an item over there spread amongst many other tokens. After she left the table, I went over to inspect it myself. As you see, she spent a great deal of time handling it and admiring it, so I thought it would be something very special. I realised then that it was special because it was an illustration of you - and it drew you to it... well, now I sound like I was creeping around watching you, but it was not like that. I simply admired you without speaking to you, not because of the way you look, but because of the way you looked at things.

'You are a stranger in a foreign place, utterly perplexed by everything around you and yet in awe of it all. You are different. In you, I see two competing energies. Like I said, you are interesting to me.'

His honesty was utterly disarming if true, and I found myself unsure in my response. An involuntary smile crept upon my lips, and despite myself, I found I trusted his sincerity. 'I'm not sure how I should respond.' Wary as I was to bring any more of Neflaug's anger upon myself, I sorely needed friends.

'I know what it is like to have many acquaintances, but few friends,' he added, squeezing my shoulders.

'There is one person, a boy I came to Aldeigjuborg on the ship with. Aside from him, there is no one else.' It was the first time I had admitted this aloud, and I realised I was lonely.

He watched me thoughtfully. 'Will you meet me here next week?'

'I will,' I agreed quickly.

'Until then,' Kjarr bid me farewell, leaving me with the brooch nestled in my hand and a smile across my face. From the corner of my eye, I saw Mikel approaching.

'Same man as last week?' he asked, bemused.

'Mm-hmm,' I nodded, watching Kjarr disappear from the marketplace.

'What did he want?'

'I think he wants to be my friend.'

'Your friend?' he exclaimed disbelievingly.

'Is that so hard to believe?'

'Be careful,' he said, taking his arm in mine as we walked towards Luca's workshop. 'This is it,' Mikel stopped in front of Luca's home.

A small fence surrounded a packed dirt courtyard where most of the work was done. There were a couple of low-lying bench seats I assumed to be places to sit and wait, though I saw no one waiting. Strewn about the area were carpentry tools, some neatly displayed hammers, and a large wooden box attached to the outer wall of the house. The home consisted of two main sections: there was the main room where Luca and his wife slept and where the kitchen was, and the second was a work area. It was a very modest abode, nothing like the home I lived in with Neflaug, and there were no separate accommodations for Mikel in the main home.

Inside the workshop were the most expensive carpentry equipment, a lathe, saws, and a vice. The floor was covered in hard straw, and I could smell its musty odour from outside. There were no closing doors, just an entrance on both the right and left wall leading straight through. In summer, it provided shade and protection from the harsh sun, but I imagined in winter it was a depressing place to work and painfully cold, barely sheltered from the elements. Like other apprentices who slept in the same place as the equipment, or animals, it was here inside this covered structure that Mikel slept each night. As Mikel had told me frequently, it was far better than sleeping on the street, which he had done many times during his childhood.

We walked inside the covered dirt area and Mikel called out, 'Luca, I've brought someone to meet you.'

A large block of wood landed on the ground near us with a bang and the copper headed Luca appeared after it. 'Too unwieldy!' he yelled at the wood before he noticed us. 'Oh, this must be Signe.' He grinned, cleaning his hands on his apron before taking my hand in greeting.

'Who else would it be? I don't have time to meet any other women,' Mikel jested.

'Welcome, welcome.' He gripped my hand in his nobbled grasp. Glancing down, I saw he was missing the top of one finger and a long-raised scar on the right side of his hand from a long-healed gash.

'Mikel speaks highly of you.'

'It must all be lies then.' He laughed, opening his mouth, showing he was missing a couple of teeth in the front.

Once a warrior? I wondered if his missing teeth resulted from combat or poor nutrition.

'I hear you are working for Neflaug,' he continued.

'That's true,' I answered.

'And you like it?'

'I like the work. It's an enjoyable challenge.'

'I hear she has grand plans for you. She was applying for you to enter the Merchant's Guild last week.'

'What an honour,' Mikel interjected excitedly. 'Why didn't you tell me?'

I shrugged, 'I didn't know.'

'Wouldn't trust that woman as far as I could throw her. She has a way of always getting what she wants,' Luca lowered his voice.

'What did she do to you?' I asked, unsure if it was rumour or reality.

'No, not me. I have never had reason to, thank the gods. I have a friend who used to sell his wool to her, and he told me she did not always give a fair price for his wool. She would go to him saying it was inferior quality when it was not. Besides that, it's just a feeling she gives me.'

'Is it possible the matter with your friend was a misunderstanding?' There was always some hard negotiating in business.

'I don't think so. The way he told it, he lost his life. Couldn't put food on the table, a child lost to hunger- a broken man now,' he said, shaking his head. 'You look after yourself,' he warned.

Mikel shuffled his feet uncomfortably.

'While you are here, Signe, would you like something to drink?' Luca asked.

'Of course, she would,' Mikel answered for me.

'Dana! Dana!' Luca called into the house. A small head belonging to Luca's wife popped out of the door. 'A drink for Mikel's friend, please Dana!'

Mikel leaned in close so as not to be overheard. 'You don't think that Neflaug could be doing something wrong, do you?' he asked. 'Do you get any sense of wrongdoing when you are working for her?'

The answer came without a thought. 'No, never.' Unflinching loyalty, I reminded myself. It seemed it was not so hard after all.

'Then why would Luca mention anything?' Mikel wondered. 'He is not one to spread words untrue.'

'This is the first I've heard of this,' I replied. Everything she had asked of me I had done, questioning none of it. Never asking questions. It wasn't worth her rage. Total loyalty, as she had commanded.

TEN

As the temperate summer neared its end, the days seemed to grow warmer. The air was still, with no breeze to provide much desired relief from the heat. Inside, the warehouse was stifling, even with the doors open. I wiped the sweat from my brow and heard Elin moan from behind me.

'It is just too hot to be working today, miss,' she spoke in my tongue, though her accent made it seem she had to force the words out of her mouth. Her bony hands pressed into her lower back as she stretched from her seat, dress sodden and clinging to her shoulders.

'Then let us take a break,' I agreed.

Hilde stopped pedalling at the spinning wheel. 'Do not let Neflaug see you all reclining like rich housevives.' A gently mewling came from the basket at her feet.

'Look, it is too hot even for the *barn*.' Elin frowned.

'She is fine.' Hilde pressed the infant to her breast and returned to spinning, one handed. 'Hmm, Signe,' she called. 'You and Helga are to go to the carpenter about a new table for the hearth room.'

'She told you that?'

Hilde nodded. 'She said she had spoken to you about it already.' She shrugged. Her rhythm did not slow despite the conversation or her nursing.

'I must have forgotten, or else she never said so.'

Helga popped her head out into the warehouse. 'We should go now, miss!'

As we walked to Luca's work yard, I racked my brain trying to remember any conversation with Neflaug about the table. 'On my life, I cannot remember Neflaug's instruction,' I confided in Helga.

'About the new table?'

'Mmmm mmm,' I nodded. 'Is it possible she did not speak to me about it?'

'She said she did,' Helga replied as we wound our way through the busy streets. 'Which way?'

I pointed to our left. 'Up there, but I swear she said nothing to me.' Was Neflaug trying to set me up for failure, trying to catch me out, give her a reason to dismiss me?

'Try not to worry now. The job will get done and she will have no cause to punish you.' Helga tried to calm my anxieties.

I took a steadying breath. Perhaps I had just forgotten.

'Is this it?' Helga asked as we stood at the gate to Luca's work area.

'My feet seemed to have carried me here without my mind.'

She patted me on the shoulder. 'That will happen when your mind is busy worrying about other things, miss.' She opened the gate and walked inside.

Luca was sitting on the bench, oiling a finished piece with a contemplative look on his face. 'Signe.' He smiled, looking up. '*Hej* Signe, what can I help you with?'

'We are here on Neflaug's business. She needs a new table.'

Luca rubbed his hands together. 'She is in luck. There isn't much work for us at the moment, so I will start right away, and I'll send the boy with an update when I have one.'

'I have the measurements Neflaug needs,' Helga stepped forward to provide them.

'The boy? You mean Mikel? These days, he is looking less like a boy and more like a man.' I laughed. 'What have you been feeding him?'

'Just good hard work,' Luca chuckled.

'Did I hear Signe?' Mikel bolted out of the door but stopped a few steps short of Helga, his eyes fixed and face flushed before the young girl.

She blushed in response and looked down at her hands.

'Mikel, this is Helga,' I said, introducing the two. 'She works for Neflaug. And Helga, this is Mikel - I told you about him. We arrived in Aldeigjuborg together.' Neither spoke nor looked at each other. Only Helga moved, looking at me with a pleading look to leave, else she might die of embarrassment.

'Come on Mikel, it's not like you to say nothing,' Luca goaded.

'It's good to meet a friend of Signe's,' Mikel mumbled.

Helga said nothing but managed a small squeak. I couldn't help but laugh.

'I think we should get back,' I said, grabbing Helga's hand and rescuing her from the situation. 'What is wrong with you?' I asked as we walked away, Helga clinging tightly to my arm.

'I am not very good at talking to boys,' she whispered.

'Mikel is a nice boy,' I said, patting her hand that was nestled in my looped arm.

'He seems so, miss,' she said with a small smile, lighting up the plain features of her face. The apples of her cheeks lifted in a way that made her look younger than her sixteen summers.

'Do you like him?'

She giggled, turning away from me to hide her reddening cheeks.

'You do! Well, I think he likes you too,' I teased.

'Shhhh, please don't tell anyone,' she pleaded.

'How can you like someone you just saw for the first time?'

'It's not the first time, miss! I've seen him before. He is so beautiful,' she sighed, clapping her hand over her mouth. 'I can't believe I just said that. Oh please, miss, don't tell.' She looked at me with tears in her eyes.

'I won't tell anyone,' I promised. 'Helga.' We stopped. 'I need to do something. If Neflaug wants me, can you tell her I went to Eryk's house early today?'

'Of course,' she agreed. 'Will you be alright on your own?'

'I need to see someone.'

She knowingly smiled, 'I'll not ask who it is, miss. That way, if she asks me, then it won't be a lie.'

'Better you do not know, Helga,' I agreed.

She threw her arms around me. 'I will see you for dinner.'

As I watched her dart away down the street, I wondered how much trouble I could get myself in. It was not difficult to find Kjarr when one knew where to look and I did, finding him leaning against the outer wall of the tavern in enrapt conversation with a foreign-looking man. After meeting my eye, he excused himself, secreting something small into the pouch at his belt.

'This is unexpected,' he said with a smile.

'You said I should find you if I ever needed to speak with you, so here I am.' My brazenness surprised even me. 'Who was that man? You were speaking another language? What was it?' I fired in quick succession.

Kjarr's green eyes blazed with amusement. 'So many questions, Signe. To answer your first question, he is an acquaintance I should hope to know better for he will help me in my next trading venture, and to answer your second- it was Arabic.'

'I have heard of the Arabic language but never heard it spoken. Eryk said that I should try to learn it, at least he is keen on teaching it to me.'

'I'm not sure what use it would be to you unless you want to trade in silver. I suspect most of the farmers you deal with speak the same language or one of those ugly dialects,' he said dismissively, continuing to lean against the tavern wall.

'My father always told me learning something is never a waste of time,' I explained defensively.

Sensing my annoyance, he checked himself. 'I am sorry. I did not mean that the learning of a language was a waste of your time. Of course, you should learn, if you want to.'

Not in the mood for holding grudges and the summer heat beckoning me for a drink and company, I shrugged his comment off. 'I will forgive you if you buy me ale.'

'Are you sure?'

I nodded, pulling him into the tavern. The air was dank, hanging with the smell of ale, sweat and roasted meats, but at least it was out of the sun. We sat at a table with two small stools, taking one each. Along one of the tavern walls were barrels of drink, but, mostly, the hall was sparsely populated. It was still early. When the evening came, lively beings would lean against these walls in different states of drunkenness. Kjarr waved to a thrall for two ales.

I felt as giddy as a child on my first adventure. 'This is my first time at the tavern.' Neflaug barely let me out of the house, except for errands and lessons.

'Is that so?' He sipped his ale, foam collecting on his top lip. Seemingly from nowhere, he produced a singular die and toyed with it between his fingers.

I took a swig of my drink. 'If you are wondering why I sought you out, well, as you said, I need a friend.' The amber liquid was cool and tasty, going down without hesitation as I gulped until the flagon was empty. My hand shot up to order another one.

'Easy there, is everything ok?'

I licked the ale foam from my lips. 'I have not had a drink in a while.'

Kjarr picked up his own cup. 'Well then, to long desired drinks,' he said, clinking his own against mine. We both drank deeply. 'So, tell me about this terrible sea journey of yours,' he prompted.

In unbecoming detail, I told him of my journey from Björkö to Aldeigjuborg.

'And why did you decide to leave your home in Birka?' he asked.

'My home is not Birka, it is Karlstad,' I corrected, my head swimming with drink as we ordered our fourth cup.

'Karlstad? My grandfather came from Orebro,' he exclaimed with a look of delight at finding some commonality between us.

'Karlstad and Orebro are close neighbours, only a couple of days' walk,' I remembered. 'Did your grandfather move his family out here?'

'He started our business. My father inherited it and so did I, each improving upon it until we were the best in the Rus' lands, well known to its lords.' His words were beginning to slur. 'Tell me, why did you leave? Was life so bad there?' He leaned in close to me.

I took another drink, feeling bold. 'It is a rather long and confusing story.' I laughed, draining my cup.

'In that case, one moment - Two more!' he shouted toward a server who scuttled over with a jug to refill our cups. 'Just leave that here,' Kjarr instructed, taking the jug and flinging more coins in his direction. 'Go on, tell me.' He grinned as he filled both cups to the rim.

Hesitating for a moment, my courage almost deserted me. 'I'm not sure I should.'

'The only thing separating reward and ruin is risk. Go on,' he encouraged me as he rolled his antler die across the table. It rocked back and forward clumsily and eventually landed on its highest score.

I took a deep breath, ready to unburden myself, but I doubted my resolve. My cup contained courage, or so I had heard men say. For luck and bravery, I downed its contents and with a steady hand; I poured more of the jug's contents into my cup. Kjarr's eyebrows lifted as he watched. 'So, you want to know?' I asked.

No words left his lips, just a nod as he watched me curiously. Fuelled by liquid courage, I dragged my stool beside him, leaning in until my lips brushed his ears and began my tale. 'I am not who I say I am.'

The sun was still high when I emerged from the tavern to stumble home, the world round under the soles of my leather slippers. I flipped my hair back over my shoulder but snagged my fingers and as my hand fought to free itself; I knew my aim of appearing sober was failing miserably. When I finally did free my fingers, my foot struck a rock, and I tripped, grabbing onto the wall of a nearby structure.

I felt giddy and free, even if terribly uncoordinated. Having unburdened myself to Kjarr felt good, but as I neared Neflaug's house, worry clawed at my insides. I had told Kjarr everything, choosing to trust my own instincts rather than keep everything hidden. I quieted the doubting voice inside my head as my feet mounted the landing to the house. Kjarr would not abuse my confidence, I told myself.

Inside the hearth room, I found Neflaug alone before a set of papers at the old table. 'How was the market?' she addressed me without looking up.

'Same as always.' I shrugged.

'And the quality of this season's wool?'

Mercifully, I had spoken with the farmers the day before, 'Good quality, perhaps better than last shipment. The fresh weather must be having an impact and the shepherds seemed to have washed the sheep well before shearing them this time,' I responded, surprised at the coherence of my answer.

'Hmm. And the price?'

'Unchanged, which I think is a good deal given the increase in quality,' I offered.

She pursed her lips unhappily. 'We need the price to be lower to make more money, despite the quality.'

'Business is doing so well at the moment,' I tried to calm her discontent.

'Could always make more money,' she growled, leaning against the wall.

'The new wool will yield a great quality product and we really are doing well at the moment.'

'We are,' she agreed.

Usually, I would have given little thought to her desire to drive down the price of wool, but Luca's warning rang in my head.

Neflaug twirled a tendril of her hair around her long finger. 'How are you coping with all the attention?' she asked, watching me from beneath her long dark eyelashes.

Her tone made me wary of where the question was leading. 'I'm not sure what you mean.'

She pointed her elegant finger at my body. 'You're getting attention in that dress, I suspect?'

'This one?' I asked, looking down at my clothing. 'It's the one you gifted to me, and I have worn it every day since. If I have received any attention recently, it would have to be because of the garment and nothing to do with me,' I continued, playing to her pride.

'That couldn't possibly be true. You are a pretty girl. I am sure someone has noticed you.' A wry smile crept across her face.

I shrugged my shoulders. 'If anyone has noticed me, they have not brought it to my attention,' I lied.

She tucked my fair hair behind my ear. 'There are many men with bad intentions in this settlement, Signe. It would be wise to be careful.' She paused. 'We have many freedoms here that we never had in our birthplaces. We must protect ourselves. If we engage in relationships, it is always the woman accused of evil influence, never the man.' She tightened her face in obvious resentment, her lips becoming a harsh line.

I nodded, accepting her caution.

'I saw you with Kjarr.' Neflaug exhaled deeply, obviously disappointed with my new friend.

'Kjarr?' I repeated, trying to sound like I had never heard the name. She pursed her lips. 'Don't pretend.'

I met her stare with fake confidence. 'He found me in the marketplace,' I answered innocently.

Neflaug's anger became motherly concern. 'Be careful around him. He does not love women honestly.' She stopped and looked at me. 'Make sure you do not relieve yourself of your wits when he is about.'

'What does that mean?'

'He lies to women to get them into his bed.'

I touched her arm. 'Don't they all? Worry not, Neflaug. I have no intention of getting into his bed.'

'I said that too, but I found myself bamboozled into a situation with him.' Neflaug turned her face away from me, taking my hand and leading me to the bench where we sat on opposite sides of the table. 'It was some time ago, and whilst I am not usually the type to engage in a casual relationship with a man, I found myself swept away by his promises and charm.' A nostalgic smile danced across her lips.

My immediate instinct was to laugh. Björn, the man from the ship that brought me to the town, was one on the list of her casual paramours, but I let her continue.

'I was younger then, and much more innocent. My husband had died the previous summer, and I was lonely,' she started. I too had been in the same position when Auden died, unsure of my position and without friends to help.

'My business was in its infancy, and I would go down to the market-place, much as you do now, and I would go about my business. At first, I did not notice him, but he noticed me, or at least he said so later. One day, he introduced himself. He told me he had watched me, and he found me to be an interesting thing to watch.' She paused. 'From then on, we met many times at the market. One day, just before the wintertime, he told me he had to go away on some important business. He suggested we meet at his home before he left, and because I was so sad at his leaving, I agreed.'

Shifting uncomfortably in my seat, I felt the retelling was about to get more personal.

'I went to him as an unknowing young girl would. He had told me his intentions were true, and I thought him a good man. In the weeks prior, I must confess, I had developed some affection for him. I recall the night so vividly. It was cold by then, but not quite the cold of winter, but the promise of the winter to come. I walked alone to his house, wrapping my shawl close around me for protection, and when I arrived, I found he lived alone. I had thought he would have some servant to keep him company, but he had none. I had only ever been alone with men who were my family or husband, I felt uncomfortable, like there was unease in my stomach.' She looked down at her hands.

'I pushed my instincts down inside myself because at the time I thought we were meant to be. Such foolish sentiments of a young woman!' she scowled at herself. Sympathy overcame me, and I leaned forward with an outstretched hand to comfort her.

'He brought me before the fire and told me how beautiful I was. I wasn't wearing anything nearly as special as the dresses I have now, but at the time I believed him. He sat close to me, and we talked. He told me he would be away for some time, and he wanted me to wait for him.'

When she said this, it felt like someone had gripped my heart tightly and hearing Neflaug talk about Kjarr spiked jealousy in me like a child whose toy I had snatched from them. The revelation of my attraction to Kjarr startled me.

'By the fireside, he took my icy hands in his, warming them with the heat of his own fingers. From nowhere, he produced a small silver ring.' She stopped. 'Well, it was not all that small. It was a pretty band with some intricate braiding of the metal. A very fine ring. He put it on my finger.' She showed me her ring finger. 'He said he wanted me to marry him and wait for him to come home when we could start our life together.'

'What happened to the ring?' I asked.

'The ring?' She looked at me, puzzled. 'Oh, I no longer have it. Why would I have any need to keep such a meaningless object?' She screwed her face up again and pursed her lips. I wondered if she meant the ring itself was worthless or if it was the sentiment she had thought to attach to it. I knew better than to ask.

'He put the ring on my finger. I let him,' she continued. 'I happily accepted his proposal, so in love with him, I agreed to wait for his return. But he said he wanted to marry me at once before he left so that he would have me to return to. The speed with which he wanted to fix the situation disturbs me now, but at the time it was flattering.' She drummed her fingers on the table.

I leaned forward, enthralled in the retelling and aching to know how it ended.

'I recall telling him we could not marry immediately, for it was a Saturday, and *Fredag* was the day gods blessed weddings, and I was quite traditional back then. We would have to wait, I insisted, but I was also worried we wouldn't have time to arrange a Gothi, and I wanted it to be formalised before I would come to him as his wife.

'He told me I shouldn't care for formalities so long as we were united in love. I should have known then that some men will say anything to get what they want. In my heart, I knew if we dishonoured the gods, they would look away from us and I would never again feel their love, but I gave in.'

Neflaug's belief in the old gods was the same as my own. The gods saw all. We understood that a ceremony was as much for the gods as it was for the people. Everyone would know that the two people uniting meant to bind themselves together, and how would anyone know this if it were done in secret with no words spoken aloud?

'I let him put that ring on my finger and kiss me, and then he said he would have me as his wife,' she finished. Fear ran through me, for I knew what she meant.

'Somehow, despite him ignoring my wishes, I still felt I loved him. When he forced himself upon me, I was not willing, but I did not struggle against his violence. I settled my anguish knowing that we would be married in front of others before too long and then I would be his and he would be mine.

'The next day when we woke, he used me again. He said he would be away for some time seeking Arabic silver and until he returned, I should keep our love and marriage a secret. I wanted nothing more than for him to return so we could be married before everyone, and I could live happily with him and bear his child.' Neflaug had never shed a tear in front of me, but as I watched her, tears streaked her beautiful face. She was a strong woman, almost devoid of emotion, and to see her in this way made me strangely protective.

She looked into my eyes. 'When springtime came, there was still no word from him. I feared he was dead. As the season ended, I saw him walk through the marketplace, head held high and with a hoard of silver in tow. He greeted people and paraded his wealth. I positioned myself in the thinning crowd, hoping he would see me and come to greet me too, but he didn't. When our eyes met, he did not acknowledge me, instead he walked directly into the arms of another. It ripped my heart out of my chest. I was a fool.' She dabbed a cloth at her tears as she spoke. 'Later that day, I went to his home and asked if we were to be wed. I will never forget what he said,' she whispered.

I drew nearer.

'He said, "I will wed another though if you wish to stay the night, I will not prevent you". He laughed at his own cleverness. But it devastated me. As I went to leave, he gave me some parting advice. "Nothing is binding unless other people know about it." I was so stupid,' Neflaug cried.

'We have all done things we regret,' I soothed, placing myself next to her and wrapping a comforting arm around her.

'You must stay away from him. Signe, promise me you will?' she implored me.

'I will,' I promised. Her description had been so like my initial meetings with Kjarr that I knew she saw my fate leading in the same direction.

She stood, breaking from her trance and shaking off my arm. 'You know better now than to break this promise,' she replied with a smile that only crooked the corner of her mouth on the right side. 'I must attend to business, so I leave you to your studies,' she said as she approached the warehouse door. 'This stays between you and me,' she instructed over her shoulder.

'Of course.' I nodded. Even if Neflaug had no fault in the incident, it could ruin her carefully built reputation if anyone ever found out what Kjarr had done to her.

He seemed so genuine. How could I let myself become so beguiled? I cursed myself for trusting so easily. 'Let another's wounds be your warning,' my father had often told me. Next time I would not be so easily led.

ELEVEN

In order to heed Neflaug's warning, I avoided Kjarr completely. No longer was she dismissive or cool with me. She had become fiercely protective. Though I knew Neflaug had little reason to tell me a lie, I could not ignore the nagging instinct that Kjarr was trustworthy. Perhaps it was my unwillingness to believe Kjarr intended to treat me the same as he had done to Neflaug, or more likely, it was my embarrassment at being deceived. Something felt amiss, but I was not willing to risk my safety or Neflaug's displeasure.

My lessons with Eryk became my only regular activity and, under his instruction, I came to understand that good business was not just about making money but maintaining a positive reputation for honest transactions. As I wandered into his house at the usual time, Eryk greeted me holding a small bronze plate, atop which three brown bug-looking things rolled about.

He shoved the platter before me, 'Try one of these, little bird,' he cooed, his smile eager to enjoy my reaction.

I inspected them with an exploratory poke. 'What do you do with them?'

He chuckled heartily. 'You eat them.'

'They're bugs.' I recoiled, screwing my face up in disgust.

'Fear not, little bird, they are not bugs. They are called dates and they come from Serkland, the land of the Abbasid Caliphate. Look,' he said as he plucked one of the dark brown dates off the plate and delicately placed it into his mouth. 'The sweetness is like nothing you would have experienced but be careful, it is hard in the centre', he explained as he chewed, pulling the pit from his mouth when he was done. Eryk certainly had a penchant for the wonderful.

He offered me the plate again, and I grasped the smallest of the offerings between my finger and thumb and held it before me, inspecting it.

'When I was much younger, I once travelled to Baghdad, the capital of that strange empire, and sampled these for the first time. Such a delight, what a marvel,' he beamed.

I raised the date to my lips, slipping the morsel between my teeth. I separated the outer from the pit, chewing gently. The taste was rich, a complex sweet flavour.

'What do you think of it?' Eryk asked.

'Food of the gods,' I mumbled, my mouth salivating.

'Undoubtedly so.'

I held the pit close to inspect it. 'Is it a nut?'

'A dried fruit.'

'It's funny that something so ugly could taste so good,' I mused as I finished the date.

'Here,' he said, taking the remaining fruit from the plate and tucking it into my hand. 'Save it for later.'

I secreted it into the small fabric bag I kept around my waist to savour at another time.

'They are extortionately expensive, but for you, little bird, anything.'

I was tired of the pet name. Eryk obviously considered me some kind of progeny to add to his collection of fine accomplishments, a reflection of his own abilities to instruct rather than of my own abilities to learn. Still, I appreciated his time and wisdom and, so long as he stayed at arm's length, I would let him continue. The only other person, aside from the other women and Eryk, which I saw, was Mikel. I suspected his visits were not for the pleasure of my conversation. Rather, he seemed to be taken with Helga as much as she was with him. I beckoned for nettle tea as I walked into the hearth room from my lesson with Eryk, taking a seat before the table.

'Do you think he likes me?' Helga asked, taking the seat next to me.

I took a sip of my tea. 'I suspect he does.'

'You did not even ask who I was referring to.'

'Do I need to?' I replied, raising one eyebrow while I blew to cool the hot liquid.

There was a quick knock on the open door before Mikel stepped over the threshold. 'Only me,' he sang as he poked his head over the threshold.

'Oh Mikel, we weren't expecting you,' I replied, wondering how much he had overheard. Helga's own thoughts must have considered the same, for her flushed face was the colour of her own pulsing blood.

'I've come with the table Neflaug ordered. Should we take this one away?' he asked, pointing to the table before me.

'Can you put it in the warehouse?' I asked, standing out of the way as Helga followed.

Luca grabbed one end of the table and Mikel the other, removing it from sight. In its place, they positioned the new table. 'Is that where she would want it?' Mikel asked.

'I hope so,' I replied, paying them from the money Neflaug had left for them.

'*Hej*, Helga.' Mikel beamed. She flashed him a beautiful smile, her face having returned to its normal pink flush. 'Would you like to take a walk with me?' he asked, offering his arm, which she accepted without another word. Arm-in-arm, they ventured out onto the street.

'Do you mind, miss?' Helga called over her shoulder, scarcely waiting for a reply as I shooed her away to enjoy her walk.

'I guess I better follow them.' Luca chortled, running after them.

Neflaug sauntered into the hearth room and flopped down at the new table, running a finger along the smooth grain of the wood. 'Where is Helga?'

'Getting some air,' I replied, covering for her absence.

'What's the name of Luca's apprentice?' she asked.

'Do you mean Mikel?'

'I am sure he is a nice boy, but I cannot help but feel it is unfitting for you to associate with someone who is so low on the rungs of our society. I am raising you amongst the most influential people in Aldeigjuborg.' She clicked her tongue disapprovingly.

'You don't want me to see him anymore?'

'If you think that would be for the best,' she said, patting my arm as she rose to leave.

'If that is what you want,' I agreed aloud, but with no intention of ignoring my friend. Mikel was the closest thing to family I had in Aldeigjuborg.

'Go on, you don't want to keep Eryk waiting again,' she said, shooing me out the door.

'Again?'

'Yes, he is expecting you. Go.' She shut the door in my face.

My feet shuffled me along the well-trodden path to Eryk's home and as he walked into the room in which I always waited for him to begin our studies; his jiggling belly hung slightly over his trousers like a sack of flour. 'Good afternoon, Signe,' he welcomed me warmly. 'You look so troubled.'

'It is Neflaug. She has directed me to sever a friendship with someone who is like family to me, but I don't really understand why,' I complained.

'Neflaug must have her reasons.'

'She said it would not be fitting for someone like me to be friends with someone like him,' I replied.

'Who would this someone be?'

'It is my friend Mikel, the boy I arrived with.'

'Perhaps she is right. Neflaug is your master, and you should not disobey her,' he cautioned. 'You are a smart woman, Signe. It will not be long before you are running the business yourself,' he counselled.

'But when?' I asked.

'Be patient. You will find you will have much more freedom when it happens.' A fatherly smile washed over his face, and I, the petulant child, was full of questions. 'Shall we begin?'

'What will we study today?' I asked, dismissing Neflaug from my mind.

'Weights, Arabic coinage, and we shall begin our study of their language,' he began. 'Silver dirhams are considered superior because each piece weighs exactly the same, so you can always be assured of the value,' Eryk explained, stacking the small pieces on top of each other, until the tower of coins tumbled onto the table.

'Do people ever counterfeit them?'

'Of course, but the Serkir won't. Islamic law prescribes the weight. Doing so would mean death,' he said solemnly.

'But if someone was not a Serkir, they could.'

'Yes, it is possible. Let's see if you can test that,' he said, picking up a few of the coins from the tumbled pile, some hack silver from a pouch, and weights from a box behind him. From under the table, he produced two scales.

I stared at the contraption, wondering what he expected of me. 'You want me to weigh the dirham to ensure it is correct?'

'I do.'

I weighed the dirham using the scale and a few small weights, making sure they balanced before nodding. 'It balances, just as you said.'

'Does it?' he asked with a small grin on his lips.

'Yes, look,' I said, motioning to the perfectly balanced scale before me.

'I loaded these scales in favour of the owner,' he said, demonstrating the fact, the scales were always out by a fraction of a *mithqal*. A slight difference in a single purchase made small difference but used over and over could make the seller a lot of money. 'Lesson for the day, little bird. Always use your own scale and never trust someone who does not allow you to check the weight.'

When the lesson was done, I made my way home via the market-place. I had barely stepped one foot inside the square, crowded as usual, before I saw him.

'Signe, where have you been? Are you well?' Kjarr asked with concern.

'I have been busy.' My answer was blunt, devoid of any courtesy.

He stopped me with a gentle hand. 'Did I offend you?'

'I'm not sure, yet,' I responded. 'There is something I need to discuss with you.' I stopped, looking around. 'Somewhere we won't be overheard.'

'Come to my home. There is no one else there,' he whispered.

I stepped back. 'Now you offend me.'

His hands shot up in front of him, defensively, 'Forgive me, it was not my intention. When you said you wanted to speak privately, it was the first place I thought of. I was not thinking,' he apologised.

'A public place will be sufficient,' I waved away his apology.

'The tavern would do. What time shall we meet?'

'For *nattmal*, let's take the night meal together and talk,' I said, turning away.

'What is this about?'

130

'All I ask is that you tell me the truth.'

'I will,' he promised.

I will find out the truth of the matter, I promised myself. Surely meeting in the tavern during such a busy night would be of no danger to me, and once I had my answer, I would know where to place my trust. I walked home intending to enter the warehouse via the large external door, or I would have had the entrance not been blocked by a man who I recognised as one who sold wool to Neflaug.

'*Hej*,' I greeted him. He nodded back at me. 'How much are you selling this wool for?'

'The usual, miss, though your master does not seem very fond of paying it,' he replied in a rough accent accustomed to speaking a tribal dialect and ill at ease with the Norse language. As he opened his mouth, I could see he was missing teeth. The two at the front were gone, so he appeared to be a sea creature with tusks.

'We must always strive to bargain,' I quipped. It was not uncommon for farmers to complain they wanted more for their product.

'No, I mean it in earnest, miss.' He looked around. 'She refuses to pay the price, and I fear she has made it so no one else will buy our wool.' He looked down at the wool, grabbing great handfuls. 'This is high-quality wool, miss, feel it,' he said, putting the wool into my hands.

I rubbed it through my fingers. It was indeed soft, clean, fine quality wool. 'It is beautiful'

'Neflaug claims it to be "inferior quality" and will not purchase it for a fair price. I told her where to go. It might be rude of me, miss, but I have a family to feed and people who rely on me.' His eyes shone with unshed tears.

'It certainly does not appear to me to be of inferior quality, but if that is what Neflaug has said, she must have a reason to say so,' I said, placing the wool gently down and smoothing it out.

'So, as I said, miss, I told her I would not sell for such a low price, and I would sell it at the market if she did not want to deal fairly and she told me.' He stopped to take a deep breath. 'She told me I had to sell to her that no one else would buy from me.' He put his hands on his hips, raising his head. 'I told her I would sell all of it, but she just laughed in my face.'

'Neflaug does not like to lose,' I lowered my tone. Neflaug bargained hard to ensure she made as much money as she could.

'That's not the worst of it, miss. I believe she has told others they may not purchase from me so that I must sell to her.' He lowered his voice even more.

'Yes, she is a tough businesswoman, but I cannot believe she has forbidden others from transacting with you,' I replied. If she had done what the farmer was claiming, Neflaug would be in trouble with the Merchant's Guild. 'Thank you for your honesty,' I said, shaking his hand.

'It's winter now and the sheep will need their wool, so I can't sell any more. If I don't make a good deal on this lot, my family may not make it through the winter. I don't know what to do,' he cried in desperation.

'What is your name?'

'I'm David, miss,' he replied, managing a small smile.

'I will find out what I can, David. Will you call back here in a week's time?' I asked. I wanted to help him, but I needed to know if his allegations were true. 'Give me a week, that's all I ask. Take this for now, to feed your family,' I said, passing him a coin.

'I will. Please, I know you will do the right thing.' He glanced at me from beneath his bushy grey eyebrows before leaving the warehouse with my promise to investigate my master. A growing sense of unease bubbled inside of me.

TWELVE

'What if you do not come home, miss?' Helga's eyes brimmed with tears; her face lined with concern.

'You know where to come and find me.'

'Are you sure you should do this? I don't mean to question you, but...'

My arms hugged her slim shoulders. 'I know the risks, Helga. This is something I must do.' The tight squeeze I have her made me no less nervous, and I felt her tense in my arms.

A final protest, 'Please don't go, miss. You cannot be sure of his intentions.'

I let her go and stood with hands on my hips. 'And I cannot be sure of my master before I hear what he has to say about it.' I had made up my mind and no talk of protecting my safety would dissuade me.

'But what if...' she trailed off.

'I have Skara with me, see,' parting my cloak to show her my axe secured in the leather belt around my waist.

'But Kjarr could overpower you before you have a chance to use it,' she cried.

'It will not come to that,' I said, hugging her again.

'You do not have to go.'

We parted, and I smiled down at her. 'I have to.'

She pulled tight to me. 'Just please be careful.'

'I will,' I agreed as I released her.

'Quick, you best go now before she sees you leaving, miss.'

I huffed. 'That will not be a problem. Of late she has been spending many nights away only to tiptoe back into the house in the early morning.' I tucked one of my neat braids behind my ear and pulled my hood over my head.

'I thought it was strange that she asked me to put the fire out before I go to sleep. Usually, she wants me to keep it going until she gets home,' Helga replied.

'Nothing is ever clear with Neflaug,' I mumbled, bundling myself out the door.

At first, I had heeded Neflaug's cautions without doubt, but as the days passed into weeks, her need for control intensified and I felt myself smothered by it, gasping for freedom. It was as if she wanted me all to herself, a desperate need to be the only one to have any influence over me.

I am a woman grown, not a child, and I know when someone is trying to blind me. The decision to seek more information was easy but, once I had it, deciphering the truth of it was a different matter entirely. I would need to trust myself.

Sunset had come, and the wind blew cold, making me glad for the double hood I wore, for it kept the unseasonable change from nipping at my face. In the days before, Neflaug had gifted me yet another fine dress, this one fit for the colder weather. Made from thick red wool, it was long, stopping to graze the ground, and I had to lift it slightly as I walked to the tavern to avoid soiling it. At the neckline, wrists, and hem, she trimmed the dress with hare fur to add extra warmth. Under my dress, thick stockings, and leather boots protected my feet. My dark cloak fastened around my shoulders clasped together with the brooch Kjarr had gifted me. It was the only one I owned, and it was a fine piece, too good to be hidden.

The streets were quiet. Most of the town were returning home for their evening meal to be with their families. My heart thundered loudly in my chest as I approached the tavern. I have to do this. I steeled myself with a deep breath and a quick glance over my shoulder. No one would recognise me with my hood drawn in the dark, but people could notice me in the tavern if I was not careful. The hubbub inside was loud, with music and people talking or slamming pitchers upon the table as they drained them. This tavern had three large central beams which bore the load of the ceiling above. Weaving between them, I found Kjarr seated at a table in the back.

Whatever he was about to tell me was going to change the way I perceived either him or Neflaug, or perhaps both of them. As I approached, he stood waiting for me to sit before he resumed his seat, a mark of respect that I had not expected.

'I was afraid you would not come,' he said. He glanced at my cloak and noticed my brooch. 'You're wearing it.'

I removed my cloak and placed it on the seat next to me. 'It is a beautiful piece, and it's a matter of practicality. I have no other pin to secure my cloak.' My response was stoic, not wanting to fan his attentions unnecessarily.

His smile tightened, obviously understanding that there would be little friendly banter before I had extracted what I discovered- if his answers were what I wanted. 'What is it you want to know? I will answer if I can.'

I had practised my approach; it took me only a moment to begin. 'By now, I am sure that you know who my master is? Neflaug, yes, I see you know that.' I watched his face for any uncontrolled reaction that would give him away. 'Is that why you first approached me?'

His eyes narrowed to gauge my meaning. 'Because you are Neflaug's woman, you think that is why I am interested in you?'

My elbows rested on the table as I leaned forward and nodded.

'What interest in Neflaug would I have? When I first saw you in the marketplace, I knew nothing of you. But I confess that after our meeting I discreetly made enquiries about you. Then I discovered your purpose for being here and who was your employer–that surprised me.'

'And yet it did not put you off?' I probed.

Kjarr glanced around the room. 'Why would it? Am I missing something?' He seemed genuinely perplexed and a little off put.

I remained silent. I had not expected him to act so oblivious.

'She is not a woman I would otherwise want to meddle with, but that does not mark you, and it certainly does not put me off pursuing you.' He smiled with a combination of mischief and confusion.

'Your pursuit of me?' I raised my eyebrows.

'Perhaps I used the wrong word. It is true I have pursued your friendship, but you know that…' he blathered.

I raised my hand to stop him. 'Let me tell you I do not want to be pursued and if you were to continue, you will find yourself frustrated in that endeavour. Tonight, I am here to ask you what has happened between you and Neflaug in the past.'

'Ah, she has told you, has she?'

I waited to see how much he would proffer without my interference. 'I suppose she has, and that is why you have been so cool towards me.'

'Do you blame me?' I retorted.

'I did nothing wrong,' he said indignantly. 'If a man does not want a woman, you can hardly blame him for trying to rid himself of her.'

'So, you admit it then?' I leaned back, thinking it might be time to leave the conversation, having learned the truth of the matter.

'Admit that I tried to get rid of her? Sure, I admit that. She is a vile woman,' he sneered. 'She is so damned persistent and does not give up. I assure you of that!' he answered, waving over two cups of ale. 'So sure of her place in Freyja's graces that she can do nothing wrong.'

'Do you blame her? You promised her marriage,' I began, coming to her defence.

He spluttered the ale from his mouth. 'Marriage? I promised her what?'

'Marriage. You put a ring on her finger and asked her to be your wife. Then you went to bed together and after, when you returned, you spurned her for another.' So much for letting him tell his own version of the events.

'I never did such a thing,' he said, leaning forward.

'You just admitted it.'

'I did not. Nor would I ever because I never did as you say. If you want to hear what really happened, you must promise to allow me to tell you without interruption,' he warned me. 'No interruptions?'

I took a sip from my cup. 'I promise.'

'This was three summers ago. I cannot recall the date more precisely than that. Neflaug was newly widowed, and her husband had been a friend of my father. I suppose you could say we had become friendly. She is a canny woman, but I was always wary of her motives, and something seemed amiss about her.

'Oftentimes, I found her hanging about the front of my father's house. Back then, I also lived with him, and I took care to be polite when I greeted her. But, when I would ask what business brought her to my house, she would never tell me. I didn't like the secretiveness, so I grew more suspicious of her. One day she came to the house I shared with my father, not just to the house, inside the house- she just walked on in. I was there alone, and I thought it was improper that a woman who was neither my kin nor my wife should be alone with me in the house. She said she did not care what other people thought, and I allowed her inside against my better judgement.'

'Did you have any forewarning that she was coming?'

'No.'

'And did she seem to know you were home alone?' I prompted.

'Yes, she did. She indicated she knew this and that she did not care. In fact, she knew my father would not be home and said she had come at a time that I would be on my own, but she gave me no reason.'

'But...'

'I thought you said you would not interrupt me,' he said sternly.

I pressed my lips tightly together and leaned in to take a sip from my cup.

He resumed, 'We engaged in some small talk by the fire, and I offered her a drink. At first, she sat a respectable distance from me, but she edged closer. Her movements made me uncomfortable, but I did not move away from her. Then, her hand was caressing my leg, and I sat fixed, as if I could not move,' he retold, shaking his head at the memories.

'She raised herself from the chair and sat in my lap and kissed me directly on the mouth. At first, I kissed her in return, then reason came upon me, and I tried to stop her. She would not move off me. Instead, she moved on top of me in a way a man might like his woman to do so. Don't get me wrong, I am not made from stone, but if I have a woman, it's by mutual want and never for any agenda.

'I pushed her off me and told her I was not interested, but she pressed herself against me. When she wouldn't move, I protested. At that moment she came to the realisation I was saying no, and her demeanour changed.' He paused as his mind recalled the details. Confusion overcame his face. 'Next, she did something strange. She cried out as if I had struck her and it shocked me. I could hardly believe what I was seeing. She cried, but I was afraid if I tried to comfort her, she would try to advance upon me once more. I was even more afraid that if she continued to cry out, someone would hear her and rush to aid her, where she may tell them I had hit her or tried to rape her. I didn't know what to do,' he remembered. 'The next day I left with my father to go on a trading mission and never spoke of it again, and it seemed she had not either, for nothing ever came of it until now.'

At least this part of the story was consistent in both versions, but I still had more questions. 'And when you returned?'

'When I returned, she was waiting amongst the people who welcomed us back. I just stared at her, still thinking her mind deranged because of the way she had acted.'

'Neflaug told me you married another when you returned.'

'There was no one else. I have never been married. The only wedding that took place after our return was my father's,' Kjarr explained.

My eyes narrowed. 'Who did your father marry?'

'Her name was Tilda. My mother died some years before and he was lonely, so he took a new wife. He had been looking for some time before settling on the woman.'

Arms folded before my chest, I sat for a moment, thinking why Neflaug would have reason to make up such a malicious rumour.

'I heard, some time ago now, that Neflaug and my father had been involved,' Kjarr said. 'But I never wanted to believe that.'

My eyes widened in disbelief. 'Your father and Neflaug?'

'I suppose it may have been possible. She certainly had been around a lot during that time and obviously I never put it all together.' He sat back, stroking his chin. 'Meaning, she probably thought whatever involvement she had with my father, if there was any, would lead to something more than it did.'

'So, you're telling me your father was with Neflaug, then she tried it on with you and then concocted a story that you had promised to marry her and that you spurned her for another?'

'That seems to be the gist of it.'

'Are you sure you were never with her?'

'I think I would remember that,' he replied with a laugh.

'Not even when you were drunk?'

'No. I want my woman sane, and I like to enjoy them when I am sober.'

'Did your father ever say anything to you about it?' I wondered, tapping my chin with my forefinger.

'No, but we never talked about things like that,' he responded. 'And that still does not explain why she came after me.'

'If not the father, perhaps the son? You might have been her backup plan.'

'Hmm, maybe.' His eyes were clouded, lost in his memories. 'You know, I thought she was always very interested in our business. At first, I thought it was reasonable mercantile curiosity, wanting to learn something from my father, hoping to better the business she inherited from her husband. There was no heir from that union. She found herself quite wealthy and perhaps she wished to do the same again, with my father. Divide us and conquer, so to say? And if she wanted to marry my father, what better way than to first rid herself of the suspicious son?' He sounded an empty laugh as if he had just come to realise that Neflaug may have, at one time, been plotting his death.

I had no doubt that she had the wits and the ability to carry out such a plan. 'Why don't we ask your father if that's what happened?' I suggested.

'I would, but he and Tilda died not long after all of this.'

'How?'

Kjarr drained his cup. 'They were heading out on a trading mission, and they never reached port. The report was that they both drowned in the Volkhov.'

I exhaled with a whistle. 'Odin's beard! This is more than I hoped to discover.' Kjarr was buried deep in his memories. 'Sorry about your father,' I said, reaching my hand across the table.

'Never would I have thought it was more than an odd encounter. Since that day, I have kept my distance from her, and nothing more ever came of it.' His eyebrows knitted together, creasing his handsome face.

'Do you swear to me that what you say is true?'

'I swear,' he promised, his eyes meeting mine with a darkness of a wronged man, who only just come into the knowledge of it.

'On the gods?'

'The gods know the truth. I fear Loki played games with my life but, Astrid,' he whispered, using my real name, 'I swear to you I tell the truth.'

'You cannot call me that here,' I worried, glancing about the room.

'I promise you I will not betray your trust or your friendship, but you must be wary of her. Please promise me that. If she is as dangerous as we suspect, then she will not want you involved with me.'

There was an unmissable sincerity in his voice. 'Why would she shower me with generosity, but broker such vicious lies?' I asked, but the answer was startlingly obvious. She hoped to control me, but to what end? I wondered. 'We must keep our friendship a secret until I untangle this mess,' I groaned as I stood to leave, my cloak parting to expose Skara.

'Were you hoping to chop me down like a tree?' Kjarr asked, motioning to the axe at my belt.

'Oh, Skara won't hurt you if you're a good boy!'

The wry smile returned to Kjarr's lips and behind his eyes I saw the reigniting of the spark that drew me to him. 'You, Astrid, are a bundle of mysteries.'

'Stop calling me that, or I might have to use her,' I threatened, my hand finding the handle of my axe.

Kjarr bowed his head in apology. 'I shall have to come up with some other name, for Signe is not a name that suits you.'

I shot a warning glare before turning to leave. 'I have had enough of pet names, thank you.'

Thirteen

The next day, after a full morning of work and an afternoon of study, I retreated to my room to rest and think over the previous night's conversation with Kjarr. In my head, I had raked over every word for the umpteenth time, considering every meaning. Kjarr's descriptions were weighed against Neflaug's as I looked for the truth. Where Neflaug had tears, Kjarr had outrage. Both were justifiable feelings in the situation. Where Kjarr seemed to have not understood significant details, Neflaug retold her version with dizzying detail and that struck me as calculating. There was one thing that I had not considered: my attraction to Kjarr. Like as I might to deny it, I wondered if it clouded my perception and gave Kjarr the unfair edge.

Father would have known. He had such a way of knowing what was within a person just by looking at them. I spun my armring, Bjarndýr, about my wrist as I thought. What Kjarr had told me seemed to make more sense, though Neflaug's story was equally plausible. Still, Kjarr seemed genuine. Surely, I would know if he was lying to me. He had been respectful and had not shied away from the details of the night, no matter how embarrassing they might have been to his manhood. Even if I believed every word he had said, it was far too early for me to move against Neflaug, not before I knew what she had planned for me. If she had lied about this one thing, it didn't mean she was evil. There had to be an explanation.

My truth finding would have to wait. Tonight, I would attend my first Guild meeting with Neflaug and acknowledged under the business.

'We must go, NOW!' Neflaug yelled as she banged on my bedroom door, pulling me from my thoughts.

I dropped my cloak on the floor and it slinked under the bed. 'Odin's beard!' I cursed, scooping it up.

'Come on,' Neflaug bellowed, her patience wearing thin. Not that she had abundance to begin with.

My foot struck the side of my shield. It, and Skara, had been hastily stowed after my return the night before.

'I'll not wait any longer,' Neflaug warned.

'My cloak, it's just not…. URGH,' I cried out in frustration as I forced the pin of my brooch through the fabric. Finally, it fastened on my third attempt.

'Signe, we must go now!' she was calling from the hearth room. She had begun walking without me.

'Please, wait!' I called, running out of my room into the hearth room, cloak billowing out behind me.

'Finally,' Neflaug said with a huff, looking me up and down.

'How do I look?' I asked, hoping I was presentable enough.

Her eyes appraised me again, sisterly annoyance written on her face. 'I would have thought that by now you would know how to dress.' She took my arm and tucked it tightly into hers, dragging me down the street. 'Tonight, as always, you reflect me, and we must always look our best.'

The night air was brutal. Wind howled and nipped at the exposed skin of my face. 'Oooh, this wind is like ice,' I raised my voice above the whistle of the air so Neflaug could hear me.

'It is fortunate then that we don't have far to walk,' Neflaug yelled above the wind as it spiralled around us, whipping my hair into a tangled heap. 'I look a mess,' Neflaug said, combing her fingers through her tangled locks as we approached the door of the guildhall. She smoothed her tousled locks with her hand but seemed distracted. Her eyes cast about the room, and she bristled with nervousness.

'I'm not sure that could ever be true,' I muttered under my breath.

Wary of her I might be, but she was the vision of beauty itself, graced by the hand of Freyja. The green of her eyes brought to life by the colour of her gown. Around her neck, a long thread of Mediterranean glass beads in various colours - a visual demonstration of her wealth. Every garment enhanced her beauty. I smoothed my hair, aware that when we entered, all eyes would be on the beauty that was Neflaug. Only after they had feasted on that sight would they see me, always the lesser vision of my charming mistress.

'When we go inside, I want you to remain at the back with the public and inductees and only come forward when you are called upon by name. Do you understand?' Neflaug asked me. 'Don't make them call on you more than once,' she warned.

I nodded. She didn't need to tell me again; I remembered. She had given me the same instruction before we left the house. I knew why I was here. She had brought me to be inducted as a member of the Guild and to be publicly acknowledged as her successor. It was undoubtedly a great honour, and what did I care if everyone thought of me as less attractive than Neflaug? My wit more than made amends.

Eryk sat at the head of the long table in the impressive guildhall. The roof was of similar construction to the inside of a ship but with beams reaching from the floor to the roof in its support. Shields, furs, and ensconced flames lined the walls. Behind the large table was a fire. Each chair was tall backed, with arms and engraved, though Eryk's chair was the largest and grandest and, even without the raised chair, he towered above the others. He inclined his head politely to Neflaug as she took a seat and smiled at me reassuringly as I shuffled to the back of the hall.

My eyes scanned the others seated at the table, where I noticed Kjarr in close conversation with an older man to his left with a bristling moustache. My right hand brushed through my hair, tucking it neatly behind my ear, the movement catching his eye, and he winked at me. Neflaug was oblivious to the exchange as my eyes darted to him. It was a dangerous game to play - whilst Kjarr held the secret of my identity, Neflaug held my livelihood in her hands. If either of them betrayed me, the result would be the same - I would lose everything.

The din of the hall dropped, showing the commencement of the night's proceedings. Most of it was mundane business points pertaining mostly to market practices, and I did my best to pay attention, but I felt myself drifting away, as I willed my mind to engage in something much more interesting. My eyes glazed over, mind drifting from the room until my imagination carried me to my thinking place on the bank of a river. The water there was calm and blue, unbroken by the wind. A small white sea bird flew low over the surface, skimming it with her wings. *Svanr*. Sven always called me that. I was his seabird, about to fly away at any moment. I had been called worse. At least she was graceful.

'*Minn Svanr*,' I heard him calling me in my daydream. A soft smile found itself across my lips as I remembered Sven in happier times.

I heard the call again and realised it was 'Signe,' being called aloud, not *minn Svanr*. You dolt! I cursed myself. Neflaug's only instruction was to pay attention, and I had failed. Forward, I urged myself, stepping towards the table with an entire room of eyes watching me. My cheeks burned with embarrassment.

'You are Signe?' asked Eryk. He was only asking as a matter of formality, and it made me uncomfortable to confirm a false name in front of so many people.

'Yes,' I said, trying to sound confident, avoiding Neflaug's piercing gaze. She would admonish me later, I was sure.

'Who supports Signe's admission into the Merchant's Guild?' he asked, casting his eyes around the table, landing expectantly on Neflaug, who then stood.

'I do,' Neflaug said with a proud smile, not a trace of annoyance or disappointment on her face. Perhaps no one had noticed my daydreaming, I hoped.

'I second that. Is there any opposition?' Eryk asked the room.

No one spoke.

'It is Neflaug's intention to recognise Signe as her successor in all things. From today Signe will hold the wool business on trust for Neflaug until she wishes Signe to own it outright.' I stood mute. It was a lot to take in. I knew Neflaug wanted me to run the business eventually, but I didn't know she intended me to own it in my name.

Two elderly looking men, with gnarled hands, which I took to be carpenters, exchanged glances.

'It seems no one objects, Signe, are now admitted to the Merchant's Guild and formally recognised as the successor to Neflaug's wool business,' he formalised.

Neflaug resumed her seat, nodded in my direction, which I took to as an order to return to the back of the room. There were a few more items of business to attend to before the conclusion of the meeting and I quickly resumed my daydreaming, safe in the knowledge I would not be called upon again. As the meeting ended, I loitered around the doorway waiting for Neflaug so we could walk home together.

'Congratulations,' Kjarr beamed as he sidled up to me.

'Thank you,' I replied, casting a glance around for Neflaug, who had disappeared.

'Have you had time to consider what I told you?'

I had spent a great deal of time thinking and I still had not decided.

'And?' he prompted.

'It puts me in a difficult position either way. I hope you can understand that.'

'Would you consider taking *nattmal* with me tonight?' he asked, cocking his head.

I was hungry and wanted to talk, so I accepted his offer. He crooked his arm and offered it for my arm to thread through. 'We cannot be too familiar,' I cautioned. 'It is one thing to be leaving but another to be found walking arm-in-arm.'

'I guess I will just follow behind you then.'

We walked into the dark street and traced the few paces across the street to the tavern. The winters, just like in Karlstad, made the days short and the nights long. It was confusing to the body that knew not when to sleep and when to be awake. A curious side effect of the endless nights was my constant, and very intense, desire to eat. My stomach grumbled gleefully in anticipation of a warm meal as we walked into the tavern, ordering two ales and some roast meat to share.

'I don't know why you would think I would lie to you,' Kjarr queried as we found a table towards the back of the hall. It was busy, but most of the people within were visiting traders conducting last business before heading home in time for the depths of winter. We took a stool each.

'I do not know which one of you is telling the whole truth,' I reminded Kjarr.

'But still, you agree to meet me.'

I shrugged. 'You have told me what you believe to be true, and I do not fear you, so I will not purposely avoid you.' A smile crept across his face and flicked his tawny hair back in a manner that told me he was pleased. 'But,' I started, 'if you give me cause to question your intentions, I will have to be wary of you as well.'

Kjarr nodded. He understood my position. 'Since our last conversation, I have been thinking a great deal,' he began.

Before us arrived two cups of ale. I gulped from my cup, feeling the liquid flow all the way down into my belly, strong and bitter.

'Why Neflaug would concoct such a story? It's been the question plaguing my mind, and the only thing I can think of is that she wanted my business or my father's business, as it would have been. Maybe she still does,' he explained, setting his cup down after drinking.

'She said she had ambitions that would take her elsewhere soon. That was her reasoning for having me inducted into the Guild, so that I may take over more of the wool business so she would be free to make her preparations.'

The tavern owner brought a large platter of roasted meat and stewed vegetables. The meat glistened in the low lighting. A couple of crisp rounds of bread appeared a moment later. I tore some off, nibbling at it before dipping it into the melted fat of the meat.

'I have heard she is working with someone important in order to achieve her aims,' he said, lowering his voice.

My eyes wandered up from the meat to Kjarr's gaze. 'What do you mean?'

'She is involved with Eryk.'

'Eryk?' I stuffed bread into my surprised mouth. My stomach grumbled louder with the anticipation of receiving food.

'Yes, I would say it began at the end of summer,' he confirmed.

'He is married, if that is what you mean by involved.' Many men, and women, had relationships with others, but Eryk was a man of the public. He should have been discreet. 'I'm not sure I believe their relationship is anything more than friendship,' I dismissed. 'They have been close for as long as I have been here, and I have seen nothing more than respect pass between them.'

'She might use this new relationship to shore up her position and her hopes for any advancement in the future,' he concluded.

'Gossip and rumour are dangerous pastimes,' I cautioned Kjarr.

'Maybe she wants to keep you locked up, so you don't hear the talk. I am sure she doesn't want you near me, but I am glad she was not too persuasive,' he said with a smile, nudging my shoulder.

'Let's not get ahead of ourselves. I still have not decided,' I said, cautioning him against rash optimism.

'Surely you see now I am telling the truth?'

'I am certain that you are, but my position is almost entirely at the mercy of Neflaug. If the situation is as you say it is, I would be most foolish not to heed her advice before she had entrusted the business to me. If I neglect her advice, it will leave me with nothing and with no one to speak for me. No, I will persist under the guise of her absolute wisdom and when the time is right, I will shake off the restraints she wishes to keep me under, and she will confine me no longer.' I sat back, considering my plan. It was not my intention to cause Neflaug harm but, I needed to protect myself if she thought to use me in some scheme of her own.

'Can I still see you?' he asked hopefully.

I smiled to myself. 'It would have to be in secret.'

'Is this not sufficient?'

'No, it's not.'

'Whilst Neflaug seems preoccupied, we should not have too much trouble and anyway, she is likely to bring herself undone in time.' Kjarr laughed. He wasn't taking this as seriously as I wanted him to.

'I am not taking any chances. She cannot know.'

'Alright,' he agreed, 'we shall no longer meet at the Skogarmaor.'

'Skogarmaor?'

His mouth twisted in an amused smile. 'Surely you knew the tavern had a name?' He waved his arm about. 'The Skogarmaor, and there is only one rule here, well maybe there is more, but Ivar.'

'The tavern owner?'

'Ivar, yes, the tavern owner. He likes this story better. The only rule of the Skogarmaor is that they will admit no Skogarmaors,' he added with raucous laughter.

That was a rule I would try my best to adhere to, though if Neflaug found me out, it could be that I found myself outcast to the forest, outside of law and without protection. A Skogarmaor, would it really come to that?

Fourteen

'Astrid!' The terse voice was unmistakably Neflaug's. 'How dare you! I will send you back to where you came from,' she snarled through bared teeth.

'No, please,' I cried, grabbing at her dress as I prostrated myself before her on the floor.

'Get off me, you liar. How can I trust anything you tell me now?'

I reached out to grab the hem of her dress, begging her for mercy. 'Everything I have done has been true. You demanded my loyalty and I've given it freely.'

'LIAR! How easily you spin lies when even now I know you've seen Kjarr behind my back and against my express command. You have been nothing but blight on my house and after everything I have done for you!' She turned her back on me.

How had she discovered my true name? Who had given me away?

There was only one- Kjarr.

He wouldn't.

'Please don't send me back, Neflaug. What will happen to me?' I pleaded with her.

'It would be a mercy to send you home. Why wouldn't you prefer that than being cast out onto the streets? she asked, rounding on me. 'Or I could cast you into the forest. Good luck surviving the vultures of the night.' She laughed maliciously. 'You might do well on your back.'

Still on the floor, I sobbed. 'Neflaug, I beg you; I have nothing, I am nothing,' I heard myself say, but could not believe the words I spoke. It was so unlike me to render myself so low.

She eyed me with contempt, then a smile crept across her lips, and I knew at once I had played right into her hands. 'You could convince me to keep you.'

I bowed my head to the floor, not daring to chance a look at her as I spoke. 'I will do anything.'

Her laugh, callous and cold, echoed in my ears. My skin beaded with moisture, but I was cold, and I heard a strange murmur as my sleeping mind wrestled with my unease, causing these lucid dreams that seemed all too real. In my nightmare, I writhed, sweat soaked beneath the furs. At Neflaug's mercy, I saw her trap and betray me. In the end, I saw myself assume the downfall of all the nefarious things Neflaug had done as she pinned it on me, and she walked away without fault.

Was that her plan all along? Was this the betrayal the seer had foretold? I wondered as my open eyes searched the darkness. Had Neflaug hoped to keep me ignorant, to use me later as a scapegoat, or had she merely hoped to use me as a puppet in a longer game? I will not allow it, I promised myself as I lay back and closed my eyes, willing for restful sleep, wrapping the furs around me and tightly squeezing shut my eyes. When I felt so alone, I longed for the commotion of the communal longhouse, the warmth of other bodies sharing my space. Still, I could not sleep.

All my instincts told me to trust Kjarr, just as they told me to be wary of Neflaug's behaviour. There seemed to be two sides to my master, and I was never quite sure which one I was speaking to. Wary as I was of Kjarr's motives, my distrust of him was not his fault alone. In him, I had reposed Sven's betrayal. Did I also judge Neflaug too harshly? I had never encountered a woman so like a man, one who controlled all facets of her own life. Perhaps she had become hardened because of the world she fought to live in, one controlled by men. Maybe she had little choice. The thought comforted me, allowing my mind to quieten and drift into sleep.

Outside, the wind howled as my imagination conjured images of houses blown away in the gust, blowing away the land, Aldeigjuborg, until nothing remained. The bed beneath me was gone with the rest of the town. Under my feet was now soft damp grass, and when I opened my eyes, I saw the familiarity of Karlstad. Fluffy white clouds drifted through the endless blue sky. The soothing rhythm of breath was audible next to me and, as I rolled to my side.

Sven lying was lying next to me, staring up at the sky. 'I've missed you, *minn Svanr*.'

'I have missed you.' The words slipped out without my meaning to speak.

He turned his face towards me, expression drawn and without his usual grin. 'I want you to know there is not a day that goes by that I don't regret what I did, how I did it,' he explained. 'It was wrong, and I hope one day you can see me for the man I am becoming because of you.'

In the sky, I saw a longship shaped cloud float by, but when I turned to point it out to Sven, he was gone. Beneath me, grass gave way to bedding furs, and the clamour of pots and pans from the hearth room displaced the gentle sounds of nature.

'Morning already?' I groaned, rolling over and pulling the blanket over my head. But the day had begun, and I rose, as expected, albeit confused and unwilling. I sat on the edge of the bed thinking about the strange dreams that plagued my sleep.

Why did I dream of Sven?

It was not the first time since my arrival. Sometimes it was just like this, sitting on the banks of the river or, once, I had relived my first meeting with Kjarr, only it was Sven's head atop Kjarr's shoulder. Bjarndýr slipped from beneath the cover of my sleeve onto my wrist.

'Why can't I stop thinking about him, about my old life?' I wondered aloud, touching my arm ring. 'What am I missing?' I asked my father as my fingers clutched Bjarndýr to feel his presence. Just as I did when I was a small girl, I curled up on the floor, gathering my knees to my chest. From under my bed, peaked my shield and axe, I reached out to touch them. Sometimes it felt as if I had forgotten my dreams of exploration, but I hadn't, though my new life provided adventure enough for the moment. The knock on my bedroom door startled me.

'*Dagmal*, miss. It's time to eat,' Helga spoke through the closed door.

'Yes, I am coming.' My finger traced the metal of Skara's head before I begrudgingly put her away.

'It will be cold, miss,' she yelled from the hearth room.

'Alright,' I grumbled under my breath as I got up to dress. Over my head, I flung my *hangerok*, striking my elbow on the small table and sending the items atop to the floor. As I picked up the cloak and pins, I noticed the Valkyrie pendant Sven had given me and something willed my fingers to take the strand and tie it around my neck. I patted the pendant, tucking it under the neckline of my dress. Perhaps the Valkyrie would protect me, lead me out of the *myrr* I was finding myself in.

The fire in the hearth room was roaring, the room cosy. Helga was busy cutting vegetables at the table.

'Is she home?' The mention of our master's name was unnecessary. We both knew there was only one woman's temper we wished to avoid.

Helga shrugged.

I sat down to a bowl of oats and discovered Helga was right; it was cold, and it was my fault.

'She didn't come home?' I asked.

'Not that I heard, miss.'

I felt my body relax. My hopes of escaping Neflaug's bad mood could continue for a little longer yet. 'How are your mother and her little *barn*?' Helga's mother had recently birthed another child, and it had been some time since I had seen her.

'She is the sweetest little girl.' Helga smiled. 'Mother is so practised at having children. I barely remember a time when she was not pregnant or nursing.'

There was no time to revel in the details. The room's door fell open and over the threshold stepped a dishevelled Neflaug with eyes underlined by dark circles. She stumbled in, catching herself on the edge of the table. Helga and I froze as Neflaug's head rise and make eye contact with us. It was Helga who spoke first, offering a bowl of sustenance to the woman.

'Something to break your fast, mistress?'

Neflaug looked away. 'No,' she replied curtly before she belched and teetered uneasily as she attempted to stand upright.

Helga and I exchanged a worried look, and I rushed to help Neflaug onto the bench. 'Are you just returning now after being out all night?' She did not need to reply. The odour of sweat and drink was overwhelmingly present on her clothing. On her skin was the unmistakable trace of a night spent with a man, but that was none of my business. I was more concerned with getting her into bed and letting her sleep off whatever malady she was experiencing. 'Are you sure you are well enough to work?'

She laid her head on her hands, mumbling into the table. 'Fine, fine, and everything is about to improve.' Her head raised, a smile crawling across her lips. Malevolence shadowed the vacancy in her eyes. Neflaug's voice was slow and even as she took great difficulty to speak each word. 'From now on, you will be the mistress here.' She raised a finger to point at me and I felt my heart still. 'You will be the master of this business and this house, in role, not name for now but…'

'From this moment? Neflaug, I am not sure I have the experience. My studies, it's not yet been a year and… I, well… I'm not sure that I have…'

My hesitation stirred her to sober. 'It does not matter what you are sure of. I have other matters to attend to and you are needed here. Remember our agreement, all the profits come straight to me, and I will work out the rest. You'll get a scrap here and there, I'll make sure, but there will be no more expansion or reinvestment when there are new opportunities on the horizon.'

Narrowing my eyes, I leaned towards her. 'How will I bring in new wool stock and continue trading without access to our profits?'

Finally accepting the bowl of food from Helga, Neflaug stuffed the meal into her mouth greedily. With a shrug, she responded, 'You'll potter along and, anyway, that's for you to figure out now, just as I have done these many years.'

'Neflaug, I just think…'

She slammed her fist on the table. 'You are not here to think, you are here to do! And if you do as you are told, there will be no trouble. Understand?'

I understood well enough that arguing with her would bring no good, so I nodded.

In silence, we watched her messily eat without a word. When she was done, she pushed the bowl towards Helga, turned to me, and with an intimidating glare, spoke so only we could hear. 'And if I find you forgetting yourself, Signe,' she hissed, 'you may find I have cause to remind you.'

I don't intend to, I thought. I have no intention of forgetting who I am.

As Neflaug stood to leave, she rounded on Helga, leering over her near the hearth. 'And you.' She jabbed her finger into the girl's shoulder. 'Do not dare breathe a word of this or you and your family will be out of work.'

With eyes downcast, Helga nodded.

Neflaug stood tall, disdain clear in her voice when she announced to the two of us, 'Shortly I will remove myself from here to live elsewhere, somewhere grander. Who knows how long I will be gone but, occasionally, I will return to see that everything is being done as I have commanded.' She waited for no response, trudging off to her room. No doubt to sleep off the effects of the night before.

When she was gone and we judged it safe to speak our minds again, Helga sat beside me, stifling a cry. 'She means to ruin us, doesn't she?'

'Why would she build up a business just to ruin it?' I asked, wrapping my arm around Helga. 'If she does that, then she will have no money either, but I have no doubt that she means to skirt that line closely.'

Helga laid her head on my shoulder. 'What will you do?'

My breath was shallow and my mind racing. 'She believes me to be under her spell. She does not think I would ever work against her.' The realisation that my reality could be worse than my nightmares came upon me. 'I will make use of her assumptions rather than blindly following her instructions,' I whispered, in case someone would overhear us. 'She underestimates me.'

Helga looked up at me, hope in her eyes.

'Send word to David, the farmer. Tell him I have not forgotten him. Ask him to come to me later this week with whatever remaining wool he has to sell.' I grabbed my cloak from a peg on the wall near the front door. Opening the door, I looked over my shoulder. 'There is someone I need to talk to. I will be back later.'

With Eryk being involved with Neflaug, I knew I could bring none of this to his attention. It was too dangerous. There was only one person who could help us who I could dare to trust. My feet led me directly to his doorstep with scarcely enough time for the sun to raise high into the sky.

'When I invited you to call on me, I didn't think it would be so soon, or so early,' Kjarr laughed when he found me at his door, rubbing his eyes.

'I assure you this is not a personal call, nor is it something that could have waited.'

His smile faded. 'You better come in then.' He moved aside to let me pass.

'I'm sorry, but there is something I would like your counsel on.' I took a seat by the dwindling fire.

Kjarr took an iron poker and stoked the flames. 'About Neflaug?'

'Is there any other that causes me such problems?' I replied with a nod. 'Just this morning she announced she is handing the business over to me to run.'

'Really?' His mouth gaped open. 'I did not expect that so soon, or if at all, she is not one to give up power. Did she say why?'

'She means for me to run everything, but for her to take the money. I believe she wishes to wait for me to become desperate. Then people make mistakes and ruin businesses. When that happens, she will leave me to take the fall whilst she remains removed from the issue. She said she has something else she is working on, a new business perhaps. Maybe she is planning to move forward with this and needs a way out of the wool trade. Who knows? Whatever it is will not be good for me or my women.'

He sat back, his hands steepled under his chin. 'Why would she think you would do that?' he asked.

'Perhaps the Signe she bargained for is ignorant, unable to understand the consequences of the decision.'

Kjarr seemed deep in thought. 'Perhaps. It may be she wishes to appear the hero to improve her current reputation, and you, dear Astrid, would be the villain in her tale.'

I shuddered. 'That is not all,' I started. 'Something happened a while ago. Since becoming familiar with the rules of the Guild, I have come to the opinion that what she did amounted to coercion.'

'That is a very serious accusation to make,' Kjarr replied, narrowing his eyes and dropping his hands into his lap.

'David, one of our farmers, told me she offered him a very low price on his last wool of the season. When he wouldn't accept it, he searched for another buyer, they offered him much more for it but before he committed to the sale, having had business dealings with Neflaug for a long time and feeling a sense of loyalty, wanted to offer her another opportunity to buy before he sold to the other merchant. She refused still, telling him the other merchant would think again before buying from her supplier. So, when David went back to the other merchant, he was told that the man would not buy from him. From my investigation,

Neflaug threatened this merchant that should he buy at a higher price than Neflaug, she would shut him down.' I paused, staring into the fire for a moment before continuing. 'Finding he had no one to sell to, David returned to Neflaug willing to accept the lower price, but when he spoke with her again, she offered half of her original offer. If that wasn't bad enough when David complained he would report her, she threatened to burn his house down and kill his flock.'

Kjarr exhaled a long-held breath, full of anxieties. 'You must be above it all. If Neflaug has done what you say, then you must not get involved.'

'I will,' I promised, 'but I cannot let her continue, not if she is doing what we think she has been.'

Kjarr sat up straight in his high-back chair. 'Leave it to me to talk to David. His family has been in this area for a long time, and he knows me. I promise you he will not starve this winter.' He reached out, touching me tenderly on the arm. I squeezed his hand in return, a smile passing between us.

My left hand went to the pendant under the neck of my dress. 'I appreciate your help in this, but I want you to know that I do not need you to rescue me. It is Aldeigjuborg, and its merchants that concern me most.'

Kjarr acted shocked. 'I would never presume to rescue you, of all people, and especially not when you have the Valkyries riding alongside for protection.'

I held the pendant out for his inspection.

'Where did you get this from?' He held the tiny figure between his thick fingers, running his fingertip over the smooth surface of the metal. Kjarr knew almost everything about my life before Aldeigjuborg. Not this, though.

'Sven gave it to me before I left.'

He finished his inspection, and a flash of what I thought might have been jealousy took harbour in the green of his eyes. 'I have never seen you wear it before.'

My mouth twisted, a small twinge of delight in his discomfort. 'I kept it in my room before now, but I realised I had almost forgotten my old self when I am most in need of her.' With a mischievous smile creeping across my lips, Loki whispering sweet goading words of devilish intent in my ears, I teased Kjarr further. 'Why? Does it make you jealous?'

'A little,' he replied honestly, removing all the fun of it. 'Does this mean I can call you Astrid in public now?'

'Odin's beard! No!' I exclaimed, tucking the Valkyrie back under my dress. 'There is far too much risk now that Neflaug will probably look for anything against me. No, it's just for strength. To make me a little bolder for the fight to come.'

PART THREE

Tell me a tale
I am not who I am.
I am not who I have been,
Nor will be again.

Have I forgotten my history,
My past and my friends?
Who knows what my story will be,
Or how it will end.

I know who I am
And slowly I learn,
That I must be true to me
No matter the cost.

FIFTEEN

WINTER 880CE, ALDEIGJUBORG, GARDARIKE

My mother was forever telling me, 'The gods have not graced you with the ability to hide your feelings, Astrid.' That much had been clear throughout my life, and she had constantly chastised me for it. 'Daughter, how will you please your husband if you cannot arrange your face into a docile smile?' she asked me, shortly after the arrangement of my marriage to Auden. I was sixteen, I remembered, and still grieving for my father.

'But I do not want to smile. I am not happy,' I complained.

She looked at me sternly, lips pursed with displeasure. 'Then you must pretend.'

'Why would I need to pretend?' I was too unworldly then to comprehend my happiness was irrelevant.

Her face relaxed. 'Your job is to be sweet and bear his children,' she told me as she smoothed my long hair down over my shoulders. If there was one thing my mother actually liked about me, it was my hair.

'Mother, I don't want to have children.'

'That is what the gods put us here for.'

'Will my husband be kind to me?' My father had taken me to Auden's hall a few times, but that was before they promised me to him, and I had never spoken to him enough to understand what kind of man he might be.

'I don't know.' She shrugged.

'I am scared, Mother.' I grasped her hand.

'I was too.'

My face burned and my eyes brimmed with tears as I further protested. 'I don't know Auden.'

She pulled her delicate hand from my desperate grasp. 'That doesn't matter.'

'You knew Father. You loved each other,' I pleaded.

She tilted her head to one side. 'Love is not always a good basis for a marriage. Perhaps if I had known then what I know now, then I would have done things differently.' Her haughty tone made me realise she would hear no further objection. My feelings had no place. I dropped myself onto a stool, defeated. 'Would you rather marry a boy of no promise? It might be exciting for a time, but your life would come to nothing but scrubbing pots and pans.'

'Marriage is not what I want! I am a warrior!' I insisted obstinately.

'Don't be stupid, Astrid. It doesn't matter what you want. I have gone to too much trouble to secure this marriage, and it is a good one. No, you will marry Auden and you better learn to hide your face if you cannot hide your feelings. Men may not care if you are happy, but they do not want to see a pained face when they come to your bed.'

My mother had been right, and I had learned how to avoid people rather than hide my feelings. I shivered, more from the memory than the cold, while I finished dressing and, as I walked into the hearth room, I knew my face bore the markings of my stress. Helga settled a cup of hot nettle tea before me at the table and I cradled the cup in my hands, my fingers nestled into the indents from the potter's own thumbprint.

'Drink. It's good for calming the spirits, miss,' she said, taking the seat opposite me.

'You don't need to call me that anymore.'

'But if Neflaug comes calling?'

I smiled sweetly. 'You do not need to worry about that anymore, I hope. Though if she does, call me by whatever name keeps you out of trouble.'

Hilde, Helga's mother, had been absent for a few days, and I had worried for her. When I asked after her mother, her answer took me by surprise. 'Mother is with child again.'

'Another? So soon after the last?' Helga could have tipped me off my seat with a feather, such was my surprise.

'Little Borris was born in the summer and Mother is in the very early stages. Oh! Signe, she does not rest at all, and I worry for her.'

'Please tell me they are both happy. Is your father pleased to add yet another to the brood?' I wondered.

'I wish I could say so, but the coming of this *barn* could not be at a worse time,' she sobbed.

'Helga,' I tried to calm her, reaching across the table to take her hand.

She looked up at me with red eyes brimming with tears. 'My father is dead.'

My mouth opened and closed. I could find no words to offer consolation.

'He was working outside, and we saw him fall to the ground, hands at his chest, but by the time we reached him, he was not breathing.'

I rushed to sit next to her, holding her in my embrace. 'Where is your mother?'

Helga raised her head a little. 'She came to the warehouse today. Shall I bring her to you?' I nodded, and she disappeared into the warehouse, re-emerging with her mother in tow.

'Hilde, I am sorry to hear of your husband,' I commiserated. 'You should go home. You do not have to be here.'

Hilde nodded, defeated. 'I vill miss him, a good man, but I am more sad for the children.'

'And you are with child again?'

'This vill be my ninth child,' she replied, patting her belly.

'A certain cause for happiness,' I responded, managing a small smile.

'*Hwala ti*,' she replied with a small smile in her native tongue. 'A child is always a blessing.'

Her strength was admirable, as was her love and care of her children. Hearing the stories from so many other women, I knew that bearing so many children took a great deal of effort from the body. 'Is there anything I could do to make you a little more comfortable?'

She climbed over the bench awkwardly and sat down opposite me. 'I'm alright.'

On her own, without her husband working the land, it would be difficult for her to feed so many mouths on her own. Yet, she was a proud woman, and I knew she would not accept help easily. I would have to be more forceful. 'It is my duty to protect you and offer you aid in time of need. If I failed to do so, you might find me in trouble.'

Her face contorted, and she glanced nervously at her daughter. 'Helga, leave us.'

Helga excused herself obediently and left the room.

'What can I do?' I asked, leaning forward once we were alone.

'I vant my daughter married.'

What had I expected Hilde to ask for? Perhaps money, surely food, even a job for another child, but marriage was a surprise. 'Who would she marry?'

'Your friend,' she replied through neat yellowing teeth.

My heart beat fast in my chest and I hoped dearly that she didn't mean for me to arrange a marriage between her daughter and Kjarr. Besides the point that they were not suited, I did not think Kjarr was looking for a wife. 'You will need to be more specific.'

'Mikel.'

'Mikel? And does this accord with Helga's wishes?' I asked.

'She talks of nothing else. It is love, I am sure, for the both of them.'

I nodded. 'I've seen them,' I agreed, 'but what can he offer her? He is still an apprentice, which prohibits him from marriage. Even if he were free to wed, he gets no wage, they would be destitute.'

'If ve leave it too long, I am vorried that they vill be man and vife in everything but name. If you understand me?' she murmured.

'I understand your meaning, but it is impossible.'

She shrugged. 'This is the only thing I vant.'

'Gods help me,' I cursed. 'I fear you place too much confidence in my ability.'

'You can do this,' she said, full of faith.

'I will not make promises, but I will try.'

She left me staring at the wall, wondering how I could work the magic that would be required to get Helga married. If I was going to succeed, getting Luca to agree would be vital. *It would get no easier with time*, I thought. Better to get the disappointment over and done with. Quick strides carried me directly to Luca's home, where I found him and Mikel working on a piece of furniture together.

'*Hej* to you both,' I greeted them.

Luca set down his tools and waved. 'Hello, Signe. What can we do for you?'

Mikel's head popped around the lathe. Taller and more square-jawed than I had ever seen him, Mikel seemed more a man than my last visit. 'It's been a while!'

'That's a surprise as you're always loitering around my home.'

Luca glanced at Mikel, not understanding what I was hinting at. 'How is Helga?' Mikel brazenly asked, the tenor of his voice unmistakably deepened.

'Well. That is why I am here,' I started, nerves causing a shake in my voice.

Luca turned to Mikel, 'Why don't you help Dana for a bit,' he suggested, sending him inside to assist with whatever Luca's wife needed help with. Once he was out of sight, he turned to me. 'What exactly is going on?' he asked, worried. 'He has not been at your hearth girl, has he?'

'Not yet,' I groaned.

Luca looked behind him, ensuring Mikel had disappeared from ear shot. 'Best tell me what is going on then.'

'Nothing too bad, I assure you. But Luca.' I hesitated, as my next question went straight to the heart of the issue. 'I must ask, why isn't Mikel a journeyman yet?'

'Been thinking about that myself recently,' he responded, and I felt myself breathe a sigh of relief. 'The boy says he has been an apprentice since he was ten.'

'That's right. I can vouch, he has told me the same. In that case, he should have passed his apprenticeship this year, he is now seventeen?' I prompted him.

'I agree, the problem is this - I have very little money to pay him. If he is no longer an apprentice, then I cannot afford to house him and pay him a wage. That's what the Guild rules require of me,' Luca said, sitting down on the bench.

My mind jumped ahead as I sat on the bench next to Luca. 'What if he could have a home of his own? Could you afford the wage?'

'That would help, but I have neither the time to help him nor the money to provide him with the materials to build that house. Why are you asking this now?'

I took a deep breath, steeling myself for refusal. 'Helga's mother has asked me to broker a marriage.'

'A matchmaker and a merchant, huh? And she wants to marry my Mikel?'

I nodded.

Luca did not hide his surprise. 'What ever happened to taking a maid to bed for fun, eh?' he questioned with mischief. 'It's not all about marriage.' He kicked at the loose ground and then stomped the small pile down with his shoe. 'Well, that would make the boy happy for sure. He speaks of her endlessly and my ears tire of it. But I worry he is too young with nothing to give.'

'Plenty marry young. I was younger than Mikel when I first married.'

'You are a woman,' Luca answered off-hand. 'Ah, don't look at me like that. You know it is different.'

I bit my lip to stop my retort but couldn't help myself. 'And how old were you and Dana when you came together?'

He considered for a moment before conceding. 'Me? A little older, not much,' he grumbled, 'and Dana, well yes, hmm, but I guess we thought we knew it all.' Luca looked up with a smile that knew when he was bested. 'Say I agreed, hey? How would we go about it?'

'If he were no longer an apprentice and was instead paid a wage, he could support a wife. Perhaps with your help I could assist with providing materials to build a house and Mikel could take a while to build it. Outside his work time, of course,' I suggested.

'It would take him some time.'

'Time enough for them to get used to the idea.'

'There is too much work to be done for me to help with construction. I'll support the boy, and if he agrees, I can certainly put him forward to the Merchant's Guild as a member and he can have a wage, but he needs someone else to help him build.'

'Leave that with me. I am sure I can find someone to assist,' I agreed, though I didn't know for sure who that would be. Helga was one of eight children, soon to be nine. Surely, she had an able-bodied brother in the ranks and, as for building materials and land, that would be the next step.

'Alright then. I suppose we should ask the boy if he agrees to it all. Should I ask him or you?'

'I'll do it,' I said, hoping to be the deliverer of good news.

Luca called Mikel out and he eyed us both suspiciously. 'Mikel, I have something to ask you. Now, try to listen and don't jump ahead.'

'Alright.'

Do I just blurt it out? How does one go about proposing marriage for someone else? My intuition told me to begin with a simple question and hope that naturally led to the crux of my mission. 'How do you feel about Helga?'

His face lit up at the mention of her name. 'Good.'

I stifled a laugh. 'No! I mean, do you like her and if so, how much?'

'I do like her. What is this about?' He looked between me and Luca, trying to figure the meaning. 'Has someone said something?' The flush started on his neck and slowly covered his face. 'I've not compromised her, I swear it.'

'Helga's mother has proposed a match between you and her daughter. I wondered if you would want that.'

For a moment, it seemed as if he had not heard the words until he erupted with a laugh and a brilliant smile. 'More than I have ever wanted anything. But,' he hesitated, 'how can it be?'

'Let us worry about that, boy. We need to know what you think,' Luca replied.

'I think it would make both of us very happy.' He grinned and at once I realised how much he had changed since we had arrived. His smile, at hearing his heart's desire, lit his face with boyish delight that echoed back to the boy I arrived in Aldeigjuborg with.

'There are a few things that need to be organised, and it may take some time. It's not a done thing yet, so please be patient. Don't go rushing into anything or causing a scandal,' I cautioned him.

'Where will we live?'

'You will have to build your own home.' Even as I said the words, I was unsure how I was going to deliver on the promise.

His smiling face turned to worry. 'With what money?'

'Consider it as a wedding gift.' I smiled. 'It will be modest, one room nothing more, but it will be yours.'

'I need someone else to help me build it. I cannot do it on my own.'

'Don't look at me. I spin wool. I don't build houses. Doesn't Helga have a brother or two who could help you?'

'She has an older brother, I think.'

'Then ask him to help you,' I suggested, gently shoving his shoulder.

'I am so happy I could burst,' he said, the smile on his face half the size of his head. 'How did you manage this for me?'

'It was Hilde who came to ask it of me, and Luca agrees, so here we are,' I replied, waving my hands about.

'Thank you,' he said as he flung his arms around me and hugged me tightly.

'I suggest you talk to Hilde soon. She is for the match, so she may encourage her boy to help you,' I said, pushing him out of the yard.

He looked back with a beaming smile. 'I will, and Signe, thank you. I will never forget this,' he sang over his shoulder as he ran off.

Luca and I smiled, but the gesture reached neither of our eyes, both overwhelmed with the task ahead of us. Whilst the consent came together quickly enough, before they could complete the union, there were many steps to get there. Still, the feeling of success caused me to float home and, as I walked in the door, I found Mikel had been and gone already, having delivered the news to Helga.

'Calm yourself daughter, it vill be next summer before you ved,' Hilde soothed, trying to calm her excited daughter.

Helga rushed to embrace her mother, then turned to me, taking me in her arms and squeezing me tightly. Though she was small and fragile as a bird, and I much taller, she took the air from me. Gasping, I escaped. 'There are still many things that need to be done before we see you wed.' I sat down on the bench, warming myself by the fire. Matchmaking was a tiring pursuit.

Helga smiled, her eyes glinting with happiness as she glanced over at Mikel. 'I can wait.' When Mikel left the house, Helga turned her attention to her daily tasks. I remained seated, exhausted. 'A drink?' she asked.

'Please.'

A steaming hot cup of nettle tea, my favourite, appeared before me. Helga placed another on the table before Hilde, who smiled happily to herself. I was glad to see a smile return to their faces after the heartache of losing their husband and father.

'My eldest sons vill help Mikel build the house ven ve are ready, though neither vill be too happy that their sister…' She stopped, noting the concern on my face.

'I can't find everyone a match.' I laughed.

'Oh no! They can find their own vives and my remaining daughters vill find husbands in good time. They are still young, but Helga here.' She tossed a glance to her daughter, who was chopping vegetables in the corner. Her mind was elsewhere. 'She needed a little help.'

'Do your sons have someone in mind?' I ventured.

'Ha! Might not just be the one. Anyvay, they could not support one even if one vas interested.'

My thoughts turned to the building of Helga and Mikel's marriage home. 'Do you think your sons will give Mikel much trouble?' I asked, concerned my friend would have to suffer the trials older brothers often put their sister's lover through. Without a substantial amount of assistance, the deal might not come to pass.

'Nothing more than he can handle. I have faith that Mikel vill show he is vorthy of their sister's love. They vill think of it as his first test being velcomed into the family.' She threw her head back with a hearty chortle.

I grinned. 'Exactly what I was afraid of.' If Helga's sons were anything like her, they would love to laugh and poke fun, but in the end, I had no concerns that they would embrace Mikel as their own.

'Vere vill they build it?'

'On the border between your land and David's,' I explained. David had been willing to sell the small amount for an initial fee and later, when Mikel had proved himself, for more. It would be little more than enough to build a small home and a small patch for a few animals and enough food for them to grow.

'Really?' Helga's head shot up; her voice full of disbelief. I had forgotten she was sitting in the corner, lost in my conversation with her mother.

Hilde stood, her eyes brimming with joyful tears. 'You are the most generous person, my beautiful Signe.' She kissed both my cheeks, squeezing my face between her hands. 'If there is anything ve can ever do for you, just say the vord.'

My heart swelled and tears gathered beneath my lashes. I swatted them away. 'Well, off with you both. I'll not excuse you from working,' I joked, ushering them through the warehouse door so I could be alone.

By mid-afternoon, David arrived at the warehouse with a small wagon full of the shorn wool of his flock, finely combed and carded. 'Good day to ye, Signe.' He whistled happily as he pulled the cart into the warehouse and began unloading it onto the table. His back hunched under the substantial weight of it.

I rose to greet him, storing my spindle in the pocket of my apron. 'This is a surprise.'

'He said ye would be expecting the delivery.'

I piled a load of wool onto the table. 'Who said?'

David stopped unloading the wool and looked at me with a puzzled expression. 'Kjarr did. The fellow came to see me and made an arrangement on your behalf,' he explained. 'I've had some time to think about it all and, if the boy needs my help, I might give a little of my time to the build as well. Such is what ye and Kjarr have done for me and my family,' he said, grinning through brown and broken teeth.

Though his face was rough and weathered from working in harsh conditions, his smile joyfully lit up his face. I smiled in return. What a week this has been, I thought. So much happiness. It almost seemed too good to be true.

'And to think of what people are saying about ye, Signe. I see that ye are a good person. I don't think it's true at all.' He shook his head as he heaped handfuls of wool on the table.

'What do you mean? Who is talking about me?'

'Well, everyone is talking. They say ye are a corrupted person, evil, maybe. Some say you have brought the influence down on Neflaug. But I know she was like that before you arrived,' he reported, knitting his bushy eyebrows together.

Standing agog, I could not comprehend what I was hearing.

Luckily, Hilde came to my defence before I could release the tirade of words that came flooding in. 'Not everyone, surely?'

He shrugged. 'It's just what I've heard, eh? Maybe not everyone, but, still, word is that ye will be the ruin and warning to stay away from ye and this business. Find someone else to trade with, they told me.'

My hands rested upon my hips. 'I certainly have no intention of ruining anyone.'

Hilde put her arm around me. 'The people saying these things do not know you.'

'That is the problem, isn't it? People think they know me, or enough about me, to form an opinion.'

Hilde brought a stool for me and sat me down, rubbing the space between my shoulder blades. 'Calm now,' she soothed. 'You will find a vay to show them otherwise.'

I would have to show people I was not who they thought I was before it was too late, or all my plans, all the promises I had made would crumble and that would only make things worse. Was this her plan all along? If Neflaug exposed me now as an imposter, it would only tarnish what little reputation I had. What then? I hid my face in my hands, ashamed of the things people must have been saying behind my back, feeling hopeless.

'Oh dear, sweet Signe, I fear I've caused ye upset. Steel ye heart! In time ye will change their minds with ye fair dealings,' he tried to comfort me.

Raising my head, I nodded. I had no other choice. 'I will make sure of it.'

As David left, I passed wads of his perfect wool to my ladies. 'Spin this long and thin. I want every thread to be perfect. It is destined for the finest fabric.' I spoke clearly. 'From now on, everything will be different.' Neflaug wanted me desperate. She wanted me to make mistakes. Desperate, though I might feel, she would not find me failing.

'So, no spinning then?' Hilde asked cheekily.

I laughed, waving her away. 'Some things will change,' I corrected.

'So, spinning, yes?'

'Spinning, yes,' I agreed with a chortle.

'What will change, then?' Helga asked, walking into the warehouse.

'To start with, I need to change the way people think of me. If people have such a poor impression of me, then I need to be more visible. I need to make connections and I need someone who can help me.'

Helga grinned. 'You already have a friend who could help you.'

'Which friend?'

She leaned in close. 'You know. The one who I shouldn't ask about.'

I rolled my eyes but knew who she meant. 'Helga, you may be right.'

'Go now,' Helga said encouragingly.

'No, I couldn't' I refused, retrieving my spindle from my apron pocket. 'There is work to be done.'

'I think you must,' Hilde piped up. 'If not for yourself, then for the rest of us. Vithout vork ve may not feed our families.'

She was right. Though I knew she made the comment to show their support, but I felt the words weighed heavy on my shoulders. Still, it was my burden to bear, and I had to do something about it now. My feet could scarcely carry me fast enough to Kjarr's home. The cloak I had wrapped myself in was insufficient for the conditions, but the speed of my travel warmed my skin enough to keep the chatter of teeth at bay. Even at the warmest part of the day, the cold seeped into the bones.

It surprised Kjarr to see me. 'Signe. What...?' he began.

'Quick,' I said, grabbing his hand and dragging him inside to the fire, his eyes alight with arousing confusion. 'Something has happened.' I explained what David had told me.

Kjarr sat back, absorbing what he had heard. After considering it all for a moment, he began. 'As a business owner, you are going to have to deal with these kinds of issues. Your reputation in business is incredibly important.'

'How did you get me the wool and make David happy?'

'I promised him you are different,' he said frankly.

I eyed him suspiciously. 'That can't be all you did.'

'And I paid him.'

'Of course, you did!' Even though I had told Kjarr I did not need rescuing, I was very glad of his help. 'Thank you, but I fear I have yet more to ask of you.' Not knowing how I would go about mending my soiled name, he had suggested getting the measure of the situation at the tavern, where everyone talked about everyone.

'So, you really want to do this then?' Kjarr asked.

'Let's go!' I agreed. 'I'm sure the Skogarmaor is the perfect place to dispel the rumours about me.' If I couldn't change the way people thought about me tonight, I could at least hear the rumours. Much of the town's business was conducted at the tavern, though some also descended into a drunken stupor as the night went on. It was still early.

I felt the blood pulsating in my ears as anger set in, remembering that Neflaug had caused so much of this trouble.

'Wait,' he yelled as I stepped onto the street, 'your cloak.' He rushed forward and placed it around my shoulders.

The afternoon wind had a chill, but the sun was warm as I turned my face to it. By the time we got to the tavern, I was glad to get out of the draughty winter air. Near the front entrance, two men played a game of hnefatafl. The board was in the middle of the table with a cluster of pieces and the king was untouched but surrounded by its opponent's pawns.

'That move is not allowed,' the older of the two men complained.

The younger brown-haired man exhaled deeply. 'You're just saying that because you're losing. I captured the king fairly.' He sat back and folded his arms. The older man heaved a sigh of defeat, slammed his cup down, rose hastily and stormed out. I stood in between the tables, looking around.

Kjarr tried to grab my hand to stop me. 'What are you doing?'

'I'm waiting for something to happen.'

He stepped back, laughing to himself. 'That's not how these things resolve themselves.'

A man wavered on the spot, drunk as man at his first feast. He was tall and might have been strong, but he was past his prime and he had grown a lazy belly. His clothes were tatty, and his brown eyes were glazed as he stared at me. He squinted in recognition before stumbling towards me, finger pointed at my chest. 'You're that Signe girl, eh?' he asked, slurring the words together. 'You're just like her,' he mumbled.

'Who?'

He tottered closer to me, close enough to smell his rank breath. 'Neflaug.'

'How do you know Neflaug?' I asked.

'How does any man know her?' he intimated, spittle collecting on his bottom lip. 'She told me about you,' he said, forcing spit out with the words. A great glob landed on my face.

'You're a stranger to me and, I assure you, I am nothing like her,' I replied calmly, though I could feel my blood growing hotter as he glared hatred at me.

'Oh, but I know the likes of you!'

I hadn't expected things to go quite like this.

He grabbed the front of my dress. 'You'll take advantage and whore yourself out. Just like her! Bloody wicked women have no place to operate in the business of men.' He drew a great breath and deliberately spat on me. A big viscous globule landed on my cheek. I wiped it away with the sleeve of my dress, rage bubbling inside me, and suddenly it blinded me. The heat of my anger took over my body, stealing my hands and balling them into fists. My right knuckle collided with the scratchy beard of my insulter, who spat blood on the floor.

'How dare you say such a thing?' I screamed, pushing him to the ground as his arms swung wildly, trying to land a hit. The dusty ground irritated my nose, and I stifled a sneeze. I straddled him, gripping his tree trunk of a neck in my hands. He was a large man, but I had the advantage of being sober and coordinated enough to land a few good punches as I sprawled him on the ground. His jaw received another heavy thud and this time he turned his face as a tooth fell from his mouth. He stopped trying to fight back, his body riddled with drink, unable to mount a coherent counterattack.

'Signe, stop,' I heard Kjarr call from behind.

My thumbs pressed into his neck where his life pulsed. The desire to extinguish the flame of his life consumed me, and it drowned sounds around me. I was alone with him, the echoes of his voice in my ears spurring me on. *I am nothing like Neflaug; I am Astrid*, I thought, pressing my thumbs harder against the thin flesh covering his life force's ebb. Two hands pulled me up from my armpits, away from the intoxicated fool.

'WHY?' I screamed angrily, flailing my arms and legs around in a futile attempt to free myself.

'Come away, before this gets out of hand,' Kjarr said, dragging me away and out of the tavern. He kept hold of me until we returned to his house and secured me inside. After handing me a drink that stole my breath, I calmed.

'So, you can fight,' Kjarr spoke quietly.

I wiped the blood from my hands, massaging my split knuckles. 'It was not exactly what I thought would happen tonight. Did you hear the things he was saying about me? And he won't be the only one to repeat such things.'

'You're nothing like Neflaug,' he began, 'and after tonight, people will understand that for sure. Neflaug is cunning, she achieves by trickery and you… well, you're more open.'

I scoffed. 'Unable to settle things with words, is that what you're saying. Now people will think I am mad.'

'Hardly. We can read you. If you are unhappy; you talk. Angry; you fight. Just like the rest of us.'

'I hope you are right,' I agreed.

'Where did you learn to fight like that?' he asked.

I took my seat next to him, body coursing with fired-up blood. 'My father thought it was an important thing for me to learn.'

'Rash and impulsive Signe. I rather like her.' Kjarr stroked his chin as a smile crept upon his lips.

'I think that part of me is Astrid, not Signe.'

Kjarr edged close. 'Then, I love Astrid even more than I ever liked Signe,' he whispered the words, his lips brushing my ear. My body responded to the touch and, although I knew it was hot with anger, not desire, I almost wished to give in. No, I can't. I wiped the perspiration from my brow, the move pushing him away.

'I rather like her too,' I agreed.

He shifted uncomfortably. 'You know, you could have killed him.'

'There was no intention of killing,' I replied, throwing my legs over his lap and laying back in the chair, surprising myself with the familiarity of the movement. Kjarr did not free himself. 'It would have stopped before it went that far.'

'Oh, but you would have if I had not been there to take you out of your blood lust.' He watched me in the firelight. 'There is a strange and dangerous beauty about you.'

'What have I done? What will people say now?' I groaned, putting my head in my hands.

Kjarr placed a finger under my chin and lifted my head. 'I don't think people will say much, actually. They'll be too worried that if they say something untrue that you, like any other man in this city, will settle a dispute with your fists to restore your honour.'

Sixteen

A few days later, I was back on Kjarr's doorstep, rapping my knuckles upon his door, hoping to rouse him. Instead of my friend, a pretty young woman stood on the threshold. I paused, confronted by her appearance, and I took a step back to make sure I was at the right house.

'Kjarr?' I ventured, 'is he home?' I asked with narrowed eyes. I'd never asked if he had a woman, just assumed his interest in me prevented the possibility.

She fluttered her long dark eyelashes at me but did not reply.

Over hanging roof, small landing, and a door with an emblem etched upon it that looked like a set of scales; it was the right house. 'Kjarr?' I tried again.

A tilt of her head and a sudden jolt of recognition in her big green eyes '*Da*, Kjarr.' She nodded and her chestnut hair tumbled over her shoulder as she turned and shut the door, leaving me outside.

What is going on? I stared at the door, confused. Was I supposed to leave or continue to wait? Inside the house, I could hear Kjarr's voice but could make out no words. The two conversed in low tones and the door opened once more. This time, it was Kjarr on the threshold.

'Come in.' His voice was rough, and his eyes looked tired.

I walked past him into the house, taking a seat at the table. 'Who is she?'

'A girl who helps me with my home,' he answered.

The pretty chestnut-headed girl disappeared. 'What is she?'

Kjarr laughed. 'She's a woman, of course.'

'You know what I mean. What kind of girl is at your house in the morning? What is she to you?' I demanded.

'Careful, I might think you were jealous,' he teased, leaning over to tuck a tendril of hair behind my ear.

'Who is she?' I pressed, knowing well that it was jealousy that caused me to push the point.

Kjarr ceased his jest. 'My father bought her when she was young and now, she makes sure that my house is in order, and I am eating my vegetables.'

I rolled my eyes. The woman was far too pretty to clean. 'And how does she keep your house so clean when I am sure you keep her too busy otherwise?'

Kjarr tutted me. 'It is not like that. She has her own family here outside the walls. When my father died, I made her a free woman. She comes now and then to make sure I am not fretting away on my own.' He pulled at the end of his tunic, flashing me with one of his intense green stares. 'But if I was, as you say, "keeping her busy," what of it? Not like I am promised to anyone, is it?'

Still irritated, I did not leave the matter, but I ignored the trap he set. 'That is very kind of her, but how do you talk to each other? She obviously had no idea what I was saying when I asked for you.'

'I converse in her dialect.' He waved his hand as if the answer were obvious.

If he wasn't telling me the truth, he had spun a moral tale, and I had no reason to think he was lying to me. Still, I felt a great degree of discomfort that such a beautiful woman was close to him. I tried to shake off the feeling. He did not owe me any loyalty, and I was not about to pledge my own.

'Alright, I didn't come here to question you about your servants,' I said, finally relenting.

Kjarr raised his eyebrows. 'Then why did you come?'

'Apparently, the Guild has heard about the incident at the tavern.'

'Hardly surprising. And their reply? Good or bad?'

'To quote Eryk, "They are pleased to hear I have dealt with this matter in a way that upholds my honour and have distinguished myself far from the dealings of women," whatever that is supposed to mean.'

Kjarr leaned forward and patted me on the shoulder. 'Well, that's good, isn't it?'

I shook my head. 'I'm not really sure.'

'Don't bother yourself too much by the comment. The incident has passed without consequence, which counts for something. And I have heard something too,' he whispered. 'It concerns Neflaug.'

'No more rumours, Kjarr.'

'No rumours, I swear. Neflaug has set herself up in a second home. She is claiming to be Eryk's handfast wife.'

My mouth hung open. 'Never!'

'At least it is what she has been telling people, but there is more. True as it may be that there is some relationship there, Eryk sees it as little more than a convenient coupling and acknowledges nothing more. To him, Neflaug is bed sport.'

'Who cares? If they are both happy with the arrangement, then it is not for us to complain. Many men have other partners, second wives even.'

Kjarr reclined, still watching me intently. 'You know Neflaug perhaps better than any other. Would she be happy without an acknowledgement, especially one that would come with influence and power?' He waited for my response.

'Do you think this was her intention when she brought me on? If it was, then her plan has failed, unless Eryk changed his mind.'

'Eryk likes pretty things, and he certainly likes to collect conquests.' Kjarr looked at me knowingly and unease struck me in the pit of my stomach. All those times Eryk had called me his little bird may have led, at some point, to his desire to add me to his collection. Bile rose in my throat.

Kjarr took a deep breath. 'I have known Eryk for a long time and, he is not the kind of man to compromise something he has worked hard for. He enjoys the sport of women but will not allow himself to be outwitted by one.' Kjarr combed his hand through his hair as he pondered. He was striking, even with worry etched on his face.

I sighed. 'All this will catch her up in the end and then I do not know what she will do to free herself from the mess. But there is nothing I can do about that now.'

Kjarr nodded thoughtfully. 'There is more. I have some news of my own.'

'Oh, yes?' The change of subject was a welcome distraction from Neflaug.

'Come summertime, I will leave for trade.'

'What I wouldn't give for an adventure,' I answered wistfully, but the sudden news of his leaving was not welcome at all.

'I knew you would say that.' He chuckled. 'Why don't you come with me?'

I laughed at the suggestion.

'I am serious,' he said without a hint of a smile.

My eyebrows raised in disbelief, 'Really?'

'Yes, I want you to come. Think of the adventures we could have together,' he said, staring off into the distance dreamily.

'I can't. I have just taken over the business from Neflaug and I need to ensure it operates.' I couldn't leave now. No matter how tempting the proposition was, there was too much to be done.

'You could do your own trading as we went,' he suggested hopefully.

'No, I really couldn't. I am needed here.' As much as I wanted to go, it was not the right time.

'You owe nothing to people here,' he tried to convince me.

'My place is here, at least at the moment.'

'I tried,' he laughed with a disappointed shrug. 'I have something for you,' he said, reaching into the pocket of his jacket. In it was a little fabric bag tied with a tiny string, inside was a ring.

I held it in my hand, feeling the coolness of the metal against my skin. 'What is this?'

'It's a ring.'

'Yes, I can see it is a ring,' I stammered. 'What does it mean?' I asked, inspecting the delicate little band, the silver gleaming brightly.

'Oh, oh, I see,' he laughed awkwardly. 'No, no, not that! Oh dear, no. This is a sample of the silver I hope to bring back in large quantities. This was to show you what I will be in search of. Did you think?'

'Oh,' I breathed, rejected. A proposal hadn't been expected, but the way he brushed it off made me feel a little unwanted.

'Unless?' He looked into my eyes. 'You could always wait for me to return.'

'I, I...' I stuttered.

'Signe, it's no secret I am interested in you, but I would expect nothing from you, and I certainly would never pressure you towards something unwanted.'

'Your serving girl. She is beautiful,' I blurted for distraction.

'Exceptionally so,' he agreed.

'You don't…. You… you never, not even before?' I asked, hinting at a deeper relationship between them despite his earlier insistence. His direct attentions were breaking my usual resolve.

'What? No!' he gasped. 'I learned something from my father's mistakes, and I know two things for certain,' he began.

I leaned in to absorb his father's wisdom.

'The first, don't play with loaded dice unless you are armed and prepared to fight. I assure you, on the first count, I am now reformed. And the second, don't take pleasure from those who serve you. It will never turn out well,' he divulged with a wink.

'I just thought… well, she is beautiful,' I mumbled, slipping the ring onto my finger.

'She is, but I only have eyes for one woman, and I fear she would sooner fight me than return my affections,' he said, as he planted a soft kiss on my forehead.

SEVENTEEN

Helga and I sat at the table in the hearth room of my house, enjoying our evening meal. Hilde had joined us, and she left her children with their siblings for her own welcome respite. As we ate in companionable silence, my mind buzzed with the words Kjarr had spoken. So much of what Neflaug had done puzzled me. I could not understand why she had put me in such a position where I held the keys to everything without her oversight. She was mad or plotting, or perhaps a little of both.

As if my mind had conjured the woman, she walked through the door. She uttered no words to Helga, Hilde, or I, and we, not having seen her for weeks, had not expected her at all. Over the threshold she stumbled, uneasy, her eyes sunken and looking like a woman who had seen little of her own bed. Still, I rushed to her side to help her to a seat.

'Neflaug, when was the last time you slept?' I asked, closing the front door against the chill of the winter wind.

She slumped over the table, head on her folded arms. Helga sent a worried glance in my direction, standing to grab a small earthenware mug from the shelf. Inside, she filled it with hot water and some herbs from the small box she kept by the fire that contained seasonings and things she had gathered from the forest to make lineaments and tinctures when they were required.

When she was done, Helga sat the cup in front of Neflaug, still slumped over. 'Here you are, mistress. It's good for women's afflictions and should help you feel a little better.' Helga looked at me with a shrug. She had done what she could.

Tiredness aside, Neflaug was not herself. Her hair was messy and her clothes hastily donned. A sure sign that all was not right. I urged her to drink, noting the snow on her boots as she looked up, her usually fierce eyes hollow, marked by the dark shadows that hung underneath.

'I am weary to my bones,' she complained in a voice that was unlike her own. Her hands came together to cradle the warm mug between her palms.

'Are you unwell?' I asked. Hilde and Helga sat silent, watching Neflaug with concern.

'My head feels full of wool and my body aches so awfully. I am tired. Oh, I am so tired.'

'Start with some sleep,' I suggested.

She stifled a sob. 'I just don't know what to do.'

I rounded the table to stand behind her, sliding my arm around her body and pulling her to stand. This time, she did not stop the crying and her body wracked with great bouts of emotion. 'It will be alright,' I lied. I did not know what was going on, but it would be anything other than alright. 'Let's put you to bed and things will be better in the morning.'

As I dragged Neflaug away to her room, I saw a knowing look pass between Helga and her mother. They had some notion of what had caused Neflaug's outburst, but they said nothing as I took Neflaug to her bed.

I pushed the door to her room open and realised I had never entered it. The room was larger than my own, with similar but grander furnishings of a bed, table, and chair, but the decorations were lavish. On the floor were exotic rugs in vivid oranges and red. The design was not local and quite uncommon. Atop her table were small bottles which I assumed contained fragrances that, even at this distance, I could smell, were heady, intoxicating scents. Neflaug had piled her bed with thick furs, which had left undisturbed in her absence. Her walls, adorned with several colourful wall hangings, all of which would have taken a long time and a large amount of coin to collect. I had only ever seen objects like this once in my life - in Eryk's home.

Neflaug was still sobbing, holding herself against the door frame. I had never seen her so vulnerable. 'Rest in your bed,' I whispered as I led her to her pallet and laid her down.

'Signe, will you stay with me?' she asked, ceasing her cries for the moment.

I held her trembling hand and nodded while she eased herself under her furs. She laid quietly, her body racked with silent sobs, while I sat next to her with one hand on her back, the other awkwardly patting her hand. My eyes cast around the room, choosing to fix upon a patch of bare wall staring at nothing at all. Finally, she slept and, easing my hand from her grasp, I crept out quietly to return to the hearth room where Hilde and Helga were waiting.

Helga set a mug down for me. 'She is asleep,' I sighed with relief.

'How is she?' Helga asked.

'Bereft. She sobbed herself to sleep.' I sipped at the tea, the warm liquid calming my nerves.

'Did she say anything?' Hilde probed.

I shook my head.

Mother and daughter glanced at one another. Helga raised her eyebrows in my direction. 'So, she said nothing of where she had been or what happened to her?'

'Not a word.'

Helga's eyes raked over me for clues but stopped, fixed on my hand. I followed her gaze and realised that she had seen the ring that Kjarr had given me still on my finger. 'Why are you wearing a ring?'

My right hand shot to cover my left. 'It means nothing.'

Her eyebrows arched with disbelief; a gesture mirrored by her mother.

'Really, it doesn't mean what you think it does. It was just a gift, but I forgot to take it off until now.' I thought about slipping the ring off my finger, but it was too late. There was no point, and besides, I didn't want to lose it. 'But I think we have a bigger issue at the moment, don't you?'

She nodded, and both women sat back on the bench and relaxed. 'I think I know what is happening,' Helga started.

I groaned. 'I am not interested in any more rumours today, so unless you know something please, do not speak.'

She sipped from her own mug, and her mother, Hilde, breathed a long breath. 'It is nothing ve have heard. It is vat ve see, something ve know.'

'Very well, go on.'

'I have seen it many times and I would know the symptoms anywhere,' Helga whispered, leaning forward. 'I believe she is with child.'

'How could you possibly think that?'

'It is obvious: the sunken eyes, the weariness, so quick to tears. It explains why she is beside herself with grief, for this would not be a child she would welcome. I don't mean to gossip, but I too have heard she is involved with Eryk and if that is true, then this child would be most inconvenient,' she said sadly.

I glanced at Hilde. She nodded her ascent.

'You may be right. It is possible Neflaug could be with child. It may explain her hurry to hand the business to me. I very much doubt that Eryk would take the child to knee and acknowledge it, and Neflaug would, somehow, have to support this one on her own. Does she even want a child?' I asked the women. 'I have never heard her say as much.'

Hilde looked down at her hands but did not answer.

Eryk could walk away from Neflaug and her child, if Helga was right and there was indeed a child on the way, but Neflaug could not do the same. Such was the plight of a woman.

Helga crept forward until she was a hand from my face. 'I believe Neflaug may have tried to rid her body of the child,' she whispered.

'No!' I gasped, tea spilling on the table. 'Helga! Why would you think such a thing?'

'Shhhh,' Hilde warned.

Still Helga went on, 'There is a woman outside of the town, perhaps half a day's walk away. She is said to be a help with these things and, I know, there are some herbs which she brews into a potion that will rid the woman's body of the baby.'

An ice-cold shudder ran down my spine.

'Some say it's not fair for a woman to be left with the seed of a man against her will. What else could she do?' she asked me frankly.

'There isn't much else she could do,' I agreed.

'If such a procedure fails, it can make the mother quite ill,' she explained.

'That may be so, but why then would you say she is still with child?'

Helga shrugged. 'Why else would she be so aggrieved?'

'No!' Hilde whispered forcefully. 'Neflaug vould never do that.'

'Of course, she would, Mother. She would do anything.' Helga's voice was tinged with spite, and she did not try to hide it.

'Not like this. I have known Neflaug for many years. I vorked for her ven she vas a young vidow and I can tell you she vould never do this.'

Hilde had never defended Neflaug in the past and I found it hard to disagree with Helga, but Hilde was so adamant that I wanted to hear why Neflaug, a woman who I thought was capable of almost anything, would not do this. 'And what was she like then?'

'Like sunshine and happiness,' Hilde replied.

The answer surprised Helga and me. My mouth fell open. 'What made her change?'

'She vas young ven she ved the master and, like many marriages, neither one understood much about the other before they came to live together. At first, he vas amused by his pretty young vife, they spent all day in bed, and he neglected his business. At the time, ve vorried a little about our positions but in time, they vould remember their duties.' She smiled at the memory. 'They vere so happy. After a time, Neflaug impressed the master vith her mind. She is smart- maybe too smart sometimes, but she vas quick to learn what he taught her.'

'Did she kill him?' Helga asked.

Hilde glared at her daughter. 'Shhh. But there vas one thing that Neflaug desired more than riches, more than power even then,' Hilde glanced at the door. It was closed. Neflaug still slept and would not hear our conversation.

'What did she want?' I asked, urging Hilde to continue her story.

'She vanted it more than being adored, nay vorshiped by her husband.'

'Neflaug is bent on getting power. What could she possibly need more than money? If it is something else, I have never seen it.'

Hilde grew frustrated with our interruptions. 'She vanted a *barn*.'

'A baby?' Helga's mouth gaped in shock.

I frowned. That would explain Hilde's insistence that Neflaug would take no steps to rid her womb of a child.

'Though the master planted many seeds, never did the voman bear fruit. If one did start to take root, she vas so desperate for it to succeed that she vould chant over her swelling belly, villing it to be strong. Sometimes I vould fetch herbs and make potions for her to drink, but nothing vould bring the babe beyond a few months. It vas hard to vatch it.' Hilde stopped, shaking her head.

'She cried and screamed each time the baby vas lost. Her mind vandered about separate from her body. Soon the master vould not touch her. At times it seemed her mind vould leave her all together. She vould act out, throw things, and scream. Soon, he took a thrall lover, and she vorked him just as Neflaug tries with Eryk. It drove Neflaug deeper into the madness. The master did not vant her in his house anymore and she convinced herself that his seed vas the poison that caused her such pain.'

'And I am convinced she killed her husband,' Helga chimed in.

'Hush child. You only saw the end and you vere too young to understand vat vas going on then. Besides, Neflaug said it vas an accident.'

Helga crossed her arms. 'Pfft.'

'It vas eventually known to her that no man's seed vould flower inside her and all she may have done vas in vain.'

'And she tried a lot of gardeners.' Helga pursed her lips and raised her eyebrows towards me.

'So, she lusted after the only things left for her?' I asked.

'Money and power,' Hilde agreed.

'And you know the rest after that,' Helga chimed in with a merry voice, a stark contrast to the dark tale told by her mother.

I heaved a sigh, turning back to Hilde. 'A woman in my village, who was a friend of my mothers, had her mind taken from her by the gods at the loss of her child. She would wander the street calling their name, looking for them as if they were simply lost. Touched by the moon, people said, but we knew she had her mind stolen by loss.'

'The loss of a child even vithin the vomb can break even the strongest of us,' Hilde whispered.

My heart broke for Neflaug's pain. It explained so much of her anguish, constantly on edge, her heart's desire unfulfilled. I found myself wondering if this child within her, if she was in fact with child, would make her whole. Would it soothe her? Would it bring forth the generous and kind woman I had seen on occasion, even if the father did not want it? I could only hope.

Even by the time the sun fell and night came, Neflaug had not emerged from her room. Helga busily ladled stew into a bowl to take to her. 'She will need to rebuild her strength.'

'I just hope she is ready to talk, and that she has learned from her mistakes,' I wished aloud.

Helga eyed me with a look that told me she harboured none of my belief that Neflaug could change her ways. I took the tray and edged up the walkway to Neflaug's room, awkwardly pushing the door open with my elbow to let me inside. Worry had consumed a good portion of my day, wondering if Neflaug had returned for good and wanted to resume being master of the business. My intention was to propose a walk in the morning by the river, if she felt up to it, and then I would coax whatever Neflaug was planning from her mind.

'Neflaug?' I called gently, thinking she was still bundled in bed, but as I set the tray down on the table, I saw the ruffled bedding and realised she was gone. *I know exactly where you are going, Neflaug,* I thought. At least if Helga was correct about Neflaug's condition, I knew where I would find her, but it was madness.

Into the hearth room, I rushed to grab my cloak from a peg on the wall. 'She is gone,' I announced.

'Mmmm,' Helga nodded, unsurprised by my announcement.

'Helga,' I stopped, turning to face her. 'How did you become so wise for someone so young?'

She shrugged. 'I listen, that's all.'

'Perhaps I should watch more and talk less, but now I have to find her and put a stop to this nonsense before she gets herself into any real trouble.'

Helga pulled my cloak around my shoulders, fastening the brooch at my right shoulder. 'Be careful then.'

She was right. I needed to be careful and there was no better protection than my long-neglected Skara. I ran back to my room and retrieved her from her hiding place. The smooth wood of her handle made me feel safe, even if I would have no need of her. So, I slipped the shaft into my belt and set off into the icy wind, whistling me along to Eryk's home. Fresh snow was whipped into the air, making it difficult to see clearly as I walked down the street. Not another person did I encounter on my journey, but the houses close by would have overheard Neflaug's cries as I rounded the corner to Eryk's home. Her admonishments rose above the whistling wind.

'Come out, you coward!' she shrieked, stooping to pick up pebbles from the street and pelting them at his front door. She grabbed wildly at anything, rocks, snow, and the wind.

'Neflaug, stop,' I called, rushing towards them before she could hurl another handful of debris.

She looked away from the door. 'He can hear me. HE CAN HEAR ME!' Tears streamed down her puffy face; eyes red from crying.

'You have been drinking,' I gasped, holding her arms against her body. She attempted to writhe out of my grasp but lacked the coordination, so simply gave a lazy slouch of her shoulders until she gave up, sobbing loudly. 'Hush now, come away with me. Come back to the house, it doesn't have to be like this,' I soothed, releasing her and leading her away. 'What is wrong?'

Neflaug, I noticed, was dangerously underdressed for the conditions. She wore nothing but a thin sleeping dress and no shoes. I wrapped my cloak around the both of us, walking awkwardly together, and felt her shiver beneath the fabric.

'He lied to me,' she sobbed on my shoulder.

'Who? Who lied to you, Neflaug?' I asked, knowing very well who she meant, but wanting to hear the truth from her lips.

She wailed, 'Eryk.'

'Shhhh, Shhhh. Let us get home.'

'He said he would leave his wife for me. We were going to be married, he said. He said he loved me!'

'They do that,' I mumbled, thinking of the advice she had given me to stay away from Kjarr. Neflaug, it seemed, was not one for taking her own advice. Cold nipped at my face and my nose ran. I sniffed. 'Forget him for now. Let's get you warm in your bed.'

My toes were frozen, and I longed for the warmth of my bedding. We stumbled side-by-side and shook the snow off ourselves. The hearth fire was still burning, banked up for the night, but Helga was smart enough to stay out of sight. Compliantly, Neflaug allowed me to lead her into her bed, where her sobs gave way to a gentle whimper.

'Close your eyes and go to sleep,' I soothed, stroking her head, my fingers twisting strands of her beautiful brown hair. 'Shhh.' Her pretty eyes fluttered sleepily as she watched my hands. Suddenly, her eyes bulged, and she sat bolt upright. She had seen the ring. I cursed myself for not having removed it earlier.

'Who gave that to you?' she demanded.

I slipped the silver band off my finger and tucked it into the pocket of my apron. 'What are you talking about?'

'Did he give it to you?'

'And who would he be?'

'Come on, little bird!' she mocked.

My mouth fell open. She meant to ask me if Eryk had given me the ring. 'Absolutely not!'

'Do not lie to me, Signe.' She slithered out of bed, her dead eyes level with mine. 'You are just as bad as all the others, all the men, all of them. You liar you, you, you…'

'Neflaug,' I stood back from her, 'I am not lying to you.'

She approached me still, causing me to step back until I was against the wall with nowhere to go. I looked around. There would be no one to come to my aid, but I had Skara at my side. Odin's beard! I could not use it against her. No, this was her grief speaking. It wasn't the real Neflaug. Still, it felt real.

BANG! Neflaug beat her fist against the wall by the side of my head. 'Oh, really?' she growled as she continued beating the wall. The rhythmic hits echoing the thudding of my heart in my chest.

'Neflaug, I have had nothing to do with Eryk except at the Guild,' I replied, still attempting to placate her.

She came closer still, until her nose grazed my own. Her drink spiked breath was hot on my face. 'I don't believe you,' she whispered, then tossed her hair over her shoulder. 'And anyway, if you have promised yourself to him, you are stupid. He will never honour the arrangement. I should know.'

'It was not Eryk who gave me the ring, it was Kjarr,' I dared to tell the truth, hoping it would weaken her anger.

Her eyes flashed with renewed spite. 'Kjarr? Kjarr? After I warned you about him? Ha! More the fool you are then, for he is nothing and if you are rutting with that man, you'll be a whore and nothing more.'

Now it was my anger that was rising. 'I have done no such thing,' I growled back at her.

She laughed, feeding from my emotion. 'Whore! You slut!' she screamed, louder and louder, repeating the words. '*Du er en hore!*' she screamed in my face, spraying spittle. 'I WILL KILL YOU BOTH AND TAKE ALL YOU HAVE.' Her fists found the wall again, banging so hard the skin of her knuckles had broken. Neflaug banged the wall with both hands, either side of my head, causing her table of perfume bottles to fall and some of the small bottles cracked, spilling their sweet-smelling contents onto the floor.

'Neflaug, STOP,' I screamed.

BANG, BANG, BANG, BANG! Her thuds were battle drums as she declared war on me. The door inched open, and Helga's face poked around the frame.

'Stay back,' I called to her. 'Neflaug's mind has become unhinged. She is mad with grief,' I warned her above Neflaug's screaming and wall thumping.

Sensing new prey, Neflaug turned, walking towards Helga.

'Go,' I screamed, and the girl disappeared.

'You are all going to be sorry you wronged me. I will kill you, and you and YOU!' she screamed, pointing to the tapestries on the wall.

The door opened again, and this time it was Hilde who entered. She strode in front of Neflaug, looking up at the woman. 'I will kill you too, old woman,' Neflaug hissed at her.

'I am not afraid of you, Neflaug. You hold no spell over me,' Hilde spoke slowly, and her words seemed to deflate some of Neflaug's rage. 'You have had too much to drink. You are angry. I can see that, but you cannot be like this, so go to sleep or leave.'

'Or what?'

'Or Signe might have to use that little axe of hers.' Hilde stood defiantly and spoke the words without so much as a waver to her voice. Even I was a little intimidated by her insistent confidence.

Neflaug glanced nervously at me, and I obligingly held my cloak open so she would glimpse Skara on my hip.

'You don't even know how to use it.'

'Are you so sure?' Hilde asked.

I could see Neflaug's eyes darting about, weighing the bluff in her mind. 'So, you may know how to use it, but you won't. Never forget this business is mine. I own everything and I can take it back and then throw you all out.'

My cloak covered Skara again, as I walked closer to the madwoman. 'I think it is you who forgets, Neflaug. Were you not the one who gifted to me, publicly, the entire business? Money and all?'

Evidently, she had forgotten, and I saw her eyes filled with fear as she understood my meaning. 'You wouldn't do that.'

'And you said you would not believe I would use my axe, either. Am I to assume that you believe I am incapable of doing anything?'

'I, I, I….' she stammered.

'So, vat vill it be, Neflaug? Vill you sleep this rage off or vill you leave this house now?' Hilde demanded a decision.

'I won't stay here with her,' she appealed to Hilde, as if she believed the old woman would throw me out in Neflaug's place.

'Then you vill leave.'

'What am I supposed to do? Where am I to live? With what money?' she pleaded.

'Neflaug, I do not want to do this, but you cannot stay if you mean to cause harm. You should have thought about that before you threatened our lives.' If the situation had been reversed, she would have thrown me out without another thought.

'There is nowhere for me to go.'

'Oh, well, that's just not true, Neflaug.' I smiled, leaning into my power over her. 'You have the entire world to explore.'

She eyed me with malice. 'You bitch,' she spat.

Hilde flashed me a warning: Don't go too far. 'Helga!' I called out, and the young girl's face popped in through the door. She must have been listening outside. 'Fetch me a handful of coins, would you?'

Helga scurried away and returned obligingly with a fistful of silver. I shoved the coins into Neflaug's open palm. 'There you go, take it. Come back when you are sober, if you must, but know this, Neflaug. All of this is now mine and I take care of my own. Anyone who threatens me and my women will know the coldness of my displeasure. Make sure you do not upset this house any further.'

Her eyes narrowed, but she did not refuse the payment. 'Take pleasure in this, and your little silver man. One day you will pay for

188

everything you have done to me,' Neflaug cursed as she stepped out of the door.

We followed her into the hearth room, Helga speeding ahead to open the front door.

I shook my head as I watched her disappear into the night. 'Oh no, Neflaug, you did this to yourself.'

EIGHTEEN

Next morning, I woke early to a frenetic buzz still lingering in the air. Neflaug had shown her hand, overplayed it, and lost. I was in ascendancy, supported by my women, but we could not get ahead of ourselves and, I knew, I would need the sage counsel of someone who could keep me grounded.

Aldeigjuborg was asleep, but I was wide awake, running through the conflict again and again. It wouldn't help to dwell. I needed to talk. Before the first rays of sunshine, I dressed myself in layers that would keep the winter chill from my bones. By the time I was swathed in fabric, only my eyes were visible. Soon the sun would rise, and on the street, dark morning mist swirled between the houses as I shivered against the brisk air despite my heavy cloak and sent a glance over my shoulder. No one was there. Still, I was uneasy. It had felt powerful to eject Neflaug, even though it had been Hilde who had done most of the commanding, but that didn't mean that Neflaug would leave me or the matter alone.

My feet led me straight to Kjarr's door. It was too early to knock; I reasoned. Better if I let myself in. I tried the lock. Open. Inside, where the fire was extinguished in the hearth and there was no sign of Kjarr's pretty serving girl. Kjarr was likely still in bed.

Did I dare go through the prettily carved arch to the room he slept in?

Agitation decided for me and led me directly to the edge of his bed, where I perched myself. 'Good morning, sleepyhead,' I whispered, pinching his toes beneath the furs.

His eyes shot open, body rigid, until he recognised me as the intruder, and relaxed. 'How?'

'You didn't lock the door last night, it seems.'

'Mmmm, good morning,' he groaned, a smile curving the edges of his mouth. 'Are you really here or is this one of my dreams?' he asked.

I laughed. 'Come on. Are you going to get out of bed?'

'Do I have to?'

For a moment, I considered retelling the previous night's incidents from under the furs. It was far more appealing than a cold hearth room devoid of fire, but I thought better of it. 'I'm sorry to stir you from your warm bed, but I insist.'

'I was having such a wonderful dream,' Kjarr moaned sleepily as he closed his eyes once more.

'Come on, get up. I'll light the fire.' I walked back into the hearth room where I took up some kindling to get the fire going again, then sat on the chair next to Kjarr's armed chair, waiting for him.

As he walked into the room, he rubbed his eyes. 'Alright, I am awake. Now you can tell me what is so important that you felt the need to appear in my dreams like a Valkyrie on the battlefield. Are you here to take my soul, as well as my heart, Astrid?'

I shook my head as he took his place beside me. 'This is serious.'

'It always is,' he replied. 'I am your friend first and a man second,' he added in a serious tone that told me he understood I had called on him for advice. 'Does this have something to do with the tavern?' he probed. 'Or the ring, really Astrid, I did not mean it to offend you. I did not intend to make you uncomfortable. It's all the joking, isn't it? I'm sorry, I will stop.'

My hand rose to silence him. 'No. It concerns Neflaug.'

'Do not let that woman be your ruin. She has done herself in well enough.'

'I have no intention of that happening, but being involved with Neflaug is like living on a rocky outcrop next to the ocean; you know it is dangerous but yet you weather the storm.' Flames licked the kindling in the hearth, and I used the iron poker to stoke them until they needed no more encouragement.

Kjarr leaned back in his chair, wrapping his fur blanket around his shoulders. 'What has she done now?'

I set the poker back in its place and paced back and forth beside it, explaining how Neflaug had returned to the house forlorn and broken, how I had followed her to Eryk's home to pull her back from the brink of madness.

'And did he come out?' Kjarr asked.

'He might not have been home, but if he had been, then he would have heard every word she screamed at those walls.'

'Eryk is avoiding her.'

'That is obvious. Do you think he has spurned her or is this a temporary frustration?' I did another lap of the room.

'Well, after we spoke about Neflaug and her dealings with the farmer David, I spoke to Eryk.' Kjarr sat forward.

'And?'

'You should find some comfort that Eryk agrees with you.'

'He does?'

'Mm-hmm, he also sees the dealings as a deliberate violation of Guild rules,' Kjarr explained, smoothing his bed hair with his hand.

'Did you show him the accounts?' I asked.

'Yes, and I stressed to him the importance of the wool trade. If they can no longer trade in this city, they will take their business elsewhere. Eryk did not need me to explain much further. He knew it would impact the market and that it could bring all business within these walls down. He is no fool, and he certainly does not suffer anyone who seeks to damage reputation or income. And, if he cares not for the finances of others, he surely cares how it will affect his own, if word spreads.'

Kjarr's sanguine knack for laying out the truth was always a comfort, and I found myself relaxed enough to sit beside him, resting my head on his shoulder. 'All that is cause enough, but I fear he may have another motive for any punishment that will be meted out to her, one that has no bearing on business.'

'Does he need another?'

'Depends on how much he liked her.'

Kjarr glanced sideways at me. 'What more could she have done?'

'It's more what they did together,' I intimated.

'Oh! You surely don't mean that Neflaug is with child?'

'I believe she is. At least that is what Hilde and Helga observed, and there is no reason to doubt them or their observations.'

'What makes you think this child would be Eryk's?' he asked, rubbing the rough stubble on his chin.

'Do you really have such little opinion of Neflaug?'

Kjarr shrugged.

I imagined that if Neflaug had pretended at rape and then murdered my father, I would distrust her too- no, I would hate her. 'Odin's beard! I am sorry for having brought this to you. I should not speak of Neflaug after all the hurt she has brought this house.'

'True, I hate her for killing my father if she did, but I do not hate her for her evil ways. I pity her.' He stopped for a moment, thoughtfully stroking his chin again. 'Let us say the child is Eryk's. Doesn't that seem awfully convenient to you?'

'I hardly think an unplanned child is convenient!' I chastised him, getting up to pace again before the fire. Only a man would say such a thing. No woman would ever think a child that was unsupported by its father was convenient. Neflaug has been reckless. There is no mistake about that, but it was not a creation of hers alone.

'That's not all. That night she went to speak with him about the situation, she truly believed he was going to repudiate his wife and take her as his partner instead. She thought he would publicly recognise their child,' I explained, stopping before him.

Kjarr leaned forward, bringing his hands closer to the fire. 'And you think he knew she was with child?'

'He must. They have seen each other. She must have told him, and that is why she returned to me so downtrodden. I am sure of it,' I replied, retaking my place next to Kjarr, though my body was still restless.

'That's why you think he agreed with me so readily?'

'No, he must agree on merit. It is strange he did not question it further, but perhaps he has observed it for himself at some point. My concern is that he will push for a more extreme punishment than if it had been any other ordinary member of the Guild. Think about it, if she remains and continues with her insistence that he recognise her, he risks exposure and ridicule.' I sighed. Neflaug had really entangled herself this time.

Kjarr exhaled heavily. 'I see. That is something I had not considered.'

'It seems I can best you in some things,' I gloated, but this was not the time to lord it over him. 'We will not wait long to find out what punishment they will decide. The meeting is tonight, is it not?'

Kjarr nodded silently.

'What are you thinking?'

'You would be right to keep her close to you and not do anything rash.'

I slumped deeper into my chair. 'Oh.'

'Astrid, tell me you didn't do something.'

My hands instinctively covered my face. 'I threw her out.'

'Why would you do that?'

I bristled. 'For one, she threatened our lives and…'

'Our lives?' If he had any residual tiredness previously, it had well and truly vanished now. His head whipped around to face me so fast I felt as if I were spinning.

'Yes.'

'Who exactly did she threaten?' Kjarr's eyes bulged with disbelief.

'Me, Helga, Hilde- well, they were both there. She threatened your life, too.'

'Me? Me? Why would she threaten me?'

Sighing, I retrieved the ring from my pouch tied to my belt and held it before him. 'Neflaug saw the ring, and she thought what I thought when you gave it to me.'

'This is not good.'

'I meant to take it off, I just…. forgot.'

'Did you explain?'

I shrugged. 'I tried, but she would not give me the chance. She was so enraged I really thought she might try to kill us, so I took my axe in, but I didn't want to use it. Then Hilde told her she needed to calm down or get out.'

'We must take this to Eryk.'

'Why?' I groaned.

'Because she has threatened the lives of four people today and I have every reason to believe, given the chance, she may try it.'

I wanted to crawl away, hide until this was all over. 'After everything that has happened, I cannot bear going to him.' I knew I should. It was not like me to shy away from the fight, but I was weary from it all.

'Astrid, you have done nothing wrong,' Kjarr said comfortingly.

Tears began spilling involuntarily from my eyes. 'Kjarr, what if we have done too much? What if we are sending her to her grave?' Eryk wielded the power in the town. As the Lawspeaker and the Guild

Master, it would be for him to pronounce judgement and deal out the consequences.

'Eryk would not put her to death. He doesn't possess the power to do that. Only the Grand Prince could, and he rarely holds court in Aldeigjuborg. No, they will punish her as they should.'

'And her child?'

'If there is one.'

'Yes, what of her child if there is one?'

'She will have to find a way for her and her child to survive. I am not sure anyone will want to help her after this.'

NINETEEN

Eryk's deep voice bellowed, the sound filling the space of the guildhall. 'Neflaug!' he called. From his tone, I gathered the sense of Neflaug's impending downfall. For me, it would be no surprise why. But for the other guild members, they gathered to watch a powerful woman tumble almost jubilantly.

Neflaug staggered forward, dishevelled, and still under the influence of drink. She refused the proffered chair, instead preferring to defy Eryk further by standing and swaying from side-to-side.

Eryk eyed his lover. 'Do as you will, woman. Stand if you must.' If there had once been affection between them, there was none evident in the moment.

She held her head aloft, bringing her eyes level to Eryk and refusing to look away.

'You are called here today on some serious charges. Do you have anything to say?'

Neflaug cast her eyes around the room. From her position at the end of the table, she could see each member of the Guild, including myself and Kjarr, seated before her. I did my best to avoid her gaze, as were most of the others. It seemed she had no friends here anymore. Realising she needed to be on the defence, she squared her shoulders, standing even taller.

'I would say,' she started, then stopped, coughing. 'These charges discuss nothing more than what should be normal business dealings.'

'We, the Guild, have concluded our own investigations and found that your actions were not appropriate and that you have conducted yourself in a way that proves the allegations against you. Are there any other factors you wish us to consider?' He was standing now, looking down his nose at her from across the table.

'What kind of investigation is it that does not allow me to speak on my behalf?' Neflaug complained.

'That is the very opportunity you have now.'

'I would speak with the Guild Master alone.' She glared, willing Eryk to accept her proposal. No doubt believing if she got him alone, he would be more amenable to her way of diffusing the situation.

Eryk flinched, feeling the eyes of all in the hall upon him. He must have known of the rumours. He knew the truth of it, and it seemed he did not enjoy being reminded indiscreetly. 'Neflaug, you may speak your case before all the members.'

She understood then there would be no opportunity but this; and took a deep breath. 'Nothing I have done has been with a heavy hand and therefore I simply cannot acknowledge these mistaken charges.'

Eryk's eyes bulged at the audacity, and even I was impressed, albeit accompanied by fear, at her own self-assuredness. 'Your lack of recognition is noted. But know this, Neflaug. You do not have to acknowledge the charges for them to be laid against you or, more importantly, for them to be proven. Your actions are against the rules and against the interests of the Guild, and that warrants punishment.' His address was cool. 'And as for the matter of you threatening the lives of your hearth women; Signe, Helga, and Hilde, in addition to the esteemed Guild member Kjarr. What say you about this?'

'Pfft.' She rolled her eyes. 'Never did I threaten them.'

Eryk slammed his fist on the table. At that moment, I saw frustration between lovers and not between authority and *kona*. 'This is a very grave matter, Neflaug, one that requires due importance.'

'You have no witnesses to this. No one would give evidence against me,' she dared.

Eryk raised one eyebrow. 'Oh, but we do.'

As if none of this mattered to her, Neflaug threw her hands in the air. 'Fine,' she screamed shrilly. 'I admit it.'

'You leave me with no choice and put me in a hard position.' The two were staring at each other as if all other presences did not matter, bodies edging towards each other across the table. 'Neflaug, I dismiss you from the Guild, effective immediately and barred for a year from reapplication.'

Neflaug laughed, 'You wouldn't, and you can't do that!'

'That we only barred you for one year, you should count yourself fortunate. It could have been longer,' Eryk warned. The men around the table nodded but stayed silent.

I watched Neflaug from the corner of my eye. Her body had slumped a little. Her head was no longer held high and, in her face, I saw fear. 'But I won't have any income,' she cried, her hand momentarily touching her belly before she moved it away to grasp the edge of the table that spanned between her and the father of the child.

'You will find some way of making money,' a grey-haired man at the table called out callously.

Neflaug walked around the table, approaching Eryk. She slammed her hands on the surface. 'You cannot do this to me, I know...I will...' she spluttered in rage.

Eryk flushed, looking around the room quickly. 'Remove Neflaug from the hall.'

No one rushed to take her.

'NOW!' he roared. 'Take her now!'

Three men rushed forward, taking her arms and dragging her out into the night. Her garbled screaming fading as they removed her to the streets. For the first time since the meeting had begun, I breathed deeply. It was over.

'I'm in sore need of a drink after tonight,' I whispered to Kjarr when everything was concluded.

'As am I,' he agreed. 'To the tavern? Now we can finally go together without worrying about what Neflaug will make of it.'

I nodded. Now Neflaug's power was waning. We did not have to be so careful. 'Still, it does not feel right.' We walked into the dimly lit ale hall and found a small table in the corner.

Kjarr pressed a cup of ale into my hand. 'You don't think she deserved it?' he asked, taking a drink for himself.

'URGH, yes. I mean, she did everything they accused her of.'

'Then why feel sorry for her?'

'You do not know her like I do.' The conflict remained in me, between a woman trying to make her mark using what was available to her and one that had gone too far.

'And does the fact you know her well redeem her?'

Hilde had painted a broader, more vivid picture of Neflaug, and it had coloured all that she had done. Some part of me still imagined that it was not only I who was being taken advantage of. Neflaug, too, had been used. Whatever had happened in the past could not excuse her behaviour now. 'No. I don't know. It's just complicated. Some things happen in our past that really change the way we see the land and people around us.'

Kjarr nodded. 'I can see this is difficult for you.'

'I don't like being involved in this, nor do I like the feeling that I was part of her downfall.' Grumbling into my cup, I shifted uncomfortably.

Kjarr dragged his stool to face me, sitting between my knees. 'You are not her downfall, Astrid.'

'Shhhh. Do not use that name here.'

'You are not her downfall, Signe. She did that on her own. You are merely one of the people who have attempted to hold her accountable, and you are not the only one.'

'But...'

'Were you the one who began her relationship with Eryk?'

'Of course not!'

'Did you extort those poor farmers? Destroying their livelihood?'

'I would never.'

'And did you threaten the lives of four people?' He lifted my chin, looking directly into my eyes.

'No.'

'Then stop inflicting yourself with this guilt.' He squeezed my knees with his hands, eliciting a small smile from me. 'Do not punish yourself for acts that were not your own.' A comforting pat on the leg and he slid his stool away, giving me space.

I grabbed for my cup. 'I will try.'

'Stop it,' he cut me off.

'But what if this is the gods playing with me? What if this is their plan?' The seer had told me so much. Over time, it had mulled in my mind, until I looked for signs in all things.

Kjarr exhaled. 'The gods give us our lives to live.'

'And for them to play with us.'

His eyes fired with amusement. 'Do you really want to torture yourself with this?'

'When I was in Uppsala, I had my runes cast and the *völva* warned I would be betrayed. What if my actions here will lead to that?'

Kjarr dragged his stool back to his side of the table and motioned for more ale. 'That may be, but if the gods have already decided, then there is nothing you can do about it. The Norns, even now, may toy with the thread of your life. How would you know?'

I shrugged and drank some more. He was right.

'A suggestion, something to distract your mind if you are interested,' he began, swirling the liquid around in his cup.

'Go on.' I narrowed my eyes.

'Have you ever considered the people here that do not believe in our gods?'

'I am not looking to abandon the old gods, even if I find myself betrayed at their pleasure.'

'No. Have you thought of what they tell themselves about their own fates?'

I shrugged. 'My own gods keep me busy enough.'

'Perhaps you should find out. In the city walls, there is a fine little Christian church. Go and see it. Maybe you will find it a suitable place to reflect.'

A flame sputtered in the corner, casting dancing shadows on the wall. 'Wouldn't it be wrong for me to step inside a Christian church?'

Kjarr tapped his cup on the table. 'You are going for the same purpose as the Christians; to reflect, to listen and speak with your gods. If there is a Christian god, I don't think he would mind that at all.'

'Maybe it is what I need,' I agreed. When I had visited Birka, I had briefly visited a Christian church, but I had never thought to do so in Aldeigjuborg. It might be the welcome distraction I needed.

Kjarr nodded to a man at the next table. 'I need to talk business with Loukas over there. Will you be alright?' he asked, standing to wave to his merchant friend across the room.

'Tomorrow I will see this church, but now I need to see my bed.'

We bid each other goodnight and, as I walked across the compacted dirt ground of the marketplace, I heard angry voices from the dark street ahead of me. Silently, I crept towards them, hiding in the dark shadows of the houses.

'What do you mean, it's not yours?' the female voice hissed.

'How could I be sure, Neflaug? After everything you have done?' Eryk spoke in a spiteful tone. I shrank into the shadows of the street so I could listen without being seen.

'You are the only man I have been with,' she cried desperately.

He laughed callously. 'And you expect me to believe that?'

'You know it is the truth.'

'Why were you not discreet? Why were you unhappy with this arrangement?' he asked disappointedly. No doubt it sounded ideal to him, having a reputable wife and children, and another woman on the side, free to alternate between the two.

'I could never have been happy with that.'

'Now you will have nothing. You need to leave, Neflaug,' he told her, his tone growing forceful again.

'No,' she replied defiantly. 'You will recognise this child as your own.'

'I will not! And if you so much as come near me or my family again, you will regret it. Be gone, Neflaug,' he said, as his heel turned, crunching the ground underneath. I heard a scuffle, but in the dark I could only see their outlines. 'Get off me,' Eryk bellowed.

Neflaug shrieked and, as I peered around the building to see what was going on, I saw the outline of her figure lurch towards Eryk. He was much larger than her, but she had the will of a woman clinging to her life. Eventually she let go, falling to the ground, and Eryk strode quickly up the street, away from the sobbing Neflaug who remained sprawled out on the ground, body racked with sobs. My heart broke watching her. I stepped from the shadows.

Neflaug looked up, dirt smeared on her face. 'Come to laugh at the fallen?' she asked me, looking up from the ground.

'Why didn't you tell me you were with child?' I asked, kneeling next to her.

'I was scared. After all these years of hoping, I did not believe it was happening,' her voice faded as tears clouded her eyes.

'I could have helped you.'

'There is this woman out of town and she...'

'Shhhh, hush Neflaug. I know of this woman, and I've also heard how you longed for a child of your own,' I whispered, taking her hand and helping her to her feet. For a moment, I wondered why I was still willing to help the woman who had threatened my life and those of my friends. In the end, she was all alone, and carrying an innocent child who should not bear the blame for the parents.

'This child is so strong, but what choice will I have if Eryk still refuses to support us? It seems I overestimated his love for me,' she cried, having finally realised the situation.

'What will you do?'

'Now that Eryk has denied me, I have no choice.'

'You always have a choice.'

'I don't see what else I can do.'

'When is your child due?'

'High summer, but I cannot be sure.'

'Take this,' I said, handing her some money and the silver ring Kjarr had given me. It was enough to leave and start anew somewhere else. 'Leave this town and make a new life for yourself.'

'What about the baby?'

'You can say you are a widow. The baby of a deceased husband is no shame.'

Neflaug hung her head. 'With a new baby, I cannot make a living. I am sure of it. No matter how much I may want her, I will not be a good mother to her.'

'You think it is a girl?'

She nodded. 'I am sure of it, as sure I am that I will fail as her mother.'

'Then find someone who will not fail her. You can find a new husband.'

'Men,' she spat. 'I'm finished with them.'

I tutted her quietly. Her insistence that she would never again be with a man was both shocking and unbelievable in equal measure. 'When she comes, you will love her. I know you will be a wonderful mother. But if you need help when labour starts, come to me and I will help you,' I said, taking her hands and warming them in mine.

'And if I don't love her?' she asked, her lip quivering.

'Do not concern yourself with that now. I have promised my help, and it is as much as I can do,' I pledged, patting her hands. Once she held her child in her arms, I was sure all her concerns would melt away. Given what Hilde had told me earlier, Neflaug had long desired motherhood and who knew, perhaps Neflaug might even find herself whole.

'Why would you do that for me?'

'A child should not suffer the mistakes of its parents.'

'I am grateful.' She smiled, removing her hand from mine. The money, she tucked into the pouch around her waist and the ring, she slotted onto her finger. 'I hope all of this works out and we never see each other again.'

She meant it kindly, and I wished the same. 'Goodbye, Neflaug.'

Twenty

After Neflaug's departure, the winter snow melted and from beneath, the plants and leaves were coming back to life. The morning held the promise of spring, and the sun, for the first time in a long time, was warm on my face as I stood in the doorway to the house that was now mine, sipping my broth. Aldeigjuborg was finally about to have her colour and scents returned to her.

Just as Kjarr had suggested, I strolled through the town toward the Christian church, outside the central marketplace but still in a prominent part of the town. Of course, I had seen it many times before, but I'd never been inside. In Birka I had seen my first Christian church and, I imagined, that one was much alike any other. From the outside it was not impressive, its wooden facade scarcely different from the other building surrounding it, save for the incline of the roof, which I heard people referred to as a steeple. Atop the roof were two lengths of wood intersecting in a cross, the symbol of the Christian God. I could not understand why or how a single god could be responsible for so much.

Inside the church, the floor was tightly compacted earth with six central wooden pillars protruding from the ground going to the ceiling, bearing the load of the roof and walls. I looked up and saw that the roof was steepled just the same as it was on the outside. It had no upper floor for storage.

What a waste of space, I thought to myself, but had to check my criticism for my house would warrant the same complaint.

The alcoves were ornately finished with wooden carvings. Sweet faces smiled down upon me and, at the front of the church, was a small dais with a table covered in richly embroidered cloth. These were the spoils a man would expect to bring home from a raid across the seas. Here and there were colourfully painted statues I assumed were dedications of their god. If Kjarr was correct and the Christian God was a man, then who was this woman? She looked gently down at a small child, who gazed lovingly upon her face.

'Hello baby god,' I greeted the infant attached to the woman statue.

Was the baby God? Or the woman? Or both? Did each member have a defined role, responsible for a different facet of life? It would naturally follow that they may worship the woman for fertility, family, and love. One might even worship her for a good harvest, but the man, forlorn and beaten, could not be a god of power, the child, even less so.

The church was empty, and, in between services worshippers were free to come and sit in peaceful silence. Between the benches was a central walkway, and I wandered along it until I was at the back of the church. Against the wall was a wooden cross to which they nailed a man. He appeared to be in a great deal of pain, with his head adorned with a crown of thorns. He looks feeble. Could that really be their god? I asked myself as I snuck another glance. Repulsed by his fragile form, I turned away from his tortured depiction to find a seat. This god on a cross looked hungry and weak, without a weapon to protect himself. Why would Christians devote themselves to a man who could not protect them? Surely, he could have used his powers to pull himself from the terrible situation he found himself in upon that cross.

My gods were powerful, and bestowed their might on their people, not only to survive but to succeed. We made offerings to our gods for their favour, and I could not see why someone would make an offering to this god. Perhaps he had nothing except his body and blood and that is why Christians consumed the same during their rituals. In consuming it, did his followers become vulnerable like their god? Did they not see the consumption of man as a wrongdoing? None of it made sense.

The seat was hard under my backside. Christians were surely more repentant because of the discomfort. For me, it would have made me reluctant to sit through a long sermon. With my head tilted back, I could see the slits in the sides of the roof, which allowed bright light to spill inside of the church. My place of worship seemed darker by comparison, at least in the recesses of my memory. I recalled the rhythmic beating of drums as I closed my eyes again, feeling the beat of my heart falling into line with my memory. Worship for me felt organic, temporal, and real.

I was alone in my comparison of beliefs until the holy man walked past me. His face was obscured by his hooded robe, so long that it brushed my feet when he passed. He inclined his head in acknowledgement and stood close to a wooden lectern, inspecting the object upon it. Curious, I stood, peering over the obstructing structure to see what he was looking at. Almost tenderly, he opened an ornate and important looking folio.

'What brings you to my church today?' he asked, looking up from its pages.

'I came to find a place to think,' I responded, taking his question as an invitation to join him.

He smiled. 'A church is a fine place to come to reflect and speak with God.'

The pages within the book's cover were richly decorated, the script illuminated with colourful depictions of life. Such a book was rare and highly valuable to those who could read. With a furrowed brow, the man studied the text, and it was obvious he possessed the skill of reading, though I did not. As I drew nearer, he made no sound or attempt to move me away as my eyes devoured the open page. Black ink was written neatly in a language unfamiliar to me, certainly not the runes I could recognise.

'Latin,' he said, noting my confusion.

'What is Latin?'

He chuckled to himself. 'The language of Rome.'

Unsure how I should address him, I used the name of a holy man of my gods. 'Gothi?' I began.

With eyebrows raised, he smiled sweetly, 'Father.'

Understanding his preferred title, I pointed to the book that lay before him. 'What is this?'

'This is the Bible, the word of God.'

'There must be a lot of words in this book,' I said, reaching out to touch the book.

'Please, don't touch the Bible,' he said, gently blocking my reaching hand.

'Oh, I....'

'No one may touch or read this Bible except for me.'

'Why?'

His chest swelled with pride. 'It is my job to bring the word of God to the people of Aldeigjuborg.'

'Father, how do people know what their god wants them to do if they cannot speak to him directly?'

'People are not meant to know the will of God. It is my role as father to my people to receive God's message and deliver it to my flock. You do not interpret the will of God, only follow it.'

'So, your followers may not talk to God?'

'Of course, they can,' he answered.

'But he may not talk to his people unless it is through you?'

'He may present his will,' he conceded.

I cocked my head to the side. 'It's only the book that people cannot see?'

He pursed his lips. 'You, I understand, are not Christian?' His patience was tested by my persistent questioning. 'I have not seen you in any of my sermons before.'

I shook my head in reply.

'Does our church interest you? We dedicate it to the venerable Saint George, the great protector of his people.'

My eyebrow arched in interest, an expression that the man did not miss.

'He is oft times depicted riding into battle on the back of his horse, weapon held aloft. Some say he vanquished a great dragon and saved many in doing so. You may find the Christian faith has much to offer you, besides the redemption of your soul.'

With a blank face, notably full of disappointment, I shrugged. It would take more than one tale of a valiant soldier to impress someone who had grown up drinking in the war stories of generations before. 'I am always interested in learning,' I hesitated, 'and in the way others do things.' Across the room, I looked at the statue of the woman and child more closely. 'But I find it difficult to believe that your god would want only to speak through one person.'

'He does not speak to only one. God has many representatives. The Pope...' he began.

'The what?'

'Pope. The father of all Christians.'

So, there was a hierarchy. 'What is his name?'

'Stephen the fifth,' he replied.

'There are five Stephens?'

'There were four of his name who were Pope before him. That is why he called Stephen the fifth,' he explained, his patience wearing thin.

'Where does he live?' I asked, looking around and wondering if he lived here or only visited.

'In Rome,' the man replied. I looked at him blankly. 'A long way from here,' he added, noting that I had likely never been to the place.

'Does he always live in Rome?'

'He does once he becomes the Pope,' he answered, returning to his book.

'If you are the only one your God speaks to, then are you an oracle, or maybe a *völva*? We have those.' I smiled, happy to have found some sort of similarity at last.

He closed his bible and huffed. 'I am nothing of the sort. A leader of the faith, I am educated and practice the enlightened, righteous religion. I am nothing like a pagan.'

His protests fell on deaf ears as I continued my questioning, thirsting for answers. 'Is it true that your god offers his body to his people? And that he makes them drink his blood and eat his flesh? Odin's beard! That is gruesome.' My hand clapped over my mouth. 'I expect I should not mention his name here.'

'I would rather you didn't.'

'Well, is it true?'

He shook his head. 'It's symbolic,' he replied, picking up a golden cup. 'We pour wine into the cup and drink from it.'

'My gods demand blood sacrifice and in return we get good crops, success in raiding, and a happy life. It seems to me that the old ways are a system of give and take. This Christian belief appears to be a bit too one sided for my liking. Why does your God give up his body to feed people when he could lead them to food or teach them to feed themselves? He does not want his people to be strong and survive on their own?' I berated him, wandering over to the front row of seats and sitting down, facing him, waiting for him to engage in our debate.

He walked to a door behind the lectern and opened it. 'You certainly have a lot of questions,' he replied. 'But I must retire for some quiet reflection.'

His suggestion has been none too subtle, but I had one more thing to ask. 'Father,' I started, turning to face him again. 'If I have any more questions, may I come and discuss them with you later?'

His face was a mix of defeat and a glimmer of hope in my eventual conversion. 'If you must.' He bowed and walked down the centre aisle and out the door of the church, leaving me alone but with far more questions than I had entered with. The only assurance I received in my visit to the church of Saint George was that the only gods I wanted to worship were my own.

TWENTY-ONE

SPRING 881CE, ALDEIGJUBORG, GARDARIKE

'Why won't this work?' Frustration constricted my voice as I glared at the earthen pot before me, filled with dull red water. As I pulled the long strings of wool from the dye bath, the muted pink colour fell short of the vibrant red I hoped for. 'I will get this right, eventually,' I sighed.

Our latest endeavour had been an attempt at mastering a lasting red dye inspired by the crimson-breasted birds I admired so much as a girl, using the process as a distraction from my unwelcome part played in Neflaug's downfall. I desperately wanted to take the colour from nature and fix it to wool. With Neflaug's departure, I had taken all the profits from our improving business and directed them back into developing new ways to advance the quality of our cloth and garments.

'If I add just a little more,' I wondered aloud, pouring powdered madder root into the solution until it was boggy. The powder seemed to do nothing more than float atop the water. My dress was tucked up about my thighs to avoid being splashed by the liquid. *It needs a good stirring*, I thought, stooping to pick up the wooden paddle. I sat on my low stool, gripping the clay pot with my legs and stirred until the powder melded into the water. The paddle fell from my palm, and I groaned at the red speckles and blotches that covered my body, giving me the appearance of having caught a rash.

'This seems much harder than it should be,' I grumbled to one of my ducks as she waddled past.

There was something missing that would make the wool hold the dye. What could I add that would make such a difference? 'Mordant!'

I shouted, knocking over my stool and startling the rest of the ducks and geese in my yard. They squawked back at me. 'Sorry, but I have finally figured it out,' I squawked back at them, dancing around the yard in celebration of my sudden solution.

Helga's voice startled me from the door. 'Signe?' she called, a bemused look on her face. 'Are you alright?'

'Oh, ha! Yes, I am, Helga. I am alright. Finally, there is a solution.'

She pointed to my arms. 'But your skin.'

'It is just dye. Really, I am fine.'

Helga laughed, inspecting my hands as I held them out to her. 'I was worried you had caught something. Look at the state of you.'

'Until now, the entire process had me sick with frustration. The dye just will not stick to the wool. I know I am missing some sort of mordant, but I can only think of one and surely....'

'You need a break. That is what you need. You have been working tirelessly since she left. Come inside and I will make you some of that nettle tea you love so much,' she suggested.

'In a moment, let me clean this up first,' I said, motioning to the mess I had created.

'I'll help you,' she said, approaching the muck.

I raised my hand to stop her. 'No use both of us ruining our clothing. Promise I will be in for tea in a moment.'

I turned to pick up the small strands of wool I had been attempting to dye. The remaining liquid in the pot would, hopefully, dry out in the sun. There was nothing I could do to clean that up. As for myself, no amount of scrubbing would remove the colour instantly. It would need a little time to fade and until then was best to keep my skin covered, so no one thought, as Helga did, that I had some sort of incurable rash. I walked around the side of the house, squeezing through the small space that separated my property from the next. The two walls of wood were barely wide enough to allow me to pass between. Here, I often found small animals hiding, a perfect place to seek shelter from the elements and ensure they were not molested. As I walked the few steps to make my way through the small space, I saw a broad dark-haired man dart in front of me and begin relieving himself against the side of the neighbouring house.

'*Hej*, what are you doing?' I yelled at him.

'Uh, uh,' he stuttered, ceasing his flow.

My initial response was anger, but then an idea sprung to mind. 'Do it in this,' I instructed, thrusting the clay pot into his hands. He gaped at me, holding the pot in one hand and his manhood in the other.

Puffed chest and upright, I stood, clarifying that "no" was not an answer I would accept. 'Go on,' I urged him. He obliged, relieving himself with an uneasy trickle into the pot.

'What do you want it for?' he asked once he was done, handing it back to me.

Stench filled my nostrils as I cradled the pot. 'What have you been drinking?'

The dark-haired man looked sheepish. 'Ale.'

I eyed the stranger askance, holding the pot at a distance.

'Been a hard week is all,' he explained defensively.

'Never mind. It will do the job.'

'What do you want it for?'

'Don't you bother yourself,' I waved him off.

His eyebrows knitted together with worry. 'It's not for some sort of spell craft, is it?'

'Ha! No. Nothing like that. Or it might be, so do not go pissing on anyone else's house.'

He loitered by the wall. 'Err, miss.'

'No, it is not for *seithr*. Now go.'

He hurried away, and I rushed back to the yard to scoop up some of the discarded madder root and put it into the pot with the urine and wool, hoping this time the liquid might offer some sort of fixing. I decided not to stay to find out but set the pot on an exposed plank of wood to keep it out of the muck and made my second pass at the narrow alley between the two houses. As I took a moment for myself, I stepped up onto the small wooden landing at the front of the house. I had not wanted to enter the warehouse. My women were probably aware of what I was up to but, for the moment, I did not want to confirm anything. Rumours could be denied but would be around the town before I had anything to show for it and, as my recent failures attested, I was not ready yet.

A smile fixed on my face; I entered the hearth room through the front door. The darkness of the room inside was jarring compared to the bright sunlight of the day. Instantly, it felt much colder inside.

'Drink?' Helga asked with a broad smile and a wave towards the table where a steaming cup filled to the brim with water and a few nettle leaves.

'Oh yes,' I replied. It reminded me of home.

Helga sat opposite me. 'You are really set on this dye business?' she asked.

'Set on it? Of that I am unsure, but I would like to produce colours that are otherwise unavailable here. It could really set us apart from the others. As you know, Helga, we can't just throw all our money into making this work- not just yet.'

'So, we will spin, weave, and dye?'

'I want to ensure we do not have to rely on anyone else for our business. My dream is to produce the most vibrant yellow, like the brightness of the sun. The type of yellow that is just like the springtime or the warmth of summer. Could you imagine seeing such a coloured fabric drifting down the streets? A garment we created,' I said dreamily. 'But first I will master this red!'

'That is quite a dream,' she said, nodding. 'You know what you are doing?'

'Not really,' I confessed.

'Then how will you make it happen?'

'Hard work? I will keep working until I know what I am doing. First, I must do some more research and then we will continue to experiment.'

'It's very exciting,' she said, a wide grin creeping over her face.

'Is it?' I asked, happy to hear that she was supportive of the venture.

'Yellow would be divine.' She smiled again, bringing her hands to her cheeks, eyes glazed with imagination. 'Can I do anything to help?'

'Well, now that you ask. Out back there is a chamber pot. Would you use it but leave the contents?'

'Leave my piss in the pot, you mean?'

Never had I heard Helga speak so crudely, but her words conveyed my meaning and as long as she did as I asked, I did not care how she explained it. 'Exactly.'

She grimaced. 'But why?'

'We need something to bind the dye and it just so happens that making water will help with the process and I need much more than I can produce myself.'

'Should I ask the other ladies to do it too?'

'Not yet, not until we understand what we are doing. No, I do not want them to know yet. For now, it will be just you and I.'

Helga was still unconvinced. 'But the smell.'

'If I remember correctly, the stench will fade when we wash and dry in the sun.'

'You best be correct, otherwise no one will buy our textiles if they stink like a festering piss pot.'

'And I really do not want to leave the house looking like this.' I motioned to my current appearance. 'I may not be able to do anything about my skin, but I can look a little less bedraggled.'

'Are you going to Kjarr?' Helga asked with a raised eyebrow.

'Do not look at me like that. It is not what you think. I trust him, and he gives me good advice.'

'Careful you do not make him fall in love with you,' she warned.

'Pfft! I do not think I am doing anything that would make anyone love me, but I fear it is too late for you to caution me against Kjarr's feelings.'

Her eyes were hopeful with girlish romance. 'Really? Do you think he will ask you to marry him?'

'Odin's beard, no! I do not intend to marry anyone.'

'But he loves you?' She couldn't hide her smile.

'Love? I am not sure about love, but there is some attraction.'

'Does it,' she paused, 'go both ways?'

Her forwardness shocked me. 'Helga!'

'Well?'

It seemed she would not give up her questioning until my answers satisfied her. 'All I know is that he is respectful, and he is a good friend to me. For now, that is all I need.'

'Just be careful.'

'I always am,' I agreed as I left the hearth room to wash and change my clothing.

As the warmer weather returned, I had changed my heavy gowns and cloaks for light and breezy dresses. I was once again back in the dress with blue trim that Neflaug had gifted me at the beginning of my life in Aldeigjuborg. My shoes were made from thin calf skin leather, perfect for the warmth, but as I made my way to Kjarr's home, they did little to protect my feet from the small sharp stones underfoot.

Visits with Kjarr no longer meant fireside conversations. The heat made it stifling inside, so we took to sitting in his yard where, like most people in town, he kept some small animals. Two ducks waddled in between our stools, digging in the mud for worms.

'From my reckoning, Neflaug will soon birth her child.' The calculation had been approximate, but it felt right. As one of Kjarr's ducks waddled past, I reached out to tickle her under her wing. She honked disapprovingly and ran in the opposite direction, earning a laugh from the both of us.

Kjarr's laughter stopped abruptly and the face he turned to me was one of disappointment. 'Why do you still think about her?'

'It is hard not to. I feel bad about it all.'

'We have been over it so many times. There is nothing more you could have done,' his voice was strained. He had admonished me time-and-time again for continuing to care. He did not understand that Neflaug had shown me great kindness in bringing me to Aldeigjuborg, albeit under false pretences, and without that opportunity, my life may have been something quite different. For me, I could not separate the person from the acts of kindness she had previously shown.

'I know you are right, but she was kind, and I thought she was my friend. She had so much evil inside of her,' I replied, watching the ducks splash around in a puddle in the yard's corner.

'You do not need to defend her. She won't be stupid enough to come back to the town.'

I nodded, 'But I think I will always wonder.'

'And that is alright,' he reminded me, patting my hand.

We sat in amiable silence while I watched the ducks chase a fat pig around the pen. The ducks flapped their wings, threatening to take flight over the swine's head. She grunted loudly then, giving up on the game, rolled heavily into the mud where she lolled in its dampness, grunting happily.

Kjarr watched me intently. I could feel his gaze even without looking. 'Where are you?' he asked. 'Off in some far off place, no doubt.'

I turned to smile. 'You know me well.'

'I'm glad to find your mind wandering for a moment. I expect you have been too busy to spend your time in daydreams of late.'

'As are you! Last week you were to leave on your trading mission.'

'I was.'

'Why do you keep delaying it?'

'I just keep finding things that keep me here.'

'How many times have you put off leaving? What is it? Maybe three times?' I asked, shoving his shoulder with my own.

'Seven,' he replied.

'Seven? I think it's time you go, or else there may be nothing for you to bring back. Everyone else would have got there first,' I teased. 'Why do you keep putting it off? Surely there is nothing more important than this?'

'More important than all the silver in the world.'

I raised my eyebrow. 'Now, what could that be?'

He shifted uncomfortably on his stool. 'Must I say it out loud?'

'Please don't say it's me.'

'You know it is.'

I met his eyes. 'You must stop putting it off or the snow will be here, and you will have to wait another year.'

'Another year stuck here with you does not sound so bad.'

'And I will miss you too, but you must go.'

'Are you sure you won't come with me?' His eyes pleaded with me, but I could not relent.

'I have too much to do here. Besides, what would I do on a trading mission other than being an additional mouth to feed, to row at the oars, to drag around to marketplaces?' Without my own purpose, I saw no reason to go.

He sighed in defeat, 'Alright, well if you really will not come with me, I guess I have to go, but it will be a long time without you.'

I was desperate to change the subject. 'Oh, I went back to that church today.'

'Really? Careful or the priest might think he is on the verge of a new convert.'

'No, no. I am not interested in it that much. I thought I might ask for some wisdom from our own gods, but I found myself distracted.'

'By what?'

'Well, for one, they have a great big roof that is a complete waste of space. There is nothing stored above, it is just left open for all to wonder why they built such a structure yet thought to leave it unfinished.'

'Is that it?' He snorted with laughter. 'You found the roof annoying?'

'Oh stop,' I said, scuffing him on the arm in reprimand. 'They could have built loft spaces to store grain, yet they didn't.'

'It was done on purpose. They have no intention of coming back to build lofts. Its use to them is to make the building close to their god.'

'But their god is so feeble. Have you seen their effigy?'

He nodded. 'I have, and I doubt the Christians would agree with you. They see their god as humble and there are many stories about God's deeds. Apparent miracles you might say: freeing slaves, surviving when others cannot, protecting or curing people from great ills.'

'You certainly know a lot about this Christian God.'

'You learn a lot when you listen.'

'You're not the first person to have told me that lately. But tell me this, Kjarr, how can their god do anything if he is dead?'

'He died, but then he rose again,' Kjarr explained.

'Like Odin when he hung himself from *Yggdrasil*, the tree of knowledge, for nine days in exchange for wisdom?' I asked.

'Not exactly. When the Christian God died, he was entombed inside some sort of crypt, and three days later he arose.' Kjarr relayed but even he was fuzzy on the details. He squinted as he tried to remember the story.

'Any wiser?'

He shook his head. 'It seems the experience did not change him at all.'

'Then why did he have to die?' I wondered, seeing this god's death as confusing and pointless.

'Apparently, he died for the sins of his people.'

'What?! He died for them?' I scoffed. And they continued to sin.

'That is what they believe. Remember, it is not dissimilar to a man volunteering to sacrifice himself to the gods at the *blót*.'

'I do not think it is the same at all!'

'Christians believe he gave up his mortal body for his spirit to rise again and sit with his father,' he tried to explain.

I scratched my head. 'But they say there is only one god?'

'There is, although they see him more in segments than as a whole.'
I shrugged, losing interest in the fickle religion. 'It's all very confusing.'
'It is,' Kjarr agreed.
'Are you Christian? I had never thought to ask you before.'
'By Thor's hammer, no! My father believed in the old gods, but I always had a keen interest in the religion of others. Did you know there are even more religions in the east?'
'Not more talk of gods,' I groaned. 'My head couldn't take any more,'
Kjarr grabbed one of my red stained hands. 'What's this? Are you sick?' he gasped.
'Nothing to concern yourself with,' I responded, freeing my palm from his grip.
'You look terrible.'
'It is just the remnants of a failed experiment with a new dye.'
He sighed with relief. 'You have a lot happening at the moment.'
I rested my face on my palm, elbow on my knee. 'I know.'
'Perhaps you should take a break.'
'You would not be the first to have suggested that to me today.'
'It seems you have received some good advice of late and it sounds like exactly what you need.'
'I have too much to do,' I complained.
'You will find when you take a little time for yourself, you are better able to get things done,' he answered wisely.
I nodded.
'What do you do when you need to take a little time?'
'I have not had the chance since I arrived in Aldeigjuborg.'
'But before?'
'Before, I would go to the practice yard with Sven and beat him with my axe and shield.' I laughed at the memory. Kjarr recoiled as if I had struck him. Did he flinch at the mention of Sven's name? As if remembering my old friend had hurt him?
He visibly shook himself off. 'Why not take that axe from under your bed and attack a tree somewhere? Just make sure it's out of sight of the walls, but not too far.'
'Do you always have the solution for everything?'
A small smile crept over his lips. 'Sadly not. I seem to just have a way of understanding you.' He stood up, pulling at my hands to

218

make me rise. 'Go on, a little hard exercise will be good. Get all those frustrations out.'

Opening the gate to leave, I looked back. 'Do you want to come with me?'

He hesitated. 'As much as I would love to, I would not want to get in your way. Anyway, I must prepare myself to leave now that you have ordered me to go.'

'Alright, I am going,' I waved as I walked away, leaving Kjarr to make his preparations as I raced home to collect Skara.

There was no point in changing. I no longer had appropriate clothing for weapon craft. Any jerkins or tunics I had access to previously were left behind long ago in my homeland. No one questioned me as I left the house, nor when I made my way through the streets and out of the town gates towards the forest in my pretty dress. Through my soft leather shoes, I could feel the pressure of every small pebble, every twig strewn upon the earth, and I cursed myself for not having selected some sturdier shoe.

Traders walked the bridge, going the opposite direction from me, and as we passed each other, we nodded in acknowledgement. Not one pair of eyes glanced below my belt where my axe was hanging, fortunate for me, for I did not know how well they would observe a merchant woman armed as a warrior. It was common enough to arm oneself while travelling for trade. Once I reached the tree line, there were fewer people. From within the pouch at my waist I took a bone pin, twisting my untethered hair into a knot on my head and slotting the pin in to secure it. I wobbled my head side-to-side to test its hold. Good enough.

Inside the forest, townspeople, and farmers alike came to forage, to walk, and more often than anywhere else, for a romp. Today, while it was still early, I would be alone. In a small clearing, I found a copse of strong trunked trees to test my aim and set to work. Sights set on a broad oak; I imagined a Saxon enemy defending their shores from my raid. We stared each other down, trying to take in the measure of one another.

My father had taught me something about fighting a man. 'Watch for the smallest of movements, some clue of their preferred hand and eye,' he had told me. My hand grasped Bjarndýr for my father's strength. 'Know your enemy's weakness,' my father had advised me when I asked for yet another morsel of wisdom from battle.

But this is a tree, I thought, and though it was true, it was the only opponent I had, so I would have to try a little harder to imbue it with the intent of ending my life. The oak's image was replaced with a dark-haired Saxon, with green eyes that were amused by his female foe. I would not be easy to conquer. He had to fight, and I watched him for any flinch that might give him away. Skara wanted to strike, and my opponent waited for me to make the first move. He grasped his sword with his right hand and pulled back into a defensive position, shifting his weight onto his back foot. I darted left, going for his unprotected side and lunged, missed! URGH. I whirled around in a circle, my axe held high to strike down. He had not expected the move, and the handle of my axe landed with a thud on his right shoulder. His leather jerkin withstood most of the hit, though it would have broken the skin beneath. It would not have been enough to sever a limb or cause any significant damage other than a momentary stun. If I had landed the head of my axe there, it could have ended him.

He bared his teeth in a snarling smile that urged me to continue my attack. 'COME AT ME!' I screamed, though if he were a Saxon, perhaps he might not understand the words. He would understand the intent, 'FIGHT ME!'

My enemy thrust his sword, and I jumped back, missing the tip of his blade. Again, he pushed forward, and I parried with my axe, this time lunging to the side and pushing him back with my shoulder. I caught my breath. I am unpractised and my strength has all but left me. That had to change. Mustering my energy and hoping to land a solid backhand, I started on my right foot and feigned a strike. This was a good move. It put many excellent warriors off their guard. Next, I transferred all my weight to my left and twisted away; I landed a hard strike on his left side. The back of my dress strained against the move, but it was hard enough to cut through his jerkin right into the soft flesh of his belly. A snarl curled my lips as I watched him clasp his hands around his spilling guts. When he dropped to his knees, he looked up, scarce believing I had undone him. Prone, he lay before me. Skara drove down hard to finish him and as the life drained from his eyes, I breathed the thrill of the fight. Aside from scraps, I had never been in actual combat. But I had imagined it and today it felt real.

As my enemy died beneath me, I leaned back, looking at the sky. My thoughts were of Sven, and I wondered if he was now looking at the same sky that I was. If he was fighting an enemy on foreign shores as we had both dreamed, perhaps he was not fighting at all. Had he fallen and was now feasting with the gods in Valhalla?

A handful of moss cleaned Skara, and she was ready to be stowed at my belt. Under the sleeve of my dress, my father's armring, Bjarndýr, was a constant reminder of my true identity. *I have to do this more often*, I thought, enjoying the thrill of blood pumping fast through my body. My breath slowed and I let my hair down over my shoulders, noticing the tie on the back of my dress had come undone. I fumbled with the laces to fasten them. 'They did not make dresses for fighting in,' I grumbled as I struggled. Try as I might, I could not get them done up. My shoulders must be tight from the axe play.

It would arouse suspicion if I re-entered the gates, partially undressed, if anyone noticed, and I could not take that chance. No, I could walk to Hilde's house. It was close by, and she could help. Hilde lived in the outlying lands and though I had never visited her home, I had no trouble in locating it. A small and tidy home, hidden behind a gate and hedge, I let myself in the gate and knocked at the door.

'Signe?' Hilde greeted me with surprise.

'I thought to come and see how you are with the new *barn*.'

'Vat a lovely surprise.'

I edged closer to her. 'And I need a little help with my dress.'

Her eyebrows shot up. 'Did something, err, happen?'

'Odin's beard, no! But dresses make poor garments for fighting and I am weary now and cannot do it up for myself,' I giggled.

'You were fighting?' Her eyes wandered to my belt.

'No, not fighting, more like practising.'

'Vith Neflaug somewhere about it is vise to be prepared,' she agreed, nodding vigorously and ushering me inside. Hilde's fingers made quick work of refastening the ties at the back of my dress as I sat on a stool in her hearth room.

I was glad of her calm assumption that my having an axe was for protection against Neflaug. 'How was the birth? Are you both well?'

'Vas not a hard birth. She came quickly. The little one is strong, and I have no time for lying about.'

Hilde was a stubborn hard worker and even if she needed the rest, I doubted she would take it.

'Do you vant to see her?' she asked.

'Of course.' I smiled as I followed her into the second room of her two-room house. It was small and dark with no windows, just a small opening in the roof to let the smoke of the fire out, just as the longhouse in Karlstad had.

'Here she is,' Hilde grinned as she picked up the infant from her box on the floor, lined with blankets. The child's eyes were shut, and her body swaddled tightly.

'Have you named her yet?'

'No name yet. My husband usually names our lot, but now that he is gone, I do not have the heart for the task.' She sniffled back a tear.

Hilde placed the sleeping babe in my arms, and I cuddled her close to my chest. 'She is beautiful.' Her downy hair was soft and fair.

'Sit, sit,' Hilde ordered, motioning to a stool next to her chair.

'Can I make a suggestion?' I asked.

'About her name?'

'Oh, no. Not about the name, about your family. I think it might help you spend more time out here rather than coming into the town to work, which might be quite impossible anyway with the new baby.'

'I have always done it before.'

'But you had your husband then.' The words tumbled from my mouth before I realised the hurt they may do. 'I am sorry. I did not mean to sound so harsh, just that you had someone to watch the children before.'

She nodded. 'I am no business voman, Signe.'

'You don't need to be. What I want is for someone to experiment with dyes. I have in mind a particular set of colours I want to achieve, but it really needs to be done outside the town where there is a lot of fresh air. So, if you do not mind a bit of stench, then…'

She did not seem immediately taken with the idea.

'I will pay you well,' I added, hoping to make the deal more attractive.

'The smell does not bother me. There is plenty of air here to take it away, but I do not know the first thing about dyeing.'

'I will teach you.'

'You know nothing about it either.' She tossed her head back and snorted as she called my bluff.

'Well then, we shall learn together.' I grinned, and we shook on our agreement.

Taking my leave of Hilde and her family, I wandered home. Instead of going directly across the bridge to the town gates, I veered off, heading for the docks. I could not say what led me there apart from a curiosity to see if it had changed much since my arrival. Since that first day, I had no reason to return to it, but today I felt a pull in that direction. Most of the town's news came aboard trading vessels, and being at the mouth of the Volkhov River meant we were the first or the last to receive information, depending on where the ship had come from.

As I ambled down the grassy slope, careful not to slip on the path, I could hear raised voices. A couple of men, pulling wagons loaded with goods, took up the path and I jumped out of their way, looking around another cart to see where the voices were coming from. A crowd of ten-or-so people had gathered around two men who I assumed to be traders.

'It was a slaughter,' the shorter of the two exclaimed to the crowd.

A small woman covered her eyes. 'What happened to them all?' she asked, peering through her fingers.

His brown eyes opened wide as he answered her, 'All gone.'

I slipped into the gathering to hear the tale.

'All five thousand?' a man asked disbelievingly.

The short trader nodded so hard his cap fell from his head. He caught it before it hit the floor. 'So they say, though I find it hard to believe.' The short man pulled on his cap, covering his eyes, his salty grey hair protruding from the hat at his ears.

'But that is the report,' his tall friend confirmed, both nodding at each other.

'How could they do that?' the small woman cried.

The tall traders' jowls flapped about as he shook his head, 'Those Franks and Carolingians see the strong Northman as a threat.'

'As well they should,' his short friend added.

The tall man shrugged and continued, 'They do not understand us, but they know our measure. Raiders will always come until those Franks learn to live with us and honour the agreements they make. They cannot make promises and then turn their backs on us!' My father had said the same many years before. It seemed this was an ongoing disagreement.

'But the Northmen fought well,' the short trader beamed.

'NORTHMEN!' The crowd erupted into unanimous cheering at the mention. 'And to Valhalla, the fallen,' a man shouted from the crowd before it dispersed.

Satisfied with the news that they had heard the gathered people left, walking up the path towards the town. I hung back, hoping for some further details that I may have missed with my late arrival.

'*Hej, Landi*,' I greeted him, recognising him as a man of my homeland.

He grasped my forearm and smiled. 'Did you hear the news?'

'Only the end and that we did not fare well in the battle. Was it news of a particular raiding party?'

He shook his head, scrunching his weathered nose in disagreement. 'No, it was a settlement.'

'Similar to Aldeigjuborg?'

'This was a settlement in its infancy, only being there for a season before the people who had granted its establishment wiped it out.'

'What land were they from? Do you know?'

'They were from a previous settlement in the Saxon lands. For reasons unknown to me, they left and set up a settlement on the Scheldt River,' he reported.

'Well, that is quite a journey from the north to the west and then to Frankia,' I mumbled.

'*Ja*,' he agreed.

I crossed my arms in front of me. 'Where is the Scheldt?'

'It is the river that marks the border between the east and west of the Frankish Empires, quite important I believe, though I've not been there myself.'

'Me neither, only heard of it in passing. And you say they are all slaughtered?'

'Who?' He scratched his cheek.

'The Northmen of that settlement on the Scheldt.'

He cracked his neck. 'I doubt they slaughtered them all. Hardly possible. Someone always gets away to tell the news to someone else. Though the Franks might well want to spread the news themselves if they think it will buy them some time without a raid. The information will reach other settlements and before we know it, there will be another battle and those Frankish scum will die by the sword and axe, just as they slaughtered ours. They should enjoy the quiet now before we bring the Lady Hel upon them,' he raged passionately. 'With Thor's help.'

'With Thor's help,' I agreed.

'*Ja.*'

'Thank you for telling me what you know. Although it is not good news, it has been a long time since I heard any talk of battles. It makes me think of my father.' I smiled fondly as I squeezed the trader's arm in farewell.

Back up the hill I ambled and over the bridge towards the town gates, nodding to the guard as I passed. The sky was full of clouds, heavy dark grey clouds. *Rain*, I thought as I hurried home.

'Just a quick kiss,' a young man said as I rounded the corner to my house.

'Not here,' I heard Helga's giggle. She pushed him away.

Mikel's shoulders slumped. 'Alright, but you have to give me kisses when you are my wife.' He chuckled, leaning into his betrothed who melted towards him.

'Oh, I will,' she promised.

Not wanting to embarrass them or make them feel like I was listening, I coughed loudly. The pair broke apart and leaned on opposite sides of the landing rail, pretending to look out at the street.

'Does Luca know you have flown the coop?' I teased Mikel.

He bowed his head. 'I may have snuck out for a moment to visit my lady.'

'I am not yours yet!' Helga smiled. 'And if Luca releases you, I might just refuse to marry a man without a position.' She giggled as he took her hand.

'Every moment without you is torture,' he whispered, gently releasing her hand from his.

Mikel ran away, down the road to return to his master. I stifled a laugh at the display of young love. 'We might have found the solution to our problems, Helga,' I said as we walked into the hearth room.

'Oh, yes?' She arched her brow, a dreamy smile still fixed on her mouth.

'Your mother.'

'And how is she the answer to our problems?'

'She has agreed to experiment with the dyes, so I do not have to do it here.'

'She will enjoy having something else to do. Now that Father is gone, she doesn't like being stuck out there on her own.'

'And we desperately need to have the process done out of town. By all accounts, it can be a pungent process. Best to be done where their air is more plentiful.'

'Did you visit her?' she asked, looking at the axe tied to my belt.

'I was on my way back from the forest. It was about time I got back to using this,' I said as I unfastened the axe from my waist, laying it upon the table.

'I have never used a weapon,' Helga whispered, admiring mine.

'Let's hope you never have to,' I replied as I moved the axe from the table and propped it up against the wall. Looking for a distraction from what I heard down at the docks, I changed the subject to business. 'The weather is warming, and the sheep will soon have their coats shorn. We need to make sure we are ready.'

'Do you want me to speak with the ladies to make sure all the preparations are being made?' she asked.

We sat at the table. 'That would be good. Helga, I need you to be my support in this.'

She nodded emphatically. 'Of course.'

'And learning a little more and taking a higher position, even when you marry Mikel.'

She blushed, and I reminded myself she was still young and prone to easy embarrassment. 'Do you think he would like that?'

'Like what?'

'Would he want me to be more than just a wife?' she asked, picking up a tuft of wool from the table.

'It matters more to me what you want.'

Helga twisted the wool in her fingers until it became a thread. 'I am not sure.'

'Be sure that you begin your marriage in the manner you wish it to continue. You should always keep some time for yourself.'

'Should I continue working as Mother did?'

'If you want to, and I hope you will do.' I smiled, reaching out for her hand.

She squeezed my fingers. 'I would like that.'

'Good, then from now I would like you to act as a go-between for myself and the staff, the women and your mother. We must ensure our product is better than whatever else is available on the market.'

She nodded; her chest puffed with pride.

'And I must put this away,' I said, motioning to the axe against the wall. 'Otherwise, people would think we were hiding a warrior within these walls.'

TWENTY-TWO

Early morning darkness could not soothe me back to sleep. I lay awake, staring at the dark figures that seemed to stand watching me in my room. They had plagued my dreams with battle scenes. I blamed my recent uptake of Skara, and my hearing of the slaughter of the settlers on the Scheldt. In my dreams I saw Sven, my onetime best friend, trapped in between two rivers of blood. My dreaming mind watched him as he became stranded to slaughter, like those who had lost their lives at Thimeon.

That was impossible, I reminded myself. He could not have been there because he was off raiding some far off coast, not a settlement of men and women from our homelands. Perhaps he had already had his adventure and, after finding wealth and renown, had contented himself with tending his mother's crops and finding a pleasant wife to have his children. Knowing Sven, he would never be content with one adventure, and he would not stop until the skalds had enshrined his name in some song of great battles. My friend, the man of such enthusiasm that he would see nothing to block his path, would always see a way through, but as I saw him standing, I sensed the danger that surrounded him.

'Sven be careful,' I called, and even though I was asleep, my scream was muffled as I yelled the warning. My hands covered my eyes against the raging river of blood, and all was calm again and my dreams took me to a field of flowers. I knew it well. Sven and I would often lay in its green pastures in the springtime, surrounded by budding *forglemmegei*, their small blue flowers that would tickle our noses until we sneezed. Unlike times before, I now wandered the field alone, following the sound of rapidly flowing water while my hands waved through the long grass. When I reached the body of water, instead of the crystal-clear water I had expected, the water ran red with blood just like the Scheldt. Thunder hammered in my chest, and in the middle of the stream, bodies were piled high, causing the water to divert to flow around the gruesome mound. The body atop the pile I recognised by his broad shoulders and fair head of hair.

'Sven? Sven, no!' I plunged myself into the fast-flowing water, racing to my friend's side. He was long dead and, even as I turned him over, I saw I could not save him, for he was covered with the deep slashes that had ended his life. I screamed, clawing at him in a desperate attempt to bring him back to life.

'No!' I yelled again at his lifeless body.

'Signe?' a soft voice called my assumed name from a distance, drawing me from the torments that were Astrid's.

My screaming continued, though now it was more of a garbled sound.

'Signe?' the voice called again as I felt my body being gently rocked from my sleep.

I wanted to stay with him, save him. How could I save him if I left now? My body thrashed against the rocking, willing myself to stay in the dreamland, to run towards my friend and hold him.

'Signe!' the voice called more urgently now as the rocking became more violent. I could feel my body slipping from my dreaming as my awareness came back to my room in the house that had once been Neflaug's and now was mine. My eyes opened, focussing on Helga standing over me, concerned etched on her face. 'You were crying out in your sleep.'

Tears threatened to come, and I blinked them back. 'Was it real? It felt so real.'

'They often do.' She calmed me, smoothing her hand over my hair. 'It must have been a terrible dream for you to cry out so loudly.'

'It was.'

'Will you try to go back to sleep? It is early, but I can stay with you until you if you like.' She slotted her hand in mine.

'I'm fine, really Helga. You go and I will follow in a moment.' I patted her hand before she left and once she had closed the door, wished a silent hope that what I had just dreamed was not some sort of seeing. The sight had never come to me before, and it was likely that Sven was off somewhere enjoying the spoils of his raid from the season before. All would be well.

Flinging the furs from the bed, I rolled to the side and slid my feet down onto the floor. The morning was cool and my underdress was thin but still I did not want to dress. It would be hours before anyone else would join us. Now it would be just Helga and me in the hearth room, and she would be too busy with her morning work to worry about my state of undress.

'What has caused these night terrors?' Helga wondered as I joined her in the hearth room, slumping down onto the bench as she busied herself at the fire.

'It must have been the stories I heard down at the dock yesterday,' I replied, rubbing my chilled hands.

'That might be the same tale I heard here in town. Tea? It's nettle, your favourite.' She smiled as she set the drink in front of me.

'Thank you.'

'Was it Anders? The old sailor?'

'I don't know his name.'

'Did he say the Frankish had killed a whole settlement of Northmen?' Helga asked.

I nodded mutely, drifting into the swirling leaves in my tea.

'You think that caused your bad dream?'

I blew on the hot drink to cool it. 'Perhaps it brought someone to mind.'

Helga looked concerned now, rushing to me. 'A friend that could be dead? In this battle?'

'No, not in Thimeon. That is not possible. Ow, the tea is hot,' I cried, nursing my burned lips. 'No, he could not have been there.'

'Then how is this dream about the battle? Or...'

'The dream was not about Thimeon. Anders, did you say that was his name? Yes, Anders said the river ran red with the blood of the settlers. In my dream, I found my friend in a pile of bodies at the fork of two rivers that flowed with blood,' I tried my best to explain.

Helga covered her eyes with her hands. 'That's worse than anything I could imagine.' She shook her head, dislodging the imagery. 'You must care very much for this person, a man?'

My voice caught in my throat. 'He was my best friend.'

'Was?'

I pushed my tea away to avoid scalding myself again. 'It has been such a long time since I have seen him. I wouldn't know what he is to me anymore. And if I did, I'm almost certain I will never see him again.'

'Did you love him?' she asked, the question coming without introduction.

'Love him as a friend and a brother? Yes! I can say that without hesitation.'

Helga stopped with her busywork and sat down, staring into my eyes. 'No, Signe. You know what I am asking. Did you love him?'

'I do not know.'

'Maybe you did not know then, but do now?' She was not holding back.

'Perhaps I loved Sven years ago but now I do not know, but I do not want him dead. Oh Helga, what if he is dead?' I asked helplessly.

She shrugged. 'He could be, and if he was, how would that change the way you felt?'

I could not answer. I had never thought of Sven as dead, only myself as gone, and being the one who left made me feel like everything had remained the same where I had left it. Certainly, Sven would have gone raiding with Jarl Soren and his men, but in my mind, he had remained the same. He did not age, he did not weaken, he would never die.

'All I know is that it hurts.' My answer was strained, and my hand clutched at the dress above my heart as if the action would still the painful beating for a moment.

'So, Signe, what will you do?' she asked mischievously, as if she had heard Loki whisper something devious in her ear.

'There is nothing I can do.'

She tutted me. 'You surprise me. It is not like you to crumple like the fallen leaves. There is always something that can be done.' She smiled, her green eyes glinting.

Her expression lightened my mood, and I laughed. 'Then tell me, oh wise Helga of Aldeigjuborg, what must I do?'

She placed her elbows on the table, bringing her fists to the space between her chin and cheeks. Her hands rolled the skin of her face, squishing it forward as she thought. 'Hmm, you go to your gods, and you ask them for a sign. Ask them for a sign of your friend's life and once you have your answer, then you will know what to do.' Helga had made an excellent suggestion.

When I had needed guidance before, I had sought answers at Uppsala from the *völva*, but this was different. There was no *völva* for me to ask, none that were visiting at least. I would have to ask the gods myself and the answers that they may provide would not be clear for me to see as they might when you consult someone with the gift, but it was the only way.

'I will,' I agreed.

'And what of Kjarr?'

I looked up at her. 'What does any of this have to do with him?'

'Do you think it is fair to make Kjarr jealous of a man he has never met and could not possibly hope to remove from your heart?' She stared at me unflinchingly.

'He is not in competition.'

Helga cocked her head to the side. 'He loves you, Signe. Are you blind to the way he looks at you?'

'You are wrong. He might want me in his bed, but love is too far.'

'I think it is you that is wrong,' she commanded. My onetime maid, now friend, looked little older than a child, yet spoke with a truth beyond her years and did not bother herself with how uncomfortable it would make me feel. I had to respect that. She seemed duty bound to make the truth as she saw it known. 'Kjarr respects you far too much to put you in that position. He would do anything for you, I know it. Whether you want to admit it, Kjarr and Sven are in competition. They are both in your mind, and in your heart.' She pressed her hand to my chest.

Kjarr's feelings had been obvious for some time, but I refused to acknowledge them and, as for my own feelings, I knew I was not ready to acknowledge them either. 'When did you become so wise, Helga?'

'A woman in love surely knows all the truth in the world,' she replied with a peaceful smile, as if she had suddenly come into the knowledge of everything. I had to return her enthusiasm. Maybe loving and being loved in return gave one the contentment that I lacked, but it was not a step I was yet prepared to take.

A knock at the door startled us both from our thoughts. Helga stood, straightening her plain brown dress, and made for the door, opening it just far enough to peer around. She looked over her shoulder, grinning widely at me.

'Who is it?' I mouthed at her.

She turned back to the door, her face masked with mock surprise. 'Oh, Kjarr! You call so early. Is everything alright?'

Suddenly aware of my lack of clothing, I pulled at my garment to gather it in front of me, hiding my body clearly visible underneath. Helga held the door fast, giving me a moment to think of something.

His voice was deep and smooth, clearly, he had been awake for some time. 'I hope it is not too early,' he spoke in a hushed voice now.

'The sun is not yet awake,' she complained. Her hair was already braided, and she had long since donned her apron.

'You are right, it is too early. I will come back later.'

Grabbing my apron from the wall, I tied it around myself, looping it over my neck, hoping to provide some modesty. 'Helga, it's alright let him in.'

She stepped back from the door and opened it widely. 'We have been awake for some time, bad dreams, I am afraid.' She set about her work again, providing small ale for us, and once she had set the cups down, she excused herself from the room.

Kjarr's eyes assessed me from across the table. 'Is everything alright?'

I shrugged. 'It is nothing more than bad dreams caused by a scary tale.'

He sipped at his drink. 'Ah! The battle at Thimeon? Yes, I heard of this too. Anyone you know?'

'No, at least I hope not.'

He nodded, and a sad smile found his lips. 'I have come to say goodbye, well, not goodbye. That sounds so final. More a farewell, for now.'

I pushed my cup from side-to-side on the table before me. 'So, you have finally decided to leave? I am glad of it.' I was happy that Kjarr would leave for this important trading mission, but now, given my discussion with Helga, I was also aware of this strange tension that lingered between us. 'When will you leave?' I asked, looking up into his sad eyes, rimmed with dark circles that marked a lack of sleep.

'Just waiting for my men now. They have been told to prepare and tend to their business. I have given them two days.'

I looked down, hoping to hide my surprise. 'So soon.'

His hand shot across the table and grasped mine. 'Will you come and see me off? If you have time, of course.'

There was a shuffle outside the door. Helga! She might have excused herself, but she was nosy enough to linger by the door to hear the words we spoke. 'I will have time. Helga will make sure of it.' I spoke loudly, letting my maid know I had discovered her overhearing us.

She walked back into the room in a huff. 'Oh, I will make sure she is there.'

Turning back to Kjarr, I managed a smile, squeezing his hand in return and releasing it. 'You might miss all the excitement while you are away.'

'The excitement of Aldeigjuborg?' Helga chimed with a laugh. 'No, I think an adventure to the heart of trade might be a little more exciting than here.'

'I always miss Aldeigjuborg when I am away.' Kjarr laughed and it sounded empty. 'Now I think I will miss it more than ever,' he said as he looked at me.

Dodging his gaze and the direction of the conversation, I pointed to Helga. 'I meant your wedding, Helga.'

Kjarr turned and threw his hands up. 'I hope to be back before then. I really don't think I will be gone that long.'

The reminder of her marriage sparked a giddy spark within Helga flitted about, collecting the half full cups of ale. 'It would depend on when you return and if my brothers and Mikel ever finish our house.'

'How are they progressing?' I asked, not having been out to visit the site myself.

'Thank God summer is here. They can start building upon the bones of the structure and once they are going with it, then it should be finished before the winter comes.'

My head nodded in agreement, but my mind stilled, disturbed by something Helga had said. 'Did you just say, "Thank God," Helga?'

'Mm-hmm,' she hummed as she returned to the pot on the fire in the hearth.

'The Christian God?'

She nodded into the bubbling pot.

'You never said you were a Christian.'

She turned to face me. 'My belief has never been an issue in this house before.'

'And it is not now, but it may be for your wedding.'

Kjarr's eyes widened, and he looked fit to burst with laughter. In their hurry to couple, I doubted Helga and Mikel had discussed their differing faiths. 'You know, Mikel believes in the old gods. He is not a Christian.'

'How very interesting.' Kjarr stroked his chin and his mouth twisted, suppressing a laugh.

Helga toyed with the edge of her apron, her mind visibly whirring. 'We have never spoken of such things before. I admit we have been a little busy and well…. I never thought to ask it.'

'Our wedding traditions may be a little different from each other,' I warned.

'You may want to decide where you want to have your wedding, and how you will do things,' Kjarr suggested.

Her interest piqued; Helga leaned towards him. 'Where do your marriages take place?'

I recalled my own marriage with a grimace, 'Outside.'

'And you have a holy man to oversee the vows?'

'Guess you could say that,' I agreed, although the priest I had met in the Aldeigjuborg church was not at all like a Gothi in my mind.

'Such an ordeal,' she exhaled in exasperation.

Kjarr patted Helga on the shoulder. 'It does not have to be. Just speak to him about it,' he suggested, smiling in my direction.

'It seems I have a lot to think about suddenly,' she said. A tiny smile crept across her lips as she looked at me. 'I expect we both do.'

TWENTY-THREE

That night, in my sleepy haze, I thought I heard knocking upon the front door.

'Not again,' I murmured into the darkness, thinking terrors were stalking me in the blackness of night yet again. Closing my eyes heightened my hearing, but as I listened, there was nothing but silence.

No one would call on me at such an hour, I thought, eyes blinking. Though yesterday, Kjarr had called long before the sun rose. This was far too early for anything decent. I closed my eyes, willing myself to return to sleep, but the sound came again. The knocking was faster this time and a little louder. Hurried. Urgent. Even desperate. Helga would not open the door at this time if she were here, but she wasn't. I was alone.

What if it was danger? I wondered, lying unmoving in my bed, deciding whether to chance my rising and answering the door. What if it was important?

The knocking continued in anguished little raps against the heavy wooden door. Rolling out of the comfort of my bed, I stumbled to the door, grabbing a shawl to guard against the coolness of the summer night's air. As I entered the hearth room, where the fire was extinguished, the knocking was frantic. Then it stopped, and a heavy thud on the landing followed the silence. My heart thumped in my chest as my hand grasped the door, turning the handle to open it to the spirit on my doorstep. A slumped woman lay in front of my door, Neflaug.

I blinked slowly, willing my vision to be a lie. 'What are you doing here?'

Her eyes were full of terror and confusion. 'The baby,' she sobbed as she clutched her massive, rounded belly.

'I cannot help you, Neflaug, but I will fetch a birthing woman to come to you.'

She slammed her hand against the door, refusing to let me shut her out. 'You made an oath. A promise to me that you would… Oowwww… Help me, when the time came.'

Cold washed over me as I realised, she had come to make good on the promise I never should have made. My father's words rang in my ear "The time will come when they call on the debt you have unwittingly accepted." Why had I not remembered his warning? Why had I been so rash to make such an oath, even one I never thought I would have to fulfil? I was no oath-breaker, and I would not have the gods think that of me, so I crouched down to Neflaug now and helped her to her feet. 'You best come in quickly.'

She stumbled into the house, groaning as she walked.

'Have you travelled far?' I asked, bending low to build the fire in the hearth. The night air was not cold, but the baby would need warmth when it arrived.

She nodded. 'I can go no further,' she moaned, breathing deeply and clutching at the end of the table. 'You promised,' she repeated, scared I would refuse her.

'I did.' She was right. I made the promise and now I was duty bound. The details I would worry about later. Fire sparked in the hearth, and I breathed life on the flame. Content that it would not go out, I laid some kindling and returned to Neflaug. 'How long have you had the birthing pains?'

Her eyes glazed over and sweat beaded upon her brow. 'Tightness,' she spoke, 'for two days.' She motioned to her middle, where the greatest breadth of the child lay. The tightness she referred to was likely the start of her labour, the squeezing that would eventually force the child out.

'Are they different now? More intense?' I recalled witnessing women in the longhouse who laboured for days and how the pains changed over time.

She nodded. 'Close together,' she breathed, as if she answered a far off voice. 'I can't do this!' she cried, her head rolling back and for a moment, she was unreachable.

'It is a little too late for that.' She turned her face from the table and vomited on the floor. 'It is alright, this is good,' I stood, walking towards her, avoiding the puddles of sick.

'Help me!' Neflaug cried, clutching my arm.

'Do not cry, it will only make it harder. Try to breathe,' I whispered, pressing my palms into the small of her back as she bent over the table.

The time that passed seemed both an eternity and only a moment. Neflaug laboured standing, crouching, and on all fours. She groaned, turned inwards silently and concentrated on breathing through the pain. All the while, we spoke of nothing more than the necessity of encouraging the baby from her body. Then the sounds changed. Her body moved into a rhythm of its own. Neflaug groaned loudly, turned her head, and then vomited once more.

'You are close now, not much longer.' In truth, I did not know if she was near her time, but the women I had seen birth their child almost always emptied their stomachs or bowels when they crossed the threshold to push the child out.

Neflaug sent out a low groan. 'I can feel pressure.'

I stood behind her as she doubled over the table. 'Where?'

Her hand motioned between her legs. 'There.'

'More than before? Oh, alright, here. Let me help you onto the table so you can lie on your back, and I can see.'

'I can't move!' she shouted at me. Neflaug slumped back into my arms, bearing down to a squat position. 'Push. I have to push.' From her came a low moan again, this time primal. I had heard it before. In this, animals and people bore little difference.

'Keep going, Neflaug, you can do it,' I urged as I bore her weight.

'Can't. No more. I can't do it,' she panted, in between breaths.

'You can,' I promised her. 'Make no noise, hold your breath and bear down,' I instructed. She did as I bid her, taking deep gasps for air in between her efforts. 'Good, good, and again.'

She sank back further into my arms and squatted low, groaning with each strain.

'It won't be long now, big push,' I told her, holding her weight on my forearms that burned like the fires of a funeral pyre.

She pushed again, but the baby did not emerge.

'Do you think you can get onto the table so I can look?' I asked.

'No,' she hissed.

Of course not, I should have known better. I considered my other options. 'Can I feel there to see if the baby is coming out?' I asked, wincing at my suggestion, but it was necessary.

She nodded.

Between her legs, I reached my hand. I could feel the soft downy hair and the dome of the infant's head. 'She's there!' I exclaimed. 'One last push should do it.'

Neflaug bore down, tucking her chin against her chest and pushed until her face was as red as a rooster's comb. The baby's crown had emerged. Now the shoulders had to pass and Neflaug could rest.

'Squat a little more,' I said, guiding her down to allow the baby to come out onto the floor without injury. 'Freyja, help me,' I begged my gods as I saw the infant's shoulder pass. Then the body slithered out without hindrance. Neflaug's head fell back, and she panted from the exertion. 'Neflaug, you did it. You have a baby girl, you were right,' I confirmed Neflaug's prediction that she would birth a girl child.

The baby squealed, looking for its mother. Neflaug turned her head away from the mewling child.

'Look at her, oh she is so beautiful,' I gushed, bending to take the baby in my arms. I sat on the floor as Neflaug birthed the afterbirth connected to the infant. In its markings, I saw *Yggdrasil*, the tree of life. The child's mouth rooted for sustenance, and I placed her on Neflaug's chest as she rested. 'Will you let her have your milk?'

Without looking at the baby, Neflaug undid the fastenings of her apron dress, taking it down to her waist and lifted her shirt, exposing her swollen breasts. The baby found its way to the nipple and there she suckled.

'You did so well,' I congratulated Neflaug. 'Will you look at her?' Once she held the baby, I thought she would feel some connection.

She remained silent.

Once the girl had her fill, she dozed sleepily against her mother's warmth, but Neflaug pushed her away and I picked up the sleeping baby. 'What will you do now?'

Neflaug crawled to her feet and stood up, her clothing stained and gait uneven. 'I don't know.'

'You could make a new life for the two of you,' I suggested, hoping she would reconsider.

She looked at me with a blank face. 'No.'

'You could. She is your child...' I began.

Neflaug walked unsteadily to the door, opening it. 'She is not mine.'

The child in my arms was powerless without her mother. I thought back to stories Hilde had told me about a young Neflaug and her desperation for offspring. Now that she had her own, how could she abandon it? I grabbed Neflaug's arm, stopping her. 'What will I tell people?'

'If you tell anyone about me, about this, I will come back for you,' she threatened, stepping out into the dark street and leaving me alone with her daughter.

The seer had been right. I recalled the wise woman's predictions as I looked down at the snoozing infant in my arms, oblivious to the surrounding turmoil. A mother, it seemed, I had become. 'Freyja,' I named her at that moment, hoping her namesake would bring us strength. 'Whatever is coming for us, we must now face together,' I whispered, cradling her against me.

Though Neflaug had done Freyja the kindness of feeding her once, I knew it would not fill the child's belly for long and if she had any hope of survival; I needed to keep her full. My feet walked the invisible line between the world that was real and the darkness I was still unsure I had really experienced. The warm bundle against my chest confirmed the truth and, as my feet mounted the steps of Hilde's house, my knuckle barely rapped against the door before I pushed it open to stand distraught in her dark house. Bleary brown eyes greeted me, deep lines around their edges and shadows below told me she too had not slept well.

'Signe?' Hilde's eyes searched the darkness behind me for danger.

Unable to speak, I shook my head, clutching at the mass at my chest. Hilde ushered me inside and sat me on a stood while her sleeping children surrounded us on the floor, still sound asleep.

'Vat are you doing here? Tell me you did not come all this vay alone?'

'I had no other choice.' I sniffed back the tears that choked my eyes and my throat.

She lowered her gaze to the tightly wrapped infant at my breast and gasped, her motherly eyes wide with disbelief. I did not know where to begin. The night had been traumatic, and I was not sure which parts to tell and which to omit. Afraid that if I opened my mouth, the entire night would tumble out and I would, at the first chance, betray my oath to Neflaug. I bowed my head, my ashen hair falling over my face, hiding my tear-filled eyes that promised to stream if I dared to speak another word.

She pulled me into her embrace, demanding only my yielding to her arms around me like a familiar blanket. Relief came as the tears streamed down my cheeks and my body wracked with sobs, but I had made the right decision. Now, I was not alone.

'Leaving the valls of the town at this time of night is very dangerous, Signe,' she whispered. The danger of a woman alone in the night had not crossed my mind. I had been too concerned with saving the child. Her life had depended on me seeking help and so I had run harder than I ever had before.

Hilde slipped a finger into the swaddling to see the infant's face. 'I von't ask vere you got the baby from, but I will ask you vat you vant to do vith it.' Her heavy accent was difficult to understand as she mumbled in hushed tones, careful not to disturb her own children from their dreams.

'I did not take it, if that's what you are asking.'

'It is not vat I thought. But it is clear she is not of your body or else you vould not be up and moving so freely,'

'I can tell you no more. A promise.'

Hilde squeezed my shoulder. 'Then I vill ask no more, though I think I know from vere the child comes, and I am both surprised and not that she gave her up to you. Give the child to me.' She held her hands out as I passed the baby over. 'Vat is her name?' she asked, inspecting the child's face.

'Freyja.'

'Is it a common name from your home?'

'The name of one of our gods. It will give her the strength to become everything her mother was not.'

Freyja roused. Her lips moved about the air, clicking her tongue. Desperation washed over me. 'She will have no strength if I cannot feed her.'

Hilde lifted her shirt and offered her nipple to the infant. 'You forget, my child is still at the breast. I can give her the milk she needs.'

The two fumbled to latch as Hilde tilted Freyja's head into position. 'At first she vill not know how to feed, only that she needs it, but in time she will get easier.' Freyja sucked loudly. 'Remember, she is new to this as vell,' Hilde replied, cradling Freyja in the crook of her arm.

'Her mother gave her the first milk but would stay no more and now, I do not know what to do,' I cried into my hands.

'She has had a good start, Signe. You have done vell. Now, leave her here vith me and go home to sleep. I vill bring her up with me, or Helga, in the morning.' A sleepy cry came from the basket next to Hilde's chair. 'Signe, can you pick up my *barn*? She also needs feeding.'

Scooping up the older baby, I passed her into her mother's care and there she also nursed, side-by-side with the newborn.

'Go home, Signe,' Hilde urged as her daughter's hungry cries were silenced by the rhythmic gulping and swallowing of milk.

Reluctantly, I stood to leave. 'You will have whatever you need. You need only name it.'

'We will speak in the morning.' Hilde rocked in her chair, gently closing her eyes as the two babies snoozed along with her.

I loitered at the door for a moment, watching their peaceful tableau. 'You shall be nothing like your mother,' I promised. The comment had been made for Freyja, but, as I wandered home in the dawning light, I realised it rang just as true for me.

PART FOUR

Will I see places
Of which I have dreamed?
Tall walls and great cities
People with strange faces,
Speak in strange voices.

The distance between us is great,
I think of you often.
The wide open spaces
Of my homeland
Still etched on my heart.

Twenty-Four

Summer 881CE, Aldeigjuborg, Gardarike

That night, between fits of restless dozing, I dreamed of my mother. She was the ever-perfect housekeeper. Her pots were the cleanest in the settlement, of that she had some renown. But maternal care was thin. She only understood her own ambitions, and for mine; she goaded me constantly.

When I was a girl, I scorned love after being burned by it. Instead, I wanted a life of my own; to make my own decisions. Now I found myself with a name I had stolen, in charge of an abandoned child, tangled and confused. At some point, I must have angered the gods. No doubt the Norns were now laughing at me. I groaned. Sleep would not come with such an active mind, and despite my efforts; I could not quieten the thoughts.

I wandered from my room into the hearth room and immediately wished I had not. Blood in pools and stained cloth lay where they had fallen mere hours before. My mind measured the time it would take to clean the mess as my body slid down the wall to the floor in a defeated heap. Woodgrain of the table took me back to Neflaug's hands clutching at its end as she birthed her daughter. There wasn't enough energy in the world that could right the mess, let alone the situation I now found myself in. The room was closing in around me. Darkness deepening like a yawning cave, with only the smallest of lights from a distance far away. Then the sobs came. I tried to hold them, but they overcame me, washing my body with grief.

'Hush, Signe.' I heard Helga's soft voice as her arms wrapped around me and she sat with me on the floor, one of her long brown braids brushing my cheek. 'Mama sent me.'

I held her tightly, never more appreciative of her warm companionship. 'She came back, didn't she?'

I nodded into her burdock scented hair. 'And swore me not to tell anyone.' Yet here I was, breaking that oath at my second opportunity. Some burdens could not be borne alone.

Helga pulled away, holding me at arm's length. Once I had thought of her as plain but, in the two summers I had known her, the beauty she held inside had illuminated the features of her face. 'I would say that I didn't believe it, but nothing Neflaug could do would surprise me anymore.' Her brown eyes held disappointment at recalling our previous master's behaviour.

'I could not let the poor *barn* die,' I cried.

Helga held me again. 'Of course, you would not do that. You have a heart, Signe.'

A heart was a curse. I was too soft, and it had come at a heavy price. Over her shoulder, I eyed the disarray. 'Will you help me?'

She stood, taking my hand and pulling me to my feet. 'Tssk. You should not have to ask.'

We set about the task on our hands and knees, a bucket of water between us and scrubbing brushes in hand. 'I am not sure we will ever get the blood out of the floor,' I complained, wringing the water from the hem of my work dress.

'We will,' Helga promised, scrubbing with a vigour that defied her stature. 'I have seen worse than this.'

The sun was high in the sky before we scrubbed the place clean, then, gathering the rags and brushes, together we set about our work.

'No one would be the wiser.' Helga smiled.

'Thank you,' I said, returning her smile. 'But we must change from these clothes, or someone will know or at least figure something has happened. I might say "burn them" but I loathe to be wasteful.'

'We will keep it for messy work in the future.'

From my rough spun dress of brown, I changed into my blue summer dress, and Helga changed into another plain work garment.

To the laundry tub, we added our soiled clothing to soak in cold water until it could be washed, leaving it out of sight in Neflaug's room.

'Now, where is my mother with that baby of yours so I can pinch her little cheeks?' Helga asked excitedly, her fingers moving nimbly as she re-plaited her hair.

'She is not really mine,' I replied, grabbing my apron from the peg on the wall and placing it over my head.

Helga put a pot over the fire, adding water and oats. 'She is now.'

'Mm-hmm,' I agreed, occupied by the substantial weight of it all. 'But I know nothing about babies.'

Helga opened the warehouse door and stepped out of sight. She emerged holding a shallow basket usually used for storing wool. 'This will serve well enough as a little cot for her, for now. Maybe I can ask Mikel and Luca to make a cradle for her.'

'I will do that later.'

With the basket on the table, Helga placed a pelt of fur inside, still attached to its hide. She carefully tucked in the excess towards the bottom of the basket.

'We will need a little blanket for her.' I joined in on the bed making, finally feeling like I was doing something of use.

'And then we will just carry her from room to room while she sleeps. Someone will always be watching over her and little *barns* do little else than sleeping for the first few weeks,' she offered helpfully. 'And when she can move a bit, you will have to learn as you go. No woman is born with knowledge. Everyone must learn.'

I walked into the warehouse, making my way through the weaving equipment to unbolt the great doors in expectation of my worker women's arrival at any moment. The sun streamed in and its warmth on my weary face was a welcome reprieve from my earthly bindings.

'Have you recovered yet?' Hilde asked, her thick accented voice jolting me from my daydream. She waddled into the warehouse laden with bags and holding a baby in each arm, both content in the embrace.

I shook my head. 'Not sure I ever will.'

'You will,' she said, thrusting Freyja into my arms. 'It is time you took to mothering.'

I stroked the pale pink cheek of the child. 'Was she good?'

Hilde tutted. 'A baby is neither good nor bad. They are all the same. They eat, they sleep, they soil themselves. That is all she vill do for the first few veeks at least.'

It was not possible for me to think weeks ahead. I was capable only of now, or it all might quickly overwhelm me. 'I made her a bed in a wool basket,' I mumbled, suddenly aware that the contribution was so small, and I felt foolish for even mentioning it.

'Good, at least she has somewhere to sleep. You bring her to me when she needs nursing,' Hilde ordered, unshouldering her heavy bag and rocking her own daughter in her unburdened arms.

'So, I just watch her and wait until she is hungry?'

She nodded. 'You still have a business to run.'

The task of watching a child somehow seemed so onerous. How could a woman manage it all and still get anything else done? 'How will I know when she needs nursing?' I asked Hilde.

'You knew vell enough that she vould need food ven you brought her to me. I think you vill know.' She gave me an understanding look. 'You need to trust yourself but she vill make a sound like "neh neh". Speaking of hunger, I need feeding myself. Making milk enough for two *barns* is hungry vork.'

I took Hilde's own child, Alva, from her arms and held her in tandem with Freyja. 'Helga is inside fixing breakfast. Eat as much as you need,' I replied, ushering Hilde into the next room.

To hold two children was heavy work, and I found it cumbersome to eat whilst one was resting against my arm and the other nearby in the basket. 'You make it look so easy, Hilde.'

I watched the woman, who shrugged as if it were nothing. Together, we filled our bellies with warm porridge as Helga gushed over the little ones. Even Helga made simple work of holding both, planting sweet kisses over their tiny faces.

'Alva, my sister, what a beauty you are and little Freyja, you are an angel,' she gushed as she surfaced from the babies' swaddling.

After we finished our meal, we sat in a comfortable silence, enjoying the respite before the day's work. I glanced over at Hilde, unsure if she was asleep in her place or merely resting her eyes. 'What will I do with Freyja at night-time?' I asked her daughter.

Hilde opened one eye and answered me. 'Each night you bring her to me so that I feed her through the night. That is important for one so young. Ven she is veaned from the milk. She can stay with you in the night, but that von't be for some time.'

'It is a lot of work for you.'

She nodded. 'Ve do vat ve must.'

'Is there anything you need? Anything I can do for you?'

'Just more food. Feeding two babies is hard on the body. It drains me.'

I heaped another helping into her bowl. 'You will have everything you need, and I hope you know how much I care for both of you.' I looked up with tears in my eyes, knowing that I had pulled these women into the tangle I had agreed to.

'We are a family now.' Helga smiled, and her mother nodded with a wink. 'But you must explain a baby, Signe. The women here know better than to ask questions of you. They will know there is a good reason, but the townspeople can be suspicious or worse, quick to make up some scandal.' She raised her eyebrows with the warning. Helga placed the babies, side-by-side in the basket. 'I don't think people will question you if you say you concealed the pregnancy, but they will want to know who the father is.'

I sighed heavily.

'They would suspect him as soon as you appeared with the babe,' Helga whispered, rubbing my shoulders.

'Who?' Hilde asked her daughter.

Helga rolled her eyes. 'You know very well, Mama.'

Freyja cried, and I recognised the "neh" sound Hilde had earlier described. I gently passed her to Hilde, who, without blinking, attached the infant to her breast.

'Signe, he leaves this afternoon,' Helga reminded me.

'Even Kjarr the wise will not have seen this coming,' I predicted as I opened the door. He was bound to be closing his house as we spoke. If not already down at the docks loading the ship, I had to hurry. 'Will you be alright without me?' I asked, looking back over my shoulder.

Helga waved me away with her hand, 'Hurry!'

Bleary-eyed and nerves affray, I stumbled to Kjarr's door. My feet retraced the steps I had trod so many times before. He answered the door without my knocking, as if he knew I would be there. His tawny hair, usually worn neatly pulled back, was hanging loosely above his shoulders in a dishevelled mess. In his eyes was his usual intensity, though I sensed he was distracted.

'Your hair, Kjarr!' I reached out a hand to tuck the loose hanging locks behind his ear.

His hand grabbed mine and clung to it. 'Come in, but be warned, I am in the middle of packing the last of my things and the house is in a state.'

Still hand-in-hand and taking a deep breath, I stepped over the threshold into his dark home. His hearth was cleaned and emptied, furniture shrouded, and window openings covered to guard against his absence. He did not overestimate the disruption of his abode. Clothes were strewn over every piece of cloth-covered furniture and rune sticks lay in piles, scattered about the floor.

Kjarr crouched over a small chest, looking up at me with eyes clouded by confusion, 'I thought you would see me off at the docks?'

'Are you leaving now? I thought it would be this afternoon?'

'It still will be. My shipmaster miscalculated the tides,' he explained as he disappeared beneath a pile of clothing.

'What did you say?'

He looked up. 'I said it doesn't bode well if my shipmaster is already making mistakes.' He laughed nervously. 'Kari comes highly recommended by a friend.'

'Is there anything I can help you with?' I asked, wading through the mess to kneel beside him.

'Hand me that comb, will you?' He pointed at the bone comb beside my knee.

I fingered the rivets which secured the teeth of the comb to its handle. Kjarr's journey would take him away for many months, far away to meet with someone from the land of the Serkir, in search of establishing a regular shipment of their silver that was equal to none. His presence would be missed, and I had come to rely on his sage advice and friendly wisdom.

'What have you done now?' Kjarr asked, eyeing me with suspicion.

I passed him the comb. 'You never miss a thing, do you?'

'With you? Never.' He stuffed the comb into the chest and slammed it shut. 'Come on, tell me.'

'Where to start?'

'Like this, "Kjarr, I did this thing," and then you say,' he began imitating me.

I shook my head. 'This is serious.'

He stopped and grasped my hand. 'You can tell me.'

'I have a baby.'

When his eyes narrowed, his mouth opened to speak. But before he could find his words, it closed again. His hand went limp around mine.

'It is not of my body, but she is mine now,' I tried to explain.

'Then how could you have a baby? Is there anything you have been hiding from me?' he asked jokingly, but I could feel his underlying fear at what I was about to divulge.

'Do you really think I could have hidden a pregnancy from my closest friends? That, I am sure, you would have noticed.'

'It's Neflaug's baby, isn't it?'

Tears welled in my eyes, threatening to spill. 'I promised I would not say.'

'You don't have to, I know it. Who else would it be?' He shrugged heavily. 'How have you become saddled with that burden?'

'An oath I never thought I would have to make good on. The gods curse me! I should have known better,' I lamented.

'Astrid, how are we going to explain this?' he worried. 'You will not face this alone; I promise you. Does the child have a name yet?'

'Freyja.'

'A girl? How nice, and a good name,' he mused, releasing my hand to rub his chin thoughtfully. 'Is our story to be that you concealed the pregnancy? Am I to be the father? Have we married in secret?' he posited aloud. 'Or.' There was a moment of hesitation. 'Is there someone else you wish to take the child?'

The suggestion took me by surprise. Even considering other options made me uncomfortable. 'Luca has long expressed the desire for offspring, though if he were to find out the child was Neflaug's, and with his dislike of her…'

'I understand.'

Could I give Freyja to another when I had made the promise? 'And how would they feed a newborn?'

'Have you a wet-nurse for the child?'

'Hilde. She has a daughter not much older, and she is willing. She does so for the care she bears for me. I could not dare assume that would transfer any further. No, Freyja stays with me.'

'Do you want me to delay the trip again? Shall I stay?' he asked me hopefully.

I put my hand against his chest. 'No, Kjarr. Not again. Really, it will be alright. Knowing I have you to help me is a great comfort, and Helga and Hilde will help me, too. Freyja will know no greater love anywhere else. With me and my women, other children will surround her.'

He sighed in relief and smoothed his hand through his ruffled hair. 'The gods already favour the child.'

'I hope so.' On the floor, next to Kjarr's chest of belongings, I sat cross-legged and picked up a scarf, toying with it to keep my hands and mind distracted.

Kjarr mused for a moment before speaking. 'I worry about something,' he began.

'More than the worries we have now?'

He stopped. 'You say your first marriage was unwanted, and when I first met you that you would never marry again. Now you find yourself in a position that demands a marriage to cover someone else's scandal. That is not what I want for you. Nor do I want you to resent me if I become your husband.'

'Do you have another plan?'

He laughed lightly. 'You could always brave the wagging tongues.'

I had thought of this also, 'But the business.'

'You are right that it might affect some people's thinking of you.'

'That cannot be. Too many depend on me for their livelihood. No. This is the only way.' Sorrow filled my eyes as I met his gaze. 'But I promise not to blame you, nor resent you in time.'

'Well,' he declared, 'if we are going to do this, we must do so properly.'

I raised my eyebrows. 'We must?'

Amusement shadowed his face, 'Not that! You have my word. A proper marriage in that manner was not my thinking, just that we conduct the process of getting married correctly.'

'We do not have the time.'

Kjarr hummed, thinking, and while I watched him, I felt a panic course through my body. Barely a year before, I had escaped a life that was headed towards my remarrying. How had I now moved towards the same fate? 'Do I really want to get married just because there is a baby that needs to be explained away?' I whined. It was hopelessly unfair.

'Of course you don't,' he spoke softly, taking me in his arms. 'Just as I do not want to take you to wife for the same reason. I will marry you because I want you as my partner. If I get a child thrown in for free, so be it. Astrid, please do not do this if it will make you unhappy. We can find another way.' His eyes were ablaze. For him, it seemed, marriage was a magnificent prize.

'My hesitation is not about you,' I replied. 'Marriage was something I thought I was done with.'

'What do you really want?' he asked, and I thought for a moment.

To raid, I almost answered, but even now I realised that was not true. The whole time I had been in Aldeigjuborg, raiding had become less attractive. Trade and merchantry had shown me another path to wealth. 'Adventure,' I mumbled, settling on the word, but still unsure if that was my heart's desire.

Kjarr's eyes softened to sympathy, and he offered a weak smile. 'Really?'

Defeated, I threw up my hands. 'If not that, then I do not know.'

'I think you do.' Kjarr smiled wittingly.

Why was this so hard? And Kjarr was making it no easier by knowing me better than myself. Frustration boiled inside me as I paced between chests and shrouded furniture. 'Urgh!' I cried, 'whatever I do, I want it to be my decision. Made by no one else but me!'

'There you go.' He chuckled at my outburst.

'How does that help me now?'

'Decide what you want to do about this situation. If you want the pretence of a marriage, then have it. Do you want this to be a business arrangement between friends or lovers? Decide the terms; I am willing to follow your lead.' Kjarr bowed his head.

That was the only way this was going to work. I could not allow myself to feel led towards any decision. It had to truly be of my making. 'It would be a commitment from you but not a promise from me that I would, uh…' I paused.

He stopped me, holding up his hand. 'I've seen you pummel a man almost to his death. I would not stake my life for a sip of honey, no matter how sweet it might be.' His body was dangerously close now. I could feel his warmth and I so desperately desired comfort to dull the shock of the previous night. 'You are the finest woman I have ever met,' Kjarr continued, 'there is no one in the world I would risk more for.'

'This feels like insanity.'

He didn't move. 'When have we ever done anything ordinarily? We are adventurers, you and I.'

'It's not insane because of that,' I breathed.

'Then why?'

The honesty he demanded broke through my reluctance. 'This marriage, I might not want it to be purely business.'

His eyebrows shot up, and a smile curved his lips as he mumbled a response, 'So, there are feelings?' he asked.

'For you?'

His face broke into a wide grin and from his mouth issued desirous laughter. 'After all this time and all this talking? I have never made it a secret that I am in love with you. But you! Do you feel the same?'

I managed a small laugh but stopped. 'This doesn't mean I want to act on it or have a genuine marriage.'

He hunched his shoulders in disappointment. 'There are all my boyish hopes dashed but you know, you are always free to choose. Always free to change your mind.'

'Thank you.'

'So, what do you say?' he asked.

'Yes,' I said.

'Yes?'

'I will marry you,' I agreed.

'You better get going then.' He stood, offering his hand to me to help me to my feet. 'There is much to attend to before I depart and precious little time to accomplish it all.'

'I can help you pack if you need,' I offered, looking around at the mess.

'Packing, no! This is organised in my own way. No, there are some, err, formalities that need to be dealt with,' he mumbled.

'Wedding related? We need not bother with that! And please no Gothi,'

'What?! Alright, I guess I can agree to a handfast union, but we cannot have people saying that I don't value you. They will have enough to talk about with our surprise baby.' He was almost giddy with excitement. I imagined if he had his way, the marriage would be an unending process of celebrations. Perhaps if he was home in time for Helga's wedding, he would want a hand in planning it. I smiled to myself as he gently pushed me towards the door.

'Fine. If you do feel the need to pay, the obligatory base standard bride price is twelve ounces of silver where I come from,' I explained, stepping over the threshold onto the landing.

His mouth hung open, and he covered it, feigning shock. 'Do you take me for a poor man, Astrid? One that does not value his woman. I will not make such a paltry offering for your hand.'

'You never stop, do you?' I couldn't help the giggle that escaped.

'Never,' he agreed. 'As a widow, I pay you the bride price and, here you need not seek permission to marry. It is your choice alone.'

'Some things are better in Aldeigjuborg.'

'Will I see you at the docks later, wife?' he asked with a wry smile.

I nodded. 'You will, husband.' The word felt strange on my tongue, but not wrong.

My feet refused to move from Kjarr's landing long after he closed the door in my face, albeit reluctantly. From inside I could hear him busily whistling a cheerful tune as he finished whatever it was, he needed to do. I found myself, despite the turbulence of the morning, feeling truly happy. He really was a good man, and I had him in my life on my own terms.

'Signe,' I heard a familiar voice call from behind me. 'Is that you?'

I turned to see Luca, Mikel's master builder. 'It is.'

'Are you well?' he asked, squinting his eyes in a manner that wondered about my sanity.

I laughed nervously and stepped down from Kjarr's landing. 'Lost in my thoughts for a moment, but I was actually heading to see you.'

'You were?'

We fell into step, walking towards his work yard. 'There is something I would like you to construct for me.'

'Not another house, I hope.' He pulled his cap down to shield against the strong morning light.

'Nothing so grand. No. It is something much smaller.' Before I could detail the work, my young friend Mikel raced up to greet me.

'Signe,' he beamed as he embraced me tightly over the fence. 'I've not seen you in a while.'

'That's because you only call to see Helga now.'

'Well, she is my betrothed.' His voice sounded older than the boy he was when we arrived in Aldeigjuborg, and his youthful, gangly frame had given way to a strong bodied man crafted by hard work.

'You have a long time to wait before she is your wife,' I replied, prodding him in the stomach. Mikel was like a younger brother to me and in all our time in Aldeigjuborg, we had remained friends. Never would I have imagined he would marry so young.

'And what brings you to see us?' he asked, glancing at Luca.

'A commission,' his master whistled through his teeth.

I steeled myself for the coming questions. 'I have come to ask you and Luca to make me a crib.'

'What for?' Mikel asked, eyes narrowing.

I leaned in. 'A baby.'

Mikel reclined against the fence of the work yard next to me as I let myself through the gate. 'I know what a crib is for, but why do you need one and why do you have a baby?'

'It's a long story, Mikel.'

'And I have all the time in Midgard,' he replied, following me as I walked into the centre of the yard.

'No, you don't,' Luca interrupted, walking in behind me. 'And if you do, I'm not sure I have enough work for an apprentice,' he playfully goaded Mikel.

'Will you do it?' I asked.

Luca needed no more information. He was not one to pry, but Mikel, I knew, would be back with questions if I did not make haste to leave. 'We would be happy to help, won't we?' Luca smiled as he elbowed Mikel, who nodded but still appeared dumbstruck.

'It will be an excellent opportunity to try out some finer work, and once I am married, I imagine the *barns* will not be too far away,' he rattled, finding his voice again as he shook off the shock.

I gasped. 'You are still a child yourself.'

'And unmarried yet!' Luca added. 'Steady lad, there will be time.' He laughed, ruffling his young apprentice's hair. 'Poor Helga.'

I made to leave, but Luca stopped me with a powerful arm. 'What is the name of the child?' The sad smile that shadowed his face softened his eyes. Perhaps he was dreaming of the child that might one day come to him and his wife.

'Freyja.'

'Oh, a little girl. I always wanted a daughter,' Luca said wistfully. Though I knew a baby would bring him much joy, the risk to Freyja was too great if I placed her with Luca. Such was his dislike and distrust of the mother who gave her life.

'Perhaps you will have one if you keep working on it,' Mikel teased.

'Careful boy,' Luca warned with a light-hearted shove. 'Say no more, leave it with us,' he said, turning back to me. 'We will make you the finest crib you've ever seen.'

'You're a good man, Luca. Thank you. When should I expect it?' I replied.

'A few weeks. I will send this one over when it is done. He will need an excuse to see his darling Helga.' Luca chortled through a gap-toothed smile as I said goodbye, heading back to my house. The door was open when I arrived. Inside, I found Helga over the fire preparing lunch and Hilde was again nursing both girls, her back against the wall as she sat on the bench.

'Is it always like this?' I asked Hilde as her own Alva gently pushed her tiny fist into the soft flesh of her breast.

'Always,' she agreed. 'Alva nurses a little less than Freyja at the moment and soon Alva vill start to eat real food and then, ven she is ready, she vill stop all together.'

'How do you know she is ready?' I asked.

'She has sprouted a tooth and there is another on the vay. Ven they can chew, they can eat,' she replied, pulling back the infant's lip to show the small white protrusion from the gum.

'Is everything sorted?' Helga asked, coming to my side and slotting her arm into mine.

I dipped my finger into the pot of stew. 'Ow, hot!' I exclaimed, licking the gravy from my scalded finger.

'Then don't stick your finger in the food before it's served.' Helga swiped me away with her spoon. 'So, is it?'

'Mm-hmm,' I replied.

'Is that a smile?' she asked with a nudge.

I turned away. 'No! Hilde, do you think I should have taken Freyja out with me? I hate to leave you with her all the time.'

'Right now, she needs me almost all the time. Try not to take her out too much until she is older. *Barns* are delicate things, and the town is too mucky.'

I nodded. It was the end of the working day and I marvelled at how Hilde could spin any wool with the care of two small ones. 'Hilde, let me take you home. You must be tired.' I brought the basket around to place Freyja in.

'I am,' she agreed. Her eyes were dark and weary.

The walk seemed longer to Hilde's when laden with babies and belongings. She trudged. 'Please stay home tomorrow and I will come to you with food for you and the children.'

I thought she would argue, but she just nodded slowly. 'Some vomen have two children at the same time. Oh, bless their veary bones!'

'It would be demanding,' I agreed as we entered her home, setting ourselves on two chairs in the hearth room, fire ablaze and well-tended by the older children. As I stared into the fire, I felt peace, and my eyelids sagged with tiredness. Hilde snored softly next to me. A small child no older than two, climbed up onto his mother's lap and started poking her in the nostril. Hilde did not stir, but I lifted the child away and sat him on the ground.

'That's not nice. Leave your mother to rest,' I chastised the boy.

He wriggled around on the floor and began playing with two sticks, ignoring. Around me, three of Hilde's nine children played, all younger than eight years.

'Odin's beard! How does she manage?' I wondered aloud. She must have spent a good deal of her life pregnant. It would have been hard enough when she had her husband around, but now she was alone, in charge of all those children. In Hilde's arms, I admired Freyja. Her dark lashes fluttered and from below her pale blue eyes, the colour of all babies, stared unfocussed in my direction. I had expected her mother's green eyes but was thankful that, for now, there would be little resemblance to her birth mother. I stroked Freyja's fluffy smattering of hair and her eyes blinked sleepily once more.

On the stool next to Hilde, I sat and let a wave of exhaustion wash over me as I closed my heavy eyelids. My tired mind pondered Hilde's age. Perhaps she was nearing her fortieth year, but hardly any older than that. But why did that matter? Sleep was coming.

I yawned. A little sleep would not hurt.

The hem of my dress pulled sharply, and I peered down at the floor where the little boy sat at my feet playing with his sticks. 'Not sleepy, little one?' I asked, combing my fingers through his light brown hair.

'Up,' he said, eyeing me expectantly.

'Huh?'

'Up,' he demanded again, thrusting his chubby arms into the air. I gathered him up as he closed his eyes and made his bed in my lap.

From beside me, Hilde laughed and looked at me through one partially open eye. 'Welcome to motherhood.'

TWENTY-FIVE

Warm afternoon sun woke me. It bathed the threshold of the open door and spilled into Hilde's small house. 'Mmmm,' I moaned, arching my back with a luxurious stretch. 'How long was I asleep?'

Hilde was again nursing the babies and was surrounded by the joyful shrieks of her other children playing both inside and out. She shrugged. 'You are awake now. Do you vant me to find you something to eat?'

I sprung from my seat. 'No, no, no,' I cried, 'am I too late?'

'Is something vrong?' Hilde called after me as I made for the door.

I spun around on my heel, knocking over the toddling boy who had earlier crawled into my lap. 'Where is Freyja?'

Hilde looked down at the infant attached to her breast. 'Still feeding,' she replied.

'I have to go,' I worried, as Freyja finished feeding and Hilde placed her into my arms.

'Vere are you going?'

'The docks. I just hope I have not missed him,' I called over my shoulder as I quickly made my way towards the water. My stride had to be steady to keep Freyja sleeping but was filled with urgency. Thankfully my feet carried me on my path to the docks with little thinking, and as Kjarr's ship came into view, I breathed a sigh of relief that it was still tethered there.

'Where have you been?' Kjarr called as I clambered clumsily onto the rocky sand near the ship's mooring. He sprang forward, his hand clasped my elbow to steady me as he scooped Freyja from my arms.

'Sorry, I, err, fell asleep,' I replied, casting a sheepish look in his direction.

'You almost missed me. But I didn't want to leave before seeing you.' He smiled broadly, peering down at the child dwarfed in his arms.

A man cleared his throat behind me. 'You certainly kept this one a secret. Why did you never tell me you had married?'

When I turned, I matched the voice with the face; Eryk. 'What are you doing here?' I asked the Master of the Guild, Neflaug's lover, and likely father of Freyja. My skin bristled with anger. This was the man who could have acknowledged his child and the only one, save Neflaug, who could have prevented my firm lodgement in this saga.

Kjarr rhythmically rocked and shushed Freyja as she stirred.

'A baby! I always thought you were a surprising woman, little bird.' Eryk's belly jiggled along with his laughter, masking a flicker of knowledge that burned within his eyes. I recalled the time he told me Neflaug had not brought me to Aldeigjuborg just to become a wife. *Look at me now*, I thought.

'We did not want to bring attention to it. We never wanted it to be anything big,' I explained, ignoring the annoying pet name he persisted with.

'You needed to keep it a secret from Neflaug. After all, she would not have taken too kindly to losing you, but we need not concern ourselves with her anymore,' he said, drawing closer to Kjarr and Freyja. 'I always thought you two would make a fine pair and I am happy that you managed it on your own.' He winked.

I looked at Kjarr for help, but he was distracted, besotted with our daughter. 'Is she not the most beautiful thing you have ever seen?' he gushed, holding the child out for Eryk's inspection.

Eryk's face flushed with discomfort, his eyes flitting between Kjarr and I. 'I'm sorry to say she doesn't look much like either of you. Babies are strange things, all squishy and unable to see the world.'

A curious comment since newborns, in my opinion, scarcely looked like anyone. It made me wonder if he recognised himself or Neflaug in Freyja's tiny features.

'Not yet, but she will,' Kjarr responded confidently. 'Who do you think she will take after? Her stubborn mother?' He stopped and kissed me on the cheek, 'Or her strong and handsome father?'

'Time will tell,' Eryk replied obtusely.

'I must make ready the ship, here,' Kjarr said, handing Freyja back to me. I watched him wave his hands about in explanation to his crew and wished he had not left me alone with the adulterous boar I had previously considered a friend.

'Many congratulations on your marriage. No one knew, my little bird.' Eryk leaned closer, touching my arm.

I shrugged off his touch. 'Like you said, Neflaug would not have cared for our union, and Kjarr is a good man,' I replied stoically, without inflection. Unlike you, the voice inside added.

'And the child, you showed no signs.'

'Fortunate in my childbearing. It was an easy pregnancy and a cold season. I was scarcely without my cloak,' I lied.

'Mm-hmm,' he hummed, nodding. 'Oh, I almost forgot, I must go. My wife is expecting me, but before I go.' He paused, lingering next to me. 'I must ask you something.'

He edged forward, and I backed away instinctively as his sour breath blew on my face. Freyja wriggled between my arms. 'You were such a promising student. Your grasp of Arabic impressive, but I could have taught you so much more than Neflaug ever could. I could have taken you to heights you would not have reached on your own and you were always so quick to learn.' He leaned even closer now, licking his lips.

I stood my ground. 'Eryk, I have a business to run, a husband and a child. Perhaps in the future, when I have more time, there may be some things I wish to learn.'

'Tssk, a pity,' he ruminated, stepping back.

My feet were rooted to the spot, eyes locked with his intense stare, determined not to be intimidated by a man who I no longer respected. Eryk nodded, turning on his heel. My disdain bore into the back of his head as I watched his swollen frame amble up the path towards the bridge to the city.

'Sorry I had to leave you with him. Is everything alright?' Kjarr asked after he had run back to us.

I nodded. 'It will be.'

His eyes were full of apology. 'It is time. I will return next summer, if the gods are with us!' he said hopefully. 'I will try to send word as often as I can, and I shall bring you back something.'

'Just bring yourself back.'

Kjarr stared silently out at the water. 'This one will be much changed when I return,' he said, looking down at Freyja.

'She will.'

Kjarr leaned towards me and planted a kiss on my cheek, pressing Freyja between us. He nuzzled my shoulder. 'I'm sorry about all of this. If it had been up to me, our first kiss would have been something a little more meaningful, and preferably in private,' he whispered into my hair.

'And it still can be,' I mustered a small smile.

A boyish energy flashed within him. 'I cannot stop bringing to mind that this morning you told me you loved me.'

'I never said that!' I laughed, aghast.

His hand shot to his chest as if an arrow had wounded him. 'Ooof, I swear you did.'

'You know I did not. I said I had feelings.'

'Oh, I know the words you spoke, but it was not what my heart heard.'

So, there was understanding between us. He would not lead me, but he heard the things that I dared not or was not ready to say. 'Whatever you need to tell yourself, Kjarr.' I had to laugh. 'Just come home quickly.' My voice was gone, lodged in my throat, as Kjarr pulled away from us, turning quickly to end the painful goodbye.

'And now I must go,' he yelled over his shoulder. He clambered aboard, slapping men on the back and taking his position on the prow, turning to wave. 'There is something at your house awaiting you,' he yelled. He must have meant my bride price.

I sighed. 'Knowing you, it will be too much.'

'To me, you are worth more than any hoard of silver I could ever muster,' he called back, not caring who heard his declaration of affection.

I waved until his ship rounded the bend out of sight and my arm grew sore from the motion, then I made for home. It was a long and lonely walk back into the town gates and when I mounted the steps to the house, my shoulders slumped with the reality that it would be a long time until the one I confided in the most returned.

Inside the house, a large chest took up most of the trestle table in my hearth room. 'Kjarr brought this for you,' Helga declared.

'He wasn't jesting,' I remarked, ogling the fortune inside.

Helga grinned and excitedly clapped her hands. 'So, does this mean you are married?'

'It would seem so,' I replied, touching some pieces inside.

Helga peered over my shoulder, stealing a peek at the box's contents. 'There has to be over fifty ounces in there.'

I rifled through the coins and jewellery. 'I would give it all back so he did not have to go.'

Helga put a cup of hot water in front of me. 'If I know love, and I do…' she began, stuffing some crushed nettle leaves into the cup. 'He will want to hurry back to you as soon as he is able.'

I took a deep, calming sip of the tea. 'There is not a better man, Helga.'

'Waiting will be difficult.'

I held the cup between my hands, inhaling the musky aroma of the nettle. 'I already miss him.'

AUTHOR'S NOTE

Vikings have long captured my interest. Years ago, I moved to a city close to York (known as Jorvik to our Viking friends) in order to explore their history, but I never really expected them to take over my life.

One day I was on the train making my way to my job in a legal office in Melbourne, when I read about a piece of wood which was found in a grave some years before. It bore runic inscriptions. Though interpreted in upwards of six different ways, owing to the basic nature of the rune structures, one interpretation stuck with me. Evidence suggests it may have belonged to a woman named Neflaug, who may have lived in Aldeigjuborg, situated in modern day Russia (the town is now known as Staraya Ladoga). Scarcely more was known about her. It sparked a curiosity that sent me to many books to learn about women's place in the settlements of the east, and from that research characters emerged and lived their own lives.

Just as today, new cities often must be ahead of their times in order to attract a workforce and new settlers. Aldeigjuborg was no different. The new residents brought with them their culture and language, but thankfully, not the rigid immovable hierarchies that plagued the old world. That is not to say that it was easy to transition between these classes. It was not, but it was possible for some. In these new settlements, rules steeped in entrenched histories were not always followed because it was simply not possible to do things the way they had always been done. In a land open to ingenuity, those who made their mark could make their fortune, the hope of all Vikings.

The Viking settlements were much more multicultural than many would first imagine. Though most in the northern regions would have conversed in Old Norse, there were also smatterings of other languages that pre-date modern Russian, such as Old East Slavic and Old Swedish, in addition to languages from further afield spoken by travelling merchants. As such, I have used a combination of these languages as relevant to the characters from those areas.

The characters in this book, though they are invented, are manifestations of what could have existed in these places. Culture and tradition could vary from household to household, the same is true for their religion. It is important to remember that Vikings were master adapters. They were quick to adopt new language, religions, and cultures to assist with their trading endeavours and, for many, hoping to secure arable farming lands abroad far away from the demanding life in the north. Most of the Scandinavian countries (and their settlements), at this point, were only lightly touched by Christianity. The religion would later take a hold on the region, but at the point at which I set this book, the old religion of the Norse gods, was still the dominating set of beliefs. This would last and later dwindle, for many years to come. The events in this book, while the daily life is based on evidence, are fiction, save for the battle of Thimeon which occurred during this time period.

I have undertaken the work on this book myself, though with copious amounts of research, which at some points were entirely daunting. Any mistakes based on interpreting archaeological evidence and written history in this book are my own.

www.meganformanek.com

If you enjoyed *Oath Undo Me*, please leave a review where you purchased the book, or on Goodreads.com. You can join the Merchant Viking, the author's monthly newsletter where she shares research, series updates, and other Viking goodies on the above website.

TITLES BY MEGAN FORMANEK

Viking Trading Lands series

Oath Undo Me

No One's Viking